THE RAMSBURGH VARIATIONS

By Julian Smart

The Hawksbridge Angels
The Train To Hawksbridge
The Ramsburgh Variations
Emma Vernon's Northminster Ghost Stories (with Harriet Smart)

THE RAMSBURGH VARIATIONS

A THOMAS RUFFORD MYSTERY: 3

by

Julian Smart

Published by Anthemion

First Edition

ISBN 978-1-907873-79-9

Made with Jutoh

PREFACE

THE recollections in this third volume of my adventures in Hawksbridge have been the hardest to commit to paper. Indeed, I have several times determined to abandon the undertaking altogether as much out of regard for your peace of mind, dear reader, as for mine: but my publisher was patient and persuasive, and their intervention successful, as you see. The volume is written with the same frankness and respect for truth as the previous ones, and it concerns events at least as uncomfortable to assimilate. Consider this fair warning!

In the darker moments of 1849, I never entirely doubted the essential nobility of the human race, but you will forgive me for coming close. At times, a sense of chaos and futility threatened to overwhelm me. I am sure you will know this feeling, especially in the aftermath of the death of a loved one, but it is especially acute in the face of evil.

Still, for all the degeneracy that is a dispiriting part of our world – yes, even in Hawksbridge, so tantalisingly near to its potential as an idyll – counterbalancing qualities are always to be found, including grace, wisdom, courage and love. I am lucky indeed to have had friends with these qualities in abundance, and more, and you shall meet them in these pages: some already familiar, and some not.

At the time depicted in this memoir, music loomed large. As you may already know, my talents and knowledge in this area may safely be described as absent – to my eternal regret – and so I must ask for your patience when I attempt musical descriptions. Indeed, I have often thought, in my more melancholic moments, that I see and hear the world through the heavy gauze of my own ignorance. I miss much nuance, to be sure. But I am not unreceptive to music's power, and I hope that I will transmit some glimmering of my remarkable experience. Strange though it is to say, there are still occasional concerts in this country and abroad that reignite that undeserved connection between myself and a discipline that remains largely a foreign, but beautiful, language to me. If you should ever by accident find yourself entranced by 'Prudence', and 'Hubris', by a person you shall meet in this book, then you and I will be as good as shaking hands.

Of my grim trials, I shall say nothing in this preface. Suffice it to say, in hesitantly shining a light on my pain and humiliation, and that of others, I justify the depiction of the ugly by inclusion of the beautiful. If any should think the light better extinguished, I refer them to my publisher, who is a far better judge of the public interest than I!

— Thomas Rufford, July 1864

Beauty is to the home what love is to the soul.

— Gabriel Forrester, from 'On the Improvement of Public Taste'

PROLOGUE

From The Hawksbridge Herald, March 29th, 1849

DOUBLE TRAGEDY IN HAWKSBRIDGE

We are sad to have to report two terrible accidents that by a sinister twist of fate occurred on the same day, March the Twenty-Seventh. In the morning of this fateful day, a young woman was crushed under the wheels of a carriage in Hawksbridge market-place while giving out pamphlets for the Society for the Emancipation of Women. It is not clear whether she was jostled into the road, or whether she saw someone she wanted to speak to, and stepped out without looking. Her legs having been badly crushed, Miss Jane Wright was initially conscious but died soon after from blood loss.

The second event happened in the early evening, when a child playing near Knight's Mount found the body of a man who had fallen from the Ramparts into the ditch some twenty-five feet below. Mr Harold Milburn, an engineer working on the new railway bridge, was pronounced dead from a broken neck, and Mrs Ninette Milburn was found wandering the Ramparts. She was so distressed she could not answer any questions, including – initially – her own name. Our own correspondent found one of the Society's pamphlets nearby, in an eerie connection with Miss Wright's unfortunate demise.

We express our heartfelt condolences to both of the families concerned.

CHAPTER ONE

April, 1849

"WELL, lad? What did you want to see me about? Nothing of a medical nature, I hope. You look healthy enough."

Dr Drummond's study conveyed a mix of comfort, taste and learning. Books and portraits lined the walls, and a faint odour of pipe smoke hung in the air, which was not unpleasant. The room reminded me of the quarters of my old academic colleagues in Oxford, except none of them had a grinning human skeleton in one corner.

"Sherry?" he said, turning to a decanter on a console table.

"Yes, please," I said. "It's about Phyllis."

"Ah," he said, smiling and bringing over our glasses. "So it is heart trouble. I thought as much."

He gestured to an upholstered chair, and took a wing armchair next to mine, lowering himself into it with a grunt.

I took a swig of sherry for courage. "I wanted to ask... I mean, Phyllis and I..."

"Spit it out, man!" said Dr Drummond, chuckling. "I know – it's not easy for a young man to talk about such things with a dour old Scotsman. You like my daughter, don't you?"

"Very much," I said. "I'm in love with her, sir, and I wanted to ask your permission to marry her."

He looked at me for a moment, as if appraising a prospective footman. "I expected it," he said. "I've been expecting it for a while. You've been tardy, my boy, but better late than never. Yes, of course you may ask Phyllis. If she desires it, then so do I."

"Thank you, sir," I said, much relieved. I had not seriously anticipated a refusal, but there was still a lingering doubt in my mind that I deserved such a prize.

"Well, I don't know anyone else who understands my daughter better," said Dr Drummond. "And she thinks highly of you, although there have been times... But I expect you've straightened everything out. And perhaps you'll calm down a little, eh? Not go careering into danger all the time? You'll have responsibilities at home, my boy."

"Yes, of course," I said. "I intend to be the best husband Phyllis could wish for." It felt strange to apply the term 'husband' to myself, but I supposed it would become more natural over time.

"To be sure, to be sure," Dr Drummond said. "I'll miss her terribly," he added. "But it's the natural way of things. I'll be content so long as she's happy – and she comes to visit her creaky old papa now and again."

I had been so wrapped in my own feelings and future that I had omitted to think of this aspect.

"I don't like to take her away from you," I said. "You could come and stay at Ramsburgh – in fact, we could build you a house on the estate!"

Dr Drummond laughed. "Oh no, lad, I won't put you to that trouble. I'm too old to move from here – I have it just so, and I will still have my housekeeper to talk to. Besides, by the time you finished it, I would doubtless have moved to a much smaller plot – for good!"

"I'm sure not –" I said, but he raised his hand to quieten me.

"Here's to Mr and Mrs Thomas Rufford!" he said. He raised his sherry glass, and I did the same.

"Assuming she'll have me," I said.

"Wheesht, man! Of course she'll have you. I don't know of any other offers, and she's not young. And you have a bonnie house."

It was a practical way of looking at things, and not entirely complimentary to me, but I was used to Dr Drummond's brusqueness. It was one of my favourite things about him.

"You'd better go and ask her," he added, "before young Dr Weldon comes calling!" He winked, and I drained my sherry glass before rising.

"Thank you, sir. I won't let either of you down."

"Indeed you won't," he said. "She'll see to that. Excuse me if I don't get up. Off you go and capture my daughter!"

~

Phyllis was sitting in the drawing room reading, and she looked up with a smile. "Whatever can you two have been talking about?" she said, with exaggerated innocence.

"My bonnie house," I said. "Care for a walk?"

"Certainly," she said. "Let me get my shawl."

It was a pleasant walk up to Knight's Mount, and standing in the spring sunshine we gazed down to the river where soon the elegant spans of a railway bridge would help link our town to the new, steel arteries that were spreading inexorably throughout the country.

"It's so still here," said Phyllis, taking my hand. "You would never know that so much is about to change."

"For the better, surely," I said. "I can't believe anything else, being with you, seeing only beauty."

I turned to face her and raised her hand to my lips. "Will you be my wife?" I said. "It's all I want in the world."

"Truly?"

"Truly." We kissed, first gently, and then passionately, wrapping our arms tightly about one another, not caring if anyone saw us.

I felt giddy as our embrace loosened.

"I love you so much," I said. "Will you marry me?"

"Yes," she said, her eyes filling with tears of happiness. "Yes, of course I'll marry you, Thomas. For some silly reason, I love you too."

"Thank you," I said, and kissed her again. "I don't remotely deserve it."

Phyllis put her head on my shoulder. "I forgive you your sins." Suddenly she straightened up and took both of my hands. "But will I be a good wife?" she said, looking at me earnestly. "I've been so self-reliant, and I realise I don't really know the first thing about marriage, even though I've written about it often enough. Now that it's my turn –"

"You will be an extraordinary wife," I said. "You don't need to worry about that. We'll play our roles by instinct. And you will still have plenty of time for your writing – I'll make sure of it."

"Good," she said, embracing me again. "It has been needling me. I didn't know if I could become Mrs Rufford, the selfless home-maker, and I was scared I would have to leave Iona Tavistock behind."

"By no means!" I said. "Miss Tavistock will be installed at Ramsburgh, and I will be the luckiest man in the county for having married two beautiful, clever women."

Phyllis smiled, which made me kiss her again several times. "In which case," she said between kisses, "I must allow you your own alter ego. Thomas Rufford, the bloodhound – the gentleman detective. But not, I trust, Thomas Rufford, the danger to women's hearts."

"Those days are behind me," I said. "And I don't suppose life will be as complicated as it has been. But – just maybe, if a distressed person came to me, I might turn my mind to their problem. I have no training or right to practise it, but somehow I seem to be of occasional help."

"I think you would be thoroughly bored if you didn't have a case in hand," said Phyllis.

"Your father strongly disapproves of that sort of thing," I said. "I as good as promised to desist."

"And yet he admires you for what you've done for Hawksbridge," said Phyllis. "He won't admit it, of course. But you're a kind of balm for trouble, and that's partly why he likes you. He just doesn't want to see you get hurt."

"And by extension, you," I said. "He's quite right. I shouldn't take risks."

"Are you not taking a large one, right now, with me?"

"If it's a risk," I said, kissing her hand, "it's a glorious one that I take without a single qualm."

~

"This one, or this?" said Francesca, holding up two samples of wallpaper and looking expectantly over the top of them. Both were striking, and showed different colour variations on a pleasing pattern of stylised leaves and flowers, one green, one blue.

"The green is more natural," I said. "But then the blue is also compelling. It almost glows."

"You're no help at all!" she said. "But yes, they are hard to choose between. I love them all," she added, flipping through a pile of further samples. "Isn't Forrester the most astonishing and talented designer?"

"I've heard him praised, but I'm afraid I've formed no opinion for myself."

"Then you should read 'On the Improvement of Public Taste'," Francesca said, putting the samples back on the pile and carefully tidying them. "It's a revelation. I'm positively shamed by my vulgar excesses in this house. I shall tear it all down as soon as I have made up my mind which papers to use."

"Redecorate? Already? But you have done everything so beautifully."

Francesca snorted. "I have seen the errors of my ways, and they are many. How could I possibly entertain Mr Forrester here with it looking like this?"

I could see little wrong with the decor – I would have to take her word for it.

"You intend to invite him?"

"But of course! He has his factory on the south side of town, and he lives near it. How lucky we are to have such a distinguished man amongst us!"

"Goodness," I said. "You have been badly bitten by the Forrester bug. He has become a sensation. Is he a handsome man?"

"Oh, a little," Francesca said, waving her hand dismissively. "But that is insignificant. His talent – no, his greatness – is far more attractive. And there's nothing he hasn't turned his hand to. His chairs are marvellous, and he designed his own house, apparently while under the influence of opium, so rumour has it!"

I scratched my head. "What is his principal insight for wallpaper design, if I may ask?"

Francesca pursed her lips and thought about this. "I couldn't possibly begin to sum it up," she said after a moment. "But I think mainly it's the observation that only natural subjects are appropriate for wall-coverings, and that we shouldn't attempt to reproduce Nature in a slavishly realistic way. The Forrester way is an elegant layering of – well, sketches of Nature, as you just saw – leaves, flowers, vines, seaweed, and so on. There's a plain honesty about it, and yet his designs are more beautiful than any other. It's obvious when you see it!"

"So, no sentimental bucolic scenes with cows and so on?"

"Precisely! Now, delightful as this conversation is, I have the feeling that you came to tell me something. What news?"

"Nothing much," I said. "Just that I have asked Phyllis to be my wife, and she has agreed."

"Oh, Thomas!" Francesca cried, flinging her arms around me. "That's so wonderful! I knew you were both made for each other. But what a loss for the single women of Hawksbridge."

She smiled at me, a little sadly. "And who will take care of my headaches?"

"The talented Mr Forrester?" I said.

"Ha!" Francesca said. "He's married, alas. And I doubt even he would be half as good as you in that respect."

"Good. That may prevent me feeling quite so inferior if I ever meet him."

"Oh, but you must!" she said. "I will invite you – and Phyllis, of course."

"I look forward to it," I said. "Now, I must think about an engagement ring. Any suggestions? I haven't yet had cause to visit a jeweller's here."

"I found a pretty necklace in Belford's. He's a rather glum man, perhaps due to being a widower, but once you get talking to him, he opens up a little. And his prices are reasonable."

"I will try Mr Belford, then. Actually..." I hesitated.

"Yes?"

"I don't know anything about jewellery. You couldn't perhaps help me choose something?"

"Of course I could," Francesca said, pressing my arm. "You poor thing! This is all a big, frightening step for you, isn't it?"

I nodded. "Yes, it is," I said, despite my bluster to Phyllis. "It's absolutely terrifying."

~

"I need you to treat it with the utmost care," the customer was saying to Mr Belford over the counter. "It belonged to my grandmother and is of great sentimental value to me. The pin has snapped off, as you can see, and it needs a good clean."

"Of course, Lady Fairfield. It's a beautiful thing. I will return it to you as good as new."

I could not see her face, but Lady Fairfield seemed a curious creature. Small in stature, she was dressed in funereal black and yet sported a hat with colourful pheasant feathers. She spoke with a high-pitched, intense tone that had the unfortunate nasal hint of a child's voice.

"Please do," she said, and seeing Mr Belford nodding at Francesca, she turned around to see who had come in.

Francesca smiled, and I bowed. "Good morning," I said.

"Oh! Good morning," she said, and narrowed her eyes at Francesca. "Your face seems very familiar. Have we met before?"

"Mrs Francesca Campbell adorns the Town Hall," I said. "However, she has hung up her wings today to go shopping."

Lady Fairfield's eyes widened. "Goodness!" she said, frowning. "The mural?"

"I'm afraid so," said Francesca. "I'm so pleased to meet you, Lady Fairfield. I have heard of your good works." She held out her hand, and Lady Fairfield shook it, still with a bemused expression on her face.

"This is my good friend Mr Thomas Rufford," Francesca went on. "You may be familiar with his investigative efforts for the town."

"Ah, yes indeed," Lady Fairfield said, shaking my hand and eyeing me with a slightly suspicious air. "Well, a gentleman with time on his hands must do what he can for the improvement of himself and the town. It is to be commended, so long as the thrill of the chase doesn't overpower one's impartiality."

I smiled and nodded indulgently, being more amused than

offended at being damned with faint praise.

"And what a time-worn business, painting the female form so immodestly!" she continued, turning to Francesca. "I must admit the likeness is a good one, and it is done with skill. But do you not feel that women should no longer submit to the whims of male desire in the matter of art? Are you not simply encouraging men to see you in a lascivious way?"

I could see Mr Belford's eyes rolling and his patience wearing thin as he drummed his fingers on the counter.

"That's a very interesting question, Lady Fairfield," Francesca replied. "One to which I cannot possibly do justice on Mr Belford's time. I hope we'll meet again socially to continue the discussion."

Lady Fairfield smiled a little coldly. "A woman should have a ready answer for such fundamental matters, you know. Anyway – you may find this of interest."

She reached into the bag she was carrying and took out two pamphlets, a copy of which she presented to each of us.

"'Female Freedom'," Francesca read aloud. "'A Manifesto for the Timely Emancipation of Women'. How fascinating! We shall study these diligently, Lady Fairfield."

"Good," said Lady Fairfield. "I think you will find them instructive. Even you, Mr Rufford."

Francesca's face suddenly changed to alarm. "But – is this the pamphlet that poor young woman...?"

Lady Fairfield nodded. "Miss Wright's loss is a blow to us at the Society," she said. "But her sacrifice will not be in vain. We will soldier on. Now, I have further errands I must attend to. It was good to meet you, Mrs Campbell, Mr Rufford. Oh, Mr Belford – would you put this poster in your window? It's for an upcoming talk of mine. It won't do you any harm at all to show your support for the advancement of your female customers."

Mr Belford grunted and reluctantly took the poster. Lady Belford left the shop, and when we could be sure we would not be seen through the window, Francesca and I looked at each other, and burst out laughing. I could even see one corner of Mr Belford's mouth turning up slightly.

"But we mustn't laugh," Francesca said. "That poor woman in the market-place – not to mention Mr Milburn, whom I'm not entirely sure wasn't another victim of this tract."

"You think it stirred the Milburns into a fatal argument?" I said.

"It's possible, isn't it? The Herald implied it. Anyway – what an astonishing, audacious character she is!"

"I'm not sure she approved of me," I said.

"And far less of me," said Francesca. "If she hadn't been so modest in height, she would have looked down her nose. You must help me come up with arguments for why sensuous art is unimpeachable, in case our paths cross in future, although something tells me we won't change her mind. Now, Mr Belford – can you help my friend find a ring for his betrothed?"

"Certainly, Mrs Campbell," he said. "There are these in this cabinet – let me get them out for you – and I will fetch some more from the back."

"Thank you," said Francesca as he arranged several rings on a red velvet cloth. "Are you well, Mr Belford?"

He looked at her with a mournful expression. "As well as can be expected," he said. "My daughter – but I won't bother you with my troubles."

"Oh, I am sorry," Francesca said. "Is she unwell?"

"In a manner of speaking," he said. "Never mind. Let me fetch the other rings."

"Oh dear," Francesca whispered. Then in a louder voice she said, "Now, Thomas. What do you think of these?"

I surveyed the little row of objects. There were plain gold rings, and others set with varying arrangements and quantities of gems. But none of them inspired me.

I shrugged. "I'm sure any of them would be fine, but..."

"Oh, Thomas!" said Francesca. "That's not very romantic. Is there not one that says 'my darling Phyllis' to you?"

I looked again, trying to picture each on Phyllis' finger. "No. Let's see what else Mr Belford brings."

He returned with a dozen or so more rings, and laid them carefully on the velvet.

"What about this one?" Francesca said. "I love opals!"

"So do I, but en masse, they look like a row of teeth," I said, and felt Francesca's elbow in my side.

Mr Belford sniffed. "What might you be looking for in particular, sir?"

"I'm afraid I don't know," I said. "Something unusual!"

"Well," Mr Belford said, fingering a box that he had left unopened. "I wasn't sure whether to show you this. I haven't priced it yet."

"Let's see it, then, Mr Belford," said Francesca.

He opened the box and placed it at the end of the red cloth. "It's quite old," he said. "Some people prefer a ring that no one else has worn, but this is – as you said, sir – unusual. Made about 1770."

I bent to examine it. Even with my inexperienced eye, I could tell that it was charming – the gold ring tapered elegantly to make room for a cluster of pearls around a red garnet, with a garnet either side. It was decorative without being flashy.

"I can see you like it," said Francesca as I stared intently at it. "It is rather lovely." She turned to Mr Belford. "Does it have a happy history?"

"It does," Mr Belford said. "The man I bought it from said that it belonged to her mother, who had a contented marriage of nearly fifty years and bore half-a-dozen healthy children. If that luck rubs off on you and your future wife, sir," he added, turning to me, "you will be fortunate indeed."

I smiled. "I'm not a superstitious man, Mr Belford, but I

do find that comforting. May I try the ring on Mrs Campbell, to give me a better idea of it?"

Mr Belford raised his eyebrows in an uncharacteristically extravagant movement of his normally quiescent features. "Certainly," he said, and he gave the ring to Francesca to try on.

"There!" said Francesca, holding out her adorned hand. "I think it's perfect. What good taste you have, Thomas. Phyllis will love it."

"In that case," I said, "I'll take it."

"I had better tell you the price first, sir," said Mr Belford. "As I said, it's an unusual piece. It won't be cheap."

"Fortunately, neither am I!" I said, with perhaps a little too much bravado. I became anxious that I had been hasty.

Mr Belford considered, and then said, "I can let you have it for thirty-five guineas."

My mind had been racing to far larger sums. "That is quite satisfactory, thank you," I said, trying not to show my relief.

"Very good, sir," Mr Belford said. "Payment within a month, if you don't mind."

"There won't be any difficulty with that," I said. "I'm grateful to you for solving my problem so quickly and painlessly!"

"It's my pleasure, sir," Mr Belford said as he wrapped the little box carefully in tissue paper. "Marriage is a wonderful thing." He sighed, and repeated in a quiet voice, "A wonderful thing."

Whether he was recalling his own marriage, now sadly consigned to the realms of memory, or whether he was contemplating some other poignant circumstance, I could not tell.

CHAPTER TWO

"LET me introduce you to my son," said Mrs Harris, ushering Flora and myself into the drawing room. "I've been wanting you to meet him for so long! And he kindly came to see how I was – all the way from Canada – when he learned of my indisposition. Well, that and a little homesickness, of course. I'll stay as long as I can, before my wretched head tells me to go to bed again. And Effie is here – did I tell you about her musical success? I can scarcely believe it."

Despite a recurrence of her migraines, and a lethargy whose source her doctor had been unable to identify, Mrs Harris had been determined to hold a party to celebrate several felicities: my engagement to Phyllis, the arrival of Captain Victor Harris, and the return of her youngest daughter, Euphemia.

Phyllis and her father were engaged in conversation with a tall and commanding fellow of about thirty years of age. His disciplined deportment and strong, confident voice spoke of a military background.

I smiled a greeting at Phyllis and Dr Drummond, and Mrs Harris introduced us.

"How do you do, Miss Davison," the Captain said. "I gather you are the creator of some spectacular wall paintings – I intend to go to the Town Hall on Monday and see them for myself! I am also told – rather mysteriously – that I am to encounter one of the models this evening. I take it that is not also you?"

"Thank you," said Flora. "But I'm no model. And I'm only one of several artists to be employed. The model in question is Mrs Campbell – I believe she has not yet arrived."

"You will enjoy Mrs Campbell," I said. "She is one of a kind. I'm very pleased to meet you, Captain Harris." I held out my hand. "Your parents have been full of your exploits in Canada."

"The honour is mine," said the Captain, taking my hand with a firm grasp. "News of your investigations has reached me via my mother's letters. I would be very glad to hear all about it. In fact, it seems that I find Hawksbridge a far more colourful place now than when I left. It must have been waiting impatiently for my absence."

"Not at all, Victor," said Mrs Harris. "When you grew up and stopped digging trenches in the garden, and blowing up your toy armies, things seemed so quiet. But certainly, since Thomas arrived we have not been bored."

"I'm sure – I hope – it was coincidence," I said. "At least, I never noticed a curse about me when I was in Oxford."

"Knowing you is hardly a curse," Mrs Harris said, affectionately touching me on the arm. "Ah! Francesca is here, and she has found Effie!"

Francesca was in the doorway talking in an animated fashion to a young woman in her late twenties. Even accounting for Francesca's love of meeting new people, her enthusiasm was notable – she can only have met Miss Harris moments before, and yet her eyes shone with admiration.

I had not yet heard any of Miss Harris' compositions, although I was aware she had impressed critics with her piano concerto, a number of nocturnes, and even a first symphony. It was a remarkable achievement in one so young, and a woman at that. The mystery that seemed to perplex even her parents was how a girl who showed some keenness for melody but little aptitude or patience for the rigour of musical theory, could now be fêted as a musical celebrity. A spell in a Parisian finishing school had – Mrs Harris said – utterly transformed her.

"Oh, Thomas!" said Francesca, guiding her new acquaintance towards me and ignoring all protocol. "Have you met Miss Harris? We have a genius in our midst! Miss Harris, this is my friend Mr Thomas Rufford."

Miss Harris was evidently bemused by the tornado that was Francesca Campbell, but she was not annoyed, and she smiled at me. She was an inch or so shorter than me, and her ample, slightly messy red hair amplified the impression of a rebel that her reputation had already indicated.

"I am delighted to meet you, Miss Harris," I said, shaking her hand. "Mrs Campbell is a great follower of yours. Francesca, did you not hear Miss Harris' piano concerto in London before coming to Hawksbridge?"

"I did indeed," said Francesca. "It was sublime. Can I ask what you're working on at the moment?"

"Thank you," Miss Harris said. "I'm thinking about another symphony. But mainly I aim to lie fallow for a while. I'm a little exhausted by a series of songs that the Conservatoire de Paris commissioned."

Mr Harris was hovering nearby. "With insufficient rests, you get crotchety, my dear! Can't have you beat, now!"

Miss Harris smiled indulgently. "Very good, Father. I'm sorry, I'm neglecting my friend and faithful assistant – where are you, Sophie?"

I had wondered who the delicate-looking young woman was by the door, hanging back diffidently. Dark-haired and slight of figure, with full lips and elegant bone structure, I instantly placed her as French.

"Come, Sophie!" Miss Harris said. "Come and meet some interesting people. I am nothing without Miss Dubois," she added. "I work her frightfully hard and I don't know why she puts up with me."

As Miss Dubois shook several hands with a shy smile, I thought I saw a trace of discomfort on Mrs Harris' face. But this soon disappeared, and introductions having been made, we were summoned for dinner.

~

I was glad to be placed next to Phyllis. "What extraordinary people there are here!" I whispered to her as the others were taking their seats. "Do you know of Miss Harris' work?"

"A little," Phyllis said. "I've been looking out for a concert with some of her pieces. There's one in Hawksbridge next week, in fact, to honour her visit. I expect she'll be too modest to mention it. They're playing her first symphony and a few other pieces."

"We shall go," I said, and Phyllis squeezed my hand.

I noticed Captain Harris casting admiring glances at Francesca. "Mrs Campbell," he said, "I was told to expect a beautiful model this evening. My parents were not wrong! Are you a regular inspiration for artists, if I may ask?"

"Thank you, Captain Harris!" said Francesca, clearly enjoying the flattery. "No, not lately, although, yes – in my younger days, I occasionally sat for friends of my late husband in London. There was one embarrassing incident – but I don't know if I should tell it..."

"Please do, Mrs Campbell," the Captain said, his eyes fixed on her. "We are all agog."

"It was such a sad humiliation," Francesca said. "It might not be kind –"

"Francesca," said Mrs Harris, "I can feel a migraine coming on and I insist you tell us before I have to retire!"

"Very well, then," Francesca said. "My husband once had a strange notion – it may even have been done for a bet, as much as out of charity – but he thought he should support an impoverished artist from a far-flung corner of England, and pay for his lodgings while he completed a portrait of me."

"That was considerate of him," I said. "Was the artist any good?"

"Unfortunately he was terrible," Francesca said, to laughter. "He was always drunk at the start of the session, and then he would pull out a flask and drink during it, and more than once he had to be laid out on a spare bed and given copious quantities of coffee. It was all rather awful."

"Good Lord," said Captain Harris. "Do you still have the portrait?"

"No," said Francesca, taking a sip of her wine. "Poor Branwell Brontë tore it up in a fit of rage, before staggering back to Bradford."

She smiled at the predictable gasps of surprise at this revelation.

"Oh, Mrs Campbell," said Miss Harris. "Can this be true? You must be pulling our legs."

"I assure you I am in earnest," Francesca replied. "I have felt bad for the poor young man ever since, and I was so saddened to learn of his death in the autumn. I didn't know about his distinguished family until everyone else found out last year. It's a tragedy, and I should not have treated his weakness and frustration so lightly."

"I must say," Miss Harris said, "I did find it strange that 'Jane Eyre' had apparently been written by a man. It's too sympathetic to the female condition."

"My sister has been urging me to read it," said the Captain, "but I haven't yet had time."

"Oh, you must," said Francesca, smiling at the Captain with a little too much warmth. "It's quite an astonishing novel. You may come to my house for tea and I shall lend you my copy."

The Captain nodded in thanks, returning her smile. It occurred to me that he could more easily have borrowed his sister's copy.

"Speaking of the female condition," said Mr Harris, no

doubt anxious to divert attention from the all-too-obvious amiability between his son and Francesca, "have you seen these tracts from the Society for the Emancipation of Women? I don't know what to make of them."

"As an acronym, it hardly speaks of radical ideas," said Miss Harris. "It sounds more like a charitable ladies' group."

"Of course, Effie!" said the Captain. "It's a clever ruse to make the organisation sound more innocuous than it is. Let them all into your hearts and homes, and boom! before you know it, women will have the vote, we'll have a female prime minister, and society as we know it will collapse in a cloud of crinoline."

"Victor, you're a misogynist pig and I detest you," said Miss Harris, giving us a little glimpse of erstwhile childhood conflict.

"You don't believe that, do you, Captain Harris?" said Francesca, with a serious expression.

"I haven't read the tracts," said Captain Harris, putting his cutlery down and leaning back, "so I speak, my dear Mrs Campbell, in jest and from a position of total ignorance on the issues. Who has read these worthy pamphlets, then? Father?"

"I've read 'A Manifesto for the Timely Emancipation of Women'," said Mr Harris. "It makes a lot of rather ridiculous demands. The female vote, of course, but also how women should be allowed to dress, the right to easier divorce, and some educational and employment reforms. It was all rather dreary, I'm afraid."

"Intriguing," I said. "A rather characterful member of the aristocracy pushed this one into my hands the other day, but I haven't read it yet."

"That sounds like Lady Fairfield," said Mr Harris. "She's the author of these leaflets. Bit of a puritan, if you ask me. I've heard her talk on the subject of alcohol and its effects on the family. She's charismatic, I'll say that about her, but I don't envy her husband, if she has one."

"She's also a great benefactor of good causes," said Mrs Harris. "I won't have a word said against her. Only last week she donated two thousand pounds to the hospital. Two thousand pounds! And she's a widow, so you should be more sympathetic. She's probably keeping herself busy to forget her misery."

"Well, the teachers of St Saviour's School seem to like her," said Mr Harris. "Most of them, at any rate. My friend Nicholas, the art master, says she's given a talk there – which he didn't care for but apparently captured the imaginations of the ladies – and is taking a party of girls on a tour of her house."

"Is she promoting women's equality, or herself, I wonder?" said Captain Harris.

Miss Dubois, whose steady consumption of wine had painted her cheeks a fetching pink, cleared her throat and said with an equally charming French accent, "I think Lady Fairfield sounds interesting. Men are always so surprised that we can do anything at all but sit quietly or make babies. I think perhaps the world shall see more of us. A woman member of your parliament – mais oui, this could happen."

"Well, Miss Dubois," said Mrs Harris, "I suggest you go along to a meeting of the Society – they are gathering at Myrtle's coffee shop every Tuesday morning. You can report back and tell us how the revolution is going!"

"Bien sûr," Miss Dubois said, shrugging. "I would like to."

"Really?" said Miss Harris, a little alarmed. "Will you have time?"

Miss Dubois shot her a defiant look, and Miss Harris' expression softened. "But of course," she said. "I cannot claim all of your time. You have done so much. Please do go. I must learn patience or I will run you ragged."

"Merci," said Miss Dubois. "I may sell some tickets for you, Effie."

"I will take at least two," I said. "Phyllis and I are coming to your concert. And you, Dr Drummond?" He nodded. "And Flora?"

"Yes, please," Flora said.

"Oh, I can't wait," said Francesca. "I've had to content myself by playing your piano nocturnes – or rather, butchering them."

"I can't guarantee it will please your ear," said Miss Harris, "either the pieces or the performance. It's only an amateur orchestra, but they are most kind to be doing it at all. The proceeds are going to St Saviour's School for their instrument fund."

"Will you be performing?" I asked.

She laughed. "Me? Good Lord, no. My forte is composing – not playing."

~

After dessert, Mrs Harris rose from the table, hand on head. "I am so sorry, everyone – the devil is dancing in my head and I must retire. It has been such fun! I hope to attend Effie's concert, but I'm not sure I'll be up to it."

She kissed her family, waved to us, and left the room, accompanied by Mr Harris.

Miss Harris sighed. "What a worry Mother is."

"Yes," said the Captain. "I'm afraid you're not helping, Effie, tinkering on the piano at all hours of the day – and night! It's driving me rather mad, let alone Mother."

"I know, I know," she said. "But I have to compose when the muse takes hold of me. I should really move out with Sophie and leave her in peace. But I can't imagine who would want us."

"Take a house?" said the Captain.

"I've looked," said Miss Harris. "There's nothing suitable – I would have to get a piano, and I don't know how long we'll be staying."

"Then you must come and stay with me!" said Francesca.

"That's very kind, Mrs Campbell," said Miss Harris, "but we wouldn't dream of imposing ourselves. And our musical habits are terrible, as Victor says."

"I'm serious, Miss Harris," said Francesca. "I have some suitable rooms for you both, and a small sitting room that we can make into a music room. I don't think I'd hear the piano from my bedroom, and I'm a heavy sleeper in any case. I would love some company – and to have pieces composed in my own house by a musical genius – it's a dream! I would be dining out on it for the rest of my life."

And it wouldn't be unpleasant for Francesca, I thought to myself, if the handsome Captain should ride out to Halfpenny House to see his sister now and again, and spend some time with her hostess for good measure.

"You are tempting me, Mrs Campbell! Victor, please stop me from imposing myself on an innocent woman and driving her to distraction."

"I couldn't possibly intervene," said the Captain. "It sounds a perfectly sensible idea."

"The Captain has spoken," said Francesca. "Will you stay with me?"

Miss Harris hesitated, running her hand through her thick red locks, and looked to Miss Dubois for an answer. She merely shrugged.

"I have to say," I put in, "Mrs Campbell's house is quite large, and absolutely delightful. You will be comfortable, assuming she's not redecorating everything, which she does rather regularly."

"Oh, I can delay that," Francesca said.

"Then... yes, please!" said Miss Harris. "That's so generous of you. We'll try to be quiet."

"Then it's settled!" said Francesca. "When would you like to move in?"

"Tomorrow?" said Miss Harris.

"Tomorrow it is," said Francesca. "We'll have such fun!"

CHAPTER THREE

I PLANTED my chair on the front lawn, well away from the house, and stared at the handsome frontage, lost in contemplation. Fox settled happily at my feet. When Phyllis' wealth was combined with mine, we could afford a grander home in which to bring up our family, entertain our friends and the local worthies, and generally live the life that our funds and status seemed to demand.

And yet, I knew that was hardly what either Phyllis or I wanted. We felt no need for a house with forty rooms, formal gardens, a couple of lakes, and a small army of servants. But should Ramsburgh perhaps be augmented a little? It was customary for landowners to regularly add wings to their houses, signalling their wealth and impeccable architectural taste. Was Ramsburgh too small for a growing family? It felt strange to imagine a Rufford brood, but I was set on that path, and I would have to give my future family all that would be expected of me.

I shaded my eyes from the morning sun and squinted at the house, trying to picture it extended on one side or another. But I could not satisfactorily visualize the house in any other way than how it presently stood. I did not want to butcher the drawing room on the west side, with its views in two directions, or demolish the arch on the east side that led into the courtyard by Flora's tower.

My mind wandered to the day before, when I had presented Phyllis with the ring on Knight's Mount where I had proposed: she had been delighted. I had judged it correctly. She was not a woman to be impressed with diamonds and sapphires, and I suspect she would have been disappointed with a ring that was showy and overly expensive. She had kissed me then with a slow, gentle intensity that had left me in no doubt about our future bliss.

I was startled out of my daydream by a figure emerging from the house, carrying something. It was my cook Catherine: an African princess, no less, who had through several twists of fate come to this continent and then my household, to the delight of all, especially my put-upon housekeeper. I enjoyed the elegance of her proud deportment as she walked across the lawn towards me.

"I saw you sitting here for so long, sir, and I thought you might like a cup of coffee."

"Thank you, Catherine! How very considerate of you." She handed me the cup and I took a sip. "Extremely good. You've certainly got the knack from your days at Myrtle's! Are you still enjoying it?"

"Yes, sir. Mrs Shannon is a fine woman to work for. She makes me laugh. Are you sure you want me to continue there, sir? Does not Mrs Felton mind cooking while I'm away? She is too good to speak of it to me."

"She's perfectly happy, I'm glad to say. She quite enjoys a couple of days' cooking, but no more. And I know you do quite a bit of preparation for her before you go to Myrtle's. Besides, it might be useful for you to hear the gossip at the coffee shop. I gather it's now the centre of a dangerous revolutionary council."

"Ah!" said Catherine, smiling. "Lady Fairfield's Society. They are serious, yes. But dangerous – no, I think. After all, they are women! What can they do?"

"Oh, they wouldn't like to hear you saying that!" I said. "Defeatism, they would cry. Do you not think they have a point about the inequalities of society?"

"I did not say they do not have a point, sir – only that as women, they have little power to change the world. I am – what is the word?"

"A realist!"

"Yes, I am a realist. I think they will only anger men if they do these things."

"Oh? What things?"

Catherine pursed her lips while she tried to remember. "Dressing in trousers, refusing their husbands their marital rights, protesting at golf clubs and inns. Some other things. Oh, I heard someone speak of breaking shop windows. I don't think these are useful things to do."

"No, I agree. They seem rather far removed from Lady Fairfield's charitable work, too."

"Yes, sir – I have served Lady Fairfield. She is clever – but I think she may have been hurt." She hesitated. "I have experience of that, as you know, sir. I might be wrong, but I think Lady Fairfield may have been treated a little as I have been treated. She is troubled."

"Interesting," I said. "Very interesting. I have briefly met the lady in question, and she certainly didn't seem the most jovial creature. But perhaps it's just her way."

"Can I ask what is wrong with the house, sir?" Catherine said. "You are worried about something."

"Not worried, exactly," I said. "I'm trying to think whether I need to enlarge the house, for when I have a family. I seem to be the only one around here who hasn't added a wing or two to their property."

"Oh!" she said, turning to look at the house. "But it's so perfect already. Would that not spoil it?"

"I know, I know," I said. "I don't want to touch it, really."

"You have the large bedroom next to yours for a nursery," Catherine said. "And there are the rooms above that for when they are older. Do you need more?"

"No – no, I don't. You're right, I don't know what I was thinking. I'm going to leave the house as it is – apart from decorations, of course. Thank you for confirming my instinct."

Catherine nodded. "Are you going to use Mr Forrester's wallpaper?"

I laughed. "You're a follower of Forrester too? Well, I might. I'll see how Mrs Campbell gets on with her redecoration."

"He is handsome," Catherine said, smiling. "I have served him, too, and his wife, on a Wednesday afternoon when men are allowed. He was trying to persuade Mrs Shannon to decorate the shop in one of his papers."

"Was she tempted?"

"She was, when he pulled out some samples and laid them on the table. I have never seen such bright colours."

"Yes, I've seen them myself," I said. "As an investor in Myrtle's, I'll have to speak to her before she puts a big dent in the shop's funds. But no doubt it would be a talking point for customers. And it would do no harm to humour the magnificent Mr Forrester."

I drained my coffee and gave the empty cup to Catherine. "That was superb. And now I have no further need to sit and stare at my house like a loon."

As Catherine returned to the house, I heard the sound of a carriage coming up the drive, and watched as it drew up by the front door. An unfamiliar, smartly-dressed man in his late thirties got out, and leaving my lonely chair on the lawn, I walked over to greet him, followed by Fox.

"William Lowick," he said, offering me his hand. "Reporter with The Hawksbridge Herald."

"Pleased to meet you, Mr Lowick," I said, shaking his hand. The man had a likeable face, clean-shaven apart from sideburns, and his brown eyes shone with a reporter's curiosity. "Thomas Rufford. What can I do for you?"

"I heard of your engagement, sir. May I congratulate you!" Running a hand through his thick and slightly unruly mane, which gave him something of the look of a poet, he cast his eye admiringly over the house. "What a fine home to bring up a family. And what a beautiful dog," he added, leaning down to stroke Fox, who was suitably appreciative.

"Thank you. I'm flattered you came all this way just for –"

"Oh, no, sir," he said, laughing and straightening up. "Not just for that. We thought that this would be a good moment for a little retrospective of your contributions to the town, which are considerable."

I frowned. "Is that of any interest to the public? Surely everything has been said by now."

"I don't believe they have, no," said Mr Lowick. "Not by you, at any rate. The accounts so far have been impersonal. We would like to write a story that starts with your arrival in Hawksbridge, paints a candid picture of your adventures from your own perspective, and ends with your engagement and prospect of a new family life. We are prepared to compensate you, of course. But I don't anticipate it taking more than two or three hours of your time. I will interview you and write the piece – submitting it for your approval, naturally."

I was silent for a few moments as I wondered what possible benefit this might have for me, and whether any harm could come of it. But Mr Lowick seemed such a pleasant and genuine fellow, standing there patiently, smiling and hopeful. I had great respect for The Herald, and I did not want to immediately crush him.

"I don't really feel the need for the money, Mr Lowick, but perhaps a charity might benefit from the fee."

"A capital idea, sir!" said the journalist enthusiastically. "That would make a good note on which to finish the article, and encourage the reader to contribute to your good cause."

"Shall we discuss it indoors?" I said, leading the way.

~

I took Mr Lowick into the ground floor study as a suitably business-like location for our discussion, but he did not appear in a hurry to talk about his article. He stood at the window with his glass of sherry looking out towards the west lawn.

"How charming and peaceful this house is, sir. Your family cannot help but be happy here."

"Thank you, Mr Lowick. Just before you came I had the foolish notion of extending it, but my excellent cook helped me out of that delusion."

"An unusual advisor, sir! You are indeed fortunate. But your house seems neither too small nor too big. I had occasion recently to visit a house that I consider outrageously out of proportion. Only a single member of one family lives there – with a few companions, admittedly – and it made me glad for my own modest home."

"Indeed," I said. "What strange creature could live like that?"

"If that is not a rhetorical question," said Mr Lowick, "I speak of Lady Esme Fairfield at Kirkheaton Hall. I'm writing an article about her charitable work, and her interest in expanding the rights of women."

"Interesting – I encountered her in Belford's, the jeweller's. She seems quite an eccentric. What do you make of her?"

"Eccentric, yes," he said, "but I find a poignancy about her situation that belies her outward toughness. She lost her husband a couple of years ago, and she never managed to have children. And now she lives nearly alone in her gilded cage. I think she needs friends, other than her admirers in the Society, who stay for long periods."

"And have you views about her Society for the Emancipation of Women?"

Mr Lowick smiled. "As a man, I feel a little unqualified to answer. I think the movement has some merit – why should a woman be considered inferior to a man, except in the matter of physical strength? – but I suspect such changes will happen slowly, and probably at the behest of enlightened men, not through strident feminine protest."

"I fear you are right," I said. "My cook Catherine was of a similar opinion."

"Good Lord," said Mr Lowick. "I envy you your philosopher-cook."

~

After an hour or so, Mr Lowick pulled out a gold pocket watch, with a little too much force so that it escaped his grasp and fell to the floor, rolling towards my feet.

"It's fortunate there was a rug here," I said, picking up the watch and examining it. "It seems to be in one piece. What a beautiful thing," I added, turning it over in my hand. The back was embellished with an attractive floral design, and the letters 'W.R.' had been engraved within a shield at the centre.

I handed it back carefully, and Mr Lowick said, "Thank you – it was a wedding present from my father-in-law. In my younger day, I had something of a reputation for wildness and unpunctuality. In a way, the watch was a gentle rebuke by my father-in-law – but the kindest rebuke possible, and I believe I've been more or less punctual ever since!"

"And the wildness?" I asked.

"Ah," he said, pushing his hand through his hair as he had earlier. "I try my best, Mr Rufford." He jumped up. "Thank you for permission to write the article. I already have some excellent material. May I return – say, on the morning of Tuesday week?"

"Certainly," I said. "I look forward to it." It had been surprisingly pleasant conversing with the journalist – I realised I did not spend a great deal of time in the company of men.

Mr Lowick drew out a neglected side of me.

After Mr Lowick's carriage had drawn away from the house, I started across the lawn to retrieve my seat of contemplation. But I soon stopped, because perched on the chair back was the regal, iridescent form of a peacock, his folded tail feathers flowing behind him like a ceremonial cloak, and his dark eyes fixed on mine.

~

If I did not care for the music, I thought as I sat in the Town Hall holding Phyllis' hand, I could at least renew my acquaintance with the murals. The concert of Euphemia Harris' pieces was well attended, in some cases probably by those simply curious to catch a glimpse of the local girl who had recently and swiftly risen to fame.

The members of the orchestra filed in, and I watched Miss Harris on the front row as she bent her head to exchange remarks with Miss Dubois. The composer turned to see how many people had come, and I caught her eye. She nodded and smiled in recognition. I wondered what kind of music this strange, red-headed beauty was capable of creating; I suspected there would be some passion in it, but I was not prepared for the reality.

When the conductor brought down his baton on the first bar, a roll of timpani signalled a blast of sound that so took the audience by surprise, I was afraid for some of the older attendees. Fortissimo chords of brass outlined a melody that was taken up by strings, and the instruments chased each other in a series of cascades, varying the melody until it was barely recognisable, before reprieving it with chords that made the hair on the back of my neck stand up.

I could see people looking at each other in a mixture of

disbelief and admiration. For a début symphony, it was supremely accomplished: even I could tell that. As the first movement progressed like a tide of churning waves, I marvelled at the energy and skill of this young woman, not yet out of her twenties. What had motivated this feat? Was it a tumultuous love affair, or simply the joy of being alive? Or perhaps, I thought, it was a noisy declaration of war against the established order.

For the second movement, a new melody started poignantly on the viola and ushered in a stunning, serene musical elegy that built to a final theme – frustratingly only hinted at thereafter, not fully repeated, but all the more intense for its rarity – with such deft counterpoint and delicacy of handling that several people, including Phyllis, were obliged to reach for their handkerchiefs. I too could feel a distinct pricking at my eyes.

After two more movements, I was exhausted and elated from the emotions and sensations that Miss Harris had made us experience, and in a state of disbelief that something of this beauty was possible at all, let alone formed in the mind of one so young and from such an unexceptional background.

A standing ovation followed, with foot-stamping from some of the young men present, and the conductor gestured for Miss Harris to stand and acknowledge the audience's enthusiasm. She was flushed with pleasure, and after a small bow, she went to Miss Dubois and brought her up to the front – although she was clearly reluctant – to share the acclamation.

The young men went wild at this, and there was whistling and more foot stomping. I began to think that I had wasted my life so far. Nothing I did could ever elicit such an intensity of emotion or invigorate the intellect in the way that Miss Harris was capable of. A woman who could not coax a note from a trumpet or play a bar on the violin could nevertheless bend an entire orchestra to her will. A mere sprinkling of dots on a page commanded an angry hurricane of sound one minute, and a lyrical, yearning melody the next.

Thus she was able to rise far above the humdrum of life, and most of her fellow men and women, by virtue of the workings of her extraordinary mind. The role that Miss Dubois played in this was unclear to me, but I thought it must have been significant for Miss Harris to acknowledge her so publicly.

There followed several more pieces of similar quality, including a string serenade and a fantasia for flute, but it was the symphony that had particularly captivated me, and I tried to recall some of the melodies. Annoyingly, they were becoming less distinct in my mind, overlaid as they were with the other compositions. I was left holding the glittering shards of Miss Harris' masterpiece, longing to piece them together again.

When the concert was over, Phyllis squeezed my hand and turned to me, her cheeks still damp with emotion. "Well," she said. "I hardly know what to say. Miss Harris is so clever. I had no idea."

"It's uncanny," I said. "She has seduced me with her symphony."

"I must be careful, then," Phyllis said. "But look – she's surrounded by young men! You have no hope, I'm afraid."

"Shall we try our luck with the throng?" I said. "We must congratulate her."

When I caught a glimpse of Miss Harris through her little knot of admirers, she was blushing but exhilarated by the success of the concert. She was signing programmes.

A fellow who had been nervously fiddling with his waistcoat buttons saw his chance and thrust his programme towards her. "Um – may we know the source of your musical inspiration, Miss Harris?" he stammered.

"Oh, everything!" she said, scribbling her name. "Nature. Art. Being happy. Appreciative listeners such as yourself." Her devotee beamed at this. "Oh, and Miss Dubois, of course," she added, putting an arm around her shy assistant's shoulders. Then she spotted us, and said, "Mr Rufford! Miss Drummond! I must know what you thought of my humble efforts." She released Miss Dubois and pushed through the human cordon, taking hold of our hands in her excitement.

"I barely know where to start," I said. "In a word – breathtaking! I need to listen to your symphony all over again, but I must wait. I'm not sure I can."

"It was all just extraordinary," said Phyllis, shaking her head in admiration.

"I'm so glad!" said Miss Harris. "I must admit, I was pleased with the symphony. Sylvie had a hard time keeping up with me – and at goodness' knows what time of night, as well! That's when the best inspiration seems to hit me. What a nuisance I am."

"Surely the end result is worth any amount of nuisance," I said.

"I must leave Sylvie to answer that," Miss Harris said.

But in her customary, enigmatic manner, Miss Dubois only shrugged.

CHAPTER FOUR

ON MONDAY, I had left a meeting with the directors of the Pottery and was idly looking in the window of Hunter's, the bookshop, when I heard my name being called. It was William Lowick.

"Mr Rufford! Good morning, sir. I see you were at Miss Harris' concert last night. What did you think?"

"Good morning, Mr Lowick. The concert – I was a little overwhelmed. I hadn't expected her music to be so..." I searched for words to describe my admiration without using hyperbole.

"So sublime?" said Mr Lowick. I nodded. "Indeed – I felt the same way. Miss Harris has a highly original mind. I noticed you talking to her – do you know her well?"

"Not really," I said, "but I expect our paths will cross further, as I'm friends with her parents and with her current hostess, Mrs Francesca Campbell."

"You lucky devil. She must be a fascinating creature."

"I think she is. Are you chasing another story?"

"In a manner of speaking," Mr Lowick said. "I'm covering today's public meeting of the Society for Emancipation of Women. It starts at twelve. Why don't you come along?"

"Well..." I hesitated. "I don't think I'm the intended audience."

"On the contrary," he said. "Lady Fairfield would say that you are exactly the sort of person she wants to reach – a man with influence in the community."

"I'm not at all sure I have any," I said.

"In that case, let me tempt you by the prospect of an

indifferent cup of coffee afterwards. And besides," he added, looking around and lowering his voice, "excessive self-righteousness can be damned amusing."

I could see that he wanted company, and I had nothing better to do, so I capitulated.

"Very well, Mr Lowick. I expect I shall learn something. And I confess I'm a little curious to see Lady Fairfield in action."

"Splendid!" he said. "It's in the Church Hall at St Ninian's."

When we arrived, Reverend Benton was talking excitedly with Lady Fairfield at the front, his hands pressed piously together as if in worship. Lady Fairfield nodded in recognition as we sat down amongst the mainly female gathering, and continued her conversation.

"Your support is much appreciated, Mr Benton," she said. "I believe the tide is turning for a more enlightened world, and the Church is in the ideal position to help spread the word."

"Indeed, Lady Fairfield," Mr Benton said. "Your work is the best example of Christian charity I know – and what better cause than a recognition of the equality of all the Lord's sheep?"

Mr Lowick leaned towards me and quietly emitted a "Baaa!" Unfortunately it was not quiet enough, and Lady Fairfield looked up, frowning. Mr Lowick adopted a neutral, innocent expression, looking around as if for the culprit.

Lady Fairfield went back to her conversation, and Mr Lowick whispered, "Sorry about that."

"An example of your wild side, I take it?" I whispered back.

"I fear so," he replied. "I'll try to be a more domesticated sheep." He took out his notebook in a studious gesture, but was soon drawing a caricature of the Rector.

As the St Ninian's clock chimed twelve, Lady Fairfield

took up her position centre-stage.

"Ladies and gentlemen," she said in her characteristically high voice, made a little shriller by the need to project to her audience, "thank you for coming. The subject today is 'Protest'. The protest at home, the protest at work, and the protest in the streets. But, my esteemed sisters, I beseech you: first protest against yourself – against the woman you are today." Lady Fairfield rested for a moment, scanning a room full of puzzled faces and letting this strange exhortation settle in her listeners' minds.

"Yes, the first protests start in front of the looking glass," she continued. "Consider the restrictions placed on your legal rights. Should you not protest against your own meekness in accepting this? Consider the unquestioning giving of yourself to your menfolk. Should you not castigate yourself in choosing to always give, while men only take? Consider the fatuous system they dare to call 'female education'. Will you truly tolerate the infantilisation of your sex? To quote that unsurpassed beacon of inspiration, Mrs Wollstonecraft: 'Strengthen the female mind by enlarging it, and there will be an end to blind obedience'."

She stopped again for the audience to absorb this statement.

"I believe education to be the key to the release from our prison," she continued. "But our struggle takes place on many fronts. In preparation for battles to come, let us grapple with our own weaknesses, and the natural but misguided inclination to accept the poisonous status quo. Let us free ourselves from the urge to submit and to take the easy path. For we are soldiers, and we must think like soldiers. We must be ruthless with ourselves. Women! Do not accept the quiet, demeaning life that men have thrust upon you. Men! Give us the rights you yourselves enjoy, and let us attain the glories we have always been capable of achieving, but for too long have been wickedly denied."

It struck me that Miss Harris had not needed permission from men before achieving her own glory, and the same went for Phyllis, but I conceded that these might be exceptions.

Lady Fairfield paused for breath, and applause broke out. The women looked rapturous, while the men looked decidedly uncomfortable, except for Mr Lowick, who wore a wry smile and scribbled in his notebook, and Mr Benton, who had been nodding and was now enthusiastically clapping. It seemed that Mr Benton was a recruit to Lady Fairfield's army.

Lady Fairfield warmed to her theme of protest, and various practical means were suggested. The proposed withdrawal of conjugal rights until equality was attained elicited frowns on several male faces, and yet Mr Benton remained as cheerful as ever. "He's obviously not getting much anyway," Mr Lowick whispered to me.

When Lady Fairfield had finished and had begun to talk to those brave enough to approach her, I turned around to see that Francesca had been sitting near the back.

"Thomas!" she said, coming towards us. "I had not expected to see you here. Who is your friend?"

"Francesca, this is William Lowick – he's kindly writing an article about me. Mr Lowick, this is Mrs Francesca Campbell."

"I'm very pleased to meet you, Mr Lowick," Francesca said. "Thomas is an excellent subject for an article, although I'm sure you're having to work hard to coax anything out of him. He's far too modest."

"He is indeed, Mrs Campbell," said Mr Lowick, "but I am trained in the dark arts of journalism. I believe I shall have my story. Mr Rufford was telling me that you know Miss Harris. I confess that for me, her concert had the edge over this meeting, passionate though Lady Fairfield is."

"Comparisons are said to be odious, Mr Lowick," said Francesca. "And this event was not meant as entertainment. But yes, Miss Harris and her music are both delightful. She and her assistant are staying at my house, and my sleep is barely disturbed at all."

Mr Lowick looked puzzled. "Your sleep?"

"Miss Harris often composes at night, apparently," I explained. "It seems to be the secret of her success."

"Curious," said Mr Lowick. "Now – I should like to speak to Lady Fairfield. Will you join me?"

Coffee was being served to the attendees. Perhaps because she was in familiar territory and clearly adored by her female followers, Lady Fairfield showed less of the prickliness she exhibited in the jeweller's. She was even in a mood to tolerate Mr Lowick, who exuded a general air of cynicism and levity despite his best efforts to behave.

"I'm glad to see you here, Mr Lowick," she said. "I'm sure that eventually you will acknowledge the wisdom of our movement. You made a good start when you came to see me. Please feel free to return – I fear I did not do justice to the Cause when you interviewed me."

"I'd be glad to, ma'am," said Mr Lowick, "since your taste in port is impeccable."

Lady Fairfield let this go with a smile, and turned to Francesca. "How nice to meet you again, Mrs Campbell," she said. "I'm anxious to know if we can count on your support. Are you not persuaded of the gross imbalance between the sexes?"

"Your talk was most intriguing, Lady Fairfield," Francesca said. "You made many good points. I consider myself better educated as a result, and I shall certainly ponder further."

"You are a master of equivocation," said Lady Fairfield. "There, you see how even language is stacked against us? But I have been unfair. You cannot be expected to change your mind in an instant. Still, I do hope you will join us."

I noticed a group of women in navy blue dresses wearing yellow sashes marked 'S.E.W.', who had held back to share Lady Fairfield with others. They now gathered around her, and they left the Church Hall together like a modern-day prophetess and her disciples.

"Lady Fairfield's sewing circle," Mr Lowick remarked. "Quite the swarm of wasps around their queen, up at Kirkheaton Hall."

CHAPTER FIVE

FRANCESCA had lost no time in issuing invitations for a dinner party at Halfpenny House to honour her musical lodgers. A note enclosed with her invitation excitedly spoke of further distinguished guests: the designer Gabriel Forrester, no less, together with his wife Penelope. I would have another chance to talk with Captain Harris, to whom I had taken a liking, and Flora and Phyllis were also invited. It promised to be a lively occasion.

On Saturday, I hired a carriage, and Flora and I went into town to fetch Phyllis.

"I want to speak intelligently to Mr Forrester," I said to Flora, "but apart from a brief look at a couple of samples, I don't know much about his work, except that everyone seems enraptured by it. Perhaps you can suggest something."

"I'm sure he'll do most of the talking. But ask him about 'Hedgerow' – it's a new design. I read an article about Mr Forrester and he's apparently very proud of it."

"'Hedgerow'," I repeated. "I'll try to drop that in. So – would you use Forrester paper? It must be right up your street, being botanically inspired."

"Some of them are beautiful," Flora said. "But they are expensive. And Mr Forrester is..."

"Yes?"

"Well, he is a little political. I'm not sure I want to be seen to cover my walls in what almost amounts to a radical manifesto."

"Interesting," I said. "I will have to watch what I say."

"Please do," Flora said. "We must try to keep the conversation light!"

"I expect Francesca will dive in head-first. Although she may rein herself in for her hero."

Flora laughed. "Have you ever known Francesca to rein herself in?"

"You have a point," I admitted.

~

Our hostess was in her element. In the drawing room, she was ensuring everyone had someone to talk to and a drink in their hand. She spotted us, and altered direction to intercept us.

"Come and meet the Forresters!" she said. "Such lovely people – they have only been here twenty minutes and I feel they are firm friends already."

Mr Forrester was a large-framed man in his early forties with a full and slightly intimidating beard. But any anxiety on my part was immediately dispelled by an enthusiastic handshake and broad smile.

"Mr Rufford, how very pleasant to meet you. In our brief acquaintance, Mrs Campbell has reminded me that you are in the habit of placing yourself in danger for the benefit of your fellow creatures. Now, if all men were built like you, what a fine world we would have! I believe this quality gives you the heart of a true socialist, Mr Rufford."

Sensing danger, Mrs Forrester intervened.

"My dear, is it not a little early in the evening for politics? Let me congratulate you both, Mr Rufford and Miss Drummond, on your engagement! I can tell just from looking at you that you will be wonderfully happy together."

"Thank you," I said, taking Phyllis' hand. "I believe we will, so long as I don't interfere with Phyllis' writing!"

"Oh! Are you a writer, Miss Drummond? Might I have read anything of yours?"

"If you have read Iona Tavistock, then yes," said Phyllis.

"No!" said Mrs Forrester, evidently shocked. "Really? But she is – you are – one of my favourite authors! How can this be? My dear Miss Drummond, you see before you a devotee. Mr Rufford, you must indeed let her continue at her usual pace, or I shall be bereft. I really cannot believe this!"

Mr Forrester also seemed impressed, and he and his wife began an interrogation about characters and plots. I did not mind being a little redundant, as I had the pleasure of watching Phyllis glow with confidence and the satisfaction of recognition.

I felt a gentle tap on my shoulder, and turned to see Miss Euphemia Harris. Her peacock-blue dress emphasised her astonishing copper hair, as well as her hourglass body. She held a nearly-empty wine glass and the contents had clearly disinhibited her.

"Good evening, Mr Rufford!" she said. "I see your fiancée is being heaped with praise. Quite right. I also feel the need for some outrageous compliments. Tell me again how you enjoyed my concert!"

"You are looking stunning," I said, "and I enjoyed your concert immensely more than any other. But these are not really compliments, merely statements of fact."

"I see," she said, smiling. "Then feel free to state facts, whenever you wish."

I noticed Miss Dubois, hanging back a little. She had dark rings around her eyes and a rather haggard look about her.

"Good evening, Miss Dubois," I said. "I'm glad to see you here. I hope you are well?"

"Merci, Mr Rufford. I am feeling a little tired," Miss Dubois said.

Miss Harris looked sheepish. "My fault, as ever. My new symphony is taking it out of her."

"Do you transcribe, Miss Dubois?" I asked.

"Bien sûr, Mr Rufford. I transcribe. I interpret. I extract –

what is a better word?"

"Tease out?" Miss Harris offered.

"Ah, oui, tease out the music that Miss Harris has inside her. It is difficile sometimes."

"You're so clever at it!" said Miss Harris. "You're the very best tease in the world." She giggled, and switched her glass with a full one on a passing tray.

Miss Dubois did not smile but said, "I think you have had sufficient, no?"

"I'll drink it slowly," Miss Harris said, as if to a parent or spouse. "I promise."

~

As the food was brought into the dining room, and there was a lull in the conversation, I tried Flora's gambit.

"Mr Forrester, Miss Davison tells me you have made a new design – 'Hedgerow'. Is this a creation of yours, or perhaps one of your colleagues?"

As Flora had predicted, Mr Forrester seemed delighted to be asked. "All my own work, I'm proud to say. I think I have caught the spirit of it – brambles, rosehips, hawthorn, and a few other elements. I confess I'm gratified at the response – we are drastically increasing production, and may be able to reduce the cost a little. I want people in all walks of life to be able to enjoy art, even in so apparently banal a setting as a wall covering. As I often say, art and life should be one and the same. I want everyone to exist in a world of artistic beauty."

He paused to relish the nods of agreement around the table.

"Now, Mr Rufford," he continued, "I dare say that with a new family life in the offing, you will be doing a spot of redecoration yourself, will you not?"

He looked slyly at Phyllis and myself, and I nodded. "Your papers will be uppermost in our minds," I said. "And I think Mrs Campbell is going to smother this entire house in the best of Forrester."

"I'm not sure 'smother' is the word, Thomas," said Francesca, "but yes – the house is currently a testament to a complete lack of imagination before my recent enlightenment, and I will shortly be redoing it all. It's so exciting! But choosing between so many beautiful patterns is agony. I might need someone to help arbitrate between competing designs."

I had noticed Captain Harris' eyes fixed firmly on Francesca since we had sat down. She appeared to be a source of fascination to him.

"I would be happy to step into that role if required," Captain Harris said. "Not that I'm an expert, but I must say these designs do hold a botanical interest for me."

"Well, thank you, Captain Harris!" Francesca said. "I may well call on you for this. It would certainly be more amusing than throwing dice to decide."

I could quite understand what amusement Francesca might have with Captain Harris. From the warm way in which she returned his gaze, it was clear that the admiration was mutual. I wondered whether trouble was brewing. Captain Harris' parents would be horrified.

"Botanical interests?" said Flora. "May we know more?"

"Botany and zoology," said Captain Harris, neatly slicing his roast beef and turning to Flora. "I'm an amateur, of course, but I'm learning. My voyages to India have unexpectedly introduced me to the wonders and immense variety of Nature. In the many tedious hours of my soldiering duties, questions have occurred to me – questions that I find I must try to answer. What is the purpose of this extraordinary variety? How does it come about? Why does it come about? How does a lizard species learn to change its colour to become invisible to its predators? How have plants come to entice their pollinators with such intricate structures, scents, colours, and even food? Questions are everywhere we look. Answers are in much shorter supply."

Captain Harris had been leaning forward during this energetic and heartfelt speech, and from the intensity in Flora's eyes, she had joined Francesca in the admiration of the prepossessing Captain.

He seemed to snap out of his earnest mood, and sat back again, stabbing his meat with his fork. "I'm sorry, I'm being far too serious. Forgive me. But I have made it my mission to advance our knowledge in this area – I have made the decision to go onto half-pay, and travel in search of some answers."

"There's no need to apologise," said Flora. "I find it fascinating – I do some botanical drawing, and these questions have occurred to me too. But I could never have the confidence to seek out the answers. That is bold."

"What a fine couple you would make," said Miss Harris, "with my brother slashing through the jungle to fetch specimens, and bringing them back to the camp for you to draw, Miss Davison!"

Flora blushed and stared at her cutlery.

"Really, Effie, you're being tiresome," said Captain Harris. "The last thing poor Miss Davison would wish to do is wander around an insect-infested jungle in the company of an obsessive ex-soldier. I can't imagine anyone would. No, I have to do this thing, and then eventually I might find some peace and become a tolerable candidate for companionship."

"What kind of soldiering did you do, Mr Harris?" Francesca asked, before sipping her wine.

"I'm just a sapper, Mrs Campbell," he said. "Royal Engineers – building bridges, repairing roads, that kind of thing. Not the most glamorous side of the army, but we had our challenges. And it has led to my other interests."

"You would make a most delightful subject for a painting," Mr Forrester declared. "The doughty soldier-engineer-biologist in his red jacket, standing in front of a half-built bridge in a war-torn landscape with a theodolite in one hand, and an exotic plant in the other. You could make a hungry young artist's career."

Francesca put down her glass and clapped her hands together. "You're so right! I can quite picture it. But theodolites are made of brass, aren't they? What muscles you would develop, posing for this."

"I'm sure Captain Harris has plenty of muscles already from a life in the army," said Mrs Forrester. The two women appeared to be savouring the conversation about Captain Harris' physique. I half-expected Francesca to go to the Captain and feel his biceps, so to avoid this unwelcome possibility, I changed the subject.

"So you intend to answer some immense questions about species, Captain Harris. Do you agree with the theory by – what's the fellow's name? – Lamarck – that characteristics acquired during a creature's lifetime can be passed to its offspring? For example, muscle strength acquired during manual labour. Might this be an adequate explanation for the variety we see?"

Captain Harris shook his head. "No, I'm afraid that theory is little better than superstition. There are many changes in species that cannot occur during an individual's lifetime. And supposing they did – such as the acquisition of wings – we would need an explanation for that. A temporary gift of wings excepted, of course," he added, referring to the Town Hall mural. "Your portrait is exquisite, Mrs Campbell. I could hardly take my eyes off it." Francesca smiled sweetly, and leant forward almost imperceptibly, as if to give the Captain a better view of what was on more forthright display in the Town Hall.

"I assume you have dismissed God as the architect of these changes," said Mrs Forrester.

"I never dismiss God lightly, of course," said Captain Harris, finally removing his gaze from Francesca. "But could

God be guiding every tiny change in species? If the secret to the variety and complexity of life on Earth is a large number of small changes, we surely have to review our idea of the Creation. It would mean a less spectacular, more arduous role for God – and perhaps one that doesn't need His constant presence."

"Well, I wish you the best of luck in unlocking these secrets," Mr Forrester said. "And I shall be interested to see what you bring back from your travels. I'm always in search of inspiration for my work."

"What was that wonderful aphorism of yours, Mr Forrester?" said Francesca. "I think it was, 'Beauty is to the home what love is to the soul.' I find that a charming sentiment."

"I assume this refers to the Forrester designs," I said. "But – forgive me – don't some people also see a whitewashed room as beautiful?"

"An interesting observation. But consider the monk in his cell." Mr Forrester paused to sip his wine, leaving puzzled expressions all around the table.

"Monks go out of their way to reject the sensual things of life," he continued. "They choose to live in stark white cells to deny themselves the temptation of beauty. Therefore they prove plain white walls to be the height of ugliness. Quod erat demonstrandum."

"He's got a point there, Thomas," said Captain Harris.

The wine had made me argumentative, and I persisted: "But are not monks and nuns the ultimate socialists? How does that accord with your beliefs?"

"A bleak kind of socialism, sir! My vision of socialism is aesthetic, not ascetic. Feed the soul, don't starve it. You might as well argue that silence is as beautiful as Miss Harris' music."

"Some may well argue that!" said Miss Harris.

"I suspect, Mr Forrester," I said, "that your definition of beauty is anything that comes out of your factories."

Mr Forrester raised his glass and smiled. "I'll drink to that definition," he said, taking a deep draught.

~

When syllabubs had been served, I glanced at Francesca. Was she really going to perform her party trick in front of such distinguished guests? What on earth would they think? She looked back at me with a wicked smile.

"Poor Thomas," she announced, "is afraid that I shall now disgrace myself with behaviour unbecoming to a lady."

"Pray demonstrate," said Captain Harris, his interest obviously piqued, "so that we may judge."

"Carry on," I said. "I don't suppose I can stop you, now that you have set up a mystery."

"Very well," she said, and proceeded to carve her syllabub, whose consistency she had no doubt been diligent in specifying. The resulting tongue, and its revolting movement, had the desired effect on Francesca's audience, and soon most of the diners – with the exception of Sylvie – were carving their own syllabub tongues, with varying degrees of success.

"Look, Sylvie!" said Miss Harris triumphantly. "How horribly real!"

Sylvie looked unamused, muttering "Dégoûtant."

Captain Harris pushed his sculpture across the table to their instructor for her approval. "How's that?" he said.

Francesca rocked the bowl and watched the tongue flop from side to side. "Most satisfactory, Captain Harris. Good shape and movement. May I?"

"Of course," said the Captain, and Francesca carefully scooped up the Captain's tongue and popped it in her mouth, slowly savouring it.

"I'm sorry, it was irresistible," she said. "You may have

mine." She pushed hers to his place, whereupon he consumed it with relish.

I looked around at the wide eyes of my fellow diners. For a few seconds, there was a shocked silence, before Mr Forrester roared with laughter and punctured the awkwardness. "An amusing ritual, Mrs Campbell. Here, Penelope, you have mine." He swapped the plates, and they both consumed the wilting remains of their dessert. "First rate taste, too, Mrs Campbell."

Phyllis had already eaten her sculpture, and said, "I wonder if Lady Fairfield has such parties. I can't quite imagine it, from what Thomas has said."

"Ah, Lady Fairfield, that energetic champion of her sex," said Mr Forrester. "And, I believe, a good socialist, in her way. I thoroughly approve of her campaign for female equality. I recently met her, and I have pledged my support."

"Really?" said Miss Harris. "I saw a gaggle of them in the market place yesterday. All yellow sashes and prim expressions, handing out their tracts, which I thankfully avoided. Do you not find them a little... odd?"

"Not at all," said Mr Forrester. "To achieve social change, one must organise. I hope to see more of their kind challenging the present order, even if it makes us a little uncomfortable. But of course, you are doing your bit for women's equality already, Miss Harris! And lifting all our spirits in the process, which is admirable. Perhaps you should give a talk about your experience in a business that is so dominated by men. Yes – I shall mention it to her, indeed."

Miss Harris smiled politely, but I could see that giving such a lecture was the last thing she wanted to do.

~

After dinner, we gathered in the drawing room, and while Mrs Forrester was talking to Flora and Phyllis, I found myself in a little group that included Mr Forrester and Miss Harris.

"I missed your concert, I'm afraid, Miss Harris," said Mr Forrester. "My wife was feeling unwell and I decided not to leave her. But everyone says it was an astonishing performance. Might you play a little for me, to give me a flavour of it?"

"My playing is indifferent, alas," said Miss Harris. "But Sylvie – would you...?"

"Si tu veux," Miss Dubois said, and we followed her to the little sitting room, now converted into a music room, where she settled herself at the piano. Without sheet music, she began to play a selection of themes from Miss Harris' first symphony. I was glad to hear them again – they were like old friends. Miss Dubois' usually impassive face twitched with emotion, and she closed her eyes as she played the final, affecting chords of this medley. She allowed herself a smile at the applause, and returned to Miss Harris' side.

"Beautifully played, and beautifully composed," said Mr Forrester. "I wonder if this piece is available anywhere for me to purchase? I would like to hear my wife take a shot at it."

"That arrangement isn't in print yet," said Miss Harris, "but we intend to submit it to a magazine. It's the delightfully named 'Ladies' Cabinet of Fashion, Music and Romance'."

"Splendid," said Mr Forrester. "My wife is already a subscriber. I will look out for it. I would like to discuss your music further, Miss Harris – but I must have a walk. Would you care for a stroll in the garden?"

Miss Harris consented, much to the evident discomfort of Miss Dubois, and they went outside in the failing evening light, while the rest of us returned to the drawing room. I tried to strike up conversation with Miss Dubois, but she was as monosyllabic as ever, and I had to admit defeat and excuse myself.

~

During a lull when Phyllis was deep in conversation with Flora about Dr Drummond's health, I wandered off to stretch my legs, and found Francesca in the small sitting room. I did not realise that Captain Harris was behind the door examining a painting, but it was too late to withdraw.

"Remarkable," Captain Harris said, and then caught sight of me. "Oh, hello, Mr Rufford. Mrs Campbell has been good enough to show me some of her pictures. She has a good eye. Please excuse me," he added. "I'm going outside for a smoke."

When he had gone, I said, "I'm sorry – I didn't know he was here."

"That's quite all right," Francesca said. "Nothing improper was taking place."

"But I don't think I was imagining a certain warmth between the two of you."

"Goodness, Thomas," said Francesca. "Are you really such a prude? A hostess is allowed to flirt a little with her guests, is she not?"

"A little, perhaps. But you were not discreet. I worry about what his parents would think of –"

"Calm yourself, my dear," said Francesca, resting her hand on mine. "I have no intention of seducing the poor Captain, even though he looks as though he needs a little... well, feminine attention. Besides, I think he would be perfect for Flora."

"You think so? Perhaps. She did seem quite interested in his zoological musings."

"Miss Harris had it right, I think," said Francesca. "I can see Flora sketching the Captain's specimens, and mopping his fevered brow as he writes his academic treatises into the night, the fireflies gathering around his lantern."

"A fine picture. Speaking of Miss Harris, have your

musicians been good guests?" I said.

"Oh, yes. But it's been extraordinary, Thomas. Extraordinary. If the public knew of..." She trailed off. "Sorry, I didn't mean to gossip. They are my guests, and they deserve privacy. Would you like more wine? People will wonder what's become of us."

"Extraordinary – in what way? If the public knew what?" I said, intrigued.

"Please forget I said anything," she said, getting up. "It has nothing to do with anyone else. Now, I have something I want to ask Mr Forrester. Isn't he fascinating?"

CHAPTER SIX

I HAD intended to resume my interrupted visit to Hunter's, but on Monday my quest for pleasure was foiled once again. As I came down the hill into Hawksbridge, the fresh morning air had turned acrid, and I could see a pall of smoke rising from the direction of Bridge Street. I hurried Celeste to the source of this disturbance, and found the skeletal, smouldering remains of The Conundrum Print Works. The fire wagon had done all it could and was being withdrawn by its crew, while a small crowd of people stood with shocked faces, whispering to each other. Standing apart from them was Mr Winston Eagle, the proprietor of the print works, whom I knew slightly from commissioning my headed notepaper and visiting cards. He held a handkerchief over his face and occasionally allowed himself a howl of anguish.

I dismounted, tied Celeste to a post, and went over to Mr Eagle and waited for the sobs to subside.

"This is a terrible sight," I said. "I take it you're insured?"

He turned to look at me, removed the handkerchief from his face, and nodded.

"Yes, Mr Rufford, thank the Lord," he said. "But I don't suppose I'll get the full amount, and not in good time, either. It took me so long to build it up. I don't know how..." He sighed. "I blame myself. I should never have taken on that silly pamphlet."

"You mean for the Society for –"

"No, no," he said, "not those. Well, perhaps those as well. But I think the fire might be in response to this." He fumbled in his pocket and drew out a crumpled paper. "I should have known better. But business is business." He handed the paper over to me.

I straightened it out and began to read. At first glance, it appeared to be a S.E.W. publication, but it quickly became obvious that it was not.

A BLUEPRINT FOR THE ELIMINATION OF MEN

A PUBLICATION OF WOMEN OF EARNESTNESS (W.O.E.)

Earnest Women of Hawksbridge, arise! Do you feel belittled? Are you cast down at the thought of your tedious maternal duties? Do you sigh with longing to join the Navy, or to take up tools on a Building Site? Are you envious of Bank Clerks and Cattle Dealers?

Be melancholy no longer! Deliverance is at hand. We need Soldiers of all Kinds! Our Pretty Soldiers will divert the men with Displays of *Ankles* and *Other Parts of Interest* so that they may be *Captured*, *Restrained* and *Punished*. Our Ugly Soldiers will do the *Manual Labour* of the country, together with the surviving *Man-Slaves*. A Glorious Future of Female Emancipation and Male Bondage awaits!

We women are stirring! We are marching!

WE ARE REVOLTING!

JOIN US NOW! FILL THE STREETS WITH W.O.E.!

There was more, presumably in a similar vein, but I got the gist of it.

"I see," I said, handing back the pamphlet with a smile. "A parody. In poor taste, perhaps, but surely it's not sufficient to prompt arson?"

Mr Eagle shrugged. "I don't know for sure. But it would rile Lady Fairfield and her followers, wouldn't it?"

I considered this. "I suppose they might feel betrayed, if you had previously printed their own pamphlets. And you don't have any idea who the wag might be?"

"None at all, except that he called himself Mr Smith," Mr Eagle said. "Business was conducted by letters, and he used a room at The Duke's Head for correspondence. I'm sure he will have used a false name."

"And the police?"

"They left a short time ago. I'm to give a written account to them at the police office – when I've recovered my wits."

As we gazed at the smouldering ruin of the print works, I heard a whistle behind me. "What a bloody awful sight."

It was William Lowick, extending a hand to Mr Eagle. "My sympathies, sir. This must be a terrible shock."

Mr Eagle wearily shook Lowick's hand, and said, "Thank you, Mr Lowick. But my misfortune is simply copy to you."

"We're not entirely heartless, Mr Lowick," said Mr Lowick, running his hand through his hair, which did not appear to have been in contact with a comb for some time. "We're still human. But our readers must keep up with events, good or bad."

"Of course, of course," said Mr Eagle, sighing. "I suppose I may as well give you your story."

"Thank you, sir. Only if you can manage it."

Mr Eagle nodded. "There's not much to say. I arrived at around six, and the blaze was going strong. Someone had alerted the brigade, and they did their best, but it was too late. There was a lot of paper in the building. The roof caved in, and most of the floors. Thank goodness it didn't spread to the neighbouring buildings." He bit his lip. "I sent my employees away. I'll have to let the poor devils go. Some of them have been with me for over ten years."

"Did you see any signs of a break-in?" Mr Lowick asked.

"Hard to say. I went round the back a few minutes ago, and there was an open door and broken windows, but that could have been from the fire."

"Any motive that you know of? Unhappy employees?"

Mr Eagle shook his head, and handed him the parody pamphlet without a word. The journalist started to guffaw.

"Not a bad effort," he said. "And you think this" – he

gestured at the ruin – "was revenge from the ladies in question?"

"I strongly suspect it," Mr Eagle said. "I can't imagine Lady Fairfield was involved herself, of course. But her followers..."

"The wasps have certainly been buzzing around lately," said Mr Lowick. "Perhaps they can sting. Not that I can put anything into print without evidence."

"I have to get to the police office," said Mr Eagle. "Good morning, Mr Rufford, Mr Lowick." He took another mournful look at the blackened building, and set off.

Mr Lowick coughed. "I don't know about you, Mr Rufford, but my throat is lined with Mr Eagle's soot. Care for an ale and a chin-wag?"

"An excellent idea," I said. "I suggest The Duke's Head."

~

Celeste having been installed at the inn's stables, we made ourselves comfortable at a table in the tap room, which we had almost to ourselves.

"Lord! but that's good," said Mr Lowick, raising his tankard to his lips.

"I think we can forgive ourselves the early hour in the circumstances," I said.

"Quite!" said Lowick. "This is entirely medicinal. So – there may be an arsonist loose in Hawksbridge. I know Lady Fairfield a little. I don't think she would risk her reputation in such a way."

"You know her? She did seem quite indulgent of you the other day."

Lowick laughed. "Yes, I do seem to get away with teasing her. I think she rather enjoys it, given the rest of the time she has her wasps fawning over her. Yes, she has her charms and her weaknesses, does the Queen Wasp of Kirkheaton Hall. I think I would know if she had criminal tendencies."

"I thought she despised all men, to hear her talk," I said.

"My dear fellow," said Lowick, leaning back in his seat as if he wanted to spend the rest of the day in idle pontification, "I'm sure by now you know it's possible for human beings to entertain entirely contradictory notions in their heads at the same time. Especially women. Yes, she hates men. But she is also capable of loving them. She was married, after all."

"Ah, yes. What happened to him?"

"Heart attack, I gather. He was a distinguished surgeon, with a reputation for removing tumours from brains. Not a very high success rate, to be sure, but no doubt his victims have helped the progression of the field."

He frowned. "Lady Fairfield showed me a room containing an extremely gruesome collection."

"Let me guess. Brains?"

Lowick nodded. "Shelves of them, pickled. She was highly delighted by my discomfort. What was it she said? Oh yes." He imitated her curious, high voice: "'In this room we have attained equality of the sexes, Mr Lowick! You will observe that a man's brain and a woman's brain have identical form and consistency.'"

His impression brought on a cough and he reached for his tankard. "Actually," he said, "the women's brains were slightly smaller, of course, but I didn't like to ruin the moment by pointing that out."

"Wise, in the circumstances," I said. "You wouldn't want to end up as an exhibit."

He smiled. "You're right, Mr Rufford, it was cowardice."

"You mentioned love," I said. "I take it that you meant friendship with men also."

"Oh yes, yes, of course," he said, swirling the remains of his drink in the tankard. "Forgive me my journalistic simplification. I think I amuse her. The wasps, however, disapprove of me. The feeling is mutual."

He signalled to the barmaid. "I'm having another. And you?"

I nodded.

The barmaid came over. She was in her late thirties, and although a little excess weight had softened her features, she was still attractive and Mr Lowick did not hide her admiration.

"Thirsty today, gentlemen?"

"Extremely, Maggie. We've just inhaled half of poor Mr Eagle's print works. In fact, I think I've still got a cinder in my eye. Care to take a look?"

"I'm not falling for that one, Mr Lowick," Maggie retorted. "Last time you had me pick up your notebook from the floor, and – well, you weren't a gentleman!"

"You're right, of course," said Lowick, slumping his shoulders in mock disappointment. "I humbly apologise. We men have had our day, after all. Two more, if you please!"

She nodded and turned to go, and then paused. "It's awful about the fire. And those two, last month." She shuddered. "The town doesn't feel the same as it did. Don't you think?"

Mr Lowick shrugged.

"It's troubling, yes," I said. "Perhaps it's too early to say there's a pattern, though. I'm sure it's just bad luck."

"Not what I've heard," said Maggie, "at least not about Mrs Milburn."

She was about to walk off, and I said, "What have you heard?"

"Oh, just that she might have had a bit of a temper. They had an argument, and she gave him a little push..."

"Then Mrs Milburn may have been slandered," said Lowick, and Maggie and I stared at him in surprise.

"Well, of course I don't know exactly what happened," he continued, "but I went to see her at St John's Asylum a few days after her husband's death. The poor woman's mind has been unbalanced by the shock. She seems to have no memory of what happened, but she's consumed by guilt."

"Oh, how horrible," said Maggie. She shook her head. "There's something evil about in Hawksbridge, mark my words!"

"I can't imagine what she must be going through," I said. "On another topic, do you happen to know if a Mr Smith collected his post here a few days ago, Maggie?"

"Ah! He arranged to, by letter. But then a small boy collected them for him. Let me get your drinks, gentlemen."

"Someone was careful," said Lowick when Maggie had gone. "But then it would be embarrassing to be identified as the satirist. It could mean loss of employment."

"True," I said. "So you saw Mrs Milburn! What did you make of her? You think she's innocent?"

"Well, I might have come too quickly to her defence just then," he said. "It's impossible to know how things went, on the ramparts, since unluckily there were no witnesses. But her mind has degenerated to a pitiful degree. I cannot stand to hear words against her when she is suffering so."

I nodded. "And I assume the police have no evidence against her?"

"None at all," he said, "and in her mental state, there could be no conviction anyway. I found my meeting with her extremely difficult. There is an unfortunate coincidence..." He paused.

"Yes?" I prompted.

"Mr Milburn and I bear a passing resemblance to one another. And Mrs Milburn's illness partly manifests in a confusion of person."

"Oh Lord," I said. "She thinks you are her husband?"

"Yes," Lowick said. He was pensive as Maggie delivered the drinks, and took up his tankard slowly. "I went to see her two days ago – she had implored them to let her go home, and they judged that she had mended sufficiently and could be looked after by her housekeeper. So they sent her home. Since I was worried about her, I called in. Perhaps that was unwise."

"Ah," I said. "She still thought...?"

"Yes," he said. "It was rather awful. She lives in a little rented terrace house on Church Street. Her housekeeper had gone out, and when Mrs Milburn answered the door she flung herself at me, calling me 'Harold'. She seemed so happy to see me that at first, I didn't correct her. She held me fast and kept saying, 'You're alive, thank God you're alive!'"

"Dear Lord in Heaven," I said. "The poor woman."

"I tried to explain, and she said, 'Of course, dear! Whatever you say,' as if she were humouring me, and made me tea, as if everything were normal. And then..."

He paused, had another draught of beer, and cleared his throat. "She came over to where I was sitting, took my hand, and said 'Come with me!' So to avoid distressing her, I did as she said, until we got to the foot of the stairs. I hesitated, and she said, 'Take me to bed, Harold! You were always so kind to me in bed.'"

I sat open-mouthed. "Oh, God."

"Naturally, I love the fairer sex, and normally I might have enthusiastically taken advantage of such an offer, but even I have my moral limits. I wrenched free of her with some difficulty, mumbled an excuse, and fled, but with her cries ringing in my ears. I can still hear them. She sounded like an injured animal. I thought she was going to follow me, but she stood at the door sobbing and howling, 'Come back to me, Harold! Come back to me!'" He shuddered at the memory.

"How terrible," I said. "And you haven't seen her since, I take it?"

He shook his head. "Goodness knows what further damage I've done to her fragile mind. But I truly meant well."

"Of course," I said. "I'm sure her housekeeper will have soothed her. Perhaps she'll recover her mind in time."

"Yes, I sincerely hope so. I confess I've been a little shaken up by all this. I expect the poor woman hates me with a vengeance, now that I've rejected and humiliated her. But I could not possibly have..."

"No," I said. "You did the right thing. But it must have been harrowing."

"And very odd," said Mr Lowick. "I'm beginning to think Maggie might be right. Maybe evil has come to Hawksbridge."

CHAPTER SEVEN

WE HAD previously agreed to meet the following day to discuss Lowick's article, so instead we took the opportunity to have this conversation over a beef sandwich.

After we had eaten and he had extracted all that he needed of my recent adventures, the journalist took a monogrammed tortoise-shell case and a box of matches from his pocket and offered me a cigarette, which I declined. Lowick struck a match with a shower of sparks, and after a puff at his cigar, stared glumly at the spent lucifer match in his hand.

"How aptly named," he said. "I suppose you know of the misery I'm helping to perpetuate by buying these infernal things?"

I was vaguely aware of the hazards of match manufacturing. "Phosphorous poisoning?" I said.

He nodded. "Phossy jaw. Women – and young girls, for goodness' sake – suffer appalling damage to their bones in these factories, while the directors grow fat. I've been meaning to write about it, but I will have to give up these things" – he waved his cigar – "before I can bear to hear any gruesome testimony." He frowned. "Some of them have to have their lower jaws removed."

"Good God," I said. "There has to be a better way to produce a flame."

Lowick shrugged and said, "Seemingly not at present. God damn it, and me," he added with feeling, and violently extinguished his cigar on the table. "I will not be complicit any longer." He ran his hands through his hair and tried to compose himself.

"Tell me," he said after a moment, "what news of Miss Harris?"

"She's in good health. I wish I could say the same about her companion. I think Miss Harris works her too hard."

"Then I would offer my assistance," Lowick said, "but alas my musical knowledge is limited to a hesitant performance of the 'Moonlight Sonata'."

"That is considerably more skill than I possess," I said. "Mr Forrester wanted Miss Harris to speak at a meeting of the Society, but she didn't seem enthused."

Lowick choked on his third beer, and spat some of it out. "My apologies, Mr Rufford," he said, wiping the table with his napkin. "But did you say Mr Forrester? You have spoken to him?"

"Yes, Mrs Campbell invited him to her last dinner party. It was interesting to meet him, although he was of course more impressed by Miss Harris than by me. Why?"

Lowick was silent for a moment. "I can't give you any details. But I would caution you – and your friends – to have nothing to do with him or his company. It's possible that his reputation may not be secure."

"Really? In what way?"

"I'm sorry," he said. "I really can't divulge at the moment. But let's just say that I have my eye on him."

~

I was unable to get anything further from Lowick to shed light on his cryptic remarks. I kept Celeste stabled at the inn and headed to Myrtle's, where it was a Mixed Company Day. A trace of smoke from the print works still hung in the air, but the breeze had dissipated the worst of it.

As I entered, I was surprised to catch sight of Miss

Dubois in a booth, talking earnestly to a woman I did not recognise. I caught Miss Dubois' eye and smiled, but although she attempted a smile, she looked a little hunted, and got up and left as I took a seat by the window.

After I had ordered a cup of coffee, Bess came through from the kitchen and sat down opposite me.

"What a nice surprise!" she said, licking a dollop of jam from her fingers. "But did you see the fire? Isn't it dreadful!"

"Yes, I spoke to poor Mr Eagle. It's difficult watching the ruination of a business. I hope he has kind friends and kin."

"Oh, yes, I do hope so," she said. "But tell me, what have you been up to? I trust you have some lovely gossip for me."

"Nothing much," I said, although there was plenty to be indiscreet about. "You're better placed for that kind of thing. I gather the Society has rather taken to Myrtle's."

"Astonishingly well!" Bess said with a smile. "They thoroughly approve of our ladies-first idea. If we hadn't done it, I'm sure Lady Fairfield would have – in fact I rather think she's a little envious."

"I'm not surprised," I said. "After all, while her Society goes around making a lot of noise and fuss, you have undertaken a quiet, polite, effective rebellion."

"I suppose I have. Well, *we* have, Mr Investor. But Lady Fairfield says that female emancipation must be fought on many fronts."

"She does? Have you spoken with her much?"

"A little," she said. "She's compelling. And she's not the dragon some people make out. She's just very driven – I can appreciate that."

My coffee arrived. "Uncommonly good, as ever," I said after a sip. "I saw Miss Harris' companion here just now – was she with a member of the Society?"

"Ah, the young French woman? Yes, she has been coming here the last few days with Miss Knowles. They are quite intense! Perhaps Miss Knowles has another recruit. Miss

Knowles is a favourite of Lady Fairfield's, judging by the tone of their conversation."

"Interesting," I said. "I'm pretty sure Miss Harris wouldn't approve. She was not exactly singing the Society's praises to Mr Forrester the other night."

Bess' eyes widened. "Oh, Thomas! Don't tell me you know Mr Forrester? You wretch! And for you to just drop his name in casually...!"

"Sorry," I said. "I suppose that is a prime piece of gossip. He was at a dinner party that Francesca organised. She is a little obsessed with him. Or rather his designs, or both, I'm not sure. He was amusing, and took some interest in Miss Harris. I hope it was her composing talents he was enthused by, not her feminine allure."

I was aware I sounded a little prim, but there was Mrs Forrester to consider.

"Well, lucky her," said Bess. "Did you know he was in here, trying to charm me into redecorating with 'Hedgerow'?"

"I heard," I said. "And did his charms work?"

"I was quite flustered, and I think I may have promised to do it!" Bess said, lowering her eyes and fidgeting with a spoon. "Sorry. I should have asked you first. But it's not that I feel obliged about the wallpaper – I should like to, anyway."

"It might be a good idea," I said, "although the shop looks good as it is. But I imagine it would be another attraction for customers, given the present mania for Forrester – so perhaps it will pay for itself. And besides, the business can well afford it. Although..."

"Although?"

I was going to mention Lowick's misgivings, but thought better of it. It would only spoil her enjoyment, and besides, he had provided no rationale.

I drained my cup, put some coins on the table, and pushed my chair back. "Although nothing. I should go! I have an appointment with my fiancée."

"I'm relieved you're not cross with me about the paper," said Bess, standing up and taking my empty coffee cup. "I was a little nervous."

I smiled as I reached for the door. "I doubt you'll ever do anything that warrants that."

~

It was splendid walking arm-in-arm with my future wife along the town walls. But there was a shadow. At Knight's Mount I would normally stray from the path and climb up the mound to stand at the edge and take in the view. This time, I kept to the path that ran to the side of the slope, and I found it hard to dismiss from my mind the image of Mr Milburn tumbling into the ditch below.

Phyllis must have understood, as she squeezed my arm and said, "I'm sure we'll be able to enjoy it again. The poor man must be remembered, of course, but... we have our own memories too."

"Yes, you're right. But to think of them courting with all the hope and happiness we have, never knowing that their marriage would be so short..." I shook my head in an attempt to expel these thoughts from my head. "Sorry. Let's talk about something else. About music, and art!"

"And literature, perhaps?" Phyllis prompted.

"Ah! yes, of course. Is the muse with you?"

"She occasionally visits. I'm making some progress. Miss Harris is quite an inspiration – such energy! Her symphony left me breathless in the concert."

"The same goes for the French horn player," I said. "He was red in the face after that opening. It was an astonishing blast of sound."

"I think she took Mr Forrester's breath away at the

party," Phyllis said, shading her eyes and looking out to sea. "But she is stunning. I hope he didn't try anything improper when they went for their walk."

"I suspect Miss Harris can look after herself," I said. "As her father might say, if he came on forte, she would bar him without quavering, presto."

"Dreadful, Thomas, quite dreadful!" Phyllis said, grimacing and then smiling at me, before turning and kissing me, her arms holding me tight. We held the kiss for several heady moments, and then she said, "I adore dear Mr Harris, but please don't turn into him. Tell me – what silly things do I do?"

"Let me see," I said, considering this. "Well, you sometimes fall into a daydream. I can tell your eyes are seeing something entirely different from the here and now. Then I long to join you, wherever you are. But alas – I fear your mind is working on a plane that I can't comprehend, let alone reach."

"What nonsense," Phyllis said. "How do you know I'm not thinking of boiled cabbage, or a hole in my dress?"

I laughed. "Do you often think of such things?"

Phyllis gazed out to sea again, narrowing her eyes in a mock reverie. "I confess I lied, to seem less intimidating. In fact, I only ever dream of ineffable mysteries and the sublime beauty and tragedy of our fleeting existence."

I could not resist the temptation to tap her on the rear for her teasing, and she yelped in a gratifying manner.

"Thomas! There might have been people looking!"

"Let them," I said. "We'll soon be married, and then the scandal would be if I never touched you at all."

"Indeed," Phyllis said. "I hope you *will* want to touch me."

"Rest assured," I said. "I shall want to. A lot. I intend to be a perfect pest."

"Only in the future? Are you not already burning with

manly passion?"

"Phyllis," I protested, "you take such things seriously enough in your books! And yet not in real life. But yes, I am rather." I sighed. "I wish we were already married. I want to take you in my arms –"

"I know," she said. "I want it too."

"Then why not throw away convention, and put us both out of our misery?"

"Oh, all sorts of reasons."

"Such as?"

"Oh, Thomas, let's not spoil this moment. All in good time."

I persisted. "One of my cottages has been done up – it's actually water-tight and comfortable now. We could meet there, with no one looking, and at least talk and read and enjoy each other's company."

"Nothing else?"

"Maybe the odd peck on the cheek."

"And a glass of wine, and then who knows what? I'm just as capable of weakness as you, Thomas, so perhaps we should not tempt fate."

"Very well," I said. "But perhaps you could think about it – how nice it would be?"

"I'll think about it," she said. "Or rather, I shall go into one of my dreams, so I can experience what cannot yet be experienced."

"Better than nothing," I said. "I will have the same dream, and we'll see if we meet in it, and give way to imagined passion. And then we can compare notes."

"We'll see," she said. "Now – I must get home, and check how poor old Papa is. He's been moaning about his aching joints today. A brandy or two will help."

"Help him, or you?"

"Possibly both," she said, squeezing my hand.

~

"I must congratulate you on your house! It has a thoroughly unpretentious grandeur. Entirely the kind of house I see myself in, when – or if – I settle down. Will you be making any changes when you marry?"

Captain Harris had put down his wine and was looking intently at me. I was reminded why I liked him enough to invite him for dinner: he was straightforward, warm, and earnest without being dry. That he was perhaps a little too hot-blooded around women I could easily forgive, recognising a shared fault.

"Thank you," I said. "I've been lucky beyond my dues. I've been thinking about extending, but I can't bring myself to spoil the house's current perfection. No doubt Phyllis will want the place freshened up a little, and I'll be happy to bow to her whims. And you must help advise, Flora, with your artist's sensibilities."

Flora smiled and shrugged. "I wouldn't dream of telling Phyllis how to decorate her own house. But if I'm pressed, I might speak my mind. So be careful what you wish for!"

The Captain shifted his affable gaze to Flora. "And you will be staying in your tower, Miss Davison? I think it will be excellent for any Rufford progeny to have an aunt so close by."

"Oh dear," said Flora. "The spinster aunt in the tower. That doesn't sound very glamorous – not that I'm ungrateful. It's just that... I hope one day my life will take a different path. Meanwhile, I'll be delighted to be a part of this little coterie. Especially now Phyllis and I are friends again. A few months ago, it might have been dreadfully awkward."

The Captain nodded. "Reconciled by a piece of beef, I heard!"

"Strangely, yes," Flora said. "That and the perspective

that age brings."

"This different path," the Captain said, drumming his fingertips on his wine glass, "do you have any plans for it? I ask as one who is contemplating changes in his own life. It's both exciting and daunting."

"I'm afraid I don't have plans as definite as yours," Flora said. "But I confess you inspired me the other day to think harder about it. I have some money put by and I would like to travel in Europe a little, and sketch. Perhaps that will lead me to something else, or perhaps I'll come gratefully back to Hawksbridge and my tower for the rest of my days."

The Captain smiled at Flora, and I could see her enjoying the steadfast attention of his gaze. "Come, come, Miss Davison, you are surely far too young to contemplate anything that lasts for the rest of your days! So much can happen to upset our plans, for the better or worse. We are never the complete masters of our own destiny."

"I can vouch for that," I put in, accepting replenishment of my glass from Catherine. "And you, Catherine, would you not say? What strange events brought an African Princess here – to my great benefit."

"God's will is a mystery, sir, but He has been good to me." She hesitated and then added, "Of late."

The Captain laughed. "Excuse me," he said. "I wasn't laughing at your misfortunes. It's just that you beautifully hint at a contradiction that we Christians face. It seems that God receives all of the credit and none of the blame. It's hardly fair."

"Perhaps I have blamed Him, sometimes," Catherine said, leaving with a tray of crockery. "May He forgive me!"

"You're plainly not afraid of God, Captain Harris," said Flora, "to challenge Him on His lack of intervention, as well as the Creation."

The Captain clearly relished Flora's inquisition, and he leaned back in his chair observing my half-sister. "The Army has taught me to be afraid of very little," he said. "Except, perhaps, of my own weaknesses, and my vast ignorance. I hope to improve in both these matters."

"By travelling the world in search of answers? Admirable," said Flora. "But as we discussed before, will you not be lonely?"

"I expect I'll be too busy to be lonely," Captain Harris said. "But you are kind to be concerned." He thought for a moment. "My sister was rather brash the other night. And yet it wouldn't be entirely unpleasant to have a travelling companion."

"Perhaps you should advertise," said Flora, deflecting the implication. "Then you might find a good match for your requirements. I imagine they would need to be a very specific type, with patience and a strong constitution."

"Yes, and a curiosity as great as mine. I think you're a curious soul, Miss Davison," he said. "That is," he hastily added, "one who has curiosity, not peculiarity!"

"Perhaps both are true," Flora said, now flushed with wine, and – I suspected – a little excitement. "I have some patience, but my constitution is not, I fear, that of an explorer."

"Oh, Miss Davison!" the Captain cried, clapping his hands together. "Despite yourself, I do believe you're considering your suitability for the position!"

"Now, Captain Harris," I said, feeling an intervention to be necessary, "let's not get carried away. Shall we change the subject? Let's talk about your talented sister, and the source of her magic."

"The less said about that, the better," the Captain replied, to my surprise. "And I shan't change the subject just yet. Miss Davison, you said you wanted to travel. You said you wished to draw. You're restless – I can feel it. If you were a man, it would be the most obvious and natural thing to come exploring with me!"

"Alas," said Flora with a barely audible sigh, "I am not a man, and the world would be scandalised."

"What a pity," Captain Harris said. "Then grant me this, at least – may I see some of your drawings?"

"Of course," said Flora. "If I may?" I nodded, and she went off to find a selection of her work.

Captain Harris leant back in his chair and lit a cheroot. "Capital girl, your sister," he said. "Wasting her talent here, I'm afraid. She needs to spread her wings."

"I've always thought so," I said. "And yet, selfishly, I want her to stay. I've not long had a sibling. I'm still getting used to the idea."

"Highly attractive, too. How come she's not been snapped up yet?"

I shrugged. "Perhaps men are afraid of her intelligence. And she's very independent-minded. But she does have a softer side – I have seen it, with an undeserving fellow who treated her badly."

"Cad! Let me at him," Captain Harris said, half in jest.

"Sheath your sword, sir – he's already dead," I said. I wondered if I should be candid. "Captain Harris –"

"Victor, please!"

"Victor. It strikes me that you are oddly alike in some ways. Intelligent, stubborn, a little restless..."

"It has occurred to me," Captain Harris said, exhaling a cloud of smoke.

"Do you like her?"

"I do," he said, without elaborating.

"As much as you like Mrs Campbell?"

He turned to me and laughed. "Now that's an entirely separate matter. And Mrs Campbell is a little old for me."

"I don't think she knows that. And she has great charms. God knows, I've had ideas myself."

"Have you, by Jove? It doesn't surprise me. Well, let's just say that I'll do my best not to let her sophisticated charms go to my head, or elsewhere."

Flora arrived with a portfolio of her drawings. "I'll take this to the drawing room," she said.

"Good idea," I said. "I'll have coffee brought in. Please excuse me for a few minutes – I have to stretch my legs."

I took a turn around the garden – it was rather an obvious move to let the two of them have some time together, but I supposed they would be too absorbed to mind.

What was that movement by the trees? I strained my eyes in the evening gloom. One – no, two large birds, carefully stepping across the lawn, then stopping suspiciously to determine if I posed a threat. My peacock had returned, this time with a female. For a moment, I fancied they had come to replace the swans that had been blasted out of existence by the former lady of the house, Mrs Kington, in a jealous rage. In any event, they were welcome adornments to Ramsburgh, I thought, notwithstanding the reputation of their raucous cries.

As I passed the drawing room, I could see Captain Harris and Flora sitting close together, their heads almost touching as they bent over Flora's drawings.

CHAPTER EIGHT

THANKFULLY, I had not drunk to excess, and so my ride to Halfpenny House in the morning was a pleasant one, accompanied by cloudless skies, birdsong, and cheerful greetings from leather-faced labourers.

The conversation about Francesca last night had made me uneasy on two accounts: first, that an inappropriate relationship was forming between her and the Captain, and second – and I report this factually, not because it was anything other than ridiculous – that this would entail a distraction from her regard for me. Naturally I knew in a rational sense that Francesca owed me no more than the courtesies and sentiments of affectionate friendship, and *vice versa.* And yet, I felt there was a particular bond between two people who had penetrated Hawksbridge society at the same time, both escaping a redundant past for an uncertain future. And then there was the preceding meeting on the train, which would scarcely have disgraced a story by my future wife in its dream-like, improbable intimacy. Francesca had a tendency to burst through the bubble that normally encloses us in the cloying restraints of propriety. In her presence, the usual rules did not apply. And I did not want the strange closeness of our friendship to be watered down.

I was jealous when I had absolutely no right to be, and I knew it, but it did not stop me going to investigate the situation at Halfpenny House. I would extract some information from Francesca, even though it was likely to cause me further discomfort. I excused my curiosity on the grounds that for the Harrises' sake, and perhaps for Flora's sake, I might be able to interpose myself between the Captain and

Francesca.

It was not Francesca I saw and heard as I approached the house. Even as Celeste crunched her hooves up the drive, the figure on the lawn did not acknowledge my arrival. As I drew close, I could see a familiar, dishevelled mop of red hair, and the owner staring heavenward – singing a glorious song that had no words, her hands outstretched. She continued even when Celeste was almost breathing down her neck, and I stopped Celeste, horse and rider both motionless and fascinated by this display.

I realised with a start that Miss Harris was not yet dressed, and wore a loose robe thrown over a white nightdress that was frothy with lace. Whether she realised it or not, a great deal of flesh was on display, and it added to my confusion at what I was witnessing. Had Miss Harris' reason been disturbed by the exertions of her work? I wondered if I should quickly summon a doctor. Where were the staff? Why was there no sign of Francesca, nor Miss Sylvie Dubois?

I looked up at the house, and at the same time that I caught sight of Miss Dubois leaning out of an upstairs window, Miss Harris stopped singing, turned her face up to her assistant and said, simply, "Yes?"

"Oui, bien sûr, je l'ais," Miss Dubois said, and withdrew from the window, closing the sash.

Miss Harris dropped her arms, and turned to me with a smile.

"My apologies, Mr Rufford," she said, in the voice of a woman perfectly possessed of her faculties. "Sometimes it helps to be dramatic. I think I have something here."

She looked down at her robe.

"Oh, sorry, I'm not even respectable. But sometimes one doesn't have time for the niceties."

"Good morning, Miss Harris," I said. "I thought for one terrible moment –"

"That I had gone stark, staring mad?" She laughed. "Poor

you – no, as far as I know I'm as sane as I shall ever be, but I have my methods. The household is getting used to them. Have you come to see Francesca? Please say you came to see me! I'm quite bored of myself now, and could use some diverting company."

"I confess I came to see Francesca," I said, dismounting. "Is she...?"

"She's out, I'm afraid," Miss Harris said. "Riding – I suppose you can guess with whom?"

"Ah – your brother?"

"The same," Miss Harris said, shaking her head. "Of course, Francesca is entitled to see whomsoever she pleases. But my brother is a red-blooded man, and dear Francesca has an unusually well-developed passion for life. I don't wish for them to get themselves into an embarrassing position."

She laughed again. "But who am I to talk? I'm standing here in the sunshine practically naked. What if I were to get dressed, and you and I were to have a stroll in the garden? Could you bear it?"

I bowed. "I could bear it very well, Miss Harris. It would be a pleasure."

"Good! Then you get Celeste stabled, and I'll try not to be too long."

She walked briskly into the house, turning briefly to give me a warm smile before disappearing.

~

"My muse manifests in strange ways," Miss Harris said as we followed the paths in the formal garden, bordered with a mass of tulips of different colours. "Today the blue skies spoke to me. Do you not sometimes feel an unaccountable joy simply looking up at the sky? Or am I being unforgivably fay?"

"Not at all; it's quite natural," I said. "There is something fundamental and primal about an intense sky, and the spring sunshine. After all, that's the source of everything, isn't it? The energy that drives all living beings."

"Quite," said Miss Harris. "I seem to need to turn raw energy, of all different kinds, into music. Sylvie understands it perfectly, and she is an essential part of this conversion."

"A catalyst?" I offered. I remembered the concept dimly from my chemistry lessons.

Miss Harris stopped and placed a hand on my arm. "Yes!" she said, her eyes sparkling. "Precisely! Sylvie is a catalyst. She is essential for anything to happen at all."

She sighed, and continued walking. "But I fear there is a difference. Sylvie is being consumed by the reaction. She is looking so tired, and yet she soldiers on. I need to give her a rest. But it's hard when I rely on her so."

"She does look a little worn out. But you must have given her a day off, as I saw her yesterday in Myrtle's with..."

I hesitated, realising too late that this might not be welcome news.

Miss Harris frowned. "With...?" she asked.

"Sorry, I should not be gossiping. With a Miss Knowles, from Lady Fairfield's Society."

Miss Harris growled. "I don't mind the poor thing having a bit of fun, a rest from her relentlessly demanding mistress. But I draw the line at the Society. I don't trust them, and I don't want Sylvie mixed up with them."

She kicked a branch from the path. "Do you not find them tiresome, Thomas? If I may call you Thomas?"

"Of course," I said. "Please do."

"Then please call me Effie."

I had the pleasant sense that my acquaintance with Miss Harris had crossed a line, albeit a faint one. "I have not yet made up my mind about the Society," I continued. "Lady Fairfield has a certain zeal that some find admirable."

"Oh, zeal! Anyone can have zeal," retorted Effie. "Directing it properly is what turns mere sound and fury into something valuable. And I do not believe she is directing it in a proper manner. She is leading women into thinking that mere protest is enough – she is encouraging a shoddy display of self-pity! And what's worse, it will give any woman like me who tries to advance herself a bad name!"

She stared at me with wide, accusing eyes, as though I were Lady Fairfield's representative and in some way responsible for the Society's shortcomings. And yet there was an intimacy about this misplaced ire that was a little thrilling.

"You have a point," I said. "I hadn't thought of it in that way."

Her expression softened. "I didn't mean to take it out on you," she said. "It's just that I have worked so hard to take my place in a man's world. I don't want to be lumped in with a bunch of humourless harridans, who will end up damaging their own cause with their silly games."

She shivered and wrapped her shawl around her. "What a fresh breeze! I need coffee. Shall we go in?"

~

"What did Mr Forrester speak with you about after dinner, if I may be so curious?" I said as Francesca's maid brought us our coffee. Of Miss Dubois there was no sign, so I assumed she was still hard at work transcribing what she had heard through the window.

"You may indeed," Effie said. "Mostly the usual enquiries into my creative practices. But I have little new to say on the subject, so I'm afraid I must have bored him horribly."

"I doubt that," I said. "I shouldn't have thought it possible."

"You are very sweet," she said, "but I assure you, I am quite human." She leaned forward and held her hand out to me. I assumed she wanted me to kiss it, so I did.

"There! The hand of a perfectly normal human female, would you not say? Capable of any human weakness, including unspeakable tedium."

"I'll have to take your word for it," I said, "since it's not at all what I have experienced of you."

She smiled in acknowledgement and raised her cup elegantly to her lips. "Then perhaps you need to get to know me better. And what of Thomas Rufford? What of his weaknesses? They are so much more interesting than a person's noble qualities, would you not say?"

I thought for a moment. "Where do I begin?" I said, and she laughed.

"Oh, Thomas," she said, "you're evidently far more exciting than I had conceived! But you are to be married. I imagine that must limit the scope for misdemeanours, at least in an honourable man."

"I hope so," I replied. My innate desires were being uncomfortably stirred by the conversation. What living male could not be affected by the company of a beautiful, talented young woman, who was admired by half the young men in the country and who looked with interest into one's eyes and smiled so charmingly? I reminded myself of Phyllis' many qualities and the wonderful life that lay ahead, so long as I behaved.

I changed the subject. "Speaking of such things, I have a new acquaintance: a Mr William Lowick, a journalist at The Hawksbridge Herald. He hints at an interesting private life, of which I know little, except that he does seem to be on good terms with Lady Fairfield. Oddly, he told me to warn you and Francesca about Mr Forrester."

"Oh? Pertaining to what?"

"He couldn't say."

"Well! What a useless warning that is. You have no idea at all?"

"Just that his reputation might be in doubt. I suppose Lowick is working on an article about him."

"How mysterious!" said Effie. "I don't know what to make of that at all. Mr Forrester seemed perfectly sound, even if he did try to convert me to socialism."

"On your walk?"

"Yes," she said. "Fortunately, I've been inoculated against it by my father. He loves nothing more than a good rant against the perils of socialism. Mr Forrester invited me to imagine a world where inequality was banished, replaced by a society where everyone simply did the work they wanted to do."

"I see. How did you counter it?"

"By observing that most people will then simply do nothing, and that by removing the incentive to improve one's situation, you remove the driving force of civilization itself, causing inevitable famine and decline back to a primitive state. And to enforce such a society, you could only do it with a ruthless authoritarian government. You would surely create a dystopia from the naivety of utopianism, I said."

"Bravo!" I said. "You surely won the argument. His reaction?"

"He smiled indulgently, as though he had a solution to all these pitfalls but he didn't want to share it, and said we'd have to agree to disagree."

"How bloody annoying," I said. "Excuse my language."

"I assure you it was extremely bloody annoying!" Effie said.

We both laughed. "I don't think he had an answer at all," I said. "He just wanted you to think he had. He realised he'd been beaten."

"Poor Mr Forrester. The most sensible and intelligent people can have the most stupid notions. In fact I wonder whether the more learned you are, the more removed your ideas are from reality."

"I can vouch for that," I said. "That's partly why I fled Oxford. I could see myself becoming too rarefied."

"That, and the incentive of inheriting a wonderful house?"

"Well, yes, that too," I admitted.

"Which I have yet to see!" Effie said, pouring more coffee. "It sounds so lovely. Might I impose on you?"

"It would be no imposition to show you my home. You and Miss Dubois," I corrected myself.

"Thank you! And of course I should like to meet your delightful sister again."

~

While I answered a call of nature, having consumed three cups of coffee, I had the leisure to reflect on the intense pleasure of forming a new friendship. I had hardly scratched the surface of it, but in this form, it was no doubt destined for a short life – marriage would necessitate some distance, and in any case, the great composer would be off on a prestigious tour or a residency, far away from genteel Hawksbridge. I would be spared the consequences of any moral failings resulting from an unwarranted admiration of Effie. In the meantime, I could allow myself conversation and the exchange of warm smiles – after all, I was not married yet. And I could see Effie and Miss Dubois occasionally gracing our dinner table in their future Hawksbridge visits. Who knows what she might have achieved in a few years' time.

As I washed my hands in the provided bowl of water, I realised that I had forgotten all about Francesca and Captain Harris. My own fickleness amused me.

When I had emerged from the water closet, I nearly bumped into Captain Harris rushing to use it. "Ah, Thomas, how agreeable to see you again so soon," he said cheerily as he slammed the door, and I went to find Francesca.

"I've been a Francesca substitute for Thomas," Effie said. "A poor one, I'm sure."

"Oh! What a nice surprise," said Francesca, pulling off her gloves. "How are you, Thomas? What news from Ramsburgh?"

"I'm very well. As for news – nothing much, although I seem to have acquired a couple of peacocks. Well, a peacock and a peahen."

"How charming! But don't they make a frightful din?"

"I quite like the sound," I said. "It makes me feel more aristocratic."

"We'll see what Phyllis has to say about that. The Captain and I have had such a lovely walk, but he had to be patient with me. My legs are not as strong as his." I had a sudden vision of Captain Harris picking up and carrying his straggling companion, Francesca's arm coiled about his neck and a smile on her face.

At that moment, Miss Dubois came into the room, and I was aghast to see her paleness, and the want of flesh on her frame. I could see the look of concern on my companions' faces.

"Madame," Miss Dubois began, and then her eyes rolled back in their sockets and she fell to the floor, unconscious. Her head had fortunately missed the furniture and was cushioned by a thick rug.

"Sylvie!" cried Effie, hastening to her side. "My poor, darling Sylvie, what have I done to you?"

Francesca rushed out of the room to find someone to fetch a doctor, and I found a cushion to place under Miss Dubois' head.

"Please fetch some water," Effie said to the maid who

had arrived, her hands over her mouth in shock. "And smelling salts, and a blanket."

~

I stayed long enough to hear from Dr Weldon that Miss Dubois was suffering from exhaustion, and would make a full recovery so long as she had plenty of rest and was encouraged to eat properly. Effie agreed to support this, although I could see from her nervous fidgeting that she was aware it would mean a severe curtailment, if not a prolonged cessation, of their creative endeavours.

I had not furthered my knowledge of Francesca's friendship with Captain Harris, except that they had taken at least one long walk together. But in the light of poor Miss Dubois' alarming state of health, this seemed a trivial matter, and I was a little ashamed of myself for my attempt to pry.

Effie's inspiring blue skies were paid for the following day with a downpour that was unrelenting. I gave Fox the briefest walk, and in the afternoon retired to my small study upstairs, fearing that the rain hurling itself upon Ramsburgh would reveal the presence of leaks in awkward places.

I was in the middle of writing a letter to Phyllis, with Fox lying heavily on my feet, when Shipley flung open the door.

"Sorry to disturb you, sir, but there's a lady downstairs, in an agitated state. Says she's Mrs Clementine Lowick."

"Good Lord," I said. "In this weather! Did she say what it's about?"

"No, sir, but it sounds urgent."

I found Mrs Lowick in the hall, dabbing her face with a handkerchief. The short distance from her carriage to the door had been enough to soak her, and it compounded her miserable demeanour.

“Mrs Lowick!” I said, stepping towards her and holding out my hand. “I’m delighted to meet you; but is everything all right?”

“Oh, Mr Rufford!” she said, grasping my hand tightly with both of hers. “I’m so worried! William – my husband – he’s not – I haven’t – I don’t know what to do!” She seemed too distraught to even form a coherent sentence.

“Won’t you come through to the drawing room, Mrs Lowick? We can have tea and you can tell me all about it. I’m sure whatever it is will come right.”

Mrs Lowick nodded, released my hand, and tried to compose herself. “What must you think of me?” she said, looking away. Then she met my gaze squarely and said, “But he’s missing, Mr Rufford! I haven’t seen him since Monday morning, and it’s now Wednesday!”

CHAPTER NINE

IN THE drawing room, Mrs Lowick was silent for a while, collecting her thoughts and drinking a reviving cup of tea. The coachman had been installed in a corner of the kitchen with a strong coffee, and his rain-battered horse had been stabled.

I decided to wait until she was ready rather than immediately mount an inquisition. I had a chance to discreetly observe her. I estimated that she was in her mid-thirties; she was of slight stature but with a strong jawline and intense eyes that together suggested a determined nature. Her brown hair had just a hint of premature grey.

Presently she cleared her throat and said, "William tells me if he's going to be away. I don't question it, although I don't like him being away from me and the children. When I do express my regret at being left alone, he reminds me – albeit gently – that I married a journalist, and stories do not arrange themselves for our convenience. But I can't think that every night he's away is to do with..."

She trailed off. "But this is beside the point," she said. "William will tell me if he will be away, and he didn't this time. And he's been away two nights. It's not like him at all. I know two nights may not seem like much – but it's totally unexpected."

"I see," I said. "That's a little worrying, to be sure. I saw him on Monday – I left him in The Duke's Head just after lunch. Have you spoken to the police?"

She nodded. "They didn't take it seriously. They said he was sure to return in a day or two. I expect they think he's just another errant husband, distracted by a night out with friends

– or worse. Or that a story has necessitated travel out of town. But it's not just one night, and this is out of character."

I nodded, and she looked out at the rain driving against the window. She suddenly looked back at me. "Oh, how foolish of me," she said. "You must be wondering why on earth I have come to you."

"No, it's perfectly –"

"But I should have explained. William was most impressed by you – he spoke of your adventures in Hawksbridge, and what a modest person you still were when you might have become – well, puffed up."

I smiled.

"I think you're a man after his own heart," she continued. "Once you have got hold of a mystery, you can't let it go until you have uncovered it. You have a reputation for it. That's why I thought you might be able to help. And because..."

"Yes?"

"Because I can't tell everything to the police."

"Ah," I said. "You need discretion. I understand."

Mrs Lowick sighed with relief. "Thank you. William was caught up in something – that is, he was investigating something. Or someone. I think it has to do with his disappearance, which is why I'm so worried. But I can't tell the police since it would compromise his investigation, and if and when he comes back, he would be furious. Not to mention the fact that the person involved would no doubt be alerted – in such a small town – and could cover up their tracks. And who knows, it could even put the children and me in danger."

"That sounds to be a serious matter, Mrs Lowick," I said, having a sinking feeling that I was about to be dragged into a complex case. "I will try to help if I can. I like William a great deal – a little more with each meeting, I have to say – and I do hope no harm has come to him. I cannot think it likely – he's a highly capable, sturdy man."

"Yes," Mrs Lowick said, "I'm sure you're right.

Nevertheless, we must find him." I was encouraged that her initial appearance of helplessness had been replaced by a calmer resolve.

"Then please tell me as much as you know, Mrs Lowick. Excuse me while I fetch a notebook. Ah, Mrs Felton – could you get more tea for Mrs Lowick? I think the pot is empty."

~

As I returned with the notebook, one of my new feathered guests let out an unearthly shriek, and Mrs Lowick jumped a little.

"Oh! Goodness – I thought it was a soul in distress. You have peacocks!"

"It seems I do, though uninvited," I said. "I quite like the company. And they seem unafraid of Fox."

"They can be quite aggressive creatures," Mrs Lowick said. "It's curious. They look strangely out of place in the English countryside, and yet perfectly at home strutting about an estate."

"Yes, more the sort of colourful beast you might find in India, I would imagine."

"I believe the Romans brought them here," Mrs Lowick said. "Did you know that William can do an uncanny impression of a peacock?"

"I did not!" I said. "I'll ask him to perform it for me. I assume you mean the call?"

Mrs Lowick laughed. "Well, yes, but now you mention it, it may be apt for his demeanour in a crowd of women. The poor man can't help himself. I find it more endearing than troublesome, if truth be told."

Then you are an unusual woman, I thought to myself.

I opened my notebook. "Is the name Gabriel Forrester

relevant here, Mrs Lowick?"

She stared at me. "He *did* tell you?"

"That's all he said – that we should beware a possible stain on his reputation. Is that what he told you?"

"Yes, not much more," said Mrs Lowick. "I suppose he was trying to protect me. But what about him? How can we help him if we don't know what trouble he's in? He said that Forrester was responsible for terrible things, and he was putting profits before lives. And yet this hardly rings true, does it? Mr Forrester is known for his socialist views."

"Ah," I said. "William reminded me on Monday that humans are capable of holding opposing views simultaneously. And a man's public view is often at odds with his private behaviour. When money is involved, a person's cherished beliefs can easily be eroded, or at least side-lined. We see it all the time in political corruption."

"True, I suppose," Mrs Lowick said, stooping to stroke Fox who had fallen asleep by her feet. "I so hate to think ill of people – especially Mr Forrester. It makes no sense."

"We must arm ourselves with knowledge," I said. "I'm afraid we must go through William's papers and learn what we can. I've found this approach fruitful in the past."

"Very well," said Mrs Lowick. "If we must, we must. Could you come to the house tomorrow? I'm sorry, I'm sure you must have many more pressing things to do than looking for a mislaid husband."

"Not really," I said. "And I've been starting to think of William as a friend. I will not rest until he is safely back at home with you."

"Oh, thank you, thank you, Mr Rufford," Mrs Lowick said. "You're just as William said – a good, generous man. Here is my card." We both got up, and I called Shipley to fetch the coachman and his horse.

"Look," Mrs Lowick said as I opened the front door. "The rain has stopped! It must be a sign. Goodbye, Mr

Rufford – until tomorrow! Shall we say eleven o'clock? I'm sure you will find us both at home then, and we shall laugh about my silliness!"

After the coach had disappeared from view, I stood for a while, appreciating the freshness of the world after the rain despite the worry of Lowick's disappearance. Could he really be in any danger? He seemed a worldly-wise man who would not unnecessarily put himself at risk. But then again, poking about the dark recesses of a man's business might well prove hazardous.

And women – women were a weakness for him, as I had gathered and Mrs Milburn had alluded to. Out of compassion, and perhaps a little fascination, he had gone beyond the journalistic necessities and strayed deeper into Mrs Milburn's life, becoming a target of her desperate emotions. I wondered whether Lowick had mentioned her to his wife. If he had, then maybe Mrs Lowick would have been less quick to focus on Mr Forrester. A woman scorned...

I decided to go and call on Mrs Milburn in the morning, before my appointment with Mrs Lowick.

~

"Yes?" said the woman at the door, who from her clothes and manner I took to be the housekeeper.

"Good morning, ma'am," I said, removing my hat. "My name is Thomas Rufford. I wonder if I might speak to Mrs Milburn for a few minutes?"

The housekeeper did not return my smile. "I'm afraid Mrs Milburn is not available, sir. She is not seeing any visitors at present. I'm sorry."

She started to close the door, so I said, "Please, ma'am – it's important. A mutual acquaintance has gone missing, and I would like to ask her if she has seen him. I will only take up a few minutes of her time."

The housekeeper hesitated, and then something seemed to dawn on her. "Mr Rufford? Have I not seen your name in the papers?"

"You may have," I said. "I resolved a couple of difficulties in the town, that is all."

"Of course!" she said, her thin lips forming the hint of a smile, and opened the door for me. "Very well – but please speak softly, and do not stay too long. Mrs Milburn's nerves are in a poor state."

I was ushered into a parlour, which was decorated with sketches of bridges, and presently Mrs Milburn appeared, moving hesitatingly into the room. She wore black, and in happier days, she must have been pretty. Now, illness had aged her complexion and movements. I stood up.

"Mrs Milburn, thank you for seeing me. My name is Thomas Rufford and I'm a friend of William Lowick."

"Good morning," she said in a small voice, and mechanically shook the hand I offered.

"You remember Mr Lowick?" I prompted.

"No, I – I don't think so," she said, taking the seat opposite mine.

I sat down again. "He's a journalist. He saw you at the... when you were being looked after, and then he came to visit you here."

"Oh," she said. "I'm sorry, my memory is not what it was. If you say he came to visit, then he must have. What did he want?"

"He came to see that you were well."

"How kind of him," she said, and then a change came over her face. "Oh! Of course. I remember now. How strange – he pretended to be my poor husband! That wasn't at all kind. Why would he do such a thing?" Her lower lip trembled, and I started to think I had made a great mistake in troubling her.

"Mrs Milburn," I said, "he didn't pretend to be him – he just looks a little like him, that's all. That's why it was confusing. It's entirely understandable."

"Oh," she said again, her mind evidently grappling with this. "I see. So he was being kind, after all?"

"Indeed he was," I said, "and I can vouch for it, having become acquainted with him recently. He's an admirable fellow."

"I see." She clasped her hands together, and stared into the empty grate.

"I'm here because I've become concerned about him. He's gone missing, you see."

She turned her gaze back to me. "Oh, no! Has he... Not the ramparts? Oh, God, no! You cannot think I did it! You cannot!"

Tears rolled down her cheeks, and she began to rock back and forth in her chair. "No, no, no! I'm not a bad woman!"

"Mrs Milburn, of course I don't think that," I said. "I just wanted to know if he called on you, that's all. Whether he might have said where he was going."

"Going?" she said, drying her eyes. "Why should I know that?"

She was like a small child. I decided that this conversation was unlikely to be productive, and stood up.

"Of course you wouldn't. I'm sorry to have troubled you, Mrs Milburn. Thank you for your time."

"Oh – you're going so soon?" She looked disappointed. She could not have had many people to talk to, and I realised I had failed to provide any comfort or stimulation that might have helped her disjointed mind.

"I don't wish to tire you, ma'am," I said, starting to move towards the door.

She moved more quickly than before, and stood at the door, blocking my path.

"But I don't want you to go yet," she said. "I hardly speak

to anyone. Mrs Spillings doesn't let me see anyone. I might as well be in prison. I might as well be dead!"

This development was a little alarming, but at the same time, I was glad to see her in a more animated state. There was fire left in her yet.

I smiled. "Well, in that case, why don't you ask Mrs Spillings if I can stay a little longer? I'm sure she has your best interests at heart."

"Yes," she said, and opened the door, looking back at me as if I were a dog in danger of wandering away. "Julia?" I heard her say. "I would like our guest to stay longer. I want to walk with him in the garden."

"I don't know..." came the reply.

"But why not?" Mrs Milburn pleaded. "You're always keeping me away from people! Just a few minutes?"

"You know what the doctors have said – it's for your own good. You will get stirred up, and it makes you unhappy. But all right. A few minutes only."

"Thank you!" Mrs Milburn said, and she appeared at the door beaming. "You may stay."

I nodded.

She remained by the doorway. "Can I show you my garden?"

"Yes, please do. I should be delighted."

To my surprise, Mrs Milburn came and grabbed hold of my hand, leading me through the house to the back door. Mrs Spillings looked on disapprovingly, shaking her head.

The garden was small, but love and care had evidently been lavished on it. There were some fruit trees, and the flower beds had been thoroughly weeded.

"I planted this rose tree for Harold," Mrs Milburn said, kneeling on the lawn and running her fingers over the velvety red petals. "It's just started to flower. He loves roses."

"I too," I said. "These are very beautiful. This garden is tremendously well kept," I added, looking around me. "You must be a dedicated gardener. I wish I had that talent."

"It's not so hard, when you have a lot of time," she said. "Do you like pansies?"

"I do have a weakness for them, yes," I said. "I used to press them when I was a child. Their patterns and shapes always appealed to me."

She went over to another corner of the garden where there was a crop of red, yellow and purple pansies.

Again she knelt and touched the petals, as though stroking a pet.

"I think they like me," she said, looking up at me. "Do they not seem friendly to you?"

"Indeed, that's exactly what they are," I said. "And quite lovely."

She looked down again, and said to the flowers, "You don't think Ninette did it, do you? Of course you don't. Ninette could never do anything like that. Even if he was being a silly old pig about it. He didn't understand at all."

As gently as I could, I said, "What didn't he understand, Mrs Milburn?"

She looked at me, puzzled at my ignorance. "Why, the Society, of course, you silly old pig." She put her hand to her mouth and giggled. "Oh, sorry! But the Society, the things we must do... but now I forget what we must do."

She stood up, brushing down her skirts. "I forget what we must do," she repeated. "We must do something. Do you know what it is?"

"I believe you're referring to the campaign for female emancipation – marches, protests, and so forth," I said.

Her eyes brightened. "Yes! That's it! Protests, and so forth. We must be free..." She trailed off, and out of the corner of my eye I saw Mrs Spillings emerging from the house.

"Now, Ninette, it's time to let this gentleman be on his way, and time for you to have a rest."

This time, Mrs Milburn did not object. "Goodbye, Mr..."

"Rufford. Thomas Rufford. Thank you for showing me your garden – it's exquisite."

"Goodbye, Mr Rufford. You will come again?"

"Of course, if you wish it," I said.

As Mrs Spillings opened the front door for me, she said, "Poor Mrs Milburn. Thank you for your patience with her. I am her only friend, and I'm afraid an inadequate one at that. But any excitement makes her worse. We have to be very careful."

"Of course, Mrs Spillings. I perfectly understand. I do hope she improves soon. If there's anything I can do..."

"Thank you, Mr Rufford. I don't think there is – she just needs peace and quiet. I'm sorry about your friend. I hope you find him."

"Yes, I'm sure I will," I said, with more confidence than I felt. "Thank you, ma'am, and good day!"

CHAPTER TEN

I LOOKED in at The Duke's Head to enquire whether Mr Lowick had been seen with anyone after I had left his company, but he had apparently left on his own. It seemed that after that, he had simply vanished into thin air.

The Lowicks lived in a modern semi-detached house on the east side of Hawksbridge. It was inoffensive enough, but the repetition of the same design along a long street made me think of a hall of mirrors. As I opened the wrought-iron gate and made my way up the stone-flagged path, I prayed fervently that I would find a jovial William, apologetic for having worried me, with his wife Clementine beside him, smiling and rosy from a night of penitent amorous attention.

But that hope was quickly dashed when, as earlier in the day, I was greeted by a solemn housekeeper, followed by an ashen-faced Mrs Lowick. I could hear children's laughter in the background that was jarring in the circumstances, for all its innocence.

"No word of William?" I asked.

She shook her head, a tense hand clutched to her breast. "Nothing," she said. "But at least you're here. Please come through to William's study. Mrs Beatty, can you get Mr Rufford some coffee?"

The housekeeper nodded, and was about to head for the kitchen, when I caught her eye. She hesitated, and gave me an intense, anxious look. A moment later, she was gone, and Mrs Lowick gestured for me to take one of the two comfortable armchairs in the study.

She noticed me eyeing William's fall-front bureau with some trepidation, and said, "I've saved you a little trouble, and taken out his papers." She pointed to three linen bags lying near the fireplace. "You can take them away and examine them – my mind is so befuddled, I won't be able to make any sense of them. Please keep the papers and their contents to yourself – oh, there's no need to say that – I'm sure you will. I will bear the consequences if William returns. I don't mind his anger, so long as I have done everything I could."

"Thank you, Mrs Lowick," I said. "Is this all?"

"Most of it will be at his office, I'm sure," Mrs Lowick said. "So I suppose we might look there too...?"

"Indeed," I said. "Although it might be hard to gain access to it. And I wonder if he trusted his colleagues enough to leave sensitive documents in the office. Well, I'll see what I can find here. I will of course secure them in my safe, and I'll let you know immediately I have found anything of interest. May I consult my fiancée – Miss Davison? She has assisted me before, and I value her advice."

"Yes, of course you may," she said. "Thank you."

"The bureau was not locked?" I asked.

"It was," she said, "but I know where he keeps the key – there, in the miniature chest of drawers on the mantel."

"Ah – I love those apprentice pieces," I said. "My father had one, and I always imagined it had been made by elves."

Mrs Lowick managed a smile, and then there was a childish scream and sobbing. "I need to attend to my own naughty elves, Mr Rufford. Please excuse me for a minute."

She had been gone only a moment when there was a knock on the door, and the housekeeper came in.

"I'm sorry to disturb you, sir, but there is something I have to give you." She looked behind her furtively. Holding out a folded piece of paper, she continued: "I took this from the master's desk on Monday, God forgive me. Mr Lowick left the house in a foul temper, and when I came in to check for dirty cups, there was this letter on his desk. I thought it must be trouble, so I took the liberty of glancing at it. And then when I saw what it said, I had to hide it from Mrs Lowick and the children. It wasn't fit for their eyes."

"I see," I said, taking the letter.

"And then hearing who you are, and how you're helping Mrs Lowick, I thought it best you should have it. Just in case, you know..."

She trailed off, and then sensing Mrs Lowick's imminent return, darted out of the room, leaving me to call "Thank you!" after her.

I put it in my pocket unread, and Mrs Lowick came back in. "Never have more than one child," she said wearily. "George is always finding ways to upset Amelia. I hope he'll grow out of it soon."

"I'm sure he will," I said. "How old is he?"

"Nine," she said. "And Amelia is six. I have told them their father is away on business."

The door opened a crack, and a small mop of unruly hair appeared, followed by the rest of George. "Hello!" he said to me, with a pleasingly impudent smile. "I'm George. Are you Mr Rufford?"

"George!" his mother said sternly. "I told you to let us talk in peace."

"But Mama, I wanted to meet Mr Rufford. The chaps at school say he's a detective. Is that true?"

I was amused that my adventures had been a matter of discussion amongst George's peers. "In a manner of speaking," I said, "but only because circumstances have led me into it – I'm not a professional detective. I just help out occasionally."

"It must be terribly exciting," George said. "Catching bad men. Did you kill any of them?"

His mother looked acutely embarrassed, but I laughed. "No, George, I haven't killed anyone, yet, and I hope never to do so."

"George, that's quite enough of that. Do go and play,

there's a good boy."

"Yes, Mama," he said, still grinning at me. "Oh, I forgot. Yesterday in the park I saw a little girl wearing Amelia's old dress. You know, the checky blue one. Isn't that funny?"

"I'm sure it couldn't have been the same one," Mrs Lowick said with a frown. "It must just have been similar."

"No, it was Amelia's dress," George persisted. "I went up and looked at the sleeves. There was a little bit of the blood stain from when that cat scratched her. And there was the patch from when she tore it on brambles. I *told* her the blackberries were too far to reach."

"Well, perhaps one of us gave it away, and forgot about it," Mrs Lowick said. "I expect it was Mrs Beatty. Now if you could please let us talk, George!"

"Yes, Mama. Goodbye, sir!" And he ran off, whistling.

"I like him," I said. "He has his father's spirit – and hair. Mrs Lowick, was there anything about your husband that you found to be... different, lately? Anything not quite right? It might help us understand his state of mind."

"You mean was he dissatisfied at home, and therefore planning to run away and leave us? No, nothing like that."

I squirmed at her misunderstanding. "I beg your pardon," I said, "that's not what I had in mind. It could be anything. Perhaps a preoccupation that might suggest to us how he was thinking, and thus where he might go. For example, was he dwelling on a particular article he was working on?"

"Apart from the Forrester business, no," she said. "But there was one strange thing. I hesitate to mention it, since it's so trivial, and yet so odd."

"Yes?"

"William has always been a great respecter of books. He's an avid reader, and writing is his trade, so it's only natural. And yet... a couple of weeks ago, he went around the house pulling books off the shelf, and then he put them on the rubbish pile in the garden, and set it alight. I asked him what he was doing, and he just shrugged."

"Good Lord," I said. "What were these books?"

"Completely harmless – some novels, including the complete works of Scott – it was a present from a dear friend. That was quite upsetting. And a book of Wordsworth poetry. And would you believe – a beautiful edition of Eliza Acton's 'Modern Cookery' – one of my favourite recipe books!"

Mrs Lowick looked pained at the memory. "It really was an extraordinary thing to do. I'm afraid we were not on good terms for several days. Do you think the balance of his mind has been upset?"

"Only if he had no rational motivation," I said. "These books must surely have something in common. Do you know what that might be?"

Mrs Lowick struggled to think, and then gave up. "No, not at all, Mr Rufford! I can't imagine. Perhaps it was a sudden attack of puritanism? That we shouldn't have such nice things? Oh, but that's too ridiculous."

"I'll give it some thought," I said, getting up, "and perhaps you could too. It may be significant. Thank you for the papers – I'll look through them this afternoon."

"I do hope you find something," Mrs Lowick said, going to the door. "I shall go down to the police office and try to talk some sense into them. Surely, after three nights, they must take me seriously."

~

"You just missed a beautiful young lady!" Mrs Felton said with a twinkle in her eye.

"Oh?" I said, dumping the bags of papers on the hall floor and removing my coat. "Which beautiful lady might that be?"

"Aren't you lucky, knowing so many? Effie! She left a note. What a pity you weren't in – I could have served tea to a famous composer. Here's her note – she took her time about it. I thought she was writing a novel!"

I took the note and unfolded it. I was surprised to find the writing spidery and uneven; all the letters I had previously received from women were neat to the point of primness. Had I not known the identity of this author, I would have deduced her to be a child.

Dear Thomas,

I am sad to find you absent from your beautiful castle! Now I have seen it briefly, I wish all the more for you to show me all of its secrets. I will return again, like a bad penny. Oh - you will be glad to know that Sylvie is a little better, and her colour is improving. Though without the use of her brain, I am at a severe loss. I did enjoy our conversation the other day. It is a relief to talk to a man who does not fawn over me.

I caught a glimpse of your wonderful peafowl and I have an idea for names for them! If you have not already christened them, that is. I will tell you when I see you again, which I hope will be soon.

Until then, I am, happily,

Your friend,

Effie

"Well, I'll be..." I said, and then realised I had said this out loud. Mrs Felton was looking at me intently as if to divine the content of the note from my expression.

"All well?" she said, expectantly.

"Yes, she says she'll call again. Excuse me – I have some reading to do."

She looked a little disappointed. "Coffee in your little study, then, my dear?"

"That would be perfect, Mrs Felton. What would I do without you?"

~

Questions hung in the air around me like restless hummingbirds. My mind did not know where to begin. In normal times, I could have spent the rest of the afternoon savouring Effie's delightful, affectionate note, perhaps writing back to her in a similar vein, inviting her to dinner and promising her a full tour of the Ramsburgh estate. I wondered at the warmness of her tone. Was my new friend simply in search of inspiration, or something more?

But today, I could only allow myself a few minutes to relish and re-read Miss Harris' note. Time was of the essence: I had to locate another friend. I tipped the contents of the first bag onto the sofa next to me, and then remembered that I had left something in my coat pocket – the mysterious letter that Mrs Beatty had given me.

On the way downstairs, I stopped at the library, lingering there and enjoying the calm elegance of the room and the quiet wisdom of a thousand writers. The question of why William had destroyed his own books pressed on me. As his wife had said, it made no sense. What possible link could there be between a renowned author, a poet, and a culinary authority?

I stood in the bay window, watching the peacock displaying his magnificent tail feathers to his mate. They shimmered with iridescent beauty in the spring sunshine, but the blasé hen, having seen it all before, wandered away in search of food. I wondered whether Mrs Milburn's trust in her husband's fidelity was justified. After all, she admitted that he was frequently away. And yet it was unkind to assume that this disappearance must be about William's failings. He could equally have been a victim of his own courage – that is, if his disappearance was indeed sinister.

I had not yet had time to contemplate my time with Mrs Milburn and draw any conclusions. It seemed unlikely that she would have had the chance or resourcefulness to cause William harm: still, I saw a little flash of passion when she stopped me from leaving her parlour. Could she have slipped away from her guard to exact a penalty for rejection at William's hand? Her housekeeper had to go out and order provisions, after all, and surely she had time off.

Coming back to William's family: what was the significance of Amelia's old dress? Perhaps none. But it seemed as though many parts of a puzzle had been laid out before me, and I simply lacked the ability to put them together. It was like discovering a stone inscribed with an ancient language; there was meaning there, if only I had the key.

I fetched the letter, and returned to my room, where I found a coffee pot waiting for me. I took a fortifying gulp, and opened the note; this was a task I had been dreading. My fears were immediately confirmed. After all, a genial communication is seldom written entirely in capitals.

SIR,

IT IS ONLY FROM A RELUCTANCE TO SEE

MORE INNOCENT PEOPLE HURT THAT I REFRAIN FROM IMMEDIATELY INFORMING YOUR WIFE OF YOUR DISGUSTING, DECEITFUL, INDEED EVIL BEHAVIOUR. YOU HAVE CONDEMNED EVERYONE WHO LOVES YOU TO ABJECT MISERY. IN SHORT, SIR, YOU HAVE MADE A DISGRACEFUL SHAMBLES OF YOUR OWN AND MANY OTHER LIVES AND ARE THEREFORE DISQUALIFIED FROM EXISTENCE IN A CIVILISED SOCIETY.

ENJOY THE LIMITED TIME YOU HAVE LEFT INFECTING GOD'S EARTH.

CHAPTER ELEVEN

I SLEPT badly, and I was relieved to see Phyllis that Friday morning. On a whim, I had invited her for breakfast when I had written to her on Wednesday. I thought it might be amusing to play husband and wife, starting the day together. It was a pity that this had to be spoilt by discussing William's disappearance, but I was grateful to share my burden.

"This is disturbing," Phyllis said, brushing crumbs from the table in the drawing room where breakfast had been laid out, and laying down the letter. "We have to conclude that William was not safe from whoever wrote this letter."

"Unfortunately, yes," I said, biting into a slice of toast. "What on earth was William up to? It's hard to get any sense of it."

"In the circumstances, I will overlook your talking with your mouth full," said Phyllis. "I'm sure that will not be your usual mode. But William – from what you've told me, he was a ladies' man. So I expect he has strayed from his marriage. How very sad for his poor family."

I was inclined to give William the benefit of the doubt. "Well, the letter doesn't mention a woman. Might it be some other indiscretion? Perhaps insulting a gentleman? Writing a scurrilous piece, perhaps? It would be easy to tread on toes in Hawksbridge. People hold much store by their reputation and position. A journalist has the power to ruin a man."

"Or in this case, perhaps a woman."

"Oh, all right, I suppose it is more likely," I admitted. "Perhaps it is consistent with his family being affected – unless that would simply be a consequence of William himself being threatened."

"We need to find out who sent the letter," Phyllis said, taking it up again and peering at it.

"I have no idea how we're going to do that," I said, draining my coffee cup and pouring more from the pot. "We have so little to go on. Just the handwriting, which will be disguised."

"I don't think handwriting can be completely be disguised," Phyllis said. "And there is something else." She held the paper close to her eyes, then got up and walked to the window for better light.

"You've got it the wrong way round," I said.

"No," she said. "There's something on the back. Look."

I pushed my chair back and went over to her, peering at the back of the letter that had appeared at first glance quite blank. I was so close to Phyllis that I could smell her violet perfume, and for a moment I was intoxicated by it. I wanted to pull her to me and kiss her; but instead I tried to focus on the sheet of paper that she held out.

"I can see some smudges," I said. "Ah – perhaps some letters. Backwards, I think."

I straightened up, looking into Phyllis' eyes. She did not look away, and I could see that for a moment, she too was tempted to indulge herself. But then she looked back at the paper. "Of course – backwards, because this letter has been resting on another, which was not quite dry."

"Interesting," I said. "There's a mirror here."

We held it up to the ornate gilded mirror, whose delicate plaster frame had seen better days. Phyllis examined the reflection.

"Something 'sitting', I think. And in front of that: M – O – N... Then it's just a squiggle. What can that mean?"

"Monday sitting? Some kind of meeting? He's an official of some kind, for a group that meets on Mondays. Perhaps a board meeting. There – doesn't that support my theory? He's ruffled important feathers. It might even be Mr Forrester." I had already explained to Phyllis that William was suspicious about the designer. "So we need to look at companies, or institutions, that meet on Mondays, starting with Forrester."

"Well, maybe," Phyllis said, doubtfully. "Perhaps it will occur to us. What about the other papers?"

"I went through them last night. There's little of interest – correspondence from previous articles, a lot of domestic receipts, some letters from his bank, that kind of thing. But there was one significant paper."

"Yes?"

"A list of names and addresses: three in London, one in York, and one in Manchester."

"But that could be about anything, from any time, surely?"

"I don't think so. William has put a cross by them – sometimes two – and a date underneath each cross. They're from this year and last year."

"Oh, Lord," said Phyllis. "That is chilling. So – deaths in a family? Related to the Forrester case?"

"It looks like it," I said. "I made a copy of the list, so we can give everything back to Mrs Lowick. Eventually the police will want to see it all – at least I hope so."

"Don't you think the police should know about William's investigation of Mr Forrester? And this awful letter?"

I hesitated. "Possibly. But were William to walk in the door five minutes after her telling the police all about the investigation, their marriage might never recover from the perceived breach of trust. And besides, we don't know what the other consequences might be. If it's as serious as William said, for all we know, it might affect more lives. I think we need to leave it to Mrs Lowick's judgement. But I agree, it makes me uncomfortable."

"We need to tell her about the letter," Phyllis said. "And then she can decide whether to show it to the police."

"Very well – no time like the present. Can I drive your

trap? I need something to do with my hands."

~

Mrs Lowick stared at the letter miserably. I had tried my best to prepare her, but it had not been much help.

"What could William possibly have done to deserve this?" she said, looking at us with wide, watery eyes. "Is it to do with Mr Forrester, do you think? Or something – someone – else?"

"It's hard to tell," I said. "There is the impression of some words on the back, but we haven't yet been able to decipher them. Will you take this to the police?"

She shook her head. "No. For all we know, that might put William, or others, in more danger. So, not until we know what we're dealing with."

"In which case, Mrs Lowick, would you mind if we kept the letter for a while?" I had an instinct – or perhaps mere hope – that with further scrutiny, something might be deduced from it.

"Of course, do keep it," she said. "And thank you for returning the rest of his papers. The list of people and dates is alarming – but at least you discovered it." She sighed. "I have spoken to the police again – they are starting to take an interest, thank goodness. They'll be coming to the house today. I suppose it will be hard to keep the truth from the children. That will be awful."

"I'm so sorry, Mrs Lowick," said Phyllis. "You must let us know if there's anything we can do. We will of course keep working on the letter."

"That's very kind of you. I'm putting you both to so much trouble..."

"It's no trouble to help friends," I said.

Mrs Lowick smiled briefly and nodded. "I also spoke to

William's colleagues at The Hawksbridge Herald this morning," she said. "They haven't seen him since last week, and when I hinted at an investigation, they professed to know nothing. It seems they give William a lot of leeway. They let me look through his papers, but there was nothing that I could see about Mr Forrester. He must be keeping that information elsewhere – unless it's all just a figment of his imagination! I'm beginning to wonder now, I really am. But that letter... Someone hates my poor William!"

~

"What else can we do?" Phyllis asked.

"Apart from squint at that damn letter again, I don't know," I said, taking the reins. "Do you suppose we would gain anything by writing to those addresses?"

"It would take a while to get any response," Phyllis said, "and at least some of them we know to be dead."

"There may still be family," I said. "But I really don't know what it'll accomplish."

"What about speaking to Mr Forrester?" Phyllis said.

"And ask him what? 'Did you do away with William Lowick?'"

"But supposing it wasn't Mr Forrester, but an employee of his. Then Mr Forrester might want to help, and perhaps could have seen him on the premises."

"Even if that were the case," I said, "remember that Mrs Lowick doesn't want anyone to know that William was investigating Forrester. We must respect her wishes. And it seems far-fetched to think that Forrester, or an employee, could be a killer. William may simply have been paranoid. Perhaps that's what being a journalist does to you."

"Yes – the books. That suggests a disordered mind.

Perhaps disordered enough to wander off into trouble."

"Good point. I hope the police make a thorough search of the area – especially the ramparts, and the river."

Phyllis shuddered. "Oh God. Poor William. Poor Clementine. And the children..." She put her arms around me, and held me tight.

~

Catherine and Mrs Felton brought us lunch, over which we failed to come up with any new ideas on the Lowick case.

"I could show you my renovated cottage," I said. "It will give us something fresh to think about."

"Hm," Phyllis said, looking suspiciously at me. "Just a tour?"

"Just a tour," I said. "It's been transformed since Johnny Falkirk used it as a hideout. I think the next occupant is going to enjoy it."

"Oh, very well, then," Phyllis said. "I'm slightly intrigued."

The peafowl were not in evidence as we walked to the cottage, which disappointed me as I wanted to show them off to Phyllis. But there would be plenty of time later for her to make friends with them.

"Goodness!" said Phyllis. "This is bright."

The sitting room had been painted a cheerful yellow, the stained ceiling covered in a fresh white coat, and the rickety furniture replaced by sturdy old pieces that I had selected myself. I had taken some of the lesser coloured engravings from the house and hung them here, and the chipped, ugly crockery had been replaced.

"What a charming home this will make," Phyllis said. "Are these new rugs, too?"

I nodded. "Come upstairs."

"If I didn't know you better, Thomas, I would be in fear for my virtue," she said. But she followed me, and admired the colourful patchwork quilt in the larger bedroom, and the pale blue walls.

She opened a cupboard. "And sheets and blankets! It really is all set. But for whom?"

I shrugged. "Probably a family from one of the other cottages, and then we'll work on improving theirs. But right now, it's ours. We can play house!"

I threw pillows from the cupboard onto the bed, got on it, and patted the other side. Phyllis made a face, but I suspected only for show, and she was soon next to me, having kicked off her shoes. I held her hand, and she rested her head on my shoulder.

"Oh, that's better," she said. "It's tiring being a detective."

"Yes, I think it's the tragedy of it that's most exhausting."

I looked around the room. "I know what's missing – a coffer at the end of the bed. Just not a wicked one."

Phyllis raised her head. "I suppose Francesca has shown you her Wicked Cassone?"

"I confess she has," I said. "It's... interesting."

"So you have been in her bedroom! I should be shocked, but I don't have the energy."

"I only looked at her chest. That is, her cassone." Phyllis slapped me playfully. "But the room is impressive. Red wallpaper, a stunning secretaire, and a four-poster bed. I expect the wallpaper has been replaced by Forrester's best by now."

"Thomas," Phyllis said, before hesitating.

"Just how... well, wicked, is the cassone?"

"Ah! Research for a future book, perhaps? It's fairly naughty. There are several paintings on it – and in it."

I described, as delicately as I could, the couple on the

front watched by the husband behind the rocks, the three people enjoying themselves inside the box, and the finely-painted, rather touching nude resting on the bottom of it.

"Good Lord," said Phyllis. "How racy." To my surprise, she reached over, turned my head towards her and kissed me with some force. My own passions were similarly roused, and we clung together for a while.

She did not protest when I unbuttoned the top of her dress to caress and kiss the exposed flesh of her breasts. "Oh dear," she whispered, but she closed her eyes and pressed my hand to her chest.

I kissed her on the lips again, and at the same time stroked her legs, moving my hand gently up beneath her dress. Her breathing became quicker, and when I reached my destination, she flinched and murmured but let me continue, smiling with pleasure as I stroked her. It did not take long. Her joy was a beautiful thing to watch, and I was happy to refrain from taking my own pleasure.

Phyllis fell asleep, and I thought about recent events, and the faint letters on the reverse of the poison pen letter. 'MON SITTING.' It made no sense. I got up and retrieved the letter which was still in my coat pocket. I went to the window and peered at it again. The 'I' had flecks of ink by it that might indicate the remnants of an 'E'. 'MON SETTING' – that was not much better. I repeated the words, gazing at Phyllis, lying in a gloriously dishevelled state and breathing rhythmically. How lucky I was to be her fiancé – how lucky, indeed, to be understood so well by another human being. The ring she wore was testament to a shared understanding of important values. We did not need the newest or the flashiest accoutrements and possessions. Pearls and a garnet, rather than diamonds.

At this thought, my brain immediately conjured up the words 'DIAMOND SETTING'. I excitedly looked again at the letter. Yes, there was space enough to allow this interpretation.

"Phyllis! Diamond setting! Couldn't that be it?"

She woke with a start. "Oh – I beg your pardon?"

"Diamond setting! Not Monday Sitting."

Phyllis blinked and sat up. "Diamond setting. Yes, that could be it! Well done. But I was having such a lovely dream about you. Oh... we... oh dear!"

She smiled at the memory and sank down on the pillow again. "I suppose we should get back to our detective work, in that case."

~

"So it could be someone who recently had some jewellery made," I said, "and this letter got mixed up with the receipt." We were back in the drawing room at Ramsburgh with tea, cake and the letter in front of us.

"But the ink was still wet," Phyllis pointed out. "If you took the receipt home, and then wrote a letter on top of it, the ink wouldn't come off, surely."

"Good point," I said. "So... the letter was written very shortly after the receipt was written, or perhaps it was from leaning on an accounts book."

"In which case, our man – or woman – is most likely a jeweller," Phyllis said.

"Good God," I said. "You're a genius at this!"

Phyllis smiled. "But of course. That's why I'm such a catch – among other reasons. Now, how are we going to narrow it down?"

"I have an idea about that," I said.

I went to find the receipt for Phyllis' ring. There were only three jewellers in Hawksbridge, as far as I knew, and so there was a good chance that I would find a match with the letter. I fervently hoped this would not be the case, because I felt sorry for Mr Belford. He seemed a decent man who had been unlucky in life, having been widowed relatively young.

Alas, Phyllis was soon finding correspondences.

"It's fortunate that the receipt is written out in capital letters," she said. "You can see the similarity here between this 'S' in the letter, and this one in the receipt. And here again with the strokes at the top and bottom of the 'N'."

"Damn," I said. "I'll have to call on Mr Belford this afternoon, if his shop is still open, and confront him with the letter. This will be unpleasant."

"I'll come with you," Phyllis said. "Perhaps he'll be more forthcoming with a female present."

"Would you? I would appreciate it. Thank you."

"Not at all," Phyllis said, wiping the crumbs off her lips with her napkin. "Well, we had better make a move. We owe it to poor Mrs Lowick to be quick."

"And to William," I said. "I hope to God this is all a wild goose chase, and he's simply been delayed somewhere."

~

We drove in silence for a few minutes, both a little uncertain what to say about our encounter in the cottage. I looked over and smiled at Phyllis. "That was heavenly earlier," I said. "Thank you."

She looked at me, narrowing her eyes. "Hm," she said. "You are trouble, Mr Rufford." Then she smiled back, and added, "But quite nice trouble, sometimes," and she patted my knee.

"I'm sorry – I've been so occupied with William that I haven't asked about your writing lately," I said. "Are you pleased with it?"

"Yes," she said. "Thank you, I am. My hero and heroine are caught up in a feud –"

"Like Romeo and Juliet?"

"Something like that. And they are having to communicate in code."

"I see," I said. "What kind of code."

"An unsophisticated one. But it does the job. They write each other letters where the real message is read from the first letter of each line."

"Good idea," I said. "I could do the same with you, and then I could write a very proper letter, with a hidden and very improper message about how I intend to behave once we are married."

"I look forward to it," Phyllis said. "Now, we must get into a more serious mood."

~

It was just before five o'clock, and the shop was not yet closed. Mr Belford's gloomy expression lightened a little when we entered, which, as we were probably about to bring him only misery, I found difficult to bear.

"Good morning, Mr Belford!" I said, as brightly as I could.

"It is indeed, sir, another lovely spring day," he said. "I trust you had no difficulty with the ring?"

"It's splendid," Phyllis said. "I couldn't be happier if I had chosen it myself."

"Oh, good," he said, visibly relieved. "It was rather one of my favourites. How may I help you today? A watch, perhaps, for sir to mark the occasion of his engagement? I have some superb ones in at present –"

"No, thank you," I said, looking around to check there

was no one else in the shop. "I'm afraid we've come about a personal matter."

"Oh!" he said, his face falling. "Oh. A personal matter? You mean personal to me, or to you?"

"Unfortunately, to you."

"To me? I don't understand."

"Mr Belford," Phyllis said gently, "no one can condemn a person for being upset when someone we love is wronged. We can all be protective – it's only human."

He stared at her and sniffed, then looked down at his shoes. "I'm sure I don't know what you're talking about, ma'am. Perhaps you have me mistaken for another?"

"I don't think so," Phyllis said, still in a soft but persistent tone. I was in awe of her composure. "I think you became upset – justifiably – and wrote a letter. Is this not the case?"

Mr Belford hesitated, and then crossed the shop and locked the door, turning the 'Open' sign to 'Closed'.

He returned, and positioned himself once more behind the counter, as if for protection.

"I'm afraid you will have to be more specific, ma'am. I don't know what you're getting at."

I reached into my pocket and held up the letter, near enough for Mr Belford to recognise it, but not so close he could grab it.

Mr Belford stared at it, and his face reddened. I could sense the cogs in his head turning like those in one of his expensive pocket watches.

"I don't know what that is."

"I think you do, Mr Belford," Phyllis said. "It's all right. We know you didn't mean what you said. But sometimes, you have to let people know that what they've done is wrong, don't you? If they think they can get away with it. They must be told what's right and what's wrong."

Phyllis' repetitive words seem to have a mesmerising effect on Mr Belford. He stared at Phyllis, his mouth slightly open, his resistance weakened by her soothing tone and by her sympathy with his plight.

Suddenly his composure failed and his face took on an expression of misery and regret. "Oh, Lord," he said, shaking his head. "I didn't mean any of it. But it's as you say – sometimes you have to write it down. I had to let it out, or I swear it would have killed me."

"Mr Lowick did you wrong?" I said.

"By God, he did me wrong. And he did Lillian wrong."

"Lillian is your daughter?" Phyllis asked.

"Yes. My only daughter, ruined by that – that – devil. The only mercy is that my dear wife is not alive to see it. She is at least spared that agony."

"Mr Belford," I said, "William Lowick has been missing for several days. I'm sorry to be blunt, but did you have anything to do with his disappearance?"

A rare smile formed on Mr Belford's face. "He's dead, sir?"

"I didn't say that – but he is missing. Do you know anything about it?"

"Praise the Lord," he said. "Praise Him indeed. I hope he's in Hell, sir, because that's where the scoundrel belongs, for seducing my Lillian, my only child. With a bastard daughter, how can she ever show her face again? I told her to give the child up, but no, she would not, out of foolish sentimentality. And now she's an outcast, and after four years, the child is too old to find a new home."

Mr Belford's knuckles were white from gripping the edge of the counter.

"But not content with one humiliation, that stinking reprobate did it again. Lillian is with child once more! I should have kicked the man's head in the first time. It was only for Lillian that I did not. But this second insult cannot be borne. No, sir, I didn't have anything to do with the man's disappearance. But I wish I had! Oh, how I wish I had! I would make him pay, sir, pay many times over." And he brought his fist down hard on the counter, rattling the display cases.

"Would you object, sir," I asked, "if we visited your daughter, to check that Mr Lowick is not there?"

He growled, and then after some hesitation, shrugged and said, "I don't see why not. She's in one of the cottages up at Pigdon Farm. That dog is paying for it. But I went yesterday, and there was no sign of him. She made no mention of him."

CHAPTER TWELVE

"OH – HAVE you any news?" Mrs Lowick asked anxiously on our second visit of the day.

"No, no news of William's whereabouts, I'm afraid," I said. "But we need to discuss the letter. I'm sorry we're calling so late."

"No, no, don't worry," she said. "Come and sit down."

Phyllis and I had the painful task of informing Mrs Lowick of what we had learned. We had agreed it should be done without delay.

"I didn't manage to tell the children," she said. "Being a dreadful coward, I've sent them to my sister in Alnwick. They were starting to ask questions. Perhaps by the time they come back, their father will be back at home."

"Good idea," I said. "It's an excellent distraction." I wondered how to begin to let Mrs Lowick down gently.

Seeing my hesitation, Phyllis said, "We found the author of the letter. The words on the back, and the handwriting, led us to Mr Belford, the jeweller."

"Oh! How clever of you!" said Mrs Lowick. "But why should he send William such a horrible letter?"

"You need to be strong, Mrs Lowick," Phyllis said gently. "There are things you didn't know about William. I'm sorry." She let Mrs Lowick absorb this information and make her own deductions before confronting her with the cruel details.

"Oh, I see, I think," said Mrs Lowick, staring at Phyllis. She was evidently trying hard to be matter-of-fact about it, when her mind must have been in turmoil. "I suppose I always knew he had his secrets. He would come home, and something in his eyes told me..." She stopped and looked away. "I believe

Mr Belford has a daughter. Is it to do with her?"

Phyllis nodded. "I'm afraid so."

"I see," Mrs Lowick said again. "I know William loves me – loves us. That I do know for sure. But he must also love this girl. It is something that happens. I'm not blind to the way the world works. Men can be strange creatures. Why cannot this" – she gestured at her home – "be enough for him?"

"It's a puzzle," I said. "But being a man, I know it can be difficult to always keep one's feelings in check. That's not to excuse him, of course, but to acknowledge that reason and instinct are often at odds."

"Thank you for being so frank with me," Mrs Lowick said. "I'm glad I didn't hear this from anyone else. I believe I'm strong enough to know more. There's a child, I take it?"

"Yes, Mrs Lowick, a young daughter," Phyllis said. "She's four years old. And..."

"And?"

Phyllis shot a desperate look at me. "Miss Belford is with child again."

Mrs Lowick looked as though she had been struck. A lone accident is one thing – it can be put down to the heat of the moment, an event that might chasten a person. But a second child, after all this time – it implied a much more serious commitment. It was akin to bigamy.

She shook her head, unable to speak. We waited, agonized, while she composed herself and dried her tears. She let out a hysterical laugh and said, "It's absurd. A second family! As if one isn't enough trouble. The silly, silly man. What was he thinking?"

"I'm sorry," is all I could think to say. "It must be hard to take. But Mr Belford is adamant that he had nothing to do with your husband's disappearance. He admitted to writing the letter, and that he would happily have done William harm, but I think he may have been telling the truth when he said he wasn't aware that William has gone missing."

"But of course," added Phyllis, "it must be for the police to judge. You will give the letter to the police? We will also give our account to them." I put the letter on the table in front of Mrs Lowick; she glanced at it briefly, and then put it in the book she was reading, as if she could not bear to be confronted by it any longer.

"Yes, yes, I'll do it in the morning, first thing," she said. "So, all this letter has done is tell me that I don't know my own husband. It brings us no further to finding him. Unless he's with *her?*"

"I think not," I said, "but I'll check tomorrow. We have the address from Mr Belford."

"Thank you," said Mrs Lowick. "Dreadful though all this is, it would be ten times harder without the two of you."

~

"We make a decent team, don't we?" I said, kissing Phyllis on the cheek and stepping out of the trap at Ramsburgh. "Thank you for your help today. You were astonishing."

"Don't mention it," Phyllis said. "And yes – I feel almost as though we're being tested. Will you speak to the police tomorrow?"

"I will, before visiting Miss Belford. You've done enough, and you must concentrate on your book. And your father will be missing you."

She nodded. "Good night! Let me know if you hear anything about William, won't you?"

Waiting for me on the hall table was a letter in a familiar hand.

Dear Thomas,

Can you bear to see your old friend so soon? I get bored so easily, don't I? - but I am having another dinner party on the 28th April, with my house guests naturally, and yes, the Captain. Don't frown and pout, Thomas, it's unbecoming and quite unnecessary. And I hope you and Phyllis and Flora can come. We will even have a representative of Lady F. in the form of Mrs Rachel Knowles, friend of Sylvie. Poor Sylvie is much better, thank goodness, if still unhealthily thin and pale, but Effie was so keen to make amends that she permitted Sylvie to invite her friend, though I could tell it was not an easy concession. Let us all keep an open mind! And I know you will be your charming self and put everyone at ease.

After the grim news in Hawksbridge of late, we deserve a little fun, do we not?

I hope you are well, my dear Thomas! Do let me know if you and your beautiful fiancée can come.

Yours affectionately,

Francesca

I smiled at the use of 'Effie'. The friendship between the two women was touching.

A dinner party was not such a bad idea – William would not wish all joy to be extinguished on account of him. And it would not be unpleasant to renew my acquaintance with Effie. So I wrote a brief note to Francesca to tell her I would be delighted to come.

~

"Thank you, Mr Rufford," said Inspector Simmons, after I had related what I knew about Mr Belford. He had the letter in front of him, as Mrs Lowick had already visited. "I see the urge to... shall we say, 'help' the troubled citizens of Hawksbridge has not left you."

Mr Simmons had the knack making admirable human qualities seem distasteful. "I'm sure you would do the same for a friend," I said. "That is, if you were not already a policeman."

He shot me a steely glance and continued: "Yet again, Mr Rufford, I have to admonish you for taking the law into your own hands. This letter should have been on my desk several days ago. Who knows what damage might have been done by this delay?"

"Mrs Lowick had a perfect right to her privacy. It was not clear what relevance it had to William's absence."

"Not clear?" said Mr Simmons, sitting up straight. "It's as clear as daylight to me. This is a death threat! And you may be sure that Mr Belford is being brought to this office for questioning as we speak. I only hope you have not aided and abetted a criminal by this delay. We are searching, and if we find a body, you may wish to reflect on your role in this."

He stood up and opened the door. "Now, no more of your heroics, please, Mr Rufford. We'll take it from here. I'm sure you don't want to see more of me than absolutely necessary. And the feeling is mutual!"

~

If William had wanted to hide Miss Belford and his own sins from the world, he had chosen his location well. A recent shower, together with the churn of cartwheels and muck from animals, had turned the track up to the farm into a midden that would have discouraged most visitors. By the same token, it would have been a chore for Miss Belford to escape her cottage for the pleasures and necessities of Hawksbridge. If William returned, I thought, I would speak to him and question his choices, to put it mildly.

As Celeste and I approached a huddled group of workers' cottages, I made a mental note of how I would improve them if they were mine. The roofs were missing a number of tiles, and the gutters were full of vegetation, which did not bode well for the interiors.

A small girl was holding a doll and playing outside one of the cottages, sitting it on an upturned pail and murmuring something to it. She wore a blue checked dress, which I was certain that, if examined, would reveal the identifying marks described by George Lowick.

A window opened, and a woman's voice called, "Matilda! Come inside! Matilda, now!"

Matilda stood and gawped at Celeste and me. "Good horsey!" she said.

"Indeed she is," I said, dismounting. "She's called Celeste, and she and I are great friends." Matilda stared at me with wide eyes, and her doll fell from the pail into the mud.

I picked the doll up and brushed it down as best I could, before handing it back. "What's she called?"

"Dolly," Matilda said, taking the doll back and clutching it to her chest.

"An excellent name," I said. "What a splendid red dress she has on."

"Matilda! I said, inside!"

Lillian Belford had appeared, and she manoeuvred her daughter towards the front door. I could well imagine how she might have appealed to William, in times when her untidy hair was more cared for and her body less mundanely clothed. And no doubt, before motherhood had made its unglamorous demands, she would have charmed him with a broad, carefree smile.

"Yes?" she demanded. "Can I help you?"

"Good morning – Miss Belford, I believe?"

She nodded, folding her arms protectively.

"I'm sorry to trouble you. I'm a friend of William's."

She frowned. "He's not supposed to go around telling people where I live," she said. "What do you want?"

"I'm afraid I have unsettling news," I said. "William has gone missing. In fact, I wondered if he might be with you."

"Missing?" she said. "No, he's not here. I haven't seen him for over a fortnight. How do you mean, missing?"

"He hasn't been seen since Monday morning. In fact, I seem to be one of the last to see him – I was drinking with him."

"In the morning? He's becoming a right old sot."

"Well, it was understandable, because of the smoke..."

"Not those horrible cigars? Well, I've never heard a sillier excuse for getting tight."

"No, it was... well, that's not relevant," I said. This was not the conversation I had planned. "The point is, Mrs Lowick hasn't seen him for five nights. It's unusual, and rather worrying."

Miss Belford snorted. "Ha! I don't see him for weeks at a time, and Clementine" – she pronounced the name with contempt – "complains after five nights? Well, see how she likes it."

"Miss Belford," I said with growing frustration, "I don't think you understand the gravity of the situation. No one has seen William, and he has left no word of his whereabouts. The police are conducting a search."

"I wish I could call on the bobbies every time I wanted Willie back in my bed!" she said with a smirk. "They wouldn't listen to me, though, would they? Seeing as I'm just a bit of trash sent off to the country to have my litter. Anyway, it's just like him to be wandering off. He does what he wants. He'll be back soon enough when he wants his thing polished!"

My look of shock chased the smile from her face. "I'm sorry. It's just that it's... hard." She fidgeted with the buttons on her dress. "How do I even know he still loves me? I don't know what I was thinking. I didn't expect much of a life, but this..."

"It must be extremely difficult," I said. "But I'm sure he loves you. I haven't known William long, but I've seen a sincerity in him – hiding behind his flippancy, to be sure."

"I don't know. Maybe. And now neither of us has him. I expect I could manage. Perhaps my father will have me back."

"I'm sure he would appreciate having you at home, and the chance to help his grandchildren grow up," I said. "But we don't know William has gone for good. We mustn't imagine the worst."

She nodded. "I expect if he died I would cry a lot, silly dope that I am. I can't feel anything right now. I'm too tired." She stretched her back, and I saw the curve that indicated a second child. "I could offer you tea, but I'm not much of a talker."

"No, that's quite all right, Miss Belford. I'll go now. You're sure you can't think of anything William said to indicate where he might be?"

"No, nothing," she said. "He never tells me anything important."

~

When I went to convey my lack of success, after a quick bite at The Dog and Hare – I could not bring myself to return to The Duke's Head where I had last seen William – Mrs Beatty asked me to wait in the hall for a moment. I could hear Mrs Lowick talking to another female, before being interrupted by Mrs Beatty, who returned and showed me to the drawing room. I was surprised by the identity of the other woman.

"Good afternoon, Lady Fairfield, Mrs Lowick," I said. "It's a pleasure to see you again, ma'am, although under wretched circumstances. I'm here to give my report, Mrs Lowick – simply that there is no sign of your husband at the location we discussed."

"You can be quite candid with Lady Fairfield, Mr Rufford," said Mrs Lowick. "I'm glad to say that we are well acquainted, via Lady Fairfield's charitable work, and I have told her everything I know."

"I came as soon as I heard about poor William's disappearance," Lady Fairfield said. "I wish I had known earlier. For all his faults and waywardness – forgive me, Clementine," she said, placing a hand on Mrs Lowick's arm, "but we have to acknowledge that in many ways, his is the weaker sex – for all his grievous sins against you, I believe William is at heart a good man. He wrote a very fair article about the Society, and he spoke warmly of you. It's simply frightening to think that a man can vanish like this, leaving no trail at all!"

She removed her hand and looked intently at Mrs Lowick. "I take it no one has seen him leave Hawksbridge? Have the police no information at all?"

Mrs Lowick shook her head. "Not as far as I'm aware. Aside from looking into Mr Belford, they are stumped."

"Dreadful," said Lady Fairfield. "But what an extraordinary coincidence for Mr Belford to send a poison-pen letter, just before William disappeared. You do think it coincidence?"

Mrs Lowick shrugged, and said, "I don't know what to think. I gather Mr Belford was already severely melancholic from the loss of his wife. And he would be within his rights to be angry, of course – the poor man's daughter..." She stopped and tightly closed her eyes, breathing deeply in a struggle to master her emotions.

"I studied the man carefully when he learned about William," I said. "I believe his surprise was genuine. But should he be responsible, I imagine he would have left some evidence. And the police will have searched his home and shop by now."

"Some evidence – quite," said Lady Fairfield. "Well, I must be leaving, my dear Clementine, but please, if there's anything I can do, send word!" She took Mrs Lowick's hand and squeezed it. "We women must help each other, as I'm sure you're tired of hearing me say."

Mrs Lowick attempted a smile, and rose to see her guest to the door.

When she came back, she sat and sighed. "A wonderful woman. Thank goodness I have such friends as her, and you!"

"Do you approve of the Society?" I said.

"Oh, how could one not?" she cried. "Her vision is correct, and inevitable, do you not think? I don't want to believe that humans should always be so unequal. It's so... primitive! Civilisation must progress."

"I can't argue with that," I said. "I just hope that her methods are equally civilised. The fire where those comic pamphlets were printed..."

She stared at me. "You can't honestly believe that was the work of the Society? Or even Lady Fairfield herself? Oh, surely not!"

"You're probably right," I said. "I'm starting to see conspiracy where bad luck or incompetence are more plausible explanations."

"I expect it's because I've run you ragged hunting for

William," Mrs Lowick said.

"Nothing that a good night's sleep won't cure," I said. "I might even be so wicked as to stay in bed late and skip church."

CHAPTER THIRTEEN

"DECENT of you to invite me, Thomas," Victor said as I ushered him into the drawing room for drinks before lunch. "It's always a pleasure to visit a hospitable man in his charming castle. I see you have new residents," he added, gesturing to the peacock and its mate strutting and foraging on the west lawn.

"Unbidden, but not unwelcome," I said. In reality, it was not me the Captain was visiting, but Flora. My half-sister had displayed a touching diffidence in asking whether Victor might come to Ramsburgh for a drawing lesson, under my watchful eye.

"Of course," I had replied, "but he must come for lunch. Then at least I can enjoy a little conversation with our new friend – and have the satisfaction of seeing you two together!"

She had blushed, but she was obviously pleased by my encouragement. I had invited Phyllis, but she had pointed out that the couple should not be crowded at this delicate stage of their acquaintance, and so she would let me be the sole chaperone.

Flora came into the room looking quite unlike a drawing master. She had not neglected her appearance, wearing her hair in a neat bun and a pearl necklace over a crimson, daringly low-cut dress that was unfamiliar to me.

"Good morning, Captain!"

The Captain turned at the sound of her voice and for a moment he was silenced, staring at Flora.

"Good Lord!" he said, and then recovered himself quickly. "Flora, you look entirely lovely. Good morning to you!"

Victor would struggle to concentrate on his drawing, I thought, unless she had a life class in mind.

"I hope you're in an artistic mood," Flora said. "If the weather holds, we can practise outside."

"I look forward to it," Victor said, fixing his unblinking gaze on her, so that she reddened a little, which added to her charm. "I might attempt a sketch of one of Ramsburgh's majestic creatures."

"Oh – the peafowl?" she said.

"Perhaps," he said, with a smile.

Mrs Felton arrived with a tray of glasses, and poured our wine.

"Oh, Miss Flora," she said. "You are a picture! Good morning, Captain. I hear you've come for a lesson – what a privilege. You've seen the Angels at the Town Hall, of course? Such talent. Really, sir, you couldn't do any better than to be taken in hand by Miss Davison."

"Mrs Felton," Victor said solemnly, taking his glass of wine, "no truer word was ever spoken." He raised his glass and looked again at Flora. "May your humble pupil prove worthy of his tutor!"

~

Captain Harris sliced the flesh off his lamb cutlet with military precision. "My draughtsmanship, such as it is, has been bound by the geometrical constraints of my work," he said. "Designs for temporary buildings, bridges, that kind of thing. The mundane and unaesthetic infrastructure of war. So I will enjoy the freedom of depicting Nature's complexity and curves."

His gaze lingered on Flora, apparently lost in thought.

"It's strange," I said, breaking his scrutiny of Flora, "that Nature has a habit of creating beautiful forms. It's almost impossible for it to be ugly. Why do you think that is?"

"Perhaps," ventured Flora, delicately dividing a new potato in half, "because humans have always defined beauty and order in terms of the appearance of Nature, ever since we were in a primitive state. Therefore Nature is already the yardstick for beauty."

"Nicely answered," said the Captain. "Hence the line by Burns: 'My love is like a red, red rose.'" He paused, starting to reach for his glass and stopping while he considered the point. "One might also say that our respect for the natural world is a necessary bond, achieved through the unifying notion of beauty, without which we would be so unhealthily preoccupied with the artifices of our human society that we would wither and die."

"That sounds an almost religious statement," I said. "And I don't believe you to be a religious man."

The Captain took a swig of wine. "Then I may need to invent my own," he said. "One with both Nature and rationality at its core. A religion based on science."

"That would be full of contradictions, surely?" I said.

"No more than any other religion you care to name," he said. "And certainly a lot less bloodthirsty. I can't tell you how sick I became of the sight of sanctimonious churchmen justifying the blood of my comrades in the name of an unseen, indifferent God. My religion would be one entirely of peace. I would need a handmaiden, of course. Or several."

"I can't imagine you leading a sect," Flora said. "You're not nearly arrogant enough for that. But then," she added slyly, "I haven't known you for long. Perhaps in a few years you will end up sacrificing virgins to your god after all, in some far-off land."

"And what an unspeakable waste of virgins that would be," said the Captain, draining his glass. "Now, this conversation is getting out of hand. You had better start schooling me, Flora, before I consume any more of your brother's excellent wine and become incapable of wielding a pencil."

~

I stood at a window in the drawing room and observed the pair with mixed feelings, as they sat and drew one of the large elm trees on the south lawn. It looked as though they had found plenty to talk about, and both were perfectly relaxed in one another's company. I was glad for them, but for all my hopes of getting better acquainted with Victor, I knew I could not compete with Flora for Victor's time.

I realised with surprise that I was a little lonely and disappointed, in a way I had not felt since last year when I had seen Victoria laughing with Dr Weldon. It was aggravated by the fact that my nascent friendship with William had been interrupted, at best, and even Effie – for whom I was beginning to feel fond – was not likely to linger for long in Hawksbridge. And Flora, too, seemed to be about to spread her wings.

True, I had my beloved Phyllis. But even then, the slight liberties she had allowed me might not be repeated for many months. Despite our engagement, she was not in a hurry to marry, while her father's health remained uncertain. And I suspected that she had much that she wanted to write before taking on the burdens and risks of motherhood.

I found myself thinking of Bess, and how easy it had been to take comfort in her welcoming bosom. Would she let me dally with her once more, for old times' sake? I imagined how pleasant that would be, my hands and lips once again enjoying her curves. Perhaps she missed me and the attentions I gave her. Perhaps no one else had come to her bed, and she was hot with lustful thoughts about me. What if I were to visit this evening, on some pretext? I might not need to try to persuade her – I could simply make her laugh, and keep close to her, my thigh brushing accidentally against hers, so she would remember how it was, until her resolve crumbled. Then she might violently kiss me, and straddle me, undoing her dress to let my warm hands cup her breasts...

"Do you need anything, my dear?" said Mrs Felton brightly.

I was suddenly aware that the effects of my erotic musings might be conspicuous, so I turned back towards the window in embarrassment.

"No, thank you, Mrs Felton, I'm quite all right."

"Very good, dear. Just let me know!"

The moment was lost, and I realised the folly of such a fantasy. My fling with Bess was forever in the past. An attempt to revive it would be stupidity of the highest order. I tried to focus my mind on serious matters instead, and whether I had done all that I could for William: this case had the air of being the first failure in my self-declared role of detective. Perhaps a concerted application of logic could make a pattern from my meagre array of facts, and so I climbed to the solitude of my second-floor study to make some notes.

Fact: William had another family, invoking the wrath of Mr Belford, the prime suspect. Who else would be aggrieved? Naturally, William's wife. Was it possible that Clementine might have found out earlier than she admitted, and had exacted revenge? It had never even occurred to me before, but it had to be considered, even though my dealings with Clementine showed no evidence of it. She had, after all, been the one to raise the alarm. And of course Lillian Belford had every right to be angry as an often-neglected mistress. I scolded myself for accepting her apparent surprise at face value: I should have gone into her home at the very least.

Fact: William was investigating serious allegations of wrongdoings by Mr Forrester or his company. William had sensed himself to be in danger – and perhaps his list of addresses held the key. But that was pure conjecture.

Fact: William had had dealings with a woman deranged by grief, Mrs Milburn, who confused him with her dead husband and had been humiliated by him, albeit unintentionally. Did he go and visit her again, or did they meet somewhere, where she killed him? Again, remotely plausible, but there was no shred of evidence of it.

Fact: William himself displayed symptoms of a disordered mind, by selecting books apparently at random and burning them. Could he have wandered off and come to some accidental mischief? Perhaps not self-murder, but erratic behaviour could have placed him in danger. And yet he had seemed rational enough when I had lunched with him on that last day – albeit displaying distress at Mr Forrester's activities as well as at the iniquities of match manufacture.

I tried to think who else figured in William's life. He must have crossed swords with a fair number of people when sating his journalistic curiosity about their work and lives; it would be an impossible task to track them all down. The only significant acquaintance I knew about was Lady Fairfield, with whom he was on good, even friendly, terms. But for all her eccentricity, there was no obvious motive for her to do him any harm, especially as he had restrained his cynicism admirably when writing about the Society.

Although I admonished myself for a certain sloppiness, I felt cheered and energised by having a plan: to talk again to Mr Belford and his daughter, and with Mrs Lowick's permission, to write to the mysterious addresses on William's list.

Mrs Lowick herself – was she truly beyond suspicion? Had she been a little hasty in raising the alarm, when William had only been gone a couple of nights? I tried to put myself in her shoes. She had got used to frequent periods of his absence, for sure. But he had apparently been meticulous in telling her how long he would be gone. A poor concession to infidelity, perhaps, but there it was: and her instinct that something was wrong had been justified.

Then again, if she had contrived to eliminate her cheating husband, she could have raised the alarm in just the same manner as if she had been truly worried.

My thoughts were now like dogs chasing their own tails, which reminded me that Fox would need his walk, as much as I needed fresh air to clear my aching head.

CHAPTER FOURTEEN

THE following day, I had barely finished my breakfast and was absorbed in a book in the drawing room when I heard a carriage draw up outside.

To my surprise, Shipley announced, "Lady Fairfield to see you, sir," and the lady in question strode purposefully into the room.

"Good morning, Mr Rufford!" she said, pulling off her gloves as I rose and opened my mouth to speak. "I'm sorry to visit so early, but I wanted to be sure to catch you in. Could I trouble you for a cup of coffee?"

"Good morning, Lady Fairfield," I said, a little put out that my pleasant post-breakfast ritual had been disturbed so boisterously. As Effie and Francesca had both enthused about 'Jane Eyre', this book had been part of my morning routine for some days, and it took me a moment to adjust to reality. "Yes, of course – let's get a fresh pot." I rang the bell, and gestured for her to sit opposite me.

"I congratulate you on your home, Mr Rufford," she said, looking about her. "It's most picturesque. Your wife will be a lucky woman, to gain both you and the comforts of this fine house."

I did not know whether to feel honoured or faintly intimidated by her visit. Exchanging a few words in passing was one thing, in the safety of other company, but having her attention fixed on me, on my own ground – that was quite another. But it was undoubtedly flattering for her to go out of her way and visit Ramsburgh.

"Thank you," I said. "A fresh pot of coffee for us, please, Catherine," I added to Catherine who had just entered.

"Of course, sir, Lady Fairfield," she said, and loaded up her tray.

"How lovely to see you, Catherine," said Lady Fairfield. "I didn't realise you were working here as well as at Myrtle's. Have you made up your mind about joining the Society, my dear, or has your employer here forbidden it?"

She said it humorously, but Catherine looked confused as to how she should answer. "It has not been discussed," she said, which I thought was a good, neutral answer. "Excuse me, ma'am."

"Oh dear!" my visitor said. "How unkind of me to put her on the spot like that. Force of habit, I'm afraid! Always the enthusiastic recruiter of females to the cause."

"Quite," I said. "So how may I help you, Lady Fairfield?"

She said nothing for a painfully long moment, but appraised me with a knowing smile and left me in no doubt that she was aware of my impatience. I wondered how the devil she managed to waltz in and take command so thoroughly. It was quite a talent.

"I thought it would be *à propos* for us to get to know one another," she said. "Especially as we are both concerned for poor Mr Lowick. William and Clementine are dear friends of mine. Oh, I applaud your taste in literature, Mr Rufford," she added, picking up my copy of 'Jane Eyre'. "What is your opinion of Miss Eyre?"

"I suppose she is commendable in many ways," I said, "but for me, her tolerance of the oaf Rochester strains credulity. It makes me think less of her, when my inclination is to like her."

Lady Fairfield laughed. "Yes, it is the pattern of this kind of novel that the more unbearable the hero, the more besotted the heroine. Well, I'm happy to say that Rochester pays for his boorishness, and Miss Eyre is shown to be the stronger of the two. I will say no more, except that it paints a picture of sufferance that most of the women in the country would recognise, to some degree."

"I sincerely hope you're wrong about that," I said, as Catherine came in with the coffee and poured it.

She shrugged, and said, "Perhaps William had just a touch of Mr Rochester about him in some aspects. I understand you may have been the last person to see him before his disappearance?"

"It's possible," I said. "I met him the morning after the fire at Mr Eagle's print works. We went into The Duke's Head and spent much of the morning there, and lunch."

"Ah, yes," she said. "Mr Eagle, of the scurrilous pamphlets." She studied my expression and lifted her coffee cup to her lips. "I see you have a question for me, Mr Rufford. Please go ahead."

"What question is that, Lady Fairfield?" I knew perfectly well, but I was not going to make it easy for her.

"You think that I torched his establishment in punishment for the leaflets. Is that not so?"

"I don't know. Did you? And would you admit it if you had?"

She smiled once more. "You are frank, and I appreciate that. No, Mr Rufford, I did not, and neither did anyone I know. Yes, you're probably right that if I were indeed the culprit, I wouldn't own up to it. However, you have my word that I had nothing to do with it. That's the best I can do to convince you. The leaflets were so childish that they damned themselves, so I think the net gain from them was on our side."

"I see," I said, taking a sip of coffee. "Well, that's good to know."

"And now that we have cleared the air on that score, I have a question to ask you."

She paused, and I said, "Forgive me, Lady Fairfield – unlike you, I cannot guess the question."

"I will be as frank as you," she said. "Did you have

anything to do with the disappearance of William Lowick?"

I spat out some coffee. "I beg your pardon? Is this a joke?"

To my consternation, she wore a serious expression. "As we have discussed, you were probably the last person to see him, that we know about. So perhaps you have more to tell? And perhaps it would be easier to tell me than the police?"

I stared at her. "What possible motive could I have for harming William? I was just getting to know him. I liked him. Indeed, I thought we could become good friends, in time."

"But journalists are apt to find out secrets, are they not? He was writing a piece about you. Perhaps he found something that you didn't want to be in his article, and he refused to omit it?"

"Absolutely not," I said, intensely resenting being interrogated like this in my own home. "We had some good conversations, and he never hinted at any gossip. He was completely professional, and I have nothing to hide."

"Come now, Mr Rufford," Lady Fairfield said with a laugh. "We all have things we want to hide. Why should you be any different?"

I stood up. "Thank you for calling, Lady Fairfield," I said coldly. "I expect your driver will be getting restless."

"Oh, sit down, you silly thing," she said, as if scolding a child. "I doubt you had anything to do with William's disappearance. But now we're straight, aren't we? Our darkest questions are posed and answered, and we've even had our first little tiff. Our relationship is progressing! Let me pour you some more coffee."

I slowly sat down, my head spinning with her quick changes in tone.

"Perhaps my approach to social intercourse is unconventional," she said. "But I can't bear wasting time. There's never enough of it." Her voice had lost the hard edge that I was accustomed to, both in her campaigning and her outrageous accusation. "You may ask me another question, so I may do penance for my rudeness."

I considered for a moment. "If you insist. Oh – that one is too personal. Let me think of another."

"No, ask away. I don't mind."

I hesitated again. "My question," I said, "was whether you are happy. But there's no need to answer – it's merely the first thing that came into my head."

She waved her hand to dismiss my embarrassment. "What a good question." She paused to take another sip of coffee. "I have long periods of contentment, certainly. I have not been truly happy – that is, blissfully happy – since my husband died."

"I'm sorry," I said. "It was tactless of me."

"Not at all – after all, it was my suggestion," Lady Fairfield said. "I loved James, and he loved me. I was devastated when he died. In fact, I lived only for him, so I was quite lost. But eventually I found a way out of my melancholy, through philanthropy and the Society. I have people around me, so I'm not as isolated as I once was. But true happiness – that's hard to achieve, is it not? I'm unsure if one is necessarily allowed a chance at bliss for a second time."

For the first time since her arrival, Lady Fairfield looked other than entirely in control of herself. She wiped away a tear, and smiled at me. "You are fortunate – you have bliss just around the corner, when you marry!"

The last thing I expected today was to be having a conversation about dead husbands and the joys of marriage with the redoubtable Lady Fairfield. "I'm sure you will find it again, Lady Fairfield," I said. "After all, when you set your mind on something, I imagine there is nothing the world can do to stop you!"

"You're very kind," she said. "And I have taken up far too much of your precious morning. My main reason for coming was to ask if you can think of anything that might illuminate William's whereabouts. We must pool our wisdom, for Clementine's sake. So if you have any inspiration, let me know, and I will let you know if I think of anything too. The police are being most dilatory – I'm certain they have not searched everywhere they could. And they seem to have given up on their main suspect."

"Mr Belford?"

"Of course. The more I think about it, the more obvious it is. The man threatens violence against William, and then William is gone. What other suspect could there be? I mean, now that we have eliminated you, Mr Rufford!" she added with a smile.

I was tempted to share my musings with her, but I had nothing concrete, and besides, I did not yet have permission to reveal the existence of William's investigation.

"As I said, I found Mr Belford's reaction convincing," I replied. "An anguished letter is entirely understandable when his daughter has been ruined."

"Then if you accept his anguish, you must accept that he could be moved to more drastic action. A man's animal nature is never far beneath the surface – a theme I intend to explore in a forthcoming lecture."

I sighed, hoping that I would not have to be present at this occasion to be reminded of my deficiencies as a male. "It's possible. He would not be sorry to see William dead, but one surely has to be a certain type to be capable of actual murder, and I simply failed to find that in him."

Lady Fairfield smiled in a pitying way. "There is your charming naivety again, Mr Rufford! To be unsullied by cynicism after all your adventures – I applaud your compassion, but I fear it may blind you to reality. However, in one respect, it may give you an advantage over me."

"Oh?"

"It may leave your mind more open to alternative avenues in this case. You have no other suspicions?"

I shook my head. "Nothing that has the remotest substance, I'm afraid."

She stood up, and said, "Then I will leave you. I have enjoyed getting to know you a little better, Mr Rufford. I hope our paths will cross again soon – even if it is too much to expect poor William also to be present. You will let me know if your detective's instincts bear any fruit?"

"It's been a pleasure, Lady Fairfield," I said, leading her to the door. "And yes, I will let you know if I find anything."

~

"We're going to have to sue, I'm afraid," said McPhee, pulling an object from a crate and removing its linen wrapper.

The managing director, Mr Lilley, sat with his arms folded, a serious expression and his eyes fixed on me, waiting for my reaction.

I examined the colourful object in front of me. It took a moment to realise that it was trying to emulate our popular Marbleware statue, 'The Hawksbridge Angels', and when recognition dawned, I burst out laughing. Mr Lilley's frown deepened, but I could see from McPhee's wry smile that he understood my response.

It was about a third of the size of the original, in a glossy glaze and painted garishly. It was a truly inept copy, and yet I was also aware of a certain charm about it. The mother-angel's face – that reproduced Francesca so well in matt, white Marbleware – was now a chubby maiden with a sentimental expression, but even that portrayal had evidently exhausted our counterfeiter, as the features of the other two angels were indistinct and distorted.

Some poor wretch in the factory had had the task of applying a rosy blush to the angels' cheeks, lips and – where exposed – the angelic nipples. The robes, wispy on the original, looked painfully stiff and solid here. The hollow form of the burning building, with its crudely painted brickwork, resembled nothing so much as –

"A flower holder, Mr Rufford!" barked Mr Lilley. "A repulsive little vase! These thieving reprobates have turned our art into a common mantelpiece ornament."

"Oh dear," I said, trying to suppress my amusement. It was a dreadful object, a vulgar piece of trash, and yet its cheerful ineptitude was not entirely unappealing. "How unfortunate. Where did you find these?"

"I had a meeting in Coventry last week," said Mr McPhee, "and as I had time to spare, I visited a market. I turned a corner, and there they were – selling pretty well, I have to say. So I bought the lot for five shillings and the promise not to report the vendor to the police for selling counterfeit goods. He was not a happy man."

"We traced the manufacturer to a company in Coventry – a John Pearson," said Mr Lilley. "Our solicitor has written to him, of course, but in the event he doesn't desist, we'll initiate legal proceedings against him. I assume you're agreeable? We need to protect our reputation from such rubbish and make an example of Pearson."

"Naturally," I said. "But..."

"Yes?" Mr Lilley demanded.

"Perhaps we should consider this market," I continued against my better judgement. "We pride ourselves on making art available to the masses. And yet we don't really, do we? Our 'Angels' are only affordable by the middle classes. Mr Pearson has spotted a market below that. I have to admire him, especially for his taste in selecting a subject."

"What are you driving at, Mr Rufford?" Mr Lilley said, rattling his coffee cup in its saucer with impatience.

"What if we were to address this market ourselves, but with a far superior offering? I think the notion of the glaze and colouring isn't entirely ridiculous – it's mainly the execution that's lacking."

Mr Lilley shook his head with pity at my naivety. "We are not in the business of making penny trinkets, Mr Rufford."

It was too late to retreat now. "We could create a separate company, if you're worried about tarnishing our good name," I said. "And it would – at least partially – head off the threat of more knock-offs."

"It's an interesting thought," McPhee said, tactfully. "We should always consider new markets. Now, if you'll excuse me, gentlemen, I have another meeting."

I nodded. "What do you intend to do with your haul of ornaments?"

"I suppose they'll be destroyed in due course," McPhee said. "Would you like some? I have two dozen."

I left with four, thinking they would make amusing presents. What would Francesca make of her rosy, shiny representation? I imagined she would pretend to be affronted, before giving way to laughter. However, Flora might be genuinely pained by the bastardisation of the work on which she had so passionately collaborated.

~

Having been released from my business obligations, I left my parcel of china in The Dog and Hare where Celeste was stabled. I thought I would visit Hunter's and finally spend a happy hour amongst books without interruption, after my previous two attempts had failed. And so it was a bitter pill when I reached the bookshop and saw that two of the window panes were boarded up, and the shop was closed. I stared gloomily at the damaged windows, which bore the signs of a deliberate and vicious attack, until my ruminations were interrupted by the sound of hooves. I turned, and saw that a police carriage had emerged from Tilton Street, which was home to Mr Belford's shop; inside, flanked by officers, was Mr Belford himself. He caught sight of me, and stared at me with a desperate, haunted look.

For a minute, I was rooted to the spot, trying to take in the broken windows and the jeweller's arrest, and wondering whether the two events were connected.

Then, thinking that Mrs Lowick might know more, I broke into a run and arrived at her home out of breath.

In the drawing room, Mrs Lowick was sitting at a little bureau.

"I've been trying to writing to the children all morning," she said. "It's so hard. I keep crying on the paper and having to start again. Do you have news?"

I relayed what I had seen.

"Arrested?" Mrs Lowick said with alarm. "Then they must have found something. Oh Lord..." She stood up, and then looked as though she was about to faint, so Mrs Beatty took her mistress to the sofa and fussed over her, putting a blanket around her and hurrying off to get some coffee.

"Do you think they've found evidence?" Mrs Lowick said. "Why else would they arrest Mr Belford?"

"I just don't know," I said. "It's possible that they merely wanted to question him again. They may have forgotten to ask him something. I don't exactly know if it was an arrest. But I admit it did look serious."

Mrs Lowick was on the verge of tears. "I don't think I can stand it," she said, looking at me with a trembling lip. "I have to know something. I have to know if he's dead. At least then I could start to grieve."

"I'm sorry," I said, "I should not have come. It's probably nothing." But even as I spoke, the front door bell rang, and I recognised the deep voice of Constable Taylor. A moment later he appeared at the door.

"I'm sorry to disturb you, ma'am – Mr Rufford. I have something we would like you to identify, ma'am. Perhaps if I could speak to you alone...?"

Mrs Lowick sighed. "I would prefer Mr Rufford to be present, please, Constable," she said.

"Certainly, ma'am. If I may take the liberty...?" She nodded, gesturing at a chair, and I went to sit next to Mrs Lowick on the sofa so that Constable Taylor could sit opposite her.

Taylor had been carrying a small object wrapped in a cloth, and he solemnly put it on the table.

"Ma'am, I'm afraid I need you to be prepared in case this item is known to you."

Mrs Lowick nodded again, and Taylor extracted the object, which I immediately recognised. It was William's tortoiseshell cigar case.

Mrs Lowick gave a small cry and put her hands to her face. "It's William's," she said. "I gave it to him on our first wedding anniversary."

"I'm very sorry, ma'am," Taylor said. "An observant member of the public saw it in Mr Belford's shop. They recognised the initials 'W.L.' on the front."

Mrs Lowick was unable to hold back the tide of her tears, and putting a reassuring hand on her arm, I waited for her to calm herself.

"Can you tell us who found it, Mr Taylor?" I asked.

"I'm afraid I'm not at liberty to disclose that, sir," he said.

"I suppose not," I said. "And Mr Belford had the audacity to try to sell the case?"

"So it would appear, sir. Inspector Simmons said that mur– I mean, criminals are apt to signal their crimes sometimes, as a matter of pride and thinking that they're cleverer than everyone else."

"Ah," I said. "Hubris."

"That's the very word the boss used, sir."

"You're saying he's dead, aren't you?" Mrs Lowick said.

Taylor looked uncomfortable. "We can't say that for sure, ma'am," he said.

"But why else would Mr Belford have his cigar case? William took it with him everywhere."

"It's possible he dropped it, ma'am," Taylor said, but he was not convincing.

"I see. Well, thank you, Constable," Mrs Lowick said. "You can tell Mr Simmons it is definitely my husband's property."

"Thank you, ma'am," he said, getting up. "You have been most helpful. And I'm very sorry – it's a terrible thing. We will do everything we can to find your husband. We hope Mr Belford will be forthcoming soon. Good afternoon, ma'am, sir."

When Taylor had gone, Mrs Lowick stood up. "I can't breathe," she said, and went to open a window.

I was suddenly reminded of William standing at the window in my study, looking out onto the lawn, relaxed and enjoying his sherry. It hit me then – I was unlikely ever to see the man again. The green shoots of our friendship were dead, all potential snuffed out. It was hard to believe that a man of such energy and lust for life was no more; but the facts were pointing inescapably to a violent end. It was senseless and cruel, and at that moment it made the meaning of my own existence harder to grasp. Tears flowed silently down my face, and I wiped them away, hoping Mrs Lowick would not see my weakness.

"Oh! My dear Thomas!" Mrs Lowick turned back from the window and sat down beside me again, her hand on my arm. "You have been so strong for me – I have barely thought about anyone beside myself. How selfish of me."

The reversal of roles seemed to give her some strength, and she was clearly touched that I shared a little of her grief at the loss of William.

"With your permission," I said after a few minutes, "I'll write to the addresses I found amongst William's documents. I feel we need to solve this particular mystery, since he thought it was important."

"Yes, I think it's time," Mrs Lowick said. "There have been too many mysteries of late. Tell me – will you be seeing Miss Belford again?"

"Yes, I'll just go and see that she's all right, and let her know about her father. I hope you don't mind –"

"No, of course not!" said Mrs Lowick. "No – I hoped you would." She got up and picked up a canvas bag that was propped up against her bureau, and handed it to me. "I wanted her to have these. Just some baby clothes, an old dress of Amelia's, and a few toys. We must think of Miss Belford and her children. She will be in a state of grief too, I know she will. And those poor children will have no father." She retrieved a handkerchief from her sleeve and dabbed her nose.

"Oh, Lord," I said, greatly touched by this. "That's good of you – she'll be very grateful."

"Well, I can do so little about anything at present. At least I can do this, and let her know that she's not been forgotten. I worry about her."

CHAPTER FIFTEEN

I DULY wrote to Whom It May Concern at each address, asking for any information pertaining to William Lowick's interest in the inhabitants at the property, as he was not currently able to continue his inquiries. I did not hold out much hope of any replies to such a vague request, and there was no particular reason for them to trust me.

Going to put my letters in the hall and wandering out into the garden to catch the last of the afternoon sunshine, I found Flora with a sketchbook, stalking the peacock. On my approach he scuttled away.

"Oh, I'm sorry," I said. "I've scared him off."

"It's fine," Flora said. "I'll get him another time. Any news of your journalist friend?"

"Not good news, unfortunately," I said. "Mr Belford has been arrested – apparently some evidence has been found."

"No! How grim for poor Mrs Lowick."

"Quite," I said. "And I have been of precious little help. Did you enjoy tutoring the Captain?"

She smiled, and I could see the answer plainly written on her face. "I did. And he proved a good student – he's not the novice he would have us believe."

"Excellent," I said. "And you're getting on well?"

"Yes," she said, starting to walk, and I followed. "Surprisingly well. I believe we're becoming the best of friends."

"I thought so, looking at you two in the garden from the drawing room. You cannot laugh like that and not be friends."

"Ah, so you were spying on us?"

"For a minute only," I said. "Then I retreated discreetly

to my lair." I squeezed her arm. "I'm so glad for you. You deserve happiness."

Flora smiled again and said, "Let's not count chickens. We shall see what we shall see. He's highly eligible, and no doubt he will have choices."

"I know a man of good taste when I meet one," I said, "and I can tell he thinks the world of you. Did you see his expression when you made your entrance before dinner? Besides, I should like him as a brother-in-law. And that would mean the talented Miss Harris would be family, too. It gets better and better."

"I can't promise to arrange things so conveniently for you," Flora said, "but I must admit, the more I see Victor, the fonder of him I become. He has so many admirable qualities... Now, that's enough sentimental talk. It must be nearly dinner time."

~

"Are you pleased with it?" I asked Bess as she brought our coffee. It was Wednesday afternoon at Myrtle's, and I had dragged Phyllis away from her writing.

Bess straightened up and looked proudly around the shop at the new blue wallpaper. "Couldn't be happier!" she said. "And I get comments all the time. You were right – I've been busier than ever. Do you like it?"

"It's... astonishing," I said, as I had not made up my mind. I had already seen samples of 'Hedgerow', an intricate collage of plants and berries, but in quantity it was a little overwhelming.

"Not quite what I asked," Bess said, smiling, "but you'll get used to it."

"Oh dear," I said when she had left. "Was I rude?"

"I'm sure you'll find something kind to say about it," Phyllis said. She sniffed her coffee. "Ah, that's good. Thank you for distracting me. This book is driving me mad. Now, tell me about Flora and the Captain! Did they kiss?"

"No, not that I saw. But I wasn't watching them the whole time."

"Oh?" said Phyllis, feigning shock. "Then who knows what happened between them!"

"They were mostly outside, so I doubt very much happened at all. However, Flora is clearly besotted. And I think Victor is too."

"Wonderful," said Phyllis. "We can look forward to an extravagant wedding."

"Let's not get our expectations up," I said. "Something may yet throw a spanner in the works."

"Francesca?"

"I hope not," I said. "But they are also friends. And I can imagine an exciting little fling would suit both of them."

Phyllis grimaced. "Oh dear. What can we do?"

"We can see how things go on Saturday, and I'll try to have a word with Francesca if need be. But you know how she is. She won't be told."

"If it's for Flora's sake, though," said Phyllis, "surely she must see sense."

I shrugged. "I expect she will. Ah – Constable Taylor!"

The constable had just come in and was sitting down at a table at the other side of the room, and he and Thomas exchanged a nod of greeting.

"I'd like to have a word," I said, "but I'll let him get settled first."

"About William?"

"Yes. He's not going to tell me much himself, but I want to try to see Mr Belford."

"You still think he might not have had anything to do with William's disappearance?" Phyllis said. "Even after the cigar case...?"

"I don't know. I just want to hear him out, and see if he needs to get a message to his daughter. Guilty or not, his is a tragic situation. And I know precisely how bleak those cells are. Besides, there's a chance – however tiny – that he might be able to tell me something that he can't say to Inspector Simmons."

After Taylor had begun to sip his coffee, I went over. "May I?" I asked, pointing to the chair opposite him.

"Of course, Mr Rufford," he said, biting into a scone. "I have a lot of time for you after what you did last year. I mean," he corrected himself, "for your advice, upon which we police acted all on our own!" He winked and smiled.

"My pleasure," I said. "I really don't mind who got the credit, so long as justice was served."

"You're a rarity, sir, and no mistake," said Taylor. "Perhaps you'd like to catch us an anarchist or two. Seems we may have got us a little infestation in Hawksbridge."

"Anarchists? Oh – the bookshop window. Anarchists were responsible for that?"

"Rumour has it," Taylor said. "It has their mark of purposeless destruction. There was trouble in The Duke's Head last night too. Smelled another little stink, I should say, and thought they'd get in on the act."

"What stink would that be?"

Taylor looked around and lowered his voice. "Probably shouldn't be saying it in this place, sir, but certain protests and... ladies have stirred things up. Gives an impression of uncertainty, I'd say – a kind of rot amongst us. Reflects badly on us police, in particular."

"Ah. You're not in favour of the Society, then."

"I've nothing against women, sir!" he said. "Far from it. But it's my job to help maintain order. I like political decisions to be made indoors in a civilised manner, not on our streets."

"Quite," I said. "But Lady Fairfield would argue that if

this fails, there's nothing for it but to march."

"I'm sure, sir. I admit they're at liberty to do it, but to my mind, give 'em an inch, and they'll take a mile. Seems like they're getting positive encouragement from some quarters."

He took some coffee and reached for another scone. "No doubt you'll be itching to know about Mr Belford – but alas, sir, you know what a stickler the boss is. I have to be extra careful."

"Yes, of course, Mr Taylor, I appreciate that. But I had a slightly different request for you. I wondered if you could take me to the police station –"

"Why, what have you done, sir?"

"Well, nothing unlawful, Mr Taylor," I said, returning his smile. "But I had hoped you might help persuade Mr Simmons to let me speak to Mr Belford."

Taylor had finished his mouthful of scone, so was able to whistle without mishap. "Bold, sir. Very bold. But seeing as you're not his lawyer, I don't know that the boss is going to be happy about it. After all, we haven't yet –" He stopped and frowned, before putting his finger to his lips.

"Got a confession? Be that as it may, I don't think I'm going to upset the machinery of justice by talking to him. I would hazard a guess that he's in an agitated state" – Taylor nodded – "and perhaps a talk with me might help calm him, especially if I can get a message to his daughter, who I'll be going to see shortly. You never know what might come out of it. After all, the interview will be supervised. You may stop it whenever you please."

Taylor grunted and took a swig of coffee. "Maybe," he said.

"I would be extremely grateful," I said. "And I know Mrs Lowick will be too."

Taylor sighed and said, "Very well, Mr Rufford. Only because it's you, mind. And I'll catch the sharp end of the Inspector's tongue for the rest of the week, I'll be bound. But yes. Just let me finish up here and have a moment to myself, and I'll take you."

"Thank you, Mr Taylor!" I said. "Can I buy you another coffee?"

"That would be bribery and corruption, sir! But it's the thought that counts."

~

Mr Simmons gave me one of his cold, withering stares. "Are you brazenly asking me if you can interfere in a police investigation, Mr Rufford? I thought I made myself clear the last time we met that you were to remember your position as an ordinary citizen of Hawksbridge: neither more, nor less."

Taylor cleared his throat. "Mr Rufford made the suggestion that talking to him on his own might calm him, boss. And also that he can relay any messages to his daughter, which is fair enough. Saves us the effort."

"Thank you, Constable – I'm sure Mr Rufford can speak for himself. Calm him, Mr Rufford? Why do you think you can do that?"

"Simply as a former customer coming for a chat and letting him vent a little. Showing a little sympathy, Inspector. It might let him open up, and it's also common decency to try to ease his soul a little."

"You do realise, sir, that in all probability this man you intend to bestow your sympathy on is a vicious murderer? Why do you think he deserves anything but due process?"

"He's not a convicted criminal yet, Inspector," I said. "He may even be entirely innocent. No harm will be done by listening to him, surely – and for Mrs Lowick's sake, it's the least I can do. And I had a visit from Lady Fairfield the other day. She was most anxious that the police do everything in their power. She was a little concerned that they might not be."

Simmons frowned. "Lady Fairfield said that?"

"Almost those words."

He considered for a moment, and then sighed. "In that case, out of deference to Lady Fairfield, and her generous support for the Police Charitable Association, I will let you have your little chat with Belford – assuming he wants to talk to you, of course. Wait here, Mr Rufford, and I'll call you. I can't let you talk to him alone, naturally – Constable Taylor will attend."

After a few minutes, I was ushered into the familiar interview room, where Mr Belford was sitting with his back to the wall and his eyes tight shut. Taylor took up a discreet position in the corner of the room, his notebook at the ready.

I sat down opposite the jeweller. "Good afternoon, Mr Belford. It's Thomas Rufford. I thought I would come and see how you are, and if there's anything you need."

Mr Belford grunted sarcastically, his eyes still closed as if in denial of the disagreeable world around him.

There was a pause. "Perhaps I can convey a message to your daughter," I said.

He opened his eyes. "Leave my daughter out of it," he said with feeling. "She's had enough trouble from your sort. What the devil has it got to do with you?" Before I could answer, he continued: "Well, I know what it's got to do with you. Why you're here. You've come to gloat at what you've done."

He leaned forward, a grimace on his face. "Isn't that right, Mr Rufford? I'm in this shit-hole because of you, and Mrs Lowick, and that ungodly husband of hers. Well, gloat away if that's what gives you pleasure."

"I don't follow," I said, glad that he was at least engaging with me. "Why do you think I'm the reason you're here?"

"I've worked it all out. Had plenty of time for it. I'm not

stupid. I know what you and Mrs Lowick are up to."

"What are we up to, Mr Belford?"

"It's plain as the nose on my face. You both want to punish me for the letter, and I'm a useful scapegoat. So Mrs Lowick takes the cigar case, hiding herself under a hood so I don't see who it is, and puts it in my shop when my back's turned. Then she calls the constable, and makes out that I'm – I'm some kind of monster."

At that, he lost control of himself and broke into sobs. Taylor kindly provided him with a clean handkerchief, and I waited for him to recover himself.

"I'm not the monster, Mr Rufford," he said after a moment, his voice thick with emotion. "I'm not the monster. Why are you doing this to me?" His aggression had been replaced by plaintive self-pity.

If this were a performance, it would have admitted him to many a theatrical company.

"I don't think you're a monster, Mr Belford," I said. "But anyone would understand why you would react violently to such an assault on your daughter's virtue."

"But I told you before, Mr Rufford. I may have wanted him dead, but I didn't go near the fellow."

"This person you said came to your shop. What happened, exactly?"

Mr Belford sniffed and gathered his thoughts. "Well, this woman came in yesterday morning. Looked like a widow, all in black with a hood, with a handkerchief pressed to her face, so I couldn't make out who it was. I asked if she needed any help, and she just shook her head and went around the shop looking at the merchandise. I felt awkward, like, as if I was intruding, so I left her to it for a minute and went into the back. When I came back, she was gone."

"And you thought nothing of it?"

"Well, she was a bit strange, but being a widower, I know what it's like – sometimes you're so low, you can't even speak, especially not to a stranger. So that's what I thought it must be. And then about half an hour later, in comes the Constable" – he pointed his thumb at Taylor – "and the Inspector. The Inspector asked me to look at the shelf where I have my cigar cases, and whether I recognised one in particular."

He shook his head. "I'm getting careless in my old age. I hadn't locked one of the cabinets – with some of my less valuable pieces – and it would have been easy to put something in there. I told the Inspector, yes, I did recognise the case – I had sold it to Mrs Lowick some years ago. She had wanted Mr Lowick's initials engraved on a silver panel on the front. And I said I didn't know why it was in my shop, because I never bought it back."

"And the Inspector didn't accept this explanation."

"No, he didn't. He accused me of taking it from Mr Lowick, dead or alive, most likely dead. I couldn't believe it. And they arrested me."

"Have they charged you?"

"No, Mr Rufford. Not yet, thank God. They know they have no right to do that."

"Good. And you believe it was Mrs Lowick who came to your shop?"

"Who else?" he said. "I bet she killed her husband herself, and was clever about hiding him. Wives have killed their husbands for less than what he did. She would have been mad with jealousy when she found out." He turned to Taylor. "Why don't you arrest her, Constable? She had the nerve to come into my shop and leave that case."

Mr Taylor remained expressionless and said nothing.

"But Mrs Lowick only found out about her husband's infidelity after he went missing," I said.

"So she says to you," Mr Belford said. "A murderer is going to be a good liar, isn't she?"

"I think she would have had a hard time disposing of Mr Lowick's body."

"She would have had help. A friend, like. A strong fellow, such as yourself, perhaps."

"You're fantasising, Mr Belford – I'm not surprised, incarcerated here as you are. But Mrs Lowick is genuinely distressed, and I am no accomplice to murder."

He shrugged. "Well, even if she didn't do it herself," he said, "it would be easy for her to get hold of the case – Mr Lowick only had to leave it behind. And she knew where it was bought, so it's a kind of message to me. It's her way of saying, 'You threaten my husband, these are the consequences.'"

"I see," I said. "But that would imply that despite having lost her husband – in one or both senses of the word – she would go to the trouble of implicating someone who may or may not have had anything to do with it. It just doesn't seem likely to me."

"Ah, but a woman in her grief, Mr Rufford, might think all kinds of strange things. If she didn't murder him herself, she probably thinks I did it, but was in danger of getting away with it. She's decided to hurry things along. Or she doesn't care who gets punished, so long as someone pays."

"Well, Mr Belford, even if I can't prove to you that she didn't murder her husband, we can safely say it was not Mrs Lowick in your shop yesterday."

"And how do you know that?"

"Because I was at her house just after you were arrested, and she had been writing letters all morning, with her housekeeper there as a witness."

There was a silence. After a moment, Mr Belford grunted.

"Do you still think I'm participating in an unjust campaign against you?" I said.

Mr Belford looked down at the table. "I don't know," he muttered. "I don't know anything any more. But you're the one who found out who the letter was by. So it stands to reason you and Mrs Lowick are..." He shrugged again.

"I can assure you, Mr Belford, that the only person I want to see accused of murder is the person responsible – if indeed Mr Lowick is dead. He still may not be, in which case, you will be released."

"Oh, he's dead all right," said Mr Belford, with a confidence that alarmed me. I noticed Taylor staring intently at him and making notes.

"Is that a confession?" I asked.

Mr Belford started to laugh, which became hysterical, and I exchanged glances with Taylor.

He tried to compose himself, and just as he was ready to speak, he was again overtaken by an incongruous fit of mirth.

"Mr Belford," I said, "Mr Lowick's disappearance is no laughing matter. What is amusing you?"

This seemed to have the desired effect. "I'm sorry," he gasped. "It's just – you have this reputation for being a clever man, Mr Rufford, so you surprised me. And I'm not myself. I didn't mean any disrespect. Don't you see why he must be dead?"

"You will need to explain yourself, I'm afraid," I said. Despite my outward optimism about William, I had drawn a similar conclusion already, but I needed to know what was going through Mr Belford's mind.

He gave me a pitying look. "Well, sir, it's like this. Either I killed him, or someone else did. Let's say you're right about Mrs Lowick, and she had nothing to do with the cigar case. So it can't be that he's just on a little trip somewhere, that he's forgotten to tell her about, and that he's accidentally left his cigar case at home for her to use against me. Yes?"

"Agreed," I said.

"So that means," said Mr Belford, now energised by his argument, "that either I am guilty of taking the cigar case off Mr Lowick, knowing he wasn't alive to retrieve it, and then trying to sell it – that would be pretty stupid of me, wouldn't it, Mr Rufford?"

I nodded.

"Or, someone else knew he was dead, and was trying to put it on me."

He was, of course, perfectly correct. Any other interpretation of the facts was untenable.

"Surely," I said, turning towards Mr Taylor, "the person we should be speaking to is our mysterious widow. I take it you know who she is, Constable?"

"Unfortunately not, sir," Taylor said. "She pressed a note into my hand, and hurried off. There was nothing to identify her."

"That's a pity," I said with a sinking heart. "And does Inspector Simmons not regard this behaviour as highly suspicious?"

"It's not for me to say, sir," he said, but aware of my unwavering gaze upon him, he added apologetically, "I'm afraid he has his suspect now."

"That figures," growled Mr Belford. "So long as you have someone to blame, that's all that matters."

My cheeks were burning with anger and I wanted to say more, but I knew it was futile. Taylor had limited power to sway the Inspector, although I knew he would do his best. Instead, I asked, "Mr Belford, would you like me to convey anything to your daughter? And to your lawyer?"

"Mr Barrowman came to see me this morning. Says I'm up before the magistrate tomorrow, to charge me or let me go," Mr Belford. "I'm sorry for what I said about you earlier. If you could see if my daughter is well... and tell her that her old papa still loves her..."

Mr Belford's eyes filled with tears, and I stood up.

"I will. Goodbye, Mr Belford. I'm sure they'll let you go tomorrow – I don't think there's enough for a charge, especially in the absence of a body. Thank you for talking to me."

He nodded, and Taylor took him back to his cell, leaving

me staring glumly at the decaying plaster on the wall and speculating in painful detail about the fate that might have befallen poor William.

CHAPTER SIXTEEN

"CEST!" said Matilda, standing in the doorway of the cottage and pointing. "Look, Mama – Cest!"

I was touched that the girl had remembered Celeste's name, more or less. Understandably, the horse had made a greater impression on her than I had.

I dismounted, tied the reins to the gatepost, and walked up the path holding Clementine's bag. Lillian Belford was now standing at the doorway, her hands on Matilda's shoulders.

"Mr Rufford, isn't it?" she said. "Have you found William?"

"I'm afraid not," I said. "Could you spare a cup of tea? I'll tell you what I know."

"Of course," she said, letting me through. "I'm sorry about the house, but..." She trailed off, contemplating the gloomy sitting room with its tattered chairs, dirty walls and bare floor.

"It's perfectly fine," I said. "It's cosy. These are a few things for you, from Mrs Lowick." I handed the bag over, and she took it suspiciously. But after shaking the contents out on the kitchen table, she held her hand to her mouth, pausing to control her emotions. In addition to the toys and clothes, Mrs Lowick had included a pork pie and a purse of coins, which Lillian had the good taste not to count in my presence.

"Look what a kind person has given you!" she said to Matilda, handing her a rag doll, which was received with a huge grin. Matilda went and sat on the doorstep to introduce her new plaything to Dolly in the sunshine. "Don't go near Celeste, please, Matilda!" Lillian said. "She might kick you."

"It's nice of Mrs Lowick," Lillian said, quietly. "I'm sorry

I was so horrible about her before."

"Don't worry," I said. "It's a curious situation. But she's genuinely concerned about you."

Lillian sighed. "Does all this mean... William is...?"

"It's not looking good, Miss Belford. I'm sorry. He's still missing."

She nodded. "I'll make the tea. Do sit."

I looked around the room. A little incongruously, a fine watercolour landscape hung on one wall, no doubt a gift from William. It depicted a dramatic mountain range, with shaggy Highland cattle in the foreground crossing a stream. It was a pity, I thought, that the light in the room did not do it justice, but that would hardly be a priority for Lillian.

Lillian put a couple of cracked and stained cups on the table, and sat down to pour from the teapot.

"So what do the police say?" she said.

"They have a possession of William's," I said. "One that he usually carried with him." I was dreading telling her where it was found, and the consequences.

"Oh," she said. "That's not good, is it?"

"I'm afraid not," I said. "It was his cigar case."

"Those damn cigars. Perhaps he just left it somewhere."

"I'm sorry to say it was found in your father's shop."

She put down her teacup. "The devil it was! What was it doing there?"

"It's hard to say, but unfortunately, the police think that your father found it."

Her eyes widened. "Papa? What are you saying?"

My mouth had gone dry at the thought of what I had to impart, and I took a gulp of tea. "Your father..." I could not yet bring myself to say it. "Your father wanted me to tell you that he loves you."

"Why would he say that? What are you not telling me, Mr Rufford?" It was obvious that she could sense that something was wrong.

"Your father has been arrested, Miss Belford. I'm extremely sorry. They think he had something to do with William's disappearance. He was charged with murder this morning at the magistrate's court."

"Oh my God!" Lillian cried. "Oh my God," she repeated, this time quietly, not wanting to frighten her daughter. She held her hand to her face again. "But he didn't, did he? Please tell me he didn't."

"I don't believe he had anything to do with it, no," I said. "The problem is that he wrote an angry and threatening letter to William. So combined with the cigar case –"

"I can't believe he would be so stupid!" Lillian said. "Well, no, I did have a horrible feeling he might try something, he was that angry. The silly, silly, man. But how did the cigar case come to be in the shop?"

"It's possible that the person who found it may have put it there," I said. "But no one knows who that person is – they kept themselves well hidden, and the police are inclined to believe they already have their man."

I hesitated, and decided I would have to confess my part in Mr Lowick's present confinement. "I'm afraid I may have made things worse. I visited your father yesterday, and he was of course adamant that he hadn't done anything. I thought it might help him to talk to me, and help me understand more about William's disappearance."

"And? How did you make things worse?"

"I went to the magistrate's court. Inspector Simmons cited three facts: that your father sent a threatening letter, that the cigar case was in his shop, and finally something your father said when speaking to me. He said at one point, 'Oh, he's dead all right,' and then laughed. Simmons took it completely out of context, implying that your father knew more about William than he was letting on. It's farcical, but the magistrate swallowed it."

"Oh God," Lillian said. "Why on earth did my father

laugh?"

"At my apparent lack of understanding. And the strangeness of his predicament, no doubt. His assessment – which was pretty much the same as mine – was that William has to be dead if someone had maliciously planted the cigar case. That person is obviously trying to blame your father."

"I see," Lillian said after a moment. "Then William really is gone."

"I fear so," I said. "If he had decided to leave both you and Mrs Lowick, I'm sure he would have sent money and a note, at least."

She sighed. "My poor papa. I must see him. I will go tomorrow."

"Do you need help getting into town?"

"No, thank you," she said. "I'll leave Matilda with my neighbour, and I don't mind walking."

She looked at Matilda play-acting with her two dolls, and shook her head. "I wish I were like her, happy in her ignorance, knowing nothing of this beastly world. Oh, Papa, Papa... can you help him, Mr Rufford?"

"I'll do everything I can," I said. "There is plenty of hope – even without another suspect, it would be hard for your father to be convicted in the absence of a body. Inspector Simmons would have to severely prejudice a jury against him."

"I'm cursed," Lillian said. "Look at all the trouble I've caused!" And she burst into tears.

"It's not your fault," I said. "It's just very bad luck."

"Bad luck that I ever met William, yes," she sniffed. "If I hadn't fallen for his stupid smile and his flattery, Papa would be in his favourite armchair now, content as can be, and I wouldn't be stuck in this hovel on my own. But," she added after a moment, "then I wouldn't have Matilda."

"Indeed – she's a delight. You're both tremendously fortunate to have each other," I said, and she managed a smile.

~

When Flora and I entered Francesca's newly decorated drawing room on Saturday evening, our hostess was – as I expected – deep in conversation with Captain Harris. But he broke away with obvious pleasure when he saw Flora, and came over to greet us.

"You are more beautiful every time I see you," he said to Flora, shaking her hand. "And since I'm an equitable fellow, your brother is looking particularly splendid too," he added, smiling at me. He pressed my shoulder in a friendly fashion, and I withdrew to let them converse.

"Phyllis has not yet arrived," said Francesca, "so I will have you all to myself for a few minutes! How are you, Thomas? Is there any news of poor Mr Lowick?"

I shook my head. "No good news." I could hear piano music coming from the small sitting room. "Is Sylvie well now?" I said.

"Well enough to help Effie again," she said. "At least, from time to time. They are less... intimate than they were. I fear Miss Knowles is partly responsible for that."

"Miss Knowles?" Then I remembered. "Ah, Sylvie's friend from the coffee shop."

"Yes, Effie is trying so hard to be friendly towards her. It's hard to watch, when she must find her so trying." She lowered her voice and said, "I rather wish I hadn't agreed to invite her now. However – now you are here, I'm sure the evening will go swimmingly! You can turn your great charm on her."

"I'll do my best," I said. "I see you finally decided on the green," I added, gesturing at the wallpaper, which was the same as that used in Myrtle's, but in green.

"I did, with a little help from Victor," Francesca said. "Otherwise I would have been paralysed with indecision. Isn't it wonderful?"

"Yes, it's quite intense," I said.

"Oh, you don't think it's too loud? But the furnishings tone it down, don't they?"

"It's perfect," I said. "It suits your temperament."

The piano music stopped, and Effie, Sylvie and Rachel Knowles appeared.

Effie was looking a little strained, but her face brightened when she saw me.

"Oh, Thomas! Let me introduce Miss Knowles. Rachel, this is Thomas Rufford, who caught me singing like a mad woman when he last visited."

"Good to meet you, Miss Knowles," I said, putting my hand out. "I believe I saw you briefly at Myrtle's with Miss Dubois."

Miss Knowles had a whiteness of complexion that was a good match for Sylvie's unhealthy pallor, in stark contrast with Effie's ruddiness, and her features had a tendency to an expression of faint and lofty amusement.

"Yes, Mr Rufford, I remember," she said, shaking my hand after a brief hesitation. "I gather you are involved in Myrtle's in some way."

"I gave it some early investment, and its name, but that's all," I replied. "I'm glad it's popular with members of your Society."

"There are too few such establishments that cater to the needs of women," Miss Knowles said, "so you and Mrs Shannon are to be congratulated. How ironic that there are hardly any times when men – and therefore you – are allowed in!" She seemed delighted at the thought of my exclusion, or perhaps merely at her own observation.

I smiled and said, "I'm just pleased that the place is thriving."

"Sylvie and I have been demonstrating some of our recent work," Effie said. "It's always good to have an early opinion from a potential member of the audience."

Miss Knowles laughed, and said, "Oh, goodness, I make a poor judge, I'm afraid. I found your pieces most diverting, of course, but I'm more likely to attend a concert of Mozart or Beethoven than try to understand modern music." Seeing the bemused expression on Effie's face, she lightly touched her arm and added, "But yours is quite delightful, Miss Harris – and Miss Dubois, of course – and I feel sure it will gain an appreciative audience amongst those more sophisticated than I."

Sylvie shrugged in her usual manner, as if to show to her indifference to her friend's musical taste; I glanced at Effie to see her reaction, and she gave me a brief, patient smile.

I sensed that Francesca would have liked to throw Miss Knowles out of the house then and there, but with a supreme effort, she said, "Well, that's the wonderful thing about music – it's so plentiful and varied that there's something for everyone. Now, let's find some wine for you all, and dinner will be ready soon."

~

Seated at the dining table, I pressed my leg against Phyllis', to which she did not object.

"How is your mother?" I enquired of Effie and Victor. "Any improvement?"

"Perhaps a little, but she's still getting those blasted headaches," the Captain said. "It goes in phases. This is a bad one."

"I'm sorry to hear that," I said. "Your parents are so hospitable – they must hate being unable to entertain."

"Very true," said the Captain. "But I expect they'll be able to resume their parties before too long, and you will once again be regaled with bad poetry, and gossip from the golfers of Hawksbridge."

"I confess I miss both," I said.

"Well, I'm sure you know this already," the Captain continued, "but my father tells me that the police have a fellow for the disappearance of your journalist friend. A jeweller, I think."

"Yes," I said, "and I believe they have the wrong man."

"Oh?" said the Captain. "You intrigue me. How so?"

"The charge is based on the scantest of evidence," I said. "An angry letter to Mr Lowick, a cigar case, and an opinion Mr Belford expressed, taken quite out of context."

"Ah, yes," said the Captain. "My father mentioned the cigar case. Found in the jeweller's shop, and belonging to Lowick. Rather damning, I should say."

"Not if someone put the case there to incriminate Mr Belford."

"How horrible," said Miss Knowles. "But why would someone do such a thing? Who would benefit from that?"

"It would divert attention from the person who knows just what has happened to Mr Lowick," I said. "The police would stop looking for the real culprit."

"Oh, heavens," said Effie. "Does this mean that we should assume the worst about Mr Lowick?"

"I fear so," I said, "although I won't give up all hope. There may still be an innocuous explanation, but it's getting harder and harder to think of a plausible one."

"It's so peculiar," said Miss Knowles. "How can a man simply disappear like that?"

"How indeed?" I said. "But I suspect foul play."

"The police have searched around the ramparts, I take it?" said the Captain. "They can be treacherous. I nearly lost my footing when I was young and drunk, in the snow. Nearly turned me to abstinence!"

Flora winced. "Don't worry, my dear!" said the Captain.

"I can hold my liquor now."

"Do you think that was the case with poor Mr Milburn?" said Francesca. "The man who fell off the ramparts. Might he have been drunk?"

"I heard his wife was the intoxicated one," said the Captain, "with propaganda from Lady Fairfield's Society. Took it all a bit literally, perhaps, and decided to strike a blow for womankind."

"Nonsense!" snapped Miss Knowles. "The Society doesn't advocate murder. That is a slander, Captain Harris, of which you are unworthy. There is no evidence that Mrs Milburn did anything of the sort, and the fact that she is still at liberty speaks for itself."

The Captain nodded and said, "Forgive me, Miss Knowles. I forgot you were an apostle of Lady Fairfield's. I was making light of the case, which I should not have. I'm sure it was just a tragic accident."

I experienced a jab of guilt at the mention of Mrs Milburn's name. I had visited her merely for my own purposes, in the investigation of William's disappearance, and had hardly given her a second thought since. But now her pitiful situation came back to me sharply, no less desperate than Mrs Lowick's. I resolved to visit her again, in case a mere conversation could lift her spirits. She had seemed quite adrift in the world.

Thankfully, the awkwardness of the moment was covered by the arrival of the venison.

I noticed that Effie had drunk her wine quickly and was soliciting another; it was hardly surprising. After another sip, she looked at me and said, "As I mentioned, I have named your peafowl. Or have you already done so yourself?"

"I haven't," I said. "Tell me your names."

"Well, he's so vain and puffed-up, and she steps around carefully, so I thought: Hubris and Prudence. Or Hu and Pru."

I laughed. "That's perfect," I said. "Hu and Pru they shall be."

"Very clever, Miss Harris," said Phyllis. "You have visited Ramsburgh?" She kept any note of suspicion out of her voice, but the motivation for her question was clear.

"I called in when passing, but Thomas was out. I saw the birds, though – such fine creatures. I'm developing a couple of melodies for them."

"Ah! I look forward to hearing your Peacock Suite," I said.

"Do you not find," Miss Knowles said, looking around at her fellow guests, "that the title of a piece is often supposed to be reflected in the music, as if one is supposed to guess the subject from the melody? And yet I can never see it – or rather hear it. My fault, I'm sure. But I always have a suspicion that a fancy name is attached to the piece purely to give it weight, and then everyone nods wisely and professes to hear how precisely the music portrays the title."

"Can you name any examples?" the Captain said.

"Oh, let me think. 'The Moonlight Sonata,' 'Fingal's Cave...' Now you've put me on the spot, of course, I can't remember any more."

"That is a sadly cynical view," said Effie. "But I think you have it the wrong way around, Miss Knowles. I don't think anyone is expecting you to divine the subject purely from the piece – but once you know what the composer was aiming to convey, or was inspired by, you can often hear the connection with the subject. After all, the composer has so many wonderful ways to create emotion in us, would you not agree? – whether it's with a melody, or a rhythm, or a pause, or tone, or – oh, there are so many ways. In 'Fingal's Cave,' I can hear swelling storms, and the majesty of the cave and mountains. But the source of a composer's inspiration doesn't necessarily result in a recognisable picture. It may just be an abstract outpouring of musical expression stemming from one idea."

"I see," said Miss Knowles. "Well, I'm not entirely sure I do, but I bow to your superior knowledge."

"It makes me so envious of you, Miss Harris," said Phyllis. "Words seem blunt instruments when you have such refined and direct means to make us cry!"

Miss Knowles had been unwise to pick an argument with Effie over music, and Effie's rebuff was satisfying. I hoped she would not be provoked further by her before the evening was finished.

"I had a distinguished visitor yesterday," Francesca said. "You'll never guess who!"

"Since I know it wasn't me," said Victor, "I can't imagine."

"Mr Forrester!" Francesca said. "He came with some samples. We had a long conversation in which he paid me overblown compliments."

Victor frowned. "The reprobate. I trust he didn't attempt to make love to you, Francesca."

"Not really, I just think it's the way he's made," said Francesca. "He's exuberant. And – if I can say it – he was a little intimate, by accident!"

"I doubt that anything he does is by accident," said Victor. "What was this intimacy, exactly?"

"He was holding up a sample to the light and he gestured for me to come closer, and his hand, which was behind me, by chance came into contact with my... lower person. I don't think he was even conscious of it, otherwise he would have pulled his hand away sooner. I didn't like to say anything! It was really quite funny. The poor man would have been mortified if he had realised what he was doing."

"At least," I said, "you may say that you have been touched by greatness."

There was laughter, but I noticed that after his initial amusement, Victor looked searchingly at Francesca.

~

During a lull in the conversation, I reached behind me for the bag I had brought with me, and handed it to Francesca.

"We have an exciting new range of ornaments at the Pottery," I said. "We're aiming to broaden our market. We've had ten thousand of these made and I'm excited to know what you think." Flora gave me a scolding look, which I ignored.

"Interesting," said Francesca. "What have you clever people been up to?"

She withdrew the object, and let out an "Oh!" Horrified, she turned the china knick-knack around in her hands, scrutinizing the caricature of her Marbleware portrait. "Well, it's very... I'm sure that... oh! I don't know quite what to say. But if that's how they see me..."

The Captain took it and examined it. "I'm sorry, Thomas," he said, "but it's perfectly hideous. This is a travesty of the original."

I burst out laughing, and Flora and Phyllis looked daggers at me, while Francesca looked confused. "I don't understand," she said. "What's going on?"

"Don't worry, Francesca," Flora said. "Thomas has played a horrible trick on you. It's nothing to do with the Pottery – it's just some cheap knock-off. The Pottery is going to sue the company responsible. Thomas, really!"

"I'm sorry," I said, getting a hold of myself. "That was unkind of me. Victor is right. And yet it has a certain charm, doesn't it?"

"Hm," said Francesca, narrowing her eyes at me, but smiling. "I suppose I'll forgive you. It is quite a funny little thing. I don't really look like that, do I?"

"Not even a little," said the Captain. "It takes a great talent to capture your beauty."

Miss Knowles took the offending item and looked it over. "Oh, Mrs Campbell," she said. "Your face was a picture. This reminds me of something – what can it be? Oh, yes – the Box Hill picnic in 'Emma'."

"How so?" said Captain Harris.

"Emma makes a joke about Miss Bates not being able to limit herself to just three dull things at once, and Miss Bates is hurt, but doesn't admit it, and is so pitiably humble. Poor Mrs Campbell! How very wicked of you, Mr Rufford."

"I don't see it at all," said the Captain, looking sternly at Miss Knowles. "Are you really comparing Miss Bates and Mrs Campbell?"

"It's quite all right, Victor," said Mrs Campbell. "I'm sure it was just a passing thought. I assure you, Miss Knowles, I'm rarely as humble as Miss Bates. And, I hope, somewhat less tedious."

"I have never known you to be in the least tedious," said the Captain. "Aside from the other delightful ladies in this room, you are the most entertaining and lively creature I know."

"Thank you, Victor," said Mrs Campbell. "I'm quite sure that's not true, but I shall try to live up to it all the same. Now, shall we withdraw? Let's retire to the small sitting room – I gather Sylvie has a little surprise for us all."

~

It seemed that Effie had not been let into the secret of this entertainment, and she was looking puzzled. Sylvie sat down at the piano, and to my alarm, Miss Knowles stood next to her, grasping a sheet of neatly-written music.

Sylvie turned in her seat to address us. "I have been working on a little song for the Society," she said. "Miss Knowles has written the words. It is called 'Rise Up and Give Voice'."

Effie's frown deepened as Sylvie played an introduction, a lively march with a passable melody. Miss Knowles took a deep breath and started to sing lustily.

For how many centuries have women been enslaved?
For how many years have we laboured in the shade?
But now is the time to rise up and give voice
To the harm that we have suffered, and to make the bravest choice.
When –

At this point Effie screamed, "How dare you!" and hurried to the piano, slamming the lid down and giving Sylvie barely a chance to remove her hands. "How dare you go off and write this dreadful... *nonsense* without telling me, Sylvie? You know my feelings about the Society."

Miss Knowles recoiled, and Sylvie turned towards Effie, plainly horrified at the violence of this outburst. "Mais, Effie –"

"You deliberately defied me," Effie continued, her face turning puce, "when you know you have limited energy for writing. You have wasted your talents on the pitiful scribblings of a shrew!"

Miss Knowles' jaw dropped.

"Tu es impossible," Sylvie cried, running out of the room, and for a moment we all stood silently, frozen in horror. Effie turned on her heel, and after she strode from the room, we could hear her crunching briskly along the gravel, striking out for who knew where. Then Miss Knowles spoke.

"Well, I'm sorry if I have inadvertently upset Miss Harris, I'm sure. I will leave. Thank you, Mrs Campbell – you were so kind to invite me."

"I'll get my groom to take you home," Francesca said. "I'm very sorry about all this excitement."

~

When Miss Knowles had left, what remained of the party sat in the drawing room exchanging glances and consuming some steadying port.

"Nil desperandum," said Victor, trying to rally the troops. "We had an excellent supper, and lively discourse."

"Far too lively," said Francesca. "I fear this party was doomed from the start. There must have been something in the air. Or perhaps the wine."

"I apologise for my stupid joke, Francesca," I said. "It was unkind."

"You are forgiven, Thomas," she said. "It *was* quite amusing. May I keep the ornament?"

"Please do," I said, "if you can bear it."

"It's sweet," she said, "and it's a conversation piece."

"Will Effie and Sylvie be all right?" Flora said.

"I'm sure they will," Francesca said. "This has happened before. Well, not in quite such an explosive way, but occasionally they become impatient with one another and have to be apart for a while."

"I'm quite used to it," said Victor. "I used to annoy her most dreadfully when we were young. And *vice versa*. But I must say, I haven't seen her as riled as that for many years."

CHAPTER SEVENTEEN

On Sunday afternoon, I decided to ease my conscience and call on Mrs Milburn. I was glad of the distraction, since the discomfort of the previous evening was nagging at me. I hoped that the partnership between Euphemia and Sylvie was not permanently fractured – it had been a terrible and public humiliation for Sylvie that would surely make a reconciliation difficult. But they had to overcome it, for the sake of their art! A petty argument could not be allowed to alter the course of musical history.

But was their falling out truly petty? I supposed it had been building for some time: it was an unequal relationship, despite its extraordinary energy and success. The seeds of its destruction may have been planted from the first moment they discovered that Sylvie could give of herself so that Effie's talents could soar. Sylvie had sacrificed many freedoms for Effie, and now she evidently saw through the Society that she could and should spread her own wings.

I might not be able to comprehend the nature of that collaboration, but they had stumbled upon a potent chemical reaction, one that now threatened to burn itself out. Could Effie find another muse, or learn to manage without one?

These thoughts brought me to Mrs Milburn's door, where I was welcomed by Mrs Spillings, the housekeeper.

"I'm sorry I didn't give advance warning," I said, "but Mrs Milburn has been on my mind, and I wanted to make sure she is well."

"She will be delighted to see you," Mrs Spillings said, ushering me into the hall and towards the sitting room. "I'm sure she's bored stiff of seeing my face. Mr Rufford to see you,

Ninette."

"Oh! Mr Rufford, how pleasant!" Mrs Milburn said, getting up from her chair. "I didn't know you were coming."

"I wanted to see that all was well with you, and to see what progress spring is making in your garden!" I said, shaking her hand.

"How kind," she said, squeezing my hand warmly. "I'm feeling much better, thank you. I have even been out in the world a little – well, in Hawksbridge, anyway!"

"What more of the world does one need?" I said. "I'm not a great one for suffering the indignities of travel."

"Indeed," she said, "but of course, the railway..."

She trailed off, lost in contemplation. I thought of Mr Milburn's work on the bridge, and how proud Mrs Milburn would have been of her husband's contribution – how she would have attended the opening ceremony, smiling as she looked up at the magnificent stone arches, a shining locomotive puffing its purposeful way across. A misstep, or perhaps a petulant shove, was all it had taken to wipe out that happy possibility, and countless others.

She recovered herself, and said, "Please do sit. Your friend... Mr Lowick, wasn't it? Is there any news?"

"There is no sign of him, unfortunately," I said, taking an armchair. "Correction – there has been one sign of him: his cigarette case."

"Oh?" she said, abstractedly plumping up a cushion on her sofa.

"It has been found in Mr Belford's jeweller's shop, and Mr Belford has been charged with murder. Wrongly, I believe."

"Oh dear," Mrs Milburn said, fiddling with the cushion frill. "But I'm sure the police wouldn't charge him without sufficient reason. I mean, not just because of a cigar case."

"I think they may have been deceived by the real culprit."

Mrs Milburn looked at me with alarm. "Oh, no! Surely

not? There must be another explanation."

"I can't think of a good one," I said.

"It's all so horrible," she said. "Let's talk about something else."

"I've brought you something to read," I said. "I don't know if you enjoy this kind of thing, but..." I pulled a book from my inside coat pocket and presented it to her.

Mrs Milburn examined the book, which I had taken from my own library, not having had time to find a new copy. I was careful to choose a story that left the reader with a sense of happy possibilities.

"Oh! Thank you!" she said. "I do enjoy Miss Tavistock's work, very much. 'The Forgiven Bride' – I haven't read this one. How sweet of you!"

"My pleasure. I found it entertaining, with a most satisfactory ending."

"Oh, good – I can't bear a tragic ending," she said. "At least, not these days." She looked a little bemused. "But I'm surprised that you – a man..."

"Like this kind of book? I hope I'm sufficiently open-minded," I said, smiling. "And they are far more than mere romances."

"Of course – I didn't mean –"

"To tell the truth, I'm prejudiced in their favour," I said. "I have the good fortune to be engaged to be married to Miss Tavistock, or rather, Miss Phyllis Drummond."

"No!" Mrs Milburn exclaimed. "You are surely pulling my leg, Mr Rufford!"

"Not a bit of it," I said. "I am due to wed a woman of far greater intellect than myself. I shall have to improve myself."

"Not at all," she said. "You are a fine man, Mr Rufford. And most certainly a kind one, to bother calling on me."

"It's my pleasure. And thank you. Can I see how your garden is coming on?"

~

It was not onerous watching Mrs Milburn proudly describe how she had nurtured her extensive family of plants. Not having much opportunity for socialising, she obviously relished having an audience.

"Let me show you my spring garden." She led me to the foot of a small tree in blossom, and I reached out and touched one of the pale pink flowers.

"That is my dear cherry tree," she said. "It has become a great friend to me, and so I planted all the prettiest things underneath for her: snake's head fritillary and aquilegias, and of course my tulips. Some of these are really rather unusual. I was lucky to get them. And such a surprise, because you plant them and you never know what will come up. Look at these red and gold ones! Aren't they delightful?"

She continued in this vein for a while, and eventually turned to me. "And that is all, I think! I hope I haven't bored you, Mr Rufford. I have rather quacked on."

"On the contrary, Mrs Milburn," I said. "Thank you for sharing the secrets of your garden with me. It's even more glorious than the last time I saw it."

"Oh! But I didn't offer you tea! What am I thinking?"

"It's perfectly all right," I said. "I must be going, anyway."

"What a pity," she said. "But let me at least give you some shortbread to take with you. It's another way I keep myself occupied! Baking is such a comfort."

She took me into the kitchen, where a large pile of shortbread lay invitingly on the table. "There – I don't know why I made so much! But it's fortunate I did. What can I wrap it in? Let me find something."

"I'm sorry – do you mind if I use your convenience?" I said.

"Of course," she said. "It's in the yard at the back there."

I was amused to find that the paper in the lavatory was made from strips of pamphlets from the Society. Was this symbolic of rejecting the Society, or had Mrs Milburn simply pushed the memory of her husband's death – and the possible role of the pamphlets – into an inaccessible recess in her mind? Or perhaps she had been given a bundle of pamphlets to distribute, and some had been put to more urgent use.

I wondered to what extent Mrs Milburn had been inveigled into the machinery of the Society; after all, she was vulnerable and lacking friends, but in possession of copious free time – just the kind of person they might want for their ranks.

My parcel of shortbread was waiting for me, tied with a blue ribbon.

"Thank you, Mrs Milburn! I shall enjoy this very much – and so will my fiancée. If I eat it all myself, I'll become tubby and far from eligible."

Mrs Milburn laughed. "I doubt that. I will be honoured to have the great Iona Tavistock sample my baking. Goodbye, Mr Rufford! Do call on me again!"

~

It was good to see that Mrs Milburn was recovering, even if sadness still lingered in her eyes. Perhaps it would be no bad thing if she were to be adopted by the Society, I thought, as a rain shower began to fall, making Celeste's ears twitch. It would give Mrs Milburn an additional sense of purpose, although of course it would encourage those who suggested that the Society's pamphlets had roused murderous sentiments in her.

I turned my face up to the rain and wished that it could disperse all that now polluted the town. William's disappearance, Mr Belford's incarceration, Mrs Milburn's misery, the fire at the printer's, the unsettling presence of anarchists, and now a disastrous rift at Halfpenny House – if only a sufficiently heavy storm could clear it all away, turning the clock that graced Hawksbridge Town Hall back to a more civilised time. It was tempting to look unfavourably on Lady Fairfield's well-meaning but often ill-fated influence. But that was unfair; most of these events were merely the unpredictable consequences of human action.

On the other hand, William's abrupt departure from Hawksbridge had all the signs of a deliberate crime, the investigation of which the police had bungled and which I was no closer to solving. It would take a while for my correspondents to reply, if indeed they ever did. Was it time to approach the lauded Mr Forrester directly? But what could I say? "Did you have Mr Lowick murdered to protect your business?" I had not the slightest evidence – only hearsay from a man who could not truthfully be characterised as reliable.

The rain abated, and at Ramsburgh, my spirits were raised by the sight of Effie Harris standing by a pony cart I recognised as belonging to Francesca. She smiled at me, just before an almighty flapping of wings above her made her duck.

"Oh! Good heavens!" she said as a large bird flew from the roof to land a few dozen yards away. "Ah, it's Hu! What a fright he gave me." She put her hand on her chest.

"Sorry! Are you all right?" I said. "I think they must be nesting up there."

"I'm fine. But that's wonderful, Thomas," she said. "Ramsburgh will have a peafowl family soon."

"So long as they don't block the gutters," I said, peering at the roof.

"Anyway, I came here on a whim and was just about to give up," she said. "Do you have a little time for me?"

"Of course," I said. "You can help banish my gloomy

thoughts."

"Gladly," she said. "Would you be so good as to take me back later?"

I nodded, and Effie dismissed her driver.

"Let's walk around your lovely house," she said. "How handsome it is! It almost makes me want to settle down in Hawksbridge, but my soul is restless. I always think that if I stop moving, my music would stop too."

After I had taken Celeste to her stable, we strolled round to the west garden. Effie turned towards the house and shaded her eyes as she looked up at the parapet. "What a satisfying roof. So many different angles and complications."

"Expensive complications when the weather tears at them," I said.

She looked back at me. "I expect you're full of complications, too, Thomas," she said. "How exciting for Phyllis to be able to discover them – the ones that you want to be discovered, of course!"

Thinking about my own past sins, and how unworthy of Phyllis they made me, was not something I wished to discuss, so I changed the subject. "I was tempted to go after you last night and see how you were. Have you made up with Sylvie?"

"Thank you, but I wasn't fit for company. I made rather a scene, didn't I? No, we haven't spoken since yesterday. I'm sorry for my outburst, but I can't abide that Knowles woman. That stupid song was no less than a prostitution of Sylvie's talents! Oh, I'm getting cross again."

She folded her arms. "Too much of me is wrapped up in Sylvie," she said. "I'm afraid the bubble will be pricked, and I'll just be Mr and Mr Harris' daughter again, irrelevant, unknown, and without any inspiration."

"Oh, surely not!" I said. "Your talent can't be taken away like that. Do you really need Sylvie so much?"

"I did," Effie said. "But I don't know any more." She shivered. "Can we go in? It's getting a little chilly."

~

Tea was served in the drawing room, and Effie stroked Fox, who was pleased to see both of us.

"It may not show," she said, "but Sylvie is a woman of great private passion – and of course masterful at orchestration. We both knew an hour after we first met that we had complementary talents. We almost immediately began a collaboration, and I found abilities I had no notion I possessed. Sylvie is able to transcribe and improve my ideas in an uncanny fashion. It's impossible to describe the delirious happiness that comes – or came – from this... this... tumultuous alliance!"

She took a sip of tea. "I'm sure you have been wondering how far our partnership goes." She looked at me, amused, as if goading me into an improper question.

"I have no wish to pry, Effie," I said, knowing she was likely to tell me anyway.

"How diplomatic," she said. "My music – our music – is borne from passion. We hold nothing back in the pursuit of our art." She looked at me intensely. "Nothing at all."

"I see," I said, my blood a little roused by this revelation.

"In so many ways, Sylvie knows exactly what I need. She knows that after my animal longings have been heightened and sated, I compose the greatest of my melodies. I conjure up – or perhaps gather up is a better term – such ideas, with so much intensity that it frightens both of us. While it drains Sylvie, it seems only to energise me further. And then we must write down what the night has produced, before I slip into a deep sleep where I dream of more music – sometimes entire movements."

"Which is why," I said, "you could not stay with your parents."

"Precisely," she said. "Dear Francesca is so

understanding, and so enlightened. She cannot be unaware of our... methods."

"In that case," I said, "I can understand how the loss of Sylvie would be painful."

"And yet," she said, her eyes shining, "while I fear it, I also welcome it! I need to start afresh. I cannot believe that only Sylvie can bring forth my music. And in the last few months I have made improvements in my transcription. I've been working to overcome the embarrassing limitation with which God has shackled me – perhaps to squash my pride. You have seen that impairment yourself, in my letter! And it's far worse when writing music."

I recalled Effie's spidery, childish handwriting.

"That must be frustrating," I said. "To hear it all in your head, and yet not be able to write it down."

"Oh, beyond measure," she said. "It's torture, and I live in terror of being declared a musical fraud. I use my own notation to remind myself of what's in my head, but it's imperfect." She retrieved a small notebook from a pocket in her dress, and opened it. I peered at it: the pages were full of wavy lines, scrawled notes, and pictograms.

"Sometimes I'll sing or play and describe my intentions to Sylvie," she continued. "Or if I'm not with her, I'll scribble like this as best I can, and we develop it together later."

She sighed. "I assure you, I would like to be like other composers, but this is my curse, or gift. Other than Sylvie, and perhaps Francesca, you are the only person alive who knows all this. What a strange relief it is to confess my limitations! But slowly, I am improving myself. And yet that is only one part of it."

She drained her tea cup, and rose. "May I see more of your home? I'm talking of nothing but myself. I want to hear about Ramsburgh and see how you live."

"Oh! Your library," she said a little while later, looking in awe at the bookshelves and the knots of comfortable furniture for pleasurable study. "If I had a room like this, I would write twice as much music. It's perfect." She walked to the window. "And there are Hu and Pru, on cue!" We both laughed, and I joined her at the window.

"I might have procured their services to impress guests," I said. "But they arrived spontaneously."

"Perhaps I was wrong about needing to travel," Effie said, staring at the grove of trees beyond the south garden. "I always thought staying still was dull and numbing. Maybe I'm finally growing up. I'm suddenly envious of the peace and quiet here."

"Well, it may not be quiet or peaceful for long if Phyllis and I..."

"True," Effie. "You will be a delightful father. For my part – I can't imagine myself as a mother, and having to be distracted from my work." She shook her head. "I was made strangely, wasn't I?"

I observed her, still staring into the distance, her red hair catching the light. It was as though she had jumped from the pages of one of the novels here: a tragic, alluring heroine, contemplating the tangled web of her life.

"You were made beautifully," I replied.

She looked at me and smiled sweetly. "Thank you. Now, what's next in my tour?"

We went into the landing. "My bedroom is next door," I began, and before I could discreetly move on, she marched into my room.

"Ah – windows on two sides, just like the drawing room," she said. "How wonderful." She walked to the west window, dragging her elegant hand over the polished mahogany surface of my chest of drawers. "Another lovely view."

She turned and said, "May I speak frankly?"

"Of course," I said, my mind searching for what frankness she could possibly have left.

"Good," she said, and walked briskly to the door, closing

it.

She stood with her back to the door. "This may seem arrogant, but I believe my work to be important. And I know what is in me is good." She closed her eyes and massaged her temples with her hands. "My heart sometimes seems infinite in capacity – and I am full of infinite notes, infinite melodies! They are just out of reach, and they must be gathered in, by an experience, by a dream, by a person's touch. It frightens me. How will I ever get it all out? What will it do to me, if I keep it all inside me, without harvesting it? I need you to help me, Thomas."

"I... I don't think –"

"It's not about thinking." She moved towards me and took my hands. "I must do whatever it takes to catch these fragments and mould them into art, or they will be wasted, and no one will ever know what might have been. Please, Thomas!"

"I don't know what you're asking me to do."

"I think you do," she said, looking into my eyes, and I found it impossible to look away. She raised her right hand and pressed my hand to her breast.

"Doesn't it pain you just a little that others get the glory?" she said softly. "Wouldn't you like to be associated forever with a work that the world loves, and which will endure for however long humanity exists?"

"Well, of course, but I don't see –"

"By helping me, Thomas. By helping draw out my music, you will forever be part of it. You will father something eternal."

This was surely a far greater temptation than anything Christ had to contend with. A beautiful woman, whose name and work were known by practically every cultured man and woman in the country, and far beyond, had chosen me to be her temporary muse, her helpmate, even her lover. She was offering me not only the untold ecstasies of the bedroom –

this very bedroom – but a kind of immortality. She knew exactly how to seduce and flatter me, and I was trembling with the fear that I might give in to her.

Her cheeks were flushed now, and her lips were parted. She pressed my hand with force against her breast, and, tilting her head, kissed me on the lips. I did not at first resist this exquisite sensation.

As Effie pressed herself against me, I suddenly thought of Phyllis in the cottage, a beatific smile on her trusting, reddened face. This memory was joined by less happy ones – visions of my past deficiencies in the face of temptation – and so, resisting the immense pressures of my sensual nature, I gently pushed her away.

"I'm sorry. I desire you – of course I do. But I'm not free to do what I want."

"Phyllis would understand," Effie whispered, grabbing my hands. "Of all people, she would understand the need to give everything, anything for the imperative of art!"

"She might forgive me," I said, "but it would be wrong to expect it of her."

I wrenched my hands free of hers.

"Please!" she said. "I don't know what I'll do otherwise! It's hurting my head! Please don't be so cruel to me!"

"Let me think about it, Effie," I said. "Give me time." I tried to trick my baser longings into thinking that I might take her offer up later. Perhaps I really would. But for now, the danger had passed.

She groaned. "Oh, what am I to do?" she said. "I will go mad." She went and sat on the bed, and hugged her knees like a child.

I grasped the door handle. "I'm sorry. I'll meet you in the drawing room," I said. "I hope we're still friends."

"Oh, of course," she said. "Please try to forget my brazenness."

"What brazenness?" I said, looking as vague as I could.

"Thank you," she said, closing her eyes tight, perhaps attempting to blot out her humiliation.

~

I took Effie back in the pony cart, and the journey helped return our friendship to its previous disposition.

"Do you think you can make up with Sylvie?" I asked when we had turned out of the drive.

"I suppose I will need to apologise," Effie said. "Bother. I won't be sincere."

"But you will have the good intention of soothing her feelings," I said. "I expect she will be thoroughly miserable and looking for a way to make up."

"I hope so," she said. "Well, you know what I mean. But that wretched Knowles woman has got her hooks into her."

"I'm sure Sylvie will see that you are far more important to her than Miss Knowles."

"Perhaps. Unless she really wants a break from me. I wouldn't blame her; I know it will happen sooner or later. It may be for the best."

"And your musical needs?" I said. "You have many male followers. Eager followers."

"Thomas, don't be so vulgar," she said, catching my meaning. "What a disgusting thought – all that leering and pawing. Anyway, I should probably be moving on. Poor Francesca must be fed up with us. We have tested even her hospitality and generosity."

"I shall miss you," I said with feeling.

"Thank you – and I you," she said, briefly pressing my arm. "And let me assure you, Thomas – you, and your castle, and your peacocks *have* been an inspiration. I promise that you will appear, somehow, somewhere, in my music!"

CHAPTER EIGHTEEN

DR WELDON did not wait for Shipley to show him in, but instead burst straight into the drawing room where I was taking my coffee after breakfast. It was the Wednesday following my memorable Sunday afternoon with Effie.

"It's Miss Harris," he said, catching his breath. He was dripping from a rain shower, and Shipley, behind him, was observing his muddy footprints with distaste. "I'm afraid she's dangerously ill, and she's asking for you. I'm sorry to intrude like this, but she may not have much time."

"Good God," I said, rising from my chair. "And they sent you? Shouldn't you be with her?"

"It was the quickest way to get a message to you," the doctor said, clenching his damp hands in agitation. "And I have done all I can think of. Mrs Campbell and Miss Dubois are tending to her."

Dr Weldon was not my favourite member of Hawksbridge society, having previously shown a romantic interest in my fiancée, followed by a barely forgivable indiscretion with a dear friend; but this was no time for grudges. He was clearly distraught. I hastily retrieved Celeste from her stable and rode her as fast as I dared, awful thoughts running through my mind. Had she tried to take her own life? Had her quarrel with Sylvie taken a dark turn? Or was I somehow responsible, because I had refused a request that most men would gladly have fulfilled?

That horrifying notion struck me like a physical blow, and I knew that, if true, it would be something for which I could never, ever forgive myself. I had failed her, when I had it in my power to soothe and help her, and when she had nowhere else to turn. What was the cost of the honour I had congratulated myself on? Was it honourable to show no mercy to a brilliant, tormented soul, and thereby cause her destruction?

Perhaps Effie had been right, and Phyllis would have understood. After all, it was not as though Phyllis imagined me to have a spotless past. In that moment of turmoil, with panic surging through me and Celeste's laboured breathing and thudding hooves in my ears, I could not at all grasp where my moral duty lay. My previous certainties had become as malleable as the mud on the rain-sodden road to Halfpenny House.

Rushed as they had been, my preparations for the journey had allowed Dr Weldon to ride ahead, and he now presided over an anxious court in Effie's bedroom. Francesca and Miss Dubois had tear-streaked faces. I was frightened to look at her, and I was shocked when I did. She looked thin, her skin was red and blotchy, and her breathing was laboured. Thankfully, she was asleep.

"I have sedated her," Dr Weldon said. "I'm afraid she has been very restless."

I knelt by the bed. "You've no idea what it might be?"

"It could be cholera," he said, and Miss Dubois let out a sob. "She has been vomiting badly, and the changes in her skin are consistent with the disease. And she has been thirsty, and complaining of stomach-ache."

"My God," I said. "No one else has been taken ill?"

He shook his head. "Not that we know of. Mrs Campbell has spoken to the servants, and they report no symptoms."

Realising that there was a strong chance that Effie's condition may not have been my responsibility, I felt an unexpected pang of relief, swiftly followed by guilt at thinking of my own comfort in such circumstances.

Without opening her eyes, Effie stirred, and whispered "Water." I poured some from the jug on the table next to her, and brought it to her lips. She struggled to lift her head, and took a few sips before lying back again. Then she opened her eyes.

"Thomas! You came – thank you!"

She stretched her hand out and I took it. "I did," I said. "Celeste has never run faster."

She managed a smile. "Good old Celeste. I will thank her when I'm better."

"We'll ride together," I said, "and no doubt you will have composed a sonata by the time we return."

"I will hold you to it," she said, and then groaned. "My stomach is on fire. And I feel so sick. I'm sorry, I think I need to be on my own for a while. But thank goodness I have such good friends."

We left Dr Weldon with Effie, and I heard her retching into a bucket.

"Let me fetch Mary to help Dr Weldon," Francesca said, and hurried to find her maid.

I went to the drawing room with Miss Dubois, where we sat silently.

"Did Effie eat or drink anything different from the rest of you?" I asked after a minute.

"No, not at all," said Miss Dubois. "We all had the same – chicken soup at lunch, and pork in the evening. There was nothing wrong with it."

"And she hadn't been out today, or yesterday?"

"No, she has been busy on her symphony."

"If I may ask – are you both...?"

"Speaking? Oui, bien sûr. We understand one another. It was just a silly thing. It happens." She wiped a tear from her face. "I wish we would not quarrel. I do not want to hurt her."

In a few minutes Dr Weldon appeared, and sat heavily in a chair.

"I have left her to rest. Mary will stay with her." He sighed. "I wish there were more we could do. She needs to have as much water as we can persuade her to have, as she has lost so much liquid. I don't think she will be able to manage food for a while."

"Euphemia's parents should be told, and Victor," I said.

"Let them know," said Dr Weldon, "but discourage them from visiting just yet. I fear that further emotional distress may be too much for her. She needs to preserve every ounce of her remaining strength."

Sylvie shut her eyes tight as if to blind herself to the horrific visions that were inevitably forming.

"Oh, Lord," Francesca said. "Thank you, Dr Weldon – you have been so kind, but you must have other patients who need you."

"If you don't mind, Mrs Campbell, yes – I will attend to my other duties, but I'll be back this evening, and if there is any change, please send for me. And I shall look in on the Harrises."

"I am so grateful," said Francesca, and Dr Weldon nodded gravely and left.

Sylvie went up to assist Mary in her vigil, and Francesca looked so dejected alone on the sofa that I joined her, and patted her arm.

"Effie is made of stern stuff," I said. "She's not going to give up without a fight. She has far too much to do."

Francesca smiled. "True. She's a force of nature. Oh, but cholera! Here! Is it something in the house? I couldn't bear it if it were my fault!"

"I've been thinking exactly the same about myself," I said.

"You? How could you have anything to do with it?" Francesca said.

"It's difficult to explain. She asked me to do something, and I refused. I can't say more than that."

"Oh," she said. "I'm afraid I can guess. She is a passionate person. And perhaps you now know what I almost told you, when we were dining with Mr Forrester."

"I think so," I said.

"What an extraordinary young woman," Francesca said, shaking her head. "But Mr Forrester also has a hidden side."

"Yes?"

"You remember I said he accidentally brushed against me when he brought some samples over?"

I nodded.

"He has been to see me a couple of times since," she continued. "It seems he has formed romantic notions about me."

"Oh, no," I said. "How inconvenient."

"More than that. On Monday, it was a sunny day, and Effie and Sylvie were picnicking in the garden and making up. It was quite touching. Then Mr Forrester arrived, full of apologies for calling without notice, and clutching a book of poetry for me. Love poetry by Ovid, of all things! I mean, I don't mind Ovid, but for a present from a man, it's a little..."

"Obvious?"

"Precisely. We talked, and he noticed a book that Victor had given me, on botany, so we talked about that. He read Victor's kind inscription in a rather mocking tone, which I didn't find funny. I wish I hadn't left it lying around. And then he turned the conversation to my Wicked Cassone. Does everyone know about the wretched thing, Thomas?"

"Everyone in Hawksbridge – yes, I would imagine so," I said. "It makes for wonderfully scandalous dinner party conversation."

"I suppose so," she said. "Anyway, he asked if he might take a look at it, and I didn't think I could refuse him."

"I see."

"So there he was in my bedroom, on his hands and knees. He spent a great deal of time examining it, and when he finally stood up, I could tell that... well, you know."

"It had inflamed him?"

"Yes. I didn't know where to look. And then he asked me to be his mistress."

"God in Heaven. What did you say?"

"I said it was very flattering, but I wasn't interested, and I reminded him he was married. To which he replied that he might not always be married to Penelope, in which case there would be a vacancy. I didn't like the implication that he could get rid of his wife just like that, Thomas."

"No – none too reassuring for any future wife, either," I said.

"Quite. When I said that it was enough to be his friend – at that moment, of course, I would have been happy never to see him again – he asked in an unpleasant tone whether Captain Harris was just a friend. And observed how friendly he had been to me at the dinner party."

"What a charming man," I said. "And this is someone lauded far and wide."

"He said: 'Captain Harris is a lazy coward and an affront to the notion of patriotism. He threw away his commission, and he will throw you away when he's done with the novelty of bedding a woman old enough to be his mother.' Or words to that effect."

"Oh, Francesca, I'm so sorry. How disgusting," I said.

"At that point, I asked him as politely as I could to leave, and then..."

She blew her nose and took a deep breath.

"And then he kissed me, and grabbed my bosom."

I squeezed her hand, unable to think of anything to say.

"I pushed him away, and he fell over the cassone. He wasn't injured, but it was most undignified, and his face was a picture of anger. However, he left without another word."

"God. What a brute. I hope he didn't damage the cassone, if that doesn't sound callous."

"Fortunately it's undamaged, as am I, apart from the shock. So there we have it. I may have to decorate in here, yet again, so I don't have to be reminded of that... creature."

"What can be done about him?" I asked. "Would an

apology from him help?"

"Oh, nothing can be done," she said. "I won't get an apology. He's the sort of man to think that the woman is at fault. I expect he usually gets what he wants."

"Well, I'm glad you taught him a lesson," I said.

"But at what cost? I'm afraid he will damage me," Francesca said. "His pride has been hurt, and he may want to hurt me back."

"He doesn't have any ammunition," I said. "Does he?"

Francesca shrugged. "Perhaps," she said. "Victor."

"So he gave you a book on botany. It's not a crime, or especially scandalous."

"But he might find out more." She looked miserable, twisting her handkerchief in her hands.

"Oh, Francesca, surely –"

"Please don't judge me," she said. "I couldn't bear it, on top of everything else."

"No – no, of course not," I said. "I'm just thinking of Flora."

"You're quite right," she said. "It was stupid of me. But he's so handsome, and funny... and I suppose I was flattered. He made me feel young."

"I can perfectly well see how compelling it might be. If it weren't for his parents, and Flora, and your reputation –"

"Yes, yes, yes," she said, getting up and pacing the length of the drawing room. "I know I'm an idiot. I'll try to restrain myself from now on. I know Victor has serious feelings for Flora, and I was just an amusement for him, of the sort that officers are accustomed to. I just hope that Forrester doesn't make things difficult. Who knows what piece of gossip he could dig up."

"I assume you kept your indiscretions to this house?" I said.

She nodded. "If it got out, it could destroy Flora's chances with Victor – oh, what have I done?" She sank back onto the sofa and put her head in her hands. "Why can I not behave like a decent person?"

~

I stayed most of the day, occasionally looking in to see Effie, but she was tossing and turning in so much discomfort that she was barely aware of me. Victor arrived, and it was hard to watch his distress, which his military training could not hide.

Before I left, I went to say goodbye. I was painfully aware that this might be a last farewell, and a tear rolled from my cheek onto hers as I bent over her. She stirred, and murmured, "It's raining, Sylvie!" before falling unconscious again.

"Goodbye, Effie," I whispered. "I'll come again soon. Be strong!"

When I got back to Ramsburgh, I informed Flora of Effie's condition, and we embraced before she went off to endure her distress in private.

"Oh, poor Miss Harris," said Mrs Felton, dabbing her eyes with her handkerchief. "Such a lovely young woman. It's too awful. But I'm sure she'll pull through, my dear. I will pray as hard as I can, and we'll ask Mr Benton to get the whole congregation praying for her."

She took my hand and squeezed it. I smiled gratefully, and said, "Might I have a coffee, Mrs Felton?"

"Of course you can, my dear. You make yourself comfortable. You've had a shock."

I sat and stared into the cold hearth. It was hard to accept that the fire of life that glowed so strongly within my friend was burning dangerously low.

Could it really be cholera? An isolated case was unusual. But if it had been something she had eaten, surely Dr Weldon would have given it weight? And anyway, why had no one else fallen ill if the meat had been bad? Perhaps it was destined to be one of the many instances where the answer was simply not forthcoming, given the ineffable complexities of biology and the limitations of medical science.

In frustration, I said, to no one in particular, "We're so damnably, pitifully fragile! What in God's name is the point of it all?"

"I know, dear," Mrs Felton said, coming in with my coffee. "It's hard to fathom. But this will make you feel better."

"Oh, thank you, Mrs Felton. Sorry, I didn't mean to say that aloud."

"Mr Rufford, you say whatever you like in your own house. You may curse the place down if it helps."

There was a loud peafowl screech from outside. "Well, quite," said Mrs Felton. "Even they are upset."

I smiled. "I know they make a racket, but I find their presence comforting. As if they're watching over us."

"The swans were nice and quiet," said Mrs Felton, "but I'm getting fond of Hu and Pru. I wonder where they came from."

"Someone's estate – I imagine the formidable Lady Fairfield must have peacocks. Perhaps they were running away from her."

"Oh, surely not," said Mrs Felton. "She's an admirable woman – very generous too. I heard she just gave a small fortune to the Hawksbridge Home for Girls. And she even took a few of them into her house! What a kind thing to do. Now, I must go and help Catherine in the kitchen. Do you need anything else, my dear?"

~

The slight improvement in my mood following my conversation with Mrs Felton was, alas, short-lived when I opened my post.

5, Barter Street, Bloomsbury, London

Dear Mr Rufford,

It was kind of you to write. I had been anticipating further correspondence with Mr Lowick - I trust he is not ill. If he is, he has my sympathies, as one who understands the scourge of infirmity.

I do not know what you have already learned, but you will appreciate that the confidences I made to Mr Lowick cannot easily be transmitted in a letter. There are people - wicked people - who will use one's words against one. But I have much to tell, and I wish to tell it while there is still time.

If you genuinely wish to find the truth then I exhort you to come to London as soon as possible and talk to me, and my poor wife. See for yourself, and then use whatever means are at your disposal to stop this terrible thing happening again.

I look forward to meeting you.

Yours faithfully,

Mr Jonathan Nesbit

P.S. Please note our new address above, as we have moved from Islington out of necessity.

CHAPTER NINETEEN

I FELT I could not undertake a trip to London to see the Nesbits while Effie was still in a dangerous condition, so I wrote back to say that I would try to visit in a week or so.

I went with Flora to see Effie the next morning. Miraculously, she had not worsened, and she was beginning to take a small amount of broth, although she did not always keep it down. Although she was still in considerable pain, she managed a weak smile, but she was too tired to utter more than a few words.

Victor had spent the night at Halfpenny House, and he had evidently had little sleep. Mr and Mrs Harris visited briefly, but mindful of Dr Weldon's advice, did not stay long.

We convened in the drawing room, a sombre party. "I dare not give her much more morphine," Dr Weldon said. "She will have to endure the pain. Truth to tell, I didn't expect her to last the night. She has a strong constitution."

"She has rarely been ill," said Victor. "Is she out of danger?"

The doctor frowned. "She's very weak. If she can't hold down her food, she will get weaker. If this is cholera, it will certainly last a good deal longer. But she has managed to drink a little, which is of course critical when there is severe dehydration. So – there is reason to be hopeful. That is all I can say, I'm afraid."

Victor nodded, and there was a gloomy silence.

Dr Weldon tried to strike a brighter note. "But I'm sure that the tenderness you have all shown, and your prayers, are helping her immensely. Seeing how much she is loved will strengthen her resolve to live, and calm her spirit."

~

After returning to Ramsburgh, I was pleasantly surprised by a visit from Phyllis and her father, on the way back from seeing Effie.

"The poor wee thing," Dr Drummond said, having lowered himself into his chair with a sigh of relief. "Cholera is a terrible disease. Very painful and messy. I haven't seen a case for a year or two, thankfully."

"Was there anything further you could suggest?" I asked.

"Alas, no," he said. "Dr Weldon is a fine doctor. She's in good hands."

"I can't bear the thought of her being in such agony," Phyllis said. "She was tossing and turning so." She bit her lip. "Awful. Was there nothing more to be done to help with that?"

"No, my dear, unless you want to finish the poor girl off with a morphine overdose."

"Well, there's plenty of hope," I said. "She's fighting this thing bravely." Racking my mind for anything of comfort, I remembered Mrs Milburn's shortbread that I had stashed in the sideboard for an appropriate moment. "Does anyone like shortbread?"

Phyllis smiled and nodded, and Dr Drummond said, "I'm a Scotsman. I think that should answer your question."

"Good," I said, and retrieved the parcel. Untying the ribbon, I opened up the paper wrapper and saw marks on the inside.

"Someone's canny," Dr Drummond said, leaning to peer at the paper. "What is that – music?"

I read the title at the top of the sheet: 'Rise Up and Give Voice.'

"Good God!" I said, and without thinking, swept the shortbread onto the table and brushed the crumbs off the sheet. "What in Heaven's name...?"

"Thomas? What's the matter?" Phyllis asked, while Dr Drummond looked from Phyllis to me and back in confusion.

I scanned the sheet up and down. There it was, the product of Miss Knowles' and Miss Dubois' joint effort. There was much crossing out, so perhaps, I thought, this was an early draft.

"What is it?" Phyllis repeated.

"Oh – sorry," I said. "It's Sylvie's song. But this cannot be."

"Whyever not, laddie?" said Dr Drummond. "This is the cause of the argument between Miss Harris and Miss Dubois, is it not? Phyllis told me all about it. Quite a steuchie. Where did you get this?"

"That's the odd thing," I said. "Mrs Milburn gave me the shortbread, and wrapped it in this paper."

"Mrs Milburn – whose husband...?" Phyllis said.

"Fell off the ramparts, yes," I said.

Dr Drummond grunted. "Or was pushed."

"I don't think so," I said. "Anyway, the point is – how did she get hold of this music? Sylvie must have given it to her. But how did they know each other?"

"Via the Society, I would imagine," said Phyllis, "Sylvie being a possible convert to the cause. And we know Mrs Milburn had a leaflet from the Society. Is there anything sinister about that?"

"Perhaps not," I conceded. "I suppose they could have met at Myrtle's, or at a talk. I just... find it odd, that's all."

"It's that inquiring, suspicious nature of yours," said Dr Drummond. "I do hope, my boy, that you will adopt a more blithe disposition when you wed my daughter."

He stared at me. "Anyway, aren't you forgetting something important?" he added.

"I am?"

"Michty me! Just hand me a piece of that shortbread,

man, before I die either of hunger or old age!"

~

Dr Drummond was dozing off, aided by a glass of whisky.

"The music is still bothering you, isn't it?" said Phyllis.

"Sorry," I said. "I didn't mean to be distant. But yes – I just think it strange that neither Mrs Milburn nor Effie mentioned Sylvie's visit, assuming that's how the song got into Mrs Milburn's possession. I think Effie was annoyed enough with Sylvie to have mentioned it – Sylvie is usually so reserved. She's not one to make friends easily."

"But in a sense, Mrs Milburn did tell you about it, didn't she? You have the sheet."

"True," I said. "Either she was trying to send me a message, or – more likely – she was absent-minded, or didn't consider it of any significance."

"Well, what significance could it have?" Phyllis said.

"That Sylvie was involved with another member of the Society, not just Miss Knowles, against Effie's wishes."

"But apart from Effie's discomfort with it, is there any real harm?"

"Probably not," I said. "Rationally, I know it's absolutely nothing. It just niggles, that's all. It's as your father says – I've become suspicious about every little thing."

Phyllis stretched out her arm and clasped my hand. "It's been difficult lately. It's hardly surprising you see shadows everywhere."

I smiled and squeezed her hand. "And there is poor Mr Belford, waiting to be tried for a crime he most probably didn't commit. It seems that any investigative talents I once had have dissolved. They were probably illusory anyway."

"Nonsense, Thomas!" Phyllis said, stroking my captured

hand with her thumb. "You have helped so many people. You have been such a support for Mrs Lowick – no one expects you to do more."

"And then there are the Nesbits," I continued. "William was in correspondence with them. They appear to be victims of Mr Forrester – but in what way, I don't know. I will try to see them in London next week."

"You really think it could shed light on William's disappearance?"

"I have no idea," I said, "but I do know I have to find out what was on William's mind. And Mr Nesbit sounds desperate to talk. Or just plain desperate."

I untangled my hand, got up, and started to pace the drawing room.

"When are we going to get married?" I said. "I want you here, as Mrs Rufford, running the place. I want to wake up next to you, so I can discuss all these things. I just need you here with me!"

"I know, I know," said Phyllis, but her expression betrayed a crushing reluctance. "There's so much going on at the moment, though – you're driven to distraction, Effie's ill, and I have Papa to look after and a book to finish. Things will become quieter soon, I'm sure."

"Will they?" I asked. "There always seems to be something. We could just have a modest wedding, and you can see as much of your father as you need. And I won't stand in the way of your writing, I promise."

"We'll see," said Phyllis. "Let's just get through the next few weeks and see how things stand. Of course I want to marry you, Thomas! But I want it to be wonderful, not fraught. I want to be able to concentrate on you, and being a wife."

I nearly added, "And being a mother?" but I thought better of it. It was natural that she should be apprehensive of the prospect, for so many reasons.

"Of course," I said, suddenly struck with the dismal, terrifying thought that Phyllis might be starting to regret her engagement. "I understand."

~

My third visit to Effie's bedside saw little improvement. Her stomach pain was still severe, allowing little energy for talking. Dr Weldon administered a small dose of morphine, but it seemed to have less effect than before. I spent some time reading aloud from Gulliver's Travels – omitting some of the more visceral passages – in the hope it would distract Effie, and it did produce the occasional smile, especially at the antics of Lagado's Academicians. I wondered whether I would be so brave if I were to be similarly afflicted.

"I would take her place if I could," said Francesca later, in the drawing room. "I would do anything to take her pain away."

"Indeed," I said. "Just how much longer is this awful thing going to continue?"

Mary came to clear away our crockery. "It's terrible, ma'am," she said. "One moment she's sipping her evening tea as usual, and the next, she's at death's door."

I stared at her. "She had tea before this? I don't remember anyone mentioning it."

"Oh!" Mary said. "No one asked me, sir. Miss Harris and Miss Dubois usually have a camomile tea before bed. Miss Dubois makes it for them both. So it was just normal, like – nothing to speak of."

I looked at Francesca. "If for some reason Sylvie didn't drink hers, and the tea was contaminated, then that would put a different complexion on things. Mary, could you please ask Miss Dubois to come down?"

Mary looked at Francesca, who nodded.

"Yes, of course, sir – ma'am," Mary said, and left.

"Oh, Lord," said Francesca. "Dr Weldon wasn't certain it was cholera."

"We're always so trusting about what we consume," I said. "But there must be so many opportunities for things to go wrong without us noticing. Anything could drop into a crate of tea. A rat could make its home in it."

Francesca shuddered. "Don't," she said, as the door opened. "Ah, Sylvie! Come and sit down. We wanted a little word about the night Effie became ill."

"Yes?" Sylvie said, frowning and taking a seat opposite us.

"Mary said you and Francesca are in the habit of taking camomile tea before bed," I said, as gently as I could. "Is that so?"

"Yes, Mr Rufford, that is correct. Is there anything wrong with that?"

"No, not at all. It's just that when Dr Weldon asked us about that evening, the tea wasn't mentioned."

"I'm sorry, Mr Rufford – but it was just so... ordinaire, I didn't think it was worth mentioning. It is such a habit."

"Quite. Is it possible that your camomile tea was contaminated?"

Sylvie looked shocked. "Oh! Surely not! No, I don't see how. I drank mine, and I was perfectly well after."

"I see. May I perhaps see the tea you have remaining, just in case there are obvious signs of contamination? It would be advisable to avoid drinking any more of it."

"That is not possible, Mr Rufford – it was the last, and I have not bought any since."

"Oh – that's a pity," I said. "And you always made the tea – no one else, this time?"

"No, no one else," she said.

"Thank you," I said. "I won't detain you any longer."

Sylvie nodded and left.

"Inconclusive," I said, drumming my fingers on the arm of my chair.

"How annoying she didn't have any left," Francesca said. "The odd rat dropping could have cleared up the mystery."

"Annoying, or convenient for her?" I said.

"Oh, Thomas! Don't be ridiculous," Francesca said. "Why on earth would Sylvie want to harm Effie? You can see how upset she is."

"But they fell out quite spectacularly. Resentment can build up over time, and Sylvie was much put upon."

"No, I won't have it," Francesca said. "They made up beautifully. If you had seen it, you wouldn't entertain such horrible thoughts."

"Maybe," I said. "I'll keep an open mind."

Francesca shook her head. "I don't like to think of you becoming cynical, Thomas. I preferred the old you, when you had just taken possession of Ramsburgh, full of optimism and youthful naiveté!"

"You're not the first person to say it," I said. "I assure you that man is still there, more or less. But I'm not letting my guard down until Effie is well again – and justice has been done for William."

~

While Francesca was sitting with Effie, I went upstairs and knocked on Sylvie's door.

"Oh – you may enter," she called. I went in; she was sitting at a writing desk with some sheets of music spread out on it.

"I'm sorry to disturb you, Miss Dubois, but there is one other matter I need to discuss."

"Yes?"

"Miss Dubois, do you know a Mrs Milburn?"

I watched her expression carefully. A flicker of alarm seemed to cross her face momentarily.

"Mrs Milburn? Let me see. Yes, I think I recognise that name."

"Might you have visited her recently?"

She looked confused. "Ah – it is possible."

"Well, have you or haven't you?"

Sylvie sighed. "Yes – yes, I have," she said quietly. "But please don't tell Effie. She doesn't like the Society. It would upset her."

"Did you have any purpose for this visit?"

"Just to talk. I don't have many friends. You may have noticed," she added, a little bitterly.

"Yes, you are kept so busy, Miss Dubois," I said. "You spoke of the Society with Mrs Milburn?"

"Yes," she said. "What meetings there will be, and marches, and so forth."

"Did you give her something?"

"Yes, some leaflets for her to give away."

"And something else?" I prompted.

"Oh," she said. "Yes, I gave her a sheet with the... the song on it. I thought it might amuse her – for the... how do you say it? – distraire –"

"To distract her from dark thoughts, perhaps."

"Exactement, Mr Rufford. To distract her. She is still grieving."

"That was kind," I said. "Thank you. I will leave you to your work."

She nodded, and returned her gaze to the little dots and lines that were Effie's scourge, and also her redemption.

CHAPTER TWENTY

I HAD ample time to think on the journey to London. I tried to make connections, but ended up constructing absurdities.

Mrs Milburn kills Mr Milburn, Sylvie tries to kill Effie, common factor: a recent introduction to the Society. But there was no hard evidence that Mrs Milburn was a murderer, and none that Sylvie deliberately tried to harm Effie.

William runs away for a new life, and uses Mr Belford and his poison letter to lend authenticity to the likelihood of his death.

Or, Mrs Lowick kills her husband, and uses Mr Belford's letter to cover her tracks, persuading someone to plant the cigar case.

Or, Mr Forrester has William killed to prevent his malpractice from being exposed.

Or, Lady Fairfield –

It was fruitless. So many different stories could be told, and all seemed equally valid, given the paucity of evidence.

I had picked up Effie's misgivings about the Society, to the extent that I had imagined them as some kind of malign force unbalancing the normal order of Hawksbridge. At times, I could see the Society egging Mrs Milburn on to dispose of her husband, who may not have been keen on the ways of the Society. I could see Miss Knowles being used to drive Sylvie and Effie apart, since Effie was also a sceptic. William and Lady Fairfield knew each other – my fevered brain did not exculpate her from involvement, for reasons unknown. And I could easily believe that the Society was responsible for the burning of Mr Eagle's printing business, after he abetted an act of sacrilege against Lady Fairfield and her followers via the parody leaflet.

And yet, there was not one iota of evidence for any of this. Mrs Milburn was a free woman, without a stain on her honour. The cause of Effie's illness was unknown. Far from skulking in the shadows as a criminal might, Lady Fairfield had given generously to many institutions and made herself very visible in the town; and her visit to Ramsburgh spoke of genuine concern for William and his wife.

To cap it all, Victor had passed on another tidbit from the ever well-informed Mr Harris. Mr Eagle was under arrest, having betrayed himself through carelessness, and then confessed to forging the parody pamphlet and burning down his own building to collect the insurance. Using The Duke's Head to communicate with the supposed author of the pamphlet had been an elaborate ruse. Mr Eagle was ill and in debt, and the building in desperate need of expensive renovation. His scheme might have avoided his bankruptcy and an impoverished old age. But the gamble had failed, and instead, the poor fellow was condemned to far greater discomfort, to spend – in all probability – the rest of his life in prison.

It might be convenient to blame everything on Lady Fairfield and her devoted wasps, but the idea did not bear scrutiny. As my train approached London, I had the disagreeable sensation of having less insight now than when I had climbed into my carriage at Newcastle.

~

In my hotel, I had an unsatisfying sleep during which my brain confused the strands of my thoughts like a cat in a basket of wool. I headed out on foot as soon as I had breakfasted, glad for the distractions of the city.

After the relative tranquillity of Hawksbridge, it was strange to be back in London. As its name suggested, Barter Street was a busy place, full of shouting, carts being unloaded, and servants hurrying to buy supplies for their employers.

As a youth I had sometimes strayed from genteel Blackheath with my friends, crossing the Thames at London Bridge to feel the noisy energy of the City, buy sweets from market stalls, and gawp with fascinated horror at the many street-walkers. So I recognised Barter Street, which, when first constructed in the early years of the century, would have been an attractive development mixing town houses for the middle class with shop premises. The mainly brick buildings were not showy but they were handsome enough, with pleasing details around the windows and doors, set on a wide road whose pavements had been planted with trees to help soften the severity of this man-made landscape.

Now, a certain shabbiness, characterized by flaking paint and stucco, foliage growing in the gutters, and uncollected rubbish, indicated that the area had relinquished any cachet it once might have had to competing developments springing up all over London. It was just as well that the architects could not see their street going to seed just as their thoughtfully placed trees were maturing.

Number 5 I found to be occupied by a coffee shop, but I tried a door to the side, which opened into a narrow stairway. An unpleasant damp smell hung in the air, and looking up, I could see a hole in the skylight that was the cause of the water pooling on the worn stairs from a recent rain shower.

The first floor apartment was labelled 'Taylor', the name above the coffee shop, so I went up to the second floor and knocked on the door, which bore no indication of the occupier's name.

A few moments passed before the door was opened by a man with blotchy, papery skin who I took to be Mr Nesbit's father.

"Yes?" he said.

"Good afternoon," I said. "I'm looking for Mr Jonathan Nesbit."

"Ah!" he said, and scrutinized me.

"Am I speaking to Mr Nesbit Senior, perhaps?" I continued.

The man laughed, before coughing. "An easy mistake to make. No, Mr Jonathan Nesbit at your service. You wouldn't be Mr Rufford, would you?"

"I am," I said. "I hope this is a convenient time. I can come back later if –"

"No, no," he said, and opened the door wider. "Now is as good a time as any. Please come in. I'm glad to see you. Emily was convinced you would never turn up."

Mr Nesbit led me from the small hall to a sitting room that had pieces of fashionable furniture that contrasted strangely with the room's faded and peeling wallpaper. He indicated an upholstered armchair.

"Would tea suffice, Mr Rufford?" he said. "I'm afraid I don't have any spirits. We just drink tea these days."

"Tea will be perfect," I said, embarrassed to be intruding. Mr Nesbit did not look well, and moved slowly. Over the small fireplace, there was a portrait of Mr Nesbit in happier times with his wife and small child. All were smiling, blissfully ignorant of their future.

"You find us in reduced circumstances," he said when he came back with a tray. "But we were able to take a few things with us from Islington. Not the staff, unfortunately. Couldn't afford them. I'm an engineer – was an engineer. Not fit for that now, but at least my wife has a small allowance."

He sat down stiffly. "Now then, Mr Rufford. It's good of you to come all this way – from Mr Forrester's town, no less." He shook his head as though this were somehow remarkable. "Do you know the reprobate socially?"

"I have only met him once," I said. "We are barely acquainted. But I have a friend who knows him better – and I have to concur with your description. From what I hear, he is not an honourable man. At least where women are concerned."

Mr Nesbit snorted. "That's the biggest understatement I've ever heard." He poured out the tea with a slightly shaking hand. "And not just with women."

He gazed at me. "Do you know what's wrong with me, Mr Rufford? And with my wife? Something tells me that you are ignorant of the basic facts of the case."

"You're right," I said. "I'm afraid I have no idea. But before you explain, please let me be clear about my own interest in this. If I gave the impression I was a colleague of William Lowick's, I apologise, but I was afraid that doors would otherwise be closed to me."

Mr Nesbit shrugged. "Well, at this point, I'm grateful for any interest from anybody. So what's your angle, Mr Rufford?"

"William Lowick is missing, feared dead," I said. "I have reason to believe he was working on a story about you, and a number of others, connected in some way with Mr Forrester."

He shook his head. "I'm sorry to hear it," he said. "I enjoyed talking to Mr Lowick. Damn it. I was putting a lot of store by his article."

"Is it possible," I said, "that whatever Mr Forrester has done to you, may have led to William being silenced? Or is that too fantastical?"

"It's not at all fantastical," Mr Nesbit said, raising his cup unsteadily to his lips. "I think it would be entirely in character. Let me explain."

He took a sip and sighed. "We moved to our Islington house two – no, two and half years ago. It was beautiful – a dream, Emily said. Newly built in the latest style, four bedrooms for us and two for the servants. All conveniences, and good-sized rooms. Respectable neighbours. The mortgage was a stretch, but I was progressing in my company, and as I say, we had Emily's allowance.

"As for the decoration, I don't really have an eye for these things. I thought the wallpaper the builders had provided was all right, but Emily didn't like it and had set her heart on particular designs. One of them was 'Wildflower Meadow', by Forrester & Co., and she had several rooms done with it, in different colours. I thought it a little extravagant – these papers aren't cheap – but I adore Emily and I couldn't refuse her this. Especially after I bought a fancy bureau.

"Well, I liked the result, and there was some paper left over, bright and cheerful as anything, so I thought I would surprise Emily. She likes to cook, even though I said she doesn't have to, and she has this great big book with all her favourite recipes copied into it, and quite a few from her mother, and her mother's mother. The cover was getting tattered and dirty, so I took her book, and..."

Mr Nesbit wiped away a tear and swallowed.

"And I covered it in this damned paper. She loved it. And I was so pleased with myself, I went and covered Viola's favourite nursery rhyme book in it, too. God forgive me!"

He stopped and sobbed into a handkerchief for a minute before recovering himself and continuing.

"We all got sick soon after. Emily and Viola had it the worst."

I was aghast. "I'm extremely sorry to hear it, Mr Nesbit. And you think the wallpaper was the culprit?"

"I don't think so, sir – I know so."

"How are your wife and child now?" I asked.

Mr Nesbit looked at the family portrait. "My wife is still very ill. I will introduce you to her shortly. My beautiful daughter Viola..."

He struggled to control himself.

"My daughter Viola is at peace. God rest her innocent soul!"

"Oh, my God," I muttered. "The poor girl."

"She's not alone, Mr Rufford. There are others of her age with her in Heaven, and all because of Mr Forrester's paper. I like to think of them playing hopscotch amongst the clouds."

The tears were pricking at my eyes. "How on earth is this allowed to continue?" I said.

"Money," Mr Nesbit said. "And arsenic poisoning can look like other diseases, so doctors can record the cause of death wrongly, either by their incompetence or through malevolence. Viola's death was put down to diphtheria. At the time I didn't know any better, but you can see for yourself. It didn't take long to work out."

He pushed a scrapbook towards me, in which he had pasted newspaper articles detailing deaths and illness where either arsenic ingestion was known, or suspicions had been raised.

"It's not just wallpaper. You can buy plenty of preparations containing arsenic," Mr Nesbit. "For the skin, for digestive problems, you name it – arsenic apparently cures it. Well, yes, in a sense it does, permanently, if you take enough of it. Imagine taking it to improve your skin, Mr Rufford! It's liking shooting yourself in the head to cure a headache."

"I had no idea," I said. "If it's so dangerous, why are people still falling for it?"

Mr Nesbit shrugged. "People are easily persuaded by confident puffery. If it's in a shop, or in their wallpaper, it couldn't possibly be harmful, could it? Everyone is too trusting. We are mostly ignorant dolts believing that everything is done for our improvement and comfort. I used to be such a dolt, too, but no more." He took back the scrapbook and leafed through it. "The world is a darker place than I ever thought possible," he said, shaking his head. "Smiling devils walk amongst us, fêted by all, but quietly killing us for profit."

"You have confronted Mr Forrester, I take it?" I said.

"Of course," he said, "and he denies any responsibility –

through his lawyer, naturally, who charmingly says that if I spread libel, I shall be sued into oblivion. I don't doubt Forrester is keeping an eye on me. If I step out of line, I wouldn't put it past him to have me – erased. I'm already ill, so finishing me off wouldn't be difficult."

He leaned towards me and whispered, "I go to a different market every time I buy provisions, Mr Rufford. Can't be too careful. Wouldn't use the market down the road, not for anything."

"I don't blame you," I said. "You said that arsenic poisoning can disguise itself as other diseases. Would cholera be one such?"

"Oh yes," Mr Nesbit said. "Similar symptoms of nausea and digestive trouble, skin darkening, headaches, and so on. When a whole family dies of it, it's an easy diagnosis to make, especially if the doctor doesn't want to make bother for himself."

My growing fear had been realised. "Effie!" I cried. "Oh, God in Heaven. My friend has been poisoned!"

~

"Thank you for coming," Mrs Nesbit said weakly from her bed. "I'm sorry I can't get up."

Mrs Nesbit lifted her thin arm and I gently shook her hand, trying not to be alarmed by the sores and scars on her face and hands. Her skin was dark and blotchy, and she had a number of warts. On her bedside table was a jug of water, a vase of lilies of the valley, and a Bible, and there was a bucket next to her bed.

"I'm pleased to meet you, Mrs Nesbit. I was very saddened to hear about the loss of your daughter."

"Thank you," she said. "I keep thinking she's here, hiding

under the bed or peeping around the door. Sometimes I hear her laugh. Maybe she's haunting us."

"She was always a mischievous one," said Mr Nesbit, "so perhaps she is. Mr Rufford says he thinks his friend has been poisoned, too."

"Oh dear," said Mrs Nesbit. "I'm sorry to hear it. Is that why you came?"

"Actually, no," I said. "I'm trying to find out why Mr William Lowick has disappeared."

"Oh yes, nice Mr Lowick! Disappeared? How awful. I liked him. He was going to write about us, and the others. I hope no harm has come to him."

"Mr Forrester's doing, mark my words," said Mr Nesbit. "He'll have known everything Mr Lowick did, almost before he did it."

"It's a distinct possibility," I said. "If he had no qualms about injuring his customers, he would appear to have an under-developed conscience."

Mrs Nesbit sighed. "It's the Devil's work. To seduce us with pretty things... deadly things. We should have paid more attention to our Bibles. Well, I have time for it now, even though my head... oh, what I wouldn't give for an hour without this headache!"

"Let me get you a poultice, dear," Mr Nesbit said, and left.

Mrs Nesbit looked at me and tried to smile. "Your friend, Mr Rufford. Is she very ill?"

"I'm afraid so, and in a lot of pain," I said. "And yet she resolutely hangs on to dear life. I am hopeful. She's a composer."

"How interesting! May I know her name?"

"Euphemia Harris."

Mrs Nesbit's eyes widened in recognition. "Oh! How wonderful that you know her – I have heard her symphony in London, only a few months ago. Such a shocking and thrilling opening! Everyone was talking about it." She frowned. "But what terrible news that she is ill. Is it from wallpaper?"

"I don't know," I admitted. "But perhaps. Where she lives now, there is Forrester wallpaper. No one else in the house has suffered yet, though."

She nodded, and Mr Nesbit came in with a damp cloth and gently applied it to her forehead.

"Ah... that's better," Mrs Nesbit said. "I'm so sorry, Mr Rufford – I think I must sleep again. But I'm glad to have met you. Please let the world know about us if you can. We can at least be a warning to others."

"I will do whatever I can," I said, and withdrew to the sitting room.

~

"What will you do?" Mr Nesbit said when he returned.

"I'll talk to Mr Forrester," I said, "both about Mr Lowick and about the poisonings. And I'll see how I can publicise the lethal use of arsenic in wallpaper and get it stopped." I realised that this was a rash offer that I was unqualified to make, but I was angry.

"Won't be easy," Mr Nesbit said. "But I know someone who can help. An expert on arsenic poisoning. He's already had his run-in with Mr Forrester, and a few others, so he has to be careful about what he says in public, but he'll tell you everything you need to know."

He went over to his desk and wrote out a name and address.

"There," he said, handing the note to me. "Dr Peter Henrick. He's a good fellow – brings us fruit every week, and takes a look at Emily, without demanding a brass farthing. Keeps both of our spirits up. I don't know if I've been any help, Mr Rufford – I wish I could say what happened to your Mr Lowick. But I would lay good money on Mr Forrester being involved."

CHAPTER TWENTY-ONE

IT WAS an easy thirty-minute walk from Barter Street to Harley Street. The images in my head of the stricken family were hard to reconcile with the cheerfulness of the spring sunshine, imbuing the city with an unwarranted sense of optimism and permanence.

A short walk it may have been, but this smart, clean street was a world away from the Nesbits' address. Judging from the architectural embellishments that included balconies and pillars along the façade, Dr Henrick's practice was doing extremely well. I informed the doctor's assistant that I did not have an appointment, but that I was prepared to wait, and that my visit concerned the Nesbits. Sure enough, this had the desired effect, and before long Dr Henrick appeared. A well-fed man in his sixties, he was white-haired and bespectacled, with a neat beard and an expression that seemed perfectly tuned to convey concerned interest.

"Mr... Rufford, was it?" he said, extending a hand. "I feel I know the name, and your face seems a little familiar, but I'm afraid I don't remember the occasion..."

"We haven't met," I said. "I'm sorry I didn't make an appointment, but I've come down from Hawksbridge and I've only just been given your name by Mr Jonathan Nesbit. I would like to discuss arsenic poisoning with you, if you can spare the time."

"Of course, of course," said the doctor. "I don't have a patient for an hour or so. But I trust there is no grave news of the Nesbits? I only saw them four or five days ago."

"I spoke to them both," I said. "They are dealing with their tragic predicament remarkably well."

Dr Henrick looked relieved, and showed me to his office, where he took up his place behind a large desk piled with journals and books, and I settled myself into a comfortable Windsor chair opposite him.

"Please excuse the chaos," he said, clearing a space and opening a notebook. "It's always like this when I'm writing a paper. Now. What is your interest in arsenic poisoning, if I might inquire, Mr Rufford?"

"It's a little indirect," I said. "I'm investigating the disappearance of a friend, who was himself looking into a matter related to Mr Gabriel Forrester, or rather to his company."

Dr Henrick nodded. "Would your friend be Mr William Lowick?" he asked.

"Yes – did he contact you?"

"Indeed, he has been to see me, and I consider him an ally in the fight against the pernicious spread of arsenic within our society. But you say he has disappeared? This is terrible news."

"Quite so. I fear the worst, since it has been weeks, and it's out of character not to contact his family." I was tempted to say 'families', but this was not the time to dwell on the complications of William's life.

"But this is awful – awful," Dr Henrick said, shaking his head. "Such a fine, energetic young man. And there is no possible indication of how...?"

"Very little," I said. "A man has been charged, on the basis of ridiculously poor evidence, but I can't see how it will hold up in court. I think it more likely that his disappearance is something to do with Mr Forrester, especially now I know that he appears to be killing off his own customers."

"Quite possibly," Dr Henrick said. "His own employees too. The poor people who manufacturer his wallpaper – mixing the dyes and handling the blocks and paper – have a shocking rate of attrition. And that's not to speak of the daily calamities in his arsenic mine."

"Mr Forrester owns an arsenic mine? The well-known socialist...?"

Dr Henrick smiled grimly. "Oh, yes. The loudest proponents of socialism are often those with the most to lose from its introduction. Perhaps it's a manifestation of guilt – or a form of moral protection, a shield against criticism. You will have to consult a philosopher or a doctor of the mind about this phenomenon, not me! But certainly Mr Forrester, for all his undoubted talents, is at best a hypocrite. He turns a blind eye, and perhaps has made himself believe his own protestations that these cases of illness are nothing to do with him."

He got up and went to a cabinet, unlocking it with a key that was chained to his belt. He extracted a pair of gloves, which he put on, and then he removed a large book and placed it on his desk.

"I have been collecting wallpaper – not out of an interest in interior design, of course, but to determine which contain arsenic, in what quantities, and how easily the pigment is shed. This volume is dedicated to Forrester's activities."

He opened the book and turned the pages, into which samples were pasted. I recognised some of the patterns.

"This recent one," he said, pointing a gloved finger at 'Hedgerow', "is a good example. It uses Scheele's Green, widely used nowadays, unfortunately. Copper arsenite. You can usually guess just by looking at a design whether it contains arsenic: it has that compelling, vibrant quality that is so sought after, and lucrative. There is a blue version of this design – here – that is equally toxic."

"Good Lord," I said under my breath.

"Sometimes contact with the wallpaper causes illness, but at other times, simply being in the same room brings on the symptoms. There may be an emission of gas, or dust. I have had patients living in a house with arsenical wallpaper who displayed symptoms, but who, when they spent time at a sea-side resort as I advised, reported an almost immediate improvement!"

"Mr Nesbit has a scrapbook of cases," I said. "They are horrifying. Surely they can't all be dismissed by the manufacturers, and the public – and indeed the authorities?"

Dr Henrick exhaled noisily, closed the book, and rose to put it back in its cabinet. "That is the crux of the matter," he said as he sat down again. "How, you ask, can such wholly preventable suffering be permitted to continue in what we think of as a civilised age? Why do the powerful not protect society from these harms? After all, we were able to abolish the evil of slavery, ahead of the rest of the world. But slavery is a clearer issue. It is plainly, absolutely wrong – there are no grey areas to debate. With a chemical such as arsenic, the water is a good deal muddier."

"Because of its use in medicine? Does it really have any medical benefit?"

"Partly that, and yes, it can be prescribed in low doses for ulcers and skin complaints, and many other things besides. In fact it's been used medicinally for hundreds of years. But there are also fraudulent and dangerous treatments, which are easily available. Now this is something that our government may be about to mitigate, in the form of a Bill on which I have been consulted. Restrictions on the ability of pharmacies to sell compounds containing arsenic will, I believe, save many lives."

"In that case," I said, "if you have the ear of members of Parliament, cannot something similar be done for the sale of poisonous wallpaper?"

"And the many other household goods containing arsenic – that is another thing entirely," said Dr Henrick. "Public perception of the chemical needs to change. One of the MPs I spoke to said this to me – I paraphrase: 'Merely crossing the road presents considerable danger, and there is no legislation disallowing all traffic, and so I hardly think that papering a room can be considered more hazardous than that.'"

"Frustrating," I said, "and glib."

"Indeed," said the doctor, "especially when you review the individual tragedies from arsenic hiding in the home. A small child licking flakes of green wallpaper pigment and dying in agony; a whole family perishing after eating a cake whose decorations were coloured with arsenic; men becoming ill from coloured playing cards; babies succumbing to the dye in their nurse's uniform. There are many examples, as you saw in Mr Nesbit's album. And it's entirely unnecessary."

He paused, his lips pursed in disgust, and sighed deeply.

"There are great forces ranged against us," he continued after a moment. "Whole industries depend upon this insidious element. I fear this is a battle that must be fought for many years – a battle in which Mr Lowick promised to be an important foot soldier, resolved as he was to put this issue firmly in the public eye."

He shook his head again. "What a loss. I sympathise with your suspicion of Mr Forrester. I have made several attempts to publicise the problem with arsenic in household decoration and furnishings, including letters to The Telegraph and other papers, and publications in a number of journals, and a couple of lectures. In response, I have received warnings from Forrester's lawyers accusing me of libel and urging me to desist mentioning either their name or the case against arsenical wallpaper in general. But they don't frighten me. I suspect they won't want to start action that brings this issue further to the public's attention. Their weakness is showing."

"Perhaps," I said, "Mr Lowick thought that Forrester would resort to violence if legal recourse were not a viable option. Perhaps that's exactly what happened."

"And that is where we leave the safe ground of hard facts, and enter a dark ocean of speculation," Dr Henrick said. "I can provide you with no evidence of this, I regret to say."

"I understand," I said. "You have already been very

helpful, Dr Henrick. Before I leave, I confess I have another motive for coming to see you. I have a friend who is seriously ill. What Mr Nesbit said made me think she has arsenic poisoning – the doctor thought it was cholera, but seemed unsure."

"I'm sorry to hear it, Mr Rufford. Please describe her symptoms to me."

"Nausea, stomach ache, digestive trouble, bad headaches, drowsiness, dark blotches on her skin. A constriction of her throat. These are the ones I know about, but there might be others."

"I see," said Dr Henrick. "These symptoms are certainly consistent with arsenic poisoning. How long has this been going on?"

"Since last Wednesday – a week."

"A week." Dr Henrick looked thoughtful. "Then she may well recover, in time. A good deal of time, mind. The dose – if it is arsenic – would appear to be moderate. Of course, she would have benefited greatly from an early diagnosis, and action to purge the poison from her body, but it can't be helped. Has anyone else in her household been affected?"

"None," I said, "but she is a guest in a house that has Forrester wallpaper in the drawing room – 'Hedgerow' in green, no less."

"Then it must be removed at once, but carefully. I suggest removing all furniture first, and ensuring no particles from the paper come into contact with the house or anything – or anyone – within it. I hope you can persuade the owner of the urgency of this. And your friend should be moved out until this is completed, and the house and drawing room walls thoroughly cleaned."

"I will advise all this, of course," I said.

"You should get her doctor to examine her again thoroughly in the light of our conversation – tell me if there is any difficulty, and I will write to him. She – and her doctor –

must be made aware that complications of the heart may follow after a week or more of illness. She must not exert herself unduly, even if she starts to feel better."

I nodded.

"Persuade him to have a lock of your friend's hair examined for traces of arsenic. A firm diagnosis is essential."

"Naturally," I said. "Is there anything that can be prescribed?"

Dr Henrick wrote down a few lines in his notebook, and ripped the page out, handing it to me. "There is little treatment at present, but this is what I have prescribed for Mr and Mrs Nesbit. I believe it is helping a little. Hydrated oxide of iron. Plenty of liquid, and chicken broth, or whatever stays down – apart from that, it's just a matter of letting the body purge itself of the poison. I warn you, it could be many weeks, or months – and perhaps years – before your friend's health is restored. In some cases, the patient's former vigour never returns. I'm sorry – I have to give you the extreme bounds of possibility. Each case is different, depending on the patient's constitution, the size of the dose, and other factors we know little about."

"Thank you," I said, pocketing the note. Finally, I might be of real use to Effie.

"Rufford, Rufford, Rufford," Dr Henrick muttered, staring at me and frowning. "That name is very familiar. And you remind me of someone. Who on earth can it be? Ah, now I have it – Dr Charles Rufford! Is he a relation of yours, by any chance?"

"My father," I said.

"Good Lord," Dr Henrick said, gazing at me. "How extraordinary. The likeness is remarkable. It's been many years since I saw him, but I admire his papers on pulmonary congestion, and he was at all the brightest dinner parties in medical circles. Is he still with us?"

"Unfortunately not," I said. "His mind declined, and he

died last year."

"I'm very sorry to hear that," Dr Henrick said. "I regret to say that I would go to my poison cabinet and make myself a final nightcap before I let myself succumb to such a terrible disease. Oh, I'm sorry, that is too morbid of me. Forgive me."

"Of course," I said. "I understand entirely. Here is my card so you can let me know how much I owe you."

"No need for payment," Dr Henrick said. "This has merely been a social call from the son of the great Dr Rufford, and I am therefore much obliged to you. But I will take your card and should any useful information come into my possession, I will write. And we must keep in touch anyway, Mr Rufford, in order to coordinate the fight against the menace of household arsenic."

I bowed. "Indeed we should, sir. I would like to help."

"And please keep me informed of progress finding Mr Lowick, and how your friend is doing. I'm afraid she's a very interesting case – too often, the victim dies immediately. In happier instances, a person recovers quickly. But in some chronic cases such as this, and indeed that of the Nesbits, the poison takes a firm hold for an extended period. It is this class of patient that I am especially preoccupied with. She will be in my prayers – as will Mr Lowick."

CHAPTER TWENTY-TWO

FOR all the grimness of my encounters, I was in better humour on my return trip to Hawksbridge. I now knew the subject of William's investigation, even if I had no direct evidence that Mr Forrester was involved in his disappearance. And I had stumbled upon a more likely diagnosis for Effie, with the prospect, perhaps, of sending her to Dr Henrick for treatment – or I might tempt the doctor to travel to Hawksbridge with an invitation to stay at Ramsburgh. Although he gave the impression that medical expertise currently had little to offer a patient such as Effie, there was always hope of new discoveries in this area. It helped to ease my helpless rage at her condition.

It was early Friday evening when I returned to Ramsburgh, and I was exhausted, but my information could not wait. I immediately fetched Celeste and rode to Halfpenny House.

Francesca was surprised to see me, but not displeased.

"You look exhausted," she said. "Would you like something to eat?"

"That would be extremely welcome," I said. "I'm famished. And then I have important news to tell you. How is Effie?"

"She's a little better, perhaps. Let me organise you some supper – then you can tell me what your mysterious news is, and see Effie."

In the dining room, I gratefully consumed the venison put in front of me, and gulped down my wine. Francesca had eaten, but had a little wine to keep me company.

"That was exquisite. I thought I was going to faint," I

said, wiping my mouth with my napkin.

"So? What did you find out?" Francesca said.

"Effie may be poisoned with arsenic. Perhaps from your Forrester wallpaper. You need to remove it, but carefully."

"Oh, God, no!" she said, clapping a hand over her mouth. "I've poisoned my wonderful guest! Oh, merciful God! But how?"

"It's not at all your fault," I said. "And it's not clear exactly how it happened. But I met a doctor in London who collected arsenic-saturated wallpaper, and your 'Hedgerow' wallpaper was in his album! Forrester is more of a rogue than you knew. And Effie's symptoms are exactly those of arsenic poisoning."

"This is too horrible," Francesca said, struggling to take it all in. "How does this change what we do for Effie?"

I explained Dr Henrick's advice, and showed her the prescription.

"It will embarrass Dr Weldon," she said. "And Dr Drummond."

"They'll get over it," I said. "I'll ride over first thing tomorrow and fetch Dr Weldon. And you should find someone to remove the wallpaper – but it should be assumed that contact between the paper and anything else will leave a residue of poison. It must be done with utmost care. Could Effie be moved while this happens?"

"She's still in pain," said Francesca. "It would be hard to move her, especially downstairs."

"True," I said, weighing up the choices. "I think on balance it would be safer to leave her in her bedroom, given the distance from the drawing room. May I see Effie?"

"Of course," Francesca said. "Sylvie is with her. Send her to me, Thomas, and I will explain to her what you have told me."

~

"Thomas!" Effie said weakly, and to my relief her smile lingered on her face. Previously she had managed only an instantaneous creasing of her pale cheeks. "I haven't seen you for ages. Where have you been?"

"To London," I said. "I've been looking for evidence of William."

"Oh! Did you find any?"

"I understand more about him and what he was doing before he disappeared. It may help. But strangely, I found something out about you."

"Really?"

"I think you've been poisoned, Effie. I don't think it's cholera, or anything like that."

"Oh," she said. "Poisoned? How? What do you mean?"

I explained what I had told Francesca. I regretted being the cause of the confusion written on her face.

"Is this good or bad?" she asked.

"I think it's good that we know more about it – that is, if Dr Weldon confirms the diagnosis. But it may take a while for the poison to leave your body."

"I see," she said. "Well, it makes sense. I certainly feel poisoned. Wallpaper, you say? How peculiar. Why on earth is it allowed?"

"Greed, I'm afraid," I said. "William was writing an article about it. I will do my best to close this awful business down. I'll speak to that villain Forrester as soon as I can. If he doesn't withdraw the papers, I'll do everything in my power to bankrupt the man. And he should compensate everyone who has been harmed by it. God damn the man to Hell!"

Effie smiled again. "You are sweet when you're indignant. Thank you. Oh, but my poor head, it never lets up."

"Shall I get a poultice?" I said, remembering Mr Nesbit's

tender treatment of his wife.

She shook her head. "Francesca said you have a talent... would you mind?"

"Of course I wouldn't," I said, without hesitation. There was no need for moral debate here. I leaned over the bed and delicately massaged Effie's head, until she fell asleep.

~

In the morning, I told Dr Weldon what I had learned, and gave him Dr Henrick's prescription. To his credit, he did not dwell on the implied slight to his professional pride. Instead, he expressed deep concern and set off immediately for Halfpenny House to look at his patient in the light of my findings.

I went on to see Phyllis, and she and her father listened intently to my account.

"Well done, my boy," Dr Drummond said. "I'm sure you're right – I should have seen it. Mea culpa."

"Arsenic seems to be able to mimic various diseases quite convincingly, so no blame should be attached to either you or Dr Weldon," I said.

Dr Drummond shrugged and grunted.

"It's curious that only Effie was affected," said Phyllis. "I assume she wasn't accustomed to licking the drawing room walls!"

"Her methods are eccentric, but perhaps not as eccentric as that," I said. "It's a mystery."

"I have been aware of some instances of arsenic poisoning from wallpaper and furnishings, from the newspapers," said Dr Drummond. "I assumed it was rather rare, and due to inadvertent defects in manufacture. But all this puts things in a different light. What an outrage perpetrated on the health of the nation! What a wretched scandal!" His agitation precipitated a coughing fit.

"Do calm yourself, Papa," Phyllis said. "Let me get you some water."

"Speaking of scandals," Dr Drummond said in a conspiratorial tone when Phyllis was out of the room, "have you seen the ditty doing the rounds in our less salubrious drinking establishments? A friend brought a copy to me. He was amused, but I was not. I'm sorry to say it, but there is talk of it being written about two friends of yours. A cruel thing, I'm afraid."

I frowned. "No, I've heard nothing about this," I said.

"Well, run along to my study and you'll find it in my desk drawer. Try to keep it from my daughter, there's a good fellow – it's a dirty little ballad. But I thought you should be warned. You'll know what to do about it, no doubt. You may keep it."

"Thank you," I said, and walked briskly to Dr Drummond's study and opened the desk drawer. Sure enough, there was a sheet containing a song whose title was 'The Angel and the Captain'. I dreaded to think what disgusting libels were contained within, and after shoving it in my pocket, I went to the water closet to conceal from Phyllis my real reason for leaving the drawing room.

"I need to let Mrs Lowick know about my trip," I said when I returned. "Please excuse the brevity of my visit."

"I'll come with you," said Phyllis. "I need a change of scene."

In the pony trap, I could feel the weight I had recently borne alone becoming less oppressive, and let out an involuntary sigh. Phyllis leaned against me, quietly understanding.

Mrs Beatty opened the door but stood on the doorstep instead of showing us in.

"Mrs Lowick is away for a while – gone to join her sister and the children in Alnwick. Well, there's not much point her moping about here any more, is there? Given the police have failed to find poor William. You haven't found him, have you, Mr Rufford?"

"Alas, no, Mrs Beatty," I said. "But I did find out what he was working on when he disappeared. I just wanted to inform Mrs Lowick – but I'll write, if you can give me the address."

Mrs Beatty went inside to fetch it, and when she came back, she said, "If you don't mind me asking, Mr Rufford – what *was* he working on?"

"Poison," I said. "Specifically, wallpaper containing arsenic pigment, that is sold freely and can cause illness and death. He was going to write about Mr Forrester, amongst others."

"Oh, Lord!" Mrs Beatty said. "No wonder he was nervous. Merciful Lord!"

~

We stood outside Myrtle's, as it was a day on which males were forbidden to enter. I spied Bess inside, and after I waved, she came out.

"Good morning, Bess!" I said. "I'm sorry to be the bearer of bad news, but I'm afraid you will have to take your wallpaper down."

She was shocked at my explanation. "But I've been having these nagging headaches since I decorated. This could be the explanation! Well, how extraordinary. I'll have it removed directly, Thomas, and as carefully as you said. I don't care if customers have to look at bare walls, I'm not having deadly poison in my shop!"

"What will you do about Mr Forrester?" Phyllis said as I took her home. "If you confront him, he will do his best to discredit you. Do we have direct evidence that Effie was poisoned by the wallpaper? Or even by arsenic at all?"

"Dr Weldon will take a sample and have it examined for arsenic," I said. "That should be conclusive, one way or the other. As for the wallpaper... well, it would be an inconceivable coincidence if there were a different source of arsenic, surely?"

"But that's not probably enough to condemn the man," said Phyllis. "At least, not from Effie's case."

"You're right," I said. "I curse the day he set up business here! Not only does he bring deadly, pretty things to seduce us all with, he's an unspeakable..." I stopped, realising that I was about to betray a confidence.

"An unspeakable what?" Phyllis said. "Thomas?"

I hesitated. "Oh, I expect you'll find out soon enough, so I may as well say. He tried to make love to Francesca – against her will, of course – and having been soundly rejected, doubtless harbours a terrible grudge."

"Good God," Phyllis said. "I feel sick."

"And I think he's already taken his revenge." I pulled the sheet out of my pocket and handed it to her. "Your father wanted me to hide it, but I need to discuss these things with you. If not you, then who? Or am I being selfish?"

"No, I want you to be able to talk to me about anything," she said. "Have you read it?"

"No, just the title," I said. "I couldn't bear to. You needn't read it. I can look at it later. Your father said it was a dirty little ballad – I think it's about Francesca and Victor. In which case I don't see any other candidate for the author but Mr Forrester."

"Ah," she said. "Does he know something, or is he speculating?"

"I think he guessed at the truth," I said.

"I see," Phyllis said. "How awful for Flora. Very well, I will read it."

The sound of the pony's hooves seemed magnified as I waited for Phyllis to finish reading. I was pained by her sharp intakes of breath and muttered expostulations: "Oh, Lord," and "Oh, how disgusting," and "The beastly man."

She got to the end, folded it up and stuffed it back in my pocket. After a moment she said, "Well, it's quite as bad as you feared. It's vile, and very obviously meant to be them."

I grimaced. "We shall have to tell Francesca – and Victor – assuming they don't already know. I don't suppose there's anything they can do, without making it worse for themselves. Distributing his bile in song form is cunning, certainly."

"Mr Forrester is a devil come to torture Hawksbridge," Phyllis said. "Is there no limit to the man's mischief?"

"Perhaps we have not yet learnt the worst of it," I said, thinking of William.

~

I headed back to Halfpenny House. Dr Weldon had gone to make up the prescription, and Victor was sitting with his sister.

"That was quick," I said to Francesca at the doorway to the drawing room, looking at the bare walls.

"My decorator was mortified that he had poisoned my home," Francesca said. "So he came immediately. And he did it just as you said, and put it all in sacks. He's off to burn the wretched stuff. Let's go into the little sitting room."

We sat down for coffee, and I wondered how I might introduce the topic of the ballad.

"Oh, blast," Francesca said. "I forgot to get him to take away the spare roll. I thought I might give away samples if my guests were interested – when I was naive and deluded about the god-like Mr Forrester. Now there are at least two reasons I don't want to touch it." She shuddered, pointing to the roll of paper sitting on a bookshelf.

I got up and walked over to it. "It's got a rather untidy

edge. Have you torn a strip off it?"

"No, I don't think so," she said. "I would have used scissors. Let me have a look." She came over. "Yes, how curious! Very messy. I don't remember it being torn like that. Could it be a mouse?"

"It would have to be a huge mouse," I said. "And it would be very dead by now. You would have tripped over it."

"Oh, don't – what a horrid thought!" Francesca said.

I greedily drained my coffee and poured another cup. "What did Dr Weldon say, if I may ask?" I said.

"Of course you may. He was sympathetic to your instinct about it, and took away a lock of Effie's hair. He was embarrassed not to have thought of it himself, naturally, but it's not really what anyone would expect, is it?"

"No. Francesca," I said, putting down my cup, "I have unpleasant news – on top of everything else."

"Oh? How alarming. Well, don't keep me in suspense!"

"It's about Mr Forrester."

"Oh, Lord," she said. "I knew it."

"Well, I assume it's his doing. It's a... song. A bawdy song, about you and Victor."

She sighed. "Just as I feared. Well, not in this precise form, of course."

"It's been turning up at various inns, apparently. Dr Drummond alerted me to it."

Francesca covered her face with her hands. "Oh, wonderful. How excruciatingly embarrassing. I'll never be able to show my face again here, will I?"

"I'm sure it's not that bad. Actually, I haven't read it yet. But Dr Drummond said it was... dirty."

"What? Let's see it, then."

I handed it over, and she scowled over it, emitting the odd bitter laugh.

"Well, well," she said, handing it back. "That settles it. Belle, for Campbell – that's pretty clear. It was nice knowing you, Thomas. I shall have to move to Italy, and be known as the infamous old Englishwoman hiding away in her palazzo, with a scandalous and mysterious past."

"Please don't," I said. "Shall I read it?"

"Be my guest."

I took a sip of coffee – wishing it were something stronger – and with trepidation, read the following verse.

THE ANGEL AND THE CAPTAIN

Young and sweet, with dainty feet, and wings to shame a dove
Belle flew with ease and toiled to please her Master from above
Her sin, it's said: to take to bed the boys and men below
She lost God's trust with dreadful lust that dealt her soul a blow.

And so like this, from kiss to kiss, our angel plied her trade
But careless flings had frayed her wings and youth began to fade.
"Why must I age?" she cried in rage, and God gave this reply:
"Now corrupt and greatly tupped, like mortals, you must die!"

Though once sublime, the marks of time lay deep on Belle's pale cheeks
She found no cheer, no man came near, her pain drew on for weeks
Until at last, to end her fast, she leapt upon a fool
With Captain's dress, and no finesse, but easy with his tool.

"Oh, Captain brave, you must me save," she gasped and bared her breast,
"No time to waste! Be quick, post haste! Please act on my request!"
With great surprise, he stripped his guise, and did his manly best;
He grasped her tight, and used his might, and then he took his rest.

As she lay prone, a wingèd crone, he felt a pang of shame
This feathered prey was old and grey, and not his usual game.
"I do declare, O creature bare, your shrivelled dugs disgust
"But I care naught, it's all in sport, and I must slake my lust."

"Oh, soldier fine," said hag divine, "no army have I spied!"
"Indeed, I fled," the Captain said, "for many men have died.
"I feel no urge to see the surge of blood upon the loam

"I have no heart to play my part; I'd rather stay at home."

Our soldier lad donned all he had and said, "Farewell, dear Belle
"I have in mind a younger bride, and she does love me well."
Belle flutters still, o'er dale and hill, to hook a willing mate
Beware, all youth, of the long in tooth – old Belle has lusts to sate.

"Good God," I said, shaking my head. "What awful dross. I'm sorry."

"Oh well, I suppose I brought it on myself," said Francesca. "I'm not so disgusting to look at, am I?"

"Not in the least," I said. "You are as beautiful as ever."

"Thank you, Thomas. Poor Victor," Francesca said, staring gloomily out of the window. "How I've led him astray. His reputation is ruined, and as for Flora..."

"But Victor and Flora were not betrothed. Yes, Flora will be hurt, but she will forgive you, I know she will. And in time she may forgive Victor. The only person who has truly acted shamefully is the author of this nonsense."

"However did that man find out about us, Thomas?" Francesca wailed. "Surely my staff wouldn't have been so loose-tongued?"

"Or maybe Victor said something indiscreet to a friend," I said, "or Mr Forrester simply guessed, based on how you looked at each other over dinner, and the botanical book."

"Well, whatever the case, Mr Forrester now has his revenge, and the town is laughing at Victor and me."

"I'm sure only the most vulgar people are giving it a second thought," I said. "And those people are beneath you."

"But Mr and Mrs Harris! How could they ever forgive me? Mr Harris is bound to have found this by now. It's too dreadful." Tears began to roll down Francesca's cheeks.

I got up and knelt by her, taking her hands. "Please don't worry," I said. "Those who love you won't turn away because of a snatched moment of happiness. Let me talk to the Harrises. I will explain how you have been a victim of revenge, and they will be sympathetic. All eyes will be on Mr Forrester and his poisonous wallpaper."

"Oh, thank you, my dear Thomas," Francesca said, smiling and wiping away her tears. "Ever-loyal Thomas, despite all the stupid things I've done – and there are so many. I don't deserve you."

CHAPTER TWENTY-THREE

"I ASSURE you, sir," the footman said icily, "that if you don't have an appointment, you will have to return at another time – after you have made an appointment."

"And I assure you," I said, "that I will wait on this doorstep all day if I have to."

"Very well, sir, have it your way," he said, and started to close the door, but someone behind him held it open.

"Who've you got there, Greene?" said a voice I recognised as belonging to Mr Forrester. "Oh, Mr Rufford! What an unexpected pleasure. Your mission must be urgent for you to call without notice on a Sunday afternoon. Let him in, Greene, let him in."

The scowling footman stepped out of the way to let me into the hall.

"Welcome to my home, Mr Rufford. I designed it myself – I would be glad of your opinion."

I had to grudgingly admit that Forrester had done a good job. Contrary to contemporary practice, where a coherent, unified design was preferred, it was built in a variety of styles, mimicking the organic growth of older houses with wings that spawned further wings, in a variety of materials and with different roof heights. It was a house that kept one guessing, and defied immediate judgement.

"It's highly unusual, Mr Forrester. I like the variety of forms."

"Good, good," he said, looking around the grand, panelled hall with pride. "I wanted a house that avoided grandstanding, a sin of which too many of our brash young architects are guilty. And I love the old traditions and styles. It would have been easier to draw a dull box, and simpler still for my builder. But I'm always suspicious of a task that is too easy! My detractors throw the word 'pastiche' at me, but they are simply envious that I have freed myself from convention."

"The result, I have to say, is charming," I said, trying to separate in my mind the building from the man.

"Thank you. Let's go into my study – the perfect room for tête-à-têtes." He directed me across the polished hall floor along a corridor that connected the main, Elizabethan portion of the building to a wing of classical appearance. It passed as the civilized home of a squire from the middle of the last century, and the furnishings were in keeping.

My host gestured at an armchair. "Would you like a glass of port? Or are you a sherry man?" he said.

"Neither, thank you," I said.

"As you wish. I'll have one myself, if you don't mind."

He poured himself a drink, and sat down opposite me.

"Now then, Mr Rufford," he said. "You seem agitated. What did you want to speak to me about?"

I cleared my throat. "Have you no qualms about selling wallpaper containing the deadly poison arsenic?"

To my surprise, he looked relieved.

"Oh!" he said, and swigged some port. "Is that all? I imagined a different topic entirely."

"What would that be, Mr Forrester?" I said.

"Nothing of consequence, I'm sure. So, arsenic. My papers are perfectly safe, Mr Rufford. I wouldn't be selling them otherwise, would I?"

"That is the assumption that your customers make, and which works in your favour," I said. "And yet people are being poisoned all the time, and you know it perfectly well."

"Do I, Mr Rufford? All I know is that a handful of people have made entirely spurious and unproven allegations. It is a disagreeable reality for anyone who has tried to improve the world by means of manufacturing, that not everyone will be grateful. Some desire to censure those who dare to dream – yes, even a few of my fellow socialists, who conflate the roar of the machine with the worst excesses of capitalism. The two are not permanent and necessary bedfellows. At the risk of boring you with philosophy, Mr Rufford: as I have expounded upon in my essay 'The Machinery of Socialism', there must be a phase when industry is in the hands of men such as myself, before a transformed society takes the reins."

He refilled his glass and continued. "But I digress. In short, there are plenty who wish to discredit me. And they will do it in any way possible."

"You mean, by becoming mortally sick?" I said. "That would be tremendously committed of them."

He laughed. "No, of course not. These people are already sick, in mind and body, and are casting around for someone to blame, or someone to pay for their treatment. Shocking stories sell newspapers, so of course these poor attention-seekers make up a cock-and-bull story about wallpaper making them ill."

"But you don't deny there is arsenic in some of your papers?"

"I don't deny it," he said. "I simply deny that it poses a risk in normal use. If you were to eat a diet of it, that would not be healthy. Naturally. But one would need to consume a great deal of it, given there is such a tiny amount in the pigment. Anything can be abused, Mr Rufford. You can use a knife for food preparation, or you can stab yourself to death with it. You can use a brick to make a house, or you can drop it on someone's head, or your own. But it is madness to curtail progress just because there is a handful of fools in the world who are determined to injure themselves, or assign blame spuriously."

"It seems that you don't need to eat the paper to succumb to arsenic poisoning, Mr Forrester. I have recently met a couple – known to you – who are severely ill from merely touching the paper, and their daughter died from it."

Mr Forrester made a dismissive gesture. "I highly doubt it."

I pressed on. "And others have become ill from merely being in rooms decorated with your paper, and their health has been restored by leaving their homes."

"Hearsay, sir, hearsay and hysteria. There are a hundred things that could account for such stories."

"And in your mines," I continued, "the rate of sickness is well documented, and heinous. Do you deny that as well?"

"I appreciate your concern, Mr Rufford, but I really don't have to be accountable to you. All industry involves a certain amount of risk. It has always been this way – it is how human society progresses. There are far more dangerous occupations – for example, building the railway to Hawksbridge that you will one day enjoy – and I'm not forcing anyone to labour in my mine."

"But you must see, sir, that arsenic is a highly toxic chemical to be introducing into a household. And all for a slightly brighter shade of green or blue! How can that possibly be worth the risk?"

"The public demands it, Mr Rufford. What the public wants, the public gets. And besides, we are not standing still. We are developing new arsenic-free pigments that are nearly as vivid."

I had not expected to hear this. "So you admit there is a problem with your arsenic-based pigments?"

He shrugged. "Removing the need for arsenic will reduce costs. I'll be able to divest myself of the mine that so offends you. And not having to waste time with baseless reports in the newspapers will be no bad thing either."

He took another swig of his port, and looked at his pocket watch, as though I was wearying him.

"But why the sudden interest, Mr Rufford? What exactly has brought you to my door on a Sunday afternoon? I think

I'm missing part of the puzzle."

"Two reasons," I said. "A friend living in a house containing your 'Hedgerow' paper has been struck down by probable arsenic poisoning. And the other reason is William Lowick."

I paused to examine Mr Forrester's reaction, but all I saw was blankness.

"The missing journalist?" he said. "I'm sorry, I don't follow. What does he have to do with me? Have they found the poor fellow yet?"

"I thought you might be acquainted with him," I said, hoping to elicit some signal that he knew more than he was saying.

"No, I never had that honour," Mr Forrester said. "Why did you think I had?"

"He was interested in cases of arsenic poisoning. Not least due to paper from your factory."

Light visibly dawned. "Oh!" he said, laughing heartily. "Oh, my Lord. You think I had something to do with Mr Lowick's disappearance. Is that it? You believe I'm a cold-blooded murderer, trying to prevent a journalist from sullying my reputation. God in Heaven, but you're a funny one. Anyway, haven't they already got someone for that?"

"Yes, but I don't think for one moment the police have the right man."

"Well, even supposing you're correct, I assure you that journalists don't bother me. I've fended off plenty of scurrilous accusations, and he wouldn't worry me unduly. Well, now I see what's going on. You're doing your little detective routine! I'm sorry to disappoint you, Mr Rufford, but you're thoroughly misguided. You need to let the police handle Mr Lowick's disappearance. I'm afraid you're well out of your depth here."

I did not care to be patronised by this man, who was undoubtedly responsible for much misery – and probably for the dirty ditty. And I still regarded him as my main suspect. But at this moment, I was firmly and infuriatingly on the back foot.

"Thank you for your time, Mr Forrester," I said, rising. "I think it only fair to let you know that I will be doing all I can to publicise the harm that your wallpaper does." I was, perhaps, making a target of myself, but not much more than I had already done in querying the ethics of his manufacturing process.

"And I will robustly defend myself, as you would expect, Mr Rufford. What a shame we cannot be friends – our acquaintance started so promisingly at Mrs Campbell's!"

How dare he mention Francesca's name? The man was beyond the pale.

~

As I returned from my futile mission to admonish Mr Forrester, I spotted Flora in the garden, pacing the south lawn with her head bowed. She came over to me as I was dismounting.

When she had come closer, I saw she had tears in her eyes.

"My poor sister!" I said, taking her hand and squeezing it. "Is it about the ballad?"

She nodded. "I have made a perfect fool of myself with Victor," she said. "How did I ever think he would respect me? I should have known that a soldier could not be trusted. I'm so furious with myself for lavishing my feelings on such an unworthy man!"

"I'm not surprised you're angry," I said. "Victor has been thoughtless and selfish. And Francesca is desperately upset with herself for hurting you. But it was just a brief flicker of a candle. You and Victor have the potential for being a roaring log fire, burning year after year."

Flora smiled at my metaphor. "But how do I know the candle won't burn for other women?"

"You can't, for sure," I said. "But if you build a strong enough alliance, you will get through whatever life hurls in your path. Even untidy, unwanted emotions. Victor loves you desperately – I can see it in his eyes."

"So why did he need Francesca?"

"He didn't need her – she was just a bauble that he reached out for. I recognise that unruly greed for sensuality in myself. Yes, he will need to curb that side of him, as I have struggled to. But I truly believe that you will show him that you are all he needs."

"I don't know," she said, stroking Celeste's neck. "But thank you."

"Has he tried to apologise?"

"Yes. I'm afraid I was rather rude. He did seem genuinely repentant... but I just can't open myself up to being hurt like that. Not again. First Henry, now Victor. I was living perfectly happily before I let my guard down."

"Perhaps not perfectly happily," I said. "You have to risk your heart. Everyone must – the potential prize is surely worth it!"

She shrugged. "I'll see how I feel in a few days. At present, I never want to see him again."

"I know. It's a platitude, but time is a great healer."

"I hope that applies to poor Effie," Flora said. "It's frightening seeing her so weak. But at least she has a proper diagnosis now. I went over this afternoon. Dr Weldon says that her hair confirms it – arsenic!"

~

Although I had suspected that my encounter with Mr Forrester was likely to be unproductive, it had still left me bruised and without a route to pursue my suspicion of him. Perhaps he had been right, and I was out of my depth. His claim not to have met William was at present hard to disprove. But Gabriel Forrester had been evasive and dismissive about the dangers of his wallpaper and his arsenic mine, which signified a chilling ruthlessness in the man.

I went to see Effie again the following day. She was still weak, but in better spirits.

"The pain in my head and stomach seems a little reduced," she said, slowly sitting up. "And I have even started to dream of music again."

"That is wonderful news!" I said, clasping her hand momentarily. "You'll be conducting your second symphony in no time."

"Perhaps not soon," Effie said. "But the fact that I believe it to be possible at all..."

I smiled. "It's all very encouraging. If Dr Weldon were here, he would probably caution you against overdoing it."

"I have no intention of doing that," Effie said, "while I can lie here and get everyone to dance attendance on me! How are Hu and Pru?"

"They are in fine fettle," I said. "And Hu is in excellent voice."

"Oh, good. They have been in my head. They have a melody each. I so look forward to seeing them again in Ramsburgh. Will you invite me to supper? Is that outrageous of me to ask?"

"Not at all," I said. It was heartening that Effie was planning small, pleasant things for when she was stronger. "Consider yourself invited. We shall have a grand time."

"We shall," she said, closing her eyes and smiling. "We shall."

~

"What an unspeakable man," Francesca said after I had described my visit to Mr Forrester. "And to think I gushed over him like a little girl. Ugh. How are we to get him to stop selling his poisonous wallpaper?"

"I'll speak to The Herald," I said. "An article is in order, to finish William's work."

"Are you sure they will want to open themselves up to the risk of litigation?"

"Then I'll find someone who will. If necessary, I will print it myself and put copies through everyone's door."

"And I'll help you," said Francesca. "We'll wander the country in our donkey cart, like itinerant preachers, declaiming in the market places."

"It may come to that," I said. "It would certainly be a good test of our friendship."

"Perhaps it would help wash away some of my many sins," Francesca said.

And tempt me into some, I thought, imagining nights in seedy inns, forced into an intimate existence, and drowsy from a day's agitation and the local ale.

This entirely inappropriate fantasy was interrupted by the arrival of Sylvie into the little sitting room.

"Mr Rufford – pardon, but might I please speak with you?"

"Of course," I said, and waited for her to continue, but she did not.

After a moment she said, "I will be in my room, if you could come when it is convenient."

"Oh – yes, I'll be up in a minute."

She nodded, and left.

"Well!" Francesca said. "That's interesting. I suppose she's lacking the affection she knew previously. Careful,

Thomas!"

"That is a terrible aspersion," I said with a smile. "I'm sure it's nothing like that. I will go and see what she wants. Perhaps she has remembered something about the night Effie became unwell. Excuse me."

I went upstairs and knocked on her door.

"Please come in," Sylvie said. She was standing anxiously by the window, fidgeting, and when she turned towards me, I could see that she had been crying.

"Miss Dubois – what's wrong?" I said as gently as I could. "What's troubling you?"

"Mr Rufford," she said after a moment, with trembling lip, "I have not been entirely truthful with you. I was afraid. I am a very bad person."

"I'm sure you had your reasons," I said. "But you want to speak now, which surely makes you a good person."

Sylvie shook her head. "I don't deserve that kindness. It is all my fault."

"I'm sure it can't be," I said. "What is your fault, exactly?"

"You must not tell anyone else," she said. "Please. If I tell you, you must not speak a word to anyone. I could not bear to tell you this if... other people were to know."

"Very well," I said, although I had misgivings about keeping her secrets. "I won't repeat what you tell me."

"Effie," she said, wiping a runaway tear from her cheek. "If it were not for me, Effie would not be sick."

"I cannot believe you meant any harm to her. How could it have been your fault?"

She started pacing up and down the room. "It was not camomile tea, you see. It was a herb tea I was given especially for Effie. For her nerves."

I easily guessed to whom she was referring. "By Miss Knowles?"

She nodded. "She gave one little bag for me, and one for Effie. She said she had prepared them especially for each of our constitutions, and that Effie was in need of herbs to bring her serenity and peace of mind. So I was eager to try it, so she would be less fâchée... less angry with me."

She blew her nose.

"It has been very difficile – she is so brilliant, yet demands so much. I wanted her to be calm, for a little while at least. And how could I know there would be anything wrong with the tea? It must be a mistake, an accident – it must be!"

"You are not to blame for this, Miss Dubois," I said. "You were not to know what the tea contained. Is there any left?"

"It was just a small amount," she said. "Just enough for one cup each."

"That is a little suspicious," I said. "It's unusual to only –"

"Oh, I know, Mr Rufford, I know! I know it looks strange, but I still can't believe Rachel would mean any harm to Effie. Why would she? Rachel was kind to me. She is not a bad woman. It must have been an accident."

"Perhaps," I said. "Perhaps not. You had become good friends with Rachel, I think?"

She sniffed. "Oui."

"Perhaps... there was a particularly intense aspect to this friendship?"

She looked at me with an expression of denial, but then gave up and shrugged her shoulders.

"So Rachel could have been jealous of your relationship with Effie, and angry that Effie had treated you harshly, as she saw it. Perhaps it seemed to Rachel that you were Effie's slave. And of course Effie was outspoken in her antipathy to the Society."

She stopped pacing. "Mon dieu!" she exclaimed, a look of horror on her face. "You cannot possibly think this."

"I hope it's not the case," I said. "But perhaps you were beginning to suspect it, which is why you have come to me."

Sylvie nodded. "There is something else." She went to the

coffer at the bottom of the bed, rummaged around in it, and took out an object covered in a linen wrapper and heavily fastened with string. She handed it to me.

"I don't know what's in it," she said. "But Rachel asked me to fetch it from Mrs Milburn's house, and keep it for her. I thought it was a little strange, but I didn't mind. And I enjoyed talking with Mrs Milburn. I taught her the song, and we had a nice afternoon."

"Mrs Milburn knew you had come for this object?"

"Yes, she had been asked to give it to me. She didn't say what it was."

"And now you think there may be something... not quite right about it?"

She nodded and said, "I... I am afraid about it. I have been worrying about what it is. Rachel said I must not open it, but if asked, to say I had found it under a hedge. And I must not mention Mrs Milburn, or Rachel, or something bad would happen to them."

"I'm afraid this rather confirms my suspicions about Miss Knowles," I said, turning the object over. "You were right to talk to me – thank you."

"I'm so sorry," Sylvie said, her eyes filling with tears. "I should have said before. But it was all so confusing."

I realised that I preferred this version of Sylvie to the one I had known. The old Sylvie appeared to me taciturn and hard to read; the Sylvie in front of me was open, vulnerable, passionate, and regretful – in a word, human.

"What's done is done," I said. "The important thing is to understand the situation, and make everything as right as it can be. We need to open this package."

"Yes – let me find scissors," she said.

The string was duly snipped, and with some trepidation I unfolded the linen wrapper. I immediately recognised the object within.

"Oh, my God," I said, recoiling. "Oh, no."

Sylvie was alarmed. "Why do you say that?" she said. "What does it mean?"

I picked up the pocket watch. "It belongs to – or belonged to – William Lowick," I said. "You can see from the engraving. I have even held it before – William dropped it, and I picked it up."

"So why did Mrs Milburn have it?" Sylvie said. "And why did Rachel want me to have it?"

I thought for a moment. "I don't know why it was in Mrs Milburn's possession, but it's a dangerous object to own, and Rachel probably didn't want it in her home. If it was found in your possession, she could deny ever having seen it. You could even act as a decoy."

Sylvie shook her head. "How can people be like that?" she said quietly. "Tell me, how?"

It occurred to me that this was a particularly hard blow for someone who was not accustomed to trusting people. Her faith in Miss Knowles had been horribly turned against her, and it could damage her greatly in future.

"I assure you, Miss Dubois, that this is not usual. Most people are not like this. You have been badly used – but not everyone will let you down, as you know from Effie."

"Thank you, Mr Rufford," she said. "I know it from you too."

"Let me take this watch and keep it at Ramsburgh. If Miss Knowles has any scheme to incriminate you, we will avoid that. I will respect your wishes for the moment, Miss Dubois, and keep your confidences, but there will come a time when I have to tell the police. I will first make my own enquiries, before Inspector Simmons blunders in." I put the watch in my pocket.

She nodded. "I understand." She came around from the opposite side of the bed, which I speculated she had been using as a shield. "Thank you."

To my surprise, she suddenly flung her arms about me.

"Thank you," she repeated, tightening her hold. "I will try to be a better person for Effie. I love her so much."

"I know," I said, returning her embrace. "And she loves you. Everything will work out for the best."

CHAPTER TWENTY-FOUR

AS I RETURNED to Ramsburgh with Miss Knowles' address and William's watch, I wondered about her motives. Could she really have wanted to harm Effie? Effie's outburst would have humiliated her – it must hurt to be called a shrew, after all. And if Miss Knowles and Sylvie had effectively been conducting an affair behind Effie's back, then emotions would be running high. It may be that Miss Knowles had only intended to make Effie a little sick, and would have been horrified to learn how close Effie had come to death.

But then there was the watch. William's cigar case had turned up, and now his watch. What was Mrs Milburn doing with it, and why had it ended up with Sylvie? Had Mrs Milburn been involved in William's disappearance after all, and was Miss Knowles trying to protect her by removing incriminating evidence? So why not keep the watch herself, or dispose of it? It was odd.

I knew that by rights, I should turn over the watch and my knowledge of the case to the police. But by violating my promise to Sylvie, she and Mrs Milburn would suffer greatly. And the police would probably draw the wrong conclusion again.

No, I would have to take on the responsibility for following wherever this evidence led. I shivered at the seriousness of this duty as Celeste carried me up the drive to Ramsburgh. Mr Forrester's words still rang in my ears: "You're well out of your depth here!" It was essential that I prove him wrong.

I knew I must interview both Miss Knowles and Mrs Milburn, but first I went to my little study and began to write two letters. The first was to Mrs Lowick, to inform her of the current state of my investigation, minus the reappearance of the watch, news of which would be more distressing than enlightening.

The second was to Lady Fairfield. I recounted my visit to London, a subject I felt sure was of interest to her as a philanthropist. Perhaps she would even be able to help my campaign against Mr Forrester. I also hinted that I had information about some eccentric behaviour on the part of Miss Knowles. I hoped that since the two were apparently friends, this might flush out further facts, without having to reveal exactly what I knew. There was a chance that Lady Fairfield, with her considerable connections, would reveal some small thing that would make sense of the current jumble of clues.

As I went downstairs with my letters, I heard sounds of raised voices in the hall.

"It is imperative that I see Miss Davison!"

"I'm sorry, sir," said Shipley, "but as I said, she's not seeing anyone today."

"You mean she's not seeing *me*?" Victor demanded. "That's what you mean, isn't it?"

"I'm afraid there's nothing I can do, sir."

"Ah, Thomas!" Victor said as he caught sight of me. "Please won't you make Flora relent and talk to me, if only for a minute? I'm going insane."

"I can try," I said, "but perhaps you and I should speak first. It seems a long time since we had a proper conversation." I wanted to put him at his ease, knowing how much he must be suffering, even if it was his own fault.

I could see a little relief in his eyes to be saved from total humiliation and ejection from the house. "Good idea, my friend – good idea," he said. "I would like that."

He followed me into my larger study, and I poured us a brandy each.

"I owe you an apology, Thomas," he said, looking bleakly into his glass. "You warned me, and foolishly I didn't listen. Instead I listened to... well, baser voices. I would complain about the difficulties of being a hot-blooded man confronted by temptation, but I know that would be to derogate from my own responsibility." He sighed and took some brandy. "I am deeply ashamed that I hurt your sister. She is so wonderful, and I have destroyed any chance I may have had with her." His gave me a mournful look. "And also, perhaps, my best chance of happiness in life. We had a rare meeting of minds."

"It may not be as bad as all that," I said. "You will have to give her time. She's wounded – but she will recover, and she may then see that forgiveness is the best course. That is," I added, "if you feel that you can master yourself in future."

Victor put his glass down, perhaps as a symbol of abstinence, and turned towards me.

"If Flora honoured me with her hand, then yes – I will swear as many oaths as she wants to never touch another woman. I know how empty such brief dalliance is. It is corrosive to the soul."

I could not help smiling. "I hope Francesca never hears that," I said.

Victor ran his hand through his hair. "Well, you know what I mean, Thomas. I'm not saying Francesca wasn't pleasant to be with. Of course she was. But the pleasure wasn't worth losing Flora for – and the disgrace of all concerned. I'm an ass."

"How many times has this been repeated in history?" I said. "Nature seems to delight in tormenting us with our own desires."

"Yes," Victor said, taking up his glass again. "No wonder the world is filled with devils and gods, pulling at our marionette strings as if we lacked control over ourselves. It's easier to believe that than take responsibility."

"The unfortunate ballad – will you do anything about it?"

I asked.

He shrugged. "I'm not sure it's worth the bother. As Forrester has no doubt calculated, making a fuss will only make me – and Francesca – look more stupid. I must say, though, it's a capital means of revenge. I might even find it amusing, were it about some other pair of unfortunates. It's annoying to think he will get away with it, of course. Perhaps I should concoct my own counter-revenge."

"I intend to make him pay for his use of poison," I said. "You may consider that sufficient retribution."

"Let's drink to that!" Victor said, raising his glass.

"And I will talk to Flora, and try to persuade her to see you."

Victor transferred his glass to his left hand. "Thomas," he said solemnly as he shook my hand, "you are a true and honourable friend, and I don't know how I will repay you."

~

It had been a while since I had visited Flora's lodgings; she had framed one of her sketches for the Town Hall mural and it now faced the window, adding a welcome sense of drama. I had forgotten how chilly the north-facing sitting room could be. The May warmth had failed to permeate the massive stone walls of the tower. I felt she deserved a better home, one filled with the sound of children, and sunshine flooding through French windows. It was all the more important that she make up with Victor.

"He's in agony, the poor devil," I said. "Could you not bear to just listen to what he has to say?"

"I already have," she said. "I don't know what a further discussion would change. He made his choice, and now he has to live with it."

I had hoped that by now she would be in a forgiving mood, but her heart seemed to have hardened.

"I understand how hurtful his behaviour has been," I said. "No one is defending it, least of all him. But are you just punishing him to make a point? If you carry on, you risk pushing him away for ever. I don't believe that's what you really want."

"What I want," Flora said, "is not to be taken advantage of. Not to be picked up and tossed away like a... like some unwanted book."

"Yes, Victor made the mistake of opening the covers of another book," I said, and Flora grimaced. "But he's barely got past the introduction of your book, and he wants to carry on reading, and re-reading, forever!"

She fiddled with the piece of embroidery in her hand. "Do you think so? Could I ever trust him again?"

"Victor has had a shock. He has seen his reflection in a piece of humiliating doggerel, and he doesn't like it. He is aware he must change. Isn't it better to have all this happen now, rather than later? Might Mr Forrester even have done you a favour, in an odd way? You can both see clearly now."

She frowned. "Well, it's a point I hadn't considered. How on earth have you managed to make a virtue of his awful lapse, Thomas? I congratulate you!"

"So you might grant him an audience?"

"Oh, I suppose so," she said. "If only to stop my brother nagging at me."

~

The next day, I failed to speak to either of my quarries. Mrs Milburn, her housekeeper told me disapprovingly, had gone to stay at Kirkheaton Hall for a few days.

"I suppose it's a kind of retreat," she had said, "where they learn to be good little campaigners. I don't think she was well enough, Mr Rufford – she is still too easily led. I don't like it, I don't mind telling you. But she insisted, and I'm not a prison guard."

At the house belonging to Miss Knowles' brother, where she stayed, the housekeeper gave me similar, although vaguer, news.

"She comes and goes, and no one can guess when she'll be here. No, I don't know where she's gone. You can try tomorrow, sir, if you want, but" – she shrugged – "who knows?"

"Not even her brother?" I asked.

"Not even him," she said. "Especially not him," she added, hinting at a difficult relationship between the pair.

I returned, irritated, to a letter from Lady Fairfield, marked 'PRIVATE & URGENT'.

Kirkheaton Hall, May 15th, 1849

Dear Mr Rufford,

I was glad to hear from you, even though your news was serious. Thank you for your descriptions of Mr Forrester's worrying business – we must discuss this further and decide how we can confront him together about the scourge of arsenic.

I too have solemn news, which I cannot fully impart in this letter. I am afraid you are in grave danger, in relation to Miss Knowles, who after an unsettling conversation has gone away. Mr Rufford, I fear for your safety if you stay at your home tonight.

I know this will appear strange, but will you please do me the honour of coming to Kirkheaton Hall as soon as you receive this letter? You must prepare for a few days' stay, and tell no one of your destination. In fact, it would be better to indicate that you are going on a trip for a while – I am sure you will be able to think of a plausible story.

Again, you will find this request odd, even perturbing: but please trust me that I have good reason. If I turn out to be mistaken, then you may berate me. But rather that than a terrible alternative. You will be comfortable in my home, and we shall have excellent discussions, I know it. Also, Mrs Milburn is currently staying, and she speaks highly of you – she will be delighted to have a little of your company.

I will arrange for a carriage to pick you up at your gates, both today (Tuesday) and, in case this letter does not reach you in time, tomorrow, at 9pm.

I look forward to welcoming you into my home, albeit in unusual circumstances!

Yours,

Esme Fairfield

I read and re-read the letter. Unusual circumstances, indeed! It seemed Lady Fairfield knew of a plot against me by the very woman I suspected of being a poisoner, and perhaps even involved in William's disappearance.

After a little thought, I found that I was not averse to staying – no doubt in some comfort – in a spectacular country home, discussing philosophy, perhaps, and the issues of our times. I would hear first-hand about Lady Fairfield's famous Society, and possibly advance my investigation into William's death and Effie's poisoning. The fact that she was willing to help campaign against arsenic wallpaper was the icing on the cake.

Deceiving my friends and staff was not so appealing, but they would no doubt understand later if my safety was at stake.

I packed a leather travelling bag, and – feeling a little queer about it – told Flora, Shipley and Mrs Felton I had further business with Dr Henrick in London. Since the coach to Newcastle started early, I would stay overnight in Hawksbridge. Shipley seemed a little puzzled about this, especially when I mentioned that my carriage to Hawksbridge would pick me up at the gates and not at the door, but he did not query it.

When I got to the Ramsburgh gates at a little before nine o'clock, the weather had turned foul, and I was quickly drenched, despite my coat and wideawake hat. As the minutes passed with no sign of transport, I was beginning to think I had been the victim of a stupid practical joke, when the dark shape of a carriage hove into view through the rain and stopped by me.

I could only see the rough shape of the caped driver, who remained silent, and there was no boy to open the door for me, so I let myself in. I had been expecting Lady Fairfield's glamorous, liveried carriage so the battered brougham was a disappointment. But it was, admittedly, discreet.

It was peculiar to be jolting through the countryside in the gloaming on a secret journey to a mysterious house party, hosted by an eccentric female campaigner. I was both apprehensive and excited, feeling that any discomfort would be rewarded by an addition to my life's experiences and the gathering of valuable information. The fact that I was avoiding some unspecified threat to my life seemed almost secondary.

After about half an hour, we turned into a drive flanked by stone gateposts of prodigious size. As we drove up to the house, the view was initially blurred by the rain running copiously down the carriage windows, but the sheer scale of the building was immediately evident.

A large central block was flanked by long colonnaded wings perpendicular to the main building, forming three sides of a square. As I got out and made my way up the flight of steps to the door, I looked up at the windowed, pedimented structure that capped the house, and thought it gave the impression of a Roman temple perched on the building. On either side of the front door stood a pair of massive columns, and each corner of the main block had a tower topped with a stone balcony.

It was impressive and ornate, but I could not call it a beautiful building. I had found that some large houses managed to convey a lightness of tone that made me forget its method of construction, but here there was no mistaking the sheer weight of masonry, whether by fault of the overall design or of the rustication. Kirkheaton Hall was frankly lumpish. Still, no doubt it was a wonder of its day, which by my estimation was during the early part of the last century.

My carriage and its ghost-like driver had moved on, and for a moment I was alone on the steps with my bag, in a stony, shadowy landscape barely illuminated by the moon. Then one of the doors opened, and a footman let me into a huge hall. It was dimly lit by oil lamps, but I could make out two rows of alcoves, the upper ones containing statues, and again I seemed to have been cast back to the Roman era, standing, perhaps, in the mausoleum of a distinguished governor.

The footman took my case. "Follow me, Mr Rufford, please – Lady Fairfield has retired, but she will receive you in the morning." The voice was feminine, and I realised I had been mistaken – the footman was a footwoman, with shortish hair in a masculine style. I wondered if my driver had also been female.

My guide took me to a staircase built into a tower, like a far grander version of Flora's stair tower at Ramsburgh, but where each step seemed to float without support, each slightly overlapping the step below it. Looking up, I could see it spiralling implausibly heavenward, and it also looped down into the bowels of the house. I felt giddy and gripped the ornate iron banister as I ascended.

On the first floor, we navigated a corridor before finally my guide opened a door, and we entered a large room adorned with tapestries which I could see only dimly by the light of the three candles that my guide lit for me.

"You'll find a jug of water, here, sir," she said, putting my bag down, "and I will bring you breakfast in the morning at half past seven. Then you will see her Ladyship at nine o'clock."

"Thank you," I said, wondering if I should ask her name before thinking better of it. I had formed the impression that anonymity was a prized quality here. "Where might I find the... er –"

"The water closet? Down the corridor this way," she said, pointing, "and it's the door on the left."

"Thank you," I said. "Good night."

"Good night, sir."

She was gone, and I was left to survey my bed, which was substantial and intricately carved. I suddenly felt exhausted, as if this monumental house had overwhelmed me, and was happy to make use of the afore-mentioned facility before quickly falling into bed and a deep slumber.

CHAPTER TWENTY-FIVE

I WAS awakened by my guide from last night, who brought me a welcome tray of toast, a couple of eggs, and coffee. She drew the curtains – I could not decide if this was a rebuke at my still being in bed, or a kindness that showed a warmer side for the first time.

For a moment, as she turned, her profile was charmingly illuminated by the bright morning sunshine, and it struck me what a strange footman she made. She was in her late twenties and pretty, with a slightly melancholy expression. Her voice conveyed a more refined upbringing than might have been expected, and altogether she looked as though she were a wife in a Restoration farce taking the guise of a servant for some foolish necessity of the plot. She was handsome in her trousers, yellow waistcoat, and tailcoat.

Hang it, I thought to myself, she is a person, not just a servant, and I should be able to address her properly. "I'm sorry, I don't know your name," I said.

"Oh – Thanes, sir," she said, looking surprised to be asked.

The name hardly became her. "Have you been working here long, Miss Thanes?"

"It's not really work, sir," she said. "I came to help Lady Fairfield – about a year ago. It gave me a purpose and freed me from – well, my difficult life. We don't really distinguish between work for the Society, and work for her Ladyship. I'm content to do both – I get board and lodging, a little money, and the knowledge that I'm useful."

"What an extraordinary thing," I said. "Well, thank you for this breakfast – it looks excellent."

She nodded and left, casting a look back at me as though I were a curiosity. Perhaps I was – after all, Lady Fairfield obviously preferred to be surrounded by women. She was living by her cause, and the strength of commitment impressed me.

I wondered what Miss Thanes – I could not think of her simply as 'Thanes' – had meant by her difficult former life. I surmised that she had been born into a genteel family, which had then fallen on hard times, perhaps necessitating immoral or at least arduous work. And then she had been rescued and swept up by Lady Fairfield and her exciting movement, becoming a loyal and grateful 'wasp', as William might have put it.

I smiled at the thought of William visiting this house, and encountering Miss Thanes. He would no doubt have been impressed by her poise, her beauty – and her unattainability. Her masculine attire might also have been alluring for him. I thought I might ask Miss Thanes about William. It would be interesting to hear how he had behaved at Kirkheaton Hall, when he had visited to research his article on the Society. Had he thoroughly charmed Lady Fairfield? Would I be a disappointment to her in comparison? I felt an obligation to live up to the grandeur of all this. But, I reminded myself, my task was to find any tidbit of information I could that illuminated William's disappearance and Miss Knowles' behaviour, not to be a court jester. No doubt the first thing I would discover was the nature of the conspiracy that required me to take sanctuary here in the first place.

At nine o'clock, Miss Thanes knocked on the door and took me down the corkscrew staircase, through several anterooms and into the grand drawing room, which was hung with family portraits and a painted ceiling resplendent with naked nymphs and satyrs.

Lady Fairfield was sitting on a sofa by a monumental stone fireplace, surrounded by three King Charles spaniels. She put down her book as I came in.

"Mr Rufford! How good of you to respond to my peculiar missive. It is a pleasure to welcome you to Kirkheaton. I trust you slept well?"

"Good morning, Lady Fairfield," I said. "Yes, and breakfast was excellent. You have a well-ordered household – and an astonishing home."

"Ah, I knew you would be tactful," she said, smiling. "Always the gentleman. I am aware the house is not, at first glance, the most lovely in the world. However, it has a charm that becomes apparent after some familiarity. Here, come and sit."

I took my place on a French upholstered armchair opposite her, and her spaniels sniffed at my ankles.

"I confess when I first came here," she continued, "as a naive young bride, the place oppressed me. It always struck me as a masculine house – grandiose and unyielding. A female architect would never have countenanced such a design, not being prone to the delusions of male self-conceit."

"No doubt the family demanded something grand and impressive," I said. "And in that the building succeeds with great aplomb. I look forward to seeing more if it – if I may."

"Of course! I will give you a tour, but not before we have had coffee. Thanes, if you please!"

Miss Thanes had been standing by the door, anticipating instruction, and she nodded and left.

"Now then," she said, scratching the head of one of her spaniels, "your letter. I was appalled to hear about Mr Forrester's wallpaper – I had formed a high regard for him, as a designer of no small genius, and a generous supporter of the Society. And indeed, as a political philosopher. What can he be thinking, exposing the public to arsenic? I was sorry to hear about Miss Harris. Is she improved?"

"Thank you – yes, a little, but it seems to be a very slow and painful recovery." Happy though I was to hear Lady

Fairfield condemn Mr Forrester, I could not help thinking that it was absurd that we were conversing as though there had been no mortal threat to me.

"Lady Fairfield," I said, "might I inquire about the reason you feared for my safety?"

"Oh, silly me," she said. "Of course you must be wondering about that. Well, I'm afraid you will think me very simple-minded. It was all an awful misunderstanding – there was a little unpleasantness between myself and Miss Knowles, and she stormed off into town, and I thought she meant one thing, when she meant quite another. She can be a little impetuous. I won't repeat what she said about Effie and you because she didn't really mean it, but I think she was still upset with Effie over her remarks, and by extension, you as her friend. But she assured me last night that I was completely overreacting. So it seems I was wrong to be worried! I do apologise that I threw you into an unnecessary panic."

"So Miss Knowles came here last night?" I said incredulously, as Miss Thanes came in with the coffee.

"Oh, yes, yes. She is somewhere about."

I sat staring at her for a moment, trying to understand how she could so lightly dismiss this.

"Well, in that case, perhaps I should make my way back to Hawksbridge," I said.

"I won't hear of it, Thomas," Lady Fairfield said, "certainly not before we have had our coffee and I have shown you the house. And now you're here, you may as well stay for another night at least – unless you have pressing business, of course."

"No, not especially," I said. I was beginning to feel a little uncomfortable, but I could not think of a plausible excuse for a hasty retreat.

Lady Fairfield poured the coffee. "So – you must tell me what it was about Rachel's – Miss Knowles' behaviour that you found alarming. I assure you it will be in the strictest confidence. She can have a temper – I have often remonstrated with her about it, and it's why I became concerned. What has she done or said?"

I remained silent, and shrugged. I really did not want to confide in her and break my word to Sylvie.

"Oh, come and sit beside me," she said. "You are too far away." I reluctantly obeyed, taking care not to tread on her dogs. "We should not have any secrets from each other," she continued, fixing me with a steadfast gaze. "After all, we need to get to the bottom of poor William's disappearance. Perhaps I will be able to help you with this doubt of yours, and easily clear things up. Yes?"

"I don't know," I said, and reached for my coffee. "I promised someone I would not mention it."

"But if the whole thing is solved, then I'm sure your friend will be more at ease. Now, Thomas – I will keep needling you, so you may as well tell me now! Out with it, and then we shall have a pleasant stroll together."

I could well believe this was true. She would keep tormenting me with her exaggerated kindness until she got it out of me.

Against my better judgement, I said, "If you insist. It concerns an object that Miss Knowles instructed... a person to obtain from Mrs Milburn."

"How intriguing," said Lady Fairfield.

"It was wrapped up, and this person had no idea what the object was."

"And do you?"

"Yes," I said. "It was William Lowick's pocket watch."

"Goodness," she said, taking a sip of coffee. "That is... remarkable. And do you suppose that Mrs Milburn is connected to William in some way?"

"They knew of one another," I said, "but I can't imagine that Mrs Milburn would be involved in anything questionable."

"I quite agree," she said. "She is never anything but a

delight. She is busy tending to the rose garden as we speak. Well, I shall ask both her and Miss Knowles about it, and I'm sure I will get a satisfactory answer from both. You leave it to me. There! That wasn't so hard, was it?"

She beamed at me, and poured me some more coffee.

I could not think of a response. If I took what she said at face value, the whole matter was inconsequential and would soon be cleared up, as though it were as simple as finding the culprit for a broken jug. "I... I think it's quite a serious business, Lady Fairfield –" I began.

"Nonsense, Thomas, I'm sure it has a perfectly dreary explanation. But I will find out, I promise you. Now, if you have finished, let's stretch our legs and you shall get your tour."

I nodded, drained my cup, and followed her, as if I were one of her spaniels.

The focus of the dining room was an ornate stone fireplace flanked with aggressive-looking lions, and on various cabinets and tables around the room stood a collection of bowls, jugs and statues carved out of what looked like purple amethyst.

"My husband's father was a great collector of Blue John," Lady Fairfield said. "It's quite rare. I don't particularly care for it, but apparently it's the biggest such collection in the country."

"Interesting," I said, peering at a statue of an elephant. "Is this where we are having lunch?"

"No," she said, "this is used by the Sisters. We will eat in the West Wing, where I have made my home in rooms more suited to my proportions."

"Sisters?" I said, with a little too much astonishment in my voice. "Are you turning Kirkheaton Hall into a monastery?"

"What would you have me call them, Thomas? 'Friends', perhaps? 'Comrades' is too military. 'Members' is redolent of a gentlemen's club. I prefer the collegiate term of 'Sisters'. It conveys both our sex and a sense of commitment to a cause."

"True," I conceded. "You are quite right."

Lady Fairfield trotted briskly from the room, and I hurried to catch up. "Now, you will have seen the hall, but not in the best light. I admit it is a little preposterous."

The Great Hall was not much less intimidating in the daylight: cavernous and stark, its height was a full two storeys, which were themselves ostentatiously lofty. I gazed up at the statues in their niches. "I take it these are your ancestors?"

"My husband's ancestors," she corrected me. "Yes, the old scoundrels stare down at me scornfully every day. I suppose you will have heard what the Fairfields got up to last century, and a little into this century, before they finally became more serious."

"I confess I have not."

"Ah!" she said. "Well, they dedicated themselves completely to their amusements, which included all manner of parties, sin and practical jokes. They were thoroughly notorious throughout the county."

"Fascinating," I said. "So this house was a playground for them."

"Yes – they even had their own theatre. They and their friends would write and perform plays of varying degrees of propriety. On that note, let me show you the Listening Room."

Lady Fairfield led me upstairs, past my own room, and then into a similar-sized bedroom with fading floral wallpaper and another large bed, its headboard carved with a coat of arms.

"Why Listening Room?" I asked.

"I'll show you," she said, leaving the room and pointing to what looked like a deep door frame, but without any doors. She pulled at a small handle in the panel, and it opened into a dark, narrow corridor.

"This runs next to the Listening Room, and half-way down is a grill behind a picture so anyone in this passageway can hear what's going on in the room."

"Good Lord," I said. "For what purpose?"

"For one of their favourite practical jokes. The Fairfields would listen to their guests' conversation at night, and the next day they would put on a play that incorporated their conversation. The expression on their guests' faces amused them, apparently."

"Delightful," I said. "What a rum lot."

"Quite so," she said. "They also liked to scare guests by dressing up as ghosts. On one occasion this led to a fatal heart attack. But enough of such nonsense. Let me show you my favourite part of the house."

We went down the stairs, and continued to descend beneath the ground floor. I found myself in a forest of columns supporting dozens of vaults, some open and some enclosed with grilles and doors.

"This continues under the whole house," she said, walking briskly along the labyrinth. "I find it a wonderfully peaceful place. We store wine and foodstuffs down here."

We came to a heavy door with a small glassless window.

"Now this is an interesting part, though it may be locked," she said, trying the door. "Ah, no, it's open. Misbehaving staff were shut down here – drunken butlers, insubordinate maids, thieving footmen, or even disagreeable guests. So you must be on your best behaviour!"

She led me to a suite of further rooms, and she pointed to a door. "My husband's specimens," she said. I recalled too well what William had said about that, and was glad that she did not offer to show me it. "One of the jail rooms," she said, indicating another door.

"Have you ever used it?" I asked, without truly wanting to know the answer.

"Not for a long time," she said, smiling at me. I could not

judge whether this was in jest.

"Well, I'm glad we live in a more civilised age," I said.

"We still have some way to go," Lady Fairfield said. "Shall we ascend?"

CHAPTER TWENTY-SIX

AFTER I had seen the stables, which were of monstrous proportions and seemingly designed for Brobdingnagian steeds, Lady Fairfield left me to explore the gardens, with a request not to disturb Mrs Milburn.

"As you know, her mind has been delicate since her husband died, and her gardening is a solace that should not be interrupted. But I have invited her to lunch, together with Miss Knowles, and you may quiz them both then. I look forward to seeing you in the West Wing at midday!"

I duly avoided Mrs Milburn as I wandered around the gardens, relieved to be on my own and able to reason without my hostess confusing my thoughts. After the apparently sinister appearance of the watch, could lunch-time conversation be as innocent and civilised as such an occasion demanded? Could their answers be satisfactory? It was tantalising, yet I was dreading a potential confrontation. Lady Fairfield would of course do her best to reassure me. After all, these 'Sisters' were under her protection, and one of them was a firm friend. Blindness to their sins would be understandable.

In any event, I told myself, I might catch them in a lie that I could take to the police. If I could not get to the bottom of these mysteries, then I could at least share the responsibility, and hope that the police would be sufficiently grateful for my evidence that Inspector Simmons would overlook my interference. Surely it was not ignominious to have tried and failed, after my previous successes.

I suddenly longed to slough off this seemingly intractable, vexing business and get back to Ramsburgh, to Fox, to my little study, to Phyllis and to Effie, who always seemed brightened by my visit. That was a small way in which I could make myself useful – and small acts were not to be sniffed at. Perhaps, like Lady Fairfield's family, I had been guilty of hubris. A belief in my own infallible investigative powers, engendered as much by luck as my own skill, was my own Great Hall – vain, arrogant, and empty. I might return empty-handed from this place, but I would return a wiser, humbler man, putting aside my obsessions and misplaced confidence, and contenting myself with friendship, preparations for marriage, and the pursuit of mental improvement.

But then I thought of the grief of Mrs Lowick, the tear-stained resignation of Lillian Belford, and Effie's broken constitution. In my mind's eye, I saw William Lowick visiting the Nesbits, imagining the compassion he would have shown, and how it kindled in him the fire to seek justice. I could not simply give up and seek refuge in the comforts of my privileged existence – I must not expect the police to solve the mysteries that I had made my burden. My self-doubt – indeed, self-pity – was too easy. No, however discomforting it was, I would need to ask difficult questions. I would not be pacified by the airs and rituals of the gentry. I would prove myself, or forever hate myself.

It was with this hardened resolve that, after a quick visit to my room, I now entered the West Wing, where voices led me to a small dining room. Lady Fairfield, Miss Knowles and Mrs Milburn were seated, and they looked up as I entered. For the purpose of social efficacy, I tried to overlook the fact that only recently, Lady Fairfield had portrayed Miss Knowles as a threat to my safety.

"Thomas!" Lady Fairfield said, smiling at me. "Have you had a nice walk? You know Miss Knowles and Mrs Milburn, of course."

"Good afternoon, ladies," I said, and they nodded and smiled. "It's very pleasant to see you both again. Yes, I had a splendid walk. Was that some kind of a mine I saw across the valley?"

"Yes, quite right – the family fortune has dirty roots, namely the extraction of coal, in addition to the farms. I intend to shut it down shortly, after some unfortunate incidents. Besides, productive seams are now few and far between. The farms are quite sufficient to fund our expenditures."

Dishes of roast chicken were brought in by another of the Sisters, and wine was poured.

"Speaking of the farms," Lady Fairfield continued, "Mr Gabriel Forrester was here last week. He suggested that he might design some workers' cottages for me, and I thought it might be amusing to indulge him, as some of my existing cottages are falling into ruin. We are like-minded in many ways."

"Yes," I said, "I can imagine that socialism and women's emancipation are similar causes. Equality for all."

"Indeed, Mr Rufford. Of course, not all adherents to socialism are fully enlightened, yet," Lady Fairfax said, picking up her wine glass. "But I'm glad to have Mr Forrester's ear. He is in a good position to convert the heathen. I suggested that we should write an educational pamphlet together that could be included with each roll of his wallpaper. Or even printed on the back! He was not altogether receptive of the notion, but I have not given up on it."

"It is such a wonderful idea," Miss Knowles said. "You are so clever."

Lady Fairfax smiled modestly, and then said, "But this was before I knew about the arsenic in his wallpaper. I will have an extremely strong word with him about that, you may be sure."

"I do hope your composer friend is feeling better, Mr Rufford," Miss Knowles said. "It was a great shock to hear about her illness. I gather it may even be due to the Forrester wallpaper that Mrs Campbell used in her house – as Lady Fairfield says, we must earnestly implore Mr Forrester to change his method of manufacture!"

I almost admired the brass neck of the woman, tackling the subject head on. She must have learned that attack is the secret of defence.

"That may well be the cause," I said. "I intend to see that arsenic is banned from use in wallpaper – somehow." I debated whether to press her on the tea, but decided that I would not use all the arrows in my quiver at once, and would instead see how the conversation developed.

"How is the rose garden, Mrs Milburn?" I asked, as we started to eat. I felt it prudent to at least attempt polite conversation with her before posing difficult questions.

"Rather wonderful, Mr Rufford!" said Mrs Milburn. "I think I have finally got out all the weeds, and the roses are starting to bloom. It's my favourite time of year."

"I was so impressed by your own garden," I said. "You are as diligent with plants as I am with mysteries!"

Mrs Milburn looked confused. "Mysteries?"

"Yes," I said, having paused for a moment to chew and swallow some chicken. "Such as how you came into possession of a pocket watch belonging to a dead man."

"Oh, Thomas," said Lady Fairfield. "How dramatic of you! I'm sure Mrs Milburn has nothing to hide. Do you, Ninette?"

Mrs Milburn had turned bright red. "Of course not, Lady Fairfield," she said, looking down at her plate. "I found it... under a hedge."

"I see," I said, gently. "And then Miss Knowles asked you to give it to someone else?"

"I..." Mrs Milburn looked imploringly at Lady Fairfield and Miss Knowles. "I don't know –"

Miss Knowles cut in: "Yes, I did, didn't I, Ninette? You remember – I didn't want anyone thinking you had come by the watch in an irregular manner, so I wrote to you telling you to wrap it up and give it to my friend."

Lady Fairfield laughed and said, "Oh, Ninette, your memory! But it's getting better all the time. More rest is required, I think."

"Oh, yes," Mrs Milburn said gratefully. "That's what happened to it, Mr Rufford. I gave it to Rachel's French friend."

"But why not give it straight to Miss Knowles?" I said.

"Because, Mr Rufford," Miss Knowles said, "I was here at Kirkheaton Hall, and thought I would see Sylvie and pick it up from her soon enough. But I haven't got around to it just yet."

"So you see, Thomas, there's nothing sinister going on here!" said Lady Fairfield, placing her cutlery neatly on her empty plate. "Tell me you're satisfied about the watch, now!"

Before I answered, I took a moment to sip my wine. "Yes, of course," I said. "So where did you find this watch, Mrs Milburn?"

"As I said, Mr Rufford – under a hedge."

"Quite, but which hedge, where?"

She shrugged. "I'm afraid I can't remember."

"The police will be disappointed," I said. "That information might be crucial."

"Oh – the police won't have to know about it, will they?" Mrs Milburn said.

"Surely not, Thomas!" said Lady Fairfield. "It will just cause unnecessary trouble, and the police have Mr Belford."

"That's exactly why they should know – because of Mr Belford," I said. "I believe he's an innocent man."

"Whyever should you think that?" asked Miss Knowles. "Mr Lowick's cigar case was found in his shop, and Mr Belford was known to hate Mr Lowick."

"That proves nothing," I said. "Merely that someone clever used the opportunity to divert attention from themselves. The person who pointed out the cigar case in Mr Belford's shop did not stop to be interviewed, and that makes me suspicious. Who was this mysterious person? If we could find her, we might come close to solving William's disappearance."

Mrs Milburn looked down at her plate again, the look on her face suggesting that she might soon be sick. Noticing this, I took the risk of distressing the poor woman further, and said, "Perhaps you have an idea who this woman was? Someone must know her, and maybe she has said something."

She vigorously shook her head, and toyed with her fork.

Lady Fairfield held up a hand to prevent me querying her further. "Mr Rufford, I think that's enough. Clearly the subject of poor William's disappearance is troubling her – I'm not surprised, given what she may have in common with Mrs Lowick where husbands are concerned. I can't think Ninette can offer any further information."

"Very well, Lady Fairfield," I said. "Perhaps you can help with another matter, Miss Knowles."

"I will certainly try," she said, solemnly.

"On the night that Miss Harris became ill, she had drunk tea that Sylvie had prepared for her. Yes?"

"If you say so, Mr Rufford. We ladies often drink something at night to help us sleep. Did you know that catmint is good for suppressing nightmares?"

"Is that what you prescribed for Miss Harris?" I said.

Miss Knowles looked as though she was having trouble recalling events as long ago as a whole fortnight. "Oh – yes, I remember now. That's exactly what I did – I gave Sylvie a camomile tea, and catmint to give to Miss Harris. I thought Miss Harris looked fraught, perhaps because of interrupted sleep" – she said this with knowing emphasis – "and might benefit from a little help."

"So," I said, "Miss Harris unwittingly took a tea she was not accustomed to taking, from a woman she had offended, and by coincidence, she immediately became dangerously ill."

"It's just awful, isn't it?" Miss Knowles said, innocently.

Suddenly she adopted a shocked expression. "You're not suggesting I deliberately poisoned poor Miss Harris? Oh, Lord!" She clapped her hand over her mouth. "What a dreadful idea! Please tell me you're not saying that, Mr Rufford! Why would I want to commit such a wicked, wicked crime?"

"Oh, Mr Rufford," said Mrs Milburn. "Why are you saying such horrible things to Rachel? I can't understand it. You were so kind to me."

"I'm sorry," I said. "But I'm simply trying to understand some very peculiar events, and quite frankly I'm struggling to believe a damned word anyone in this room is saying."

Mrs Milburn began sobbing quietly into a handkerchief, while Miss Knowles had abandoned her shocked look and she and Lady Fairfield sat in stony silence, staring at me.

Had I gone too far? Perhaps, but I could not suppress my misgivings. Even I had not wanted to believe it, but on the basis of Miss Knowles' too-polished performance, it seemed more plausible than ever that she was the agent of Effie's illness, and implicated in concealing evidence.

I was beginning to think, too, that Mrs Milburn knew more about the watch than she was letting on. She gave the impression of a woman reluctantly coached in untruths. How else had she been used by Miss Knowles? No sooner had I formed a supposition when I put it to Mrs Milburn.

"What if, Mrs Milburn, you were in fact the widow seen in Mr Belford's shop? What if you had placed the cigar case in the shop, and were the one to alert the police about it? I expect you were persuaded to do it, when you were in no position to object. And then the watch, which for some reason was not left in the shop, was put to good use as a means of drawing Miss Dubois into the darker aspects of the Society, by making her an accomplice."

Mrs Milburn's sobbing became louder, and Lady Fairfield exclaimed, "Enough, Thomas! This is outrageous of you. I invite you to my house out of the kindness of my heart, and this is how you behave?"

Two of the Sisters had heard raised voices, and now stood in the doorway, watching.

"But was it out of kindness, Lady Fairfield?" I said. "Perhaps it was simply a ruse to find out what I knew."

It was at that moment that I suddenly realised that if this were the case, I was in terrible danger. But it was too late. I could not retract the suspicions that I had so forcefully, indeed gleefully expressed. So I had little choice but to plough on.

"Was it you in the shop, Mrs Milburn?" I said.

"Ignore anything she says," Miss Knowles said. "She is not in full possession of her faculties."

At this Mrs Milburn stopped sobbing and looked up at Miss Knowles. "You must not say that! I am well again! And I lied, I lied, I lied! There, I said it! It *was* me in the shop. Rachel gave me the watch and the cigar case. I placed the cigar case on a shelf, but I was scared, and stupidly fumbled with the watch and dropped it, and could not put it on the shelf in time, so I snatched it up and fled. So I wrote to Miss Knowles and she told me to give it to Miss Dubois. That's all that happened, Mr Rufford. I don't know anything else. I did it for the Society, because Lady Fairfield has helped me so much. At the time, I didn't mind doing what I was asked to do, but now I'm not sure, and I do mind lying. I was taught never to lie."

"Go!" Lady Fairfield shrieked. "Go to your room! Be sure that you will be punished for your dreadful insolence. Leave immediately, you ungrateful, demented witch!"

Mrs Milburn cried out as though she had been hit, and fled. I wanted to follow her and give her whatever comfort I could, but I knew instinctively that this would not be allowed.

Lady Fairfield got up from the table and started to pace around the room while Miss Knowles glared at me.

"Oh, Thomas," she said. "What a disappointment. We were getting on so well. Why must you spoil everything with your incessant questions? It's a terrible habit, always trying to worm out every last secret. You should have minded your own business, married your fiancée, and enjoyed that fine house of yours."

I tried desperately to think how I might make an escape. But even if I made it to the door past my lunch companions, I would be caught by the two Sisters in the doorway. Perhaps I could launch a chair through one of the windows and flee that way? How strong was the window?

But behind me, on one of her perambulations across the room, Lady Fairfield had picked up a heavy silver candlestick and was bringing it down forcefully on my head.

CHAPTER TWENTY-SEVEN

I WAS awakened by a fearful headache, and when I reached to touch my head, I found it to be sticky with drying blood. Opening my eyes, I surveyed my surroundings. I was lying on a straw bed in a small, cold and malodorous room whose unplastered walls I recognised as one of the dungeons Lady Fairfield had shown me earlier in the day. Assuming it was even the same day, of course. By one wall, there was a bucket for calls of nature, a jug of water, and a china mug.

What looked like evening light was coming from a small, high window that offered no possibility of egress. I stood up, painfully, and tried the thick oak door. It was locked, of course, and no doubt also bolted on the other side. I looked through the grille in the door, but could see nobody.

I tried to gather my thoughts, although my thudding head made it difficult. I had walked straight into a trap, laid by a woman about whom I had had far too few suspicions. I realised it was unlikely that Lady Fairfield would let me tell the world what I had learned, especially after I had been assaulted. But the fact that I was still alive surely meant that I had a chance. She was making up her mind what to do with me, I thought. I might therefore be able to influence my fate, if I could discover her motivations.

Lady Fairfield and William had known each other, but how well? When I had seen them together after her talk on the subject of 'Protest', I had noted a hint of informality. Had William turned the full force of his charm on Lady Fairfield when he had been to interview her? Or was he connected with another resident of Kirkheaton Hall? Or had he simply discovered something unsavoury that would compromise Lady

Fairfield's reputation?

My speculations were interrupted by the sound of a bolt being drawn and a key turning in the lock. I saw movement behind the grille, and I was chilled by the awareness that these could be my last seconds on Earth. I sat down on my straw bed and braced myself for whatever horror might now be visited upon me.

"Good evening, Thomas!" Lady Fairfield said, brightly, as if she were a nurse visiting me in hospital. The door closed behind her, and she sat down on the ancient stool that had been provided for me. "How is your head? I'm sorry that was necessary. It's all very regrettable, but I'm sure you will eventually see that I had little choice."

I touched my head again and winced. "I didn't take you for a common thug," I said. "It seems I misjudged you."

She tutted and shook her head. "I'll make an allowance, just this once, Thomas, but you must be more polite to your betters in future, or things will only get worse for you. Now, I need to explain a few things. You are a guest in my home indefinitely. If you make any attempt to leave, Mrs Milburn will suffer dreadfully. I believe you feel a certain regard and pity for her, and so this offers a straightforward mechanism to prevent any unnecessary scheming on your part. Put any idea of leaving out of your head, Thomas, and you will find more peace of mind. Is that understood?"

I nodded.

"Good. I have a few ideas for how you can be of service to the Society, but I'm afraid you will have to get used to a restricted life."

"You cannot surely hope to keep me a prisoner here, undetected, for any length of time?"

Lady Fairfield smiled and said, "You must hope that that is exactly what I am able to do. The alternative is too disagreeable to contemplate. I assure you that the Sisters are extremely loyal. Each has her reasons to believe that her fate and mine are inextricably linked."

I wondered whether I would be able to overpower Lady Fairfield and use her to obtain my freedom.

"What has the world done to you," I asked, "that you should behave in this extraordinary manner?"

"Oh, too many things," Lady Fairfield said. "If I am in the mood, I may tell you about them. But I don't need you to understand me. You just need to know what part to play. I will take care of everything else."

She frowned. "But I will tell you this, because there is a tiny, irrational part of me that cares what you think of me, however stupid that impulse. I am only doing what has become necessary due to one indiscretion. My work is too important for it to be destroyed by a caprice of emotion, and so I must protect what I love. It doesn't give me any pleasure to cause pain. But many women look up to me, and I must continue my campaign."

She stood up and gazed solemnly at me. "I believe history will look kindly on me, and any difficult decisions I have made in the fulfilment of my destiny will be forgiven and forgotten. I cannot shirk this call, whatever the cost. I hope you will come to understand that. Anyway, Thomas, I will have some food brought to you, and arrange for a better bed – that looks most uncomfortable."

"I would appreciate it," I said, "and perhaps one of your... Sisters might be able to clean my wound."

She nodded. "Open, please, Rachel," she said, and the door opened to let her out, quickly slamming shut again.

I lay back on my bed, relieved that the threat of my execution had abated. I was granted a little time I could use to plot an escape. But Lady Fairfield had been clever in picking Mrs Milburn as her hostage. I could not risk her mistreatment, or even murder, at the hands of Lady Fairfield's obedient troops. However, I was buoyed by the thought that the chance might arise of taking her with me. An infinitesimal chance, certainly, but it was enough to give me hope.

My supper consisted of bread and the luxury of beer, and one of the Sisters – evidently sworn to silence, no matter how polite my questions – tidied up my wounded head, so that at least my early demise from an infection was rendered less likely.

An ugly little bed was found – perhaps from a servant's room – and despite the dampness of the mattress, it was Heaven compared with my straw bed. But my sleep, such as it was, was full of nightmares, as you may imagine, and when the sun once more penetrated my pathetic cell and woke me, my prospects were hardly better than the grim unreality my dreams had depicted.

~

A few hours after dawn – I was unable to precisely gauge time – I was visited again by Lady Fairfield.

"You are lucky today, Thomas!" she said, standing by the partly open door. "I will allow you a treat."

"I'm agog," I said. "What delights do you have in store for me?"

"None if you continue with your sarcasm," she said, starting to retreat.

"I'm sorry. Please continue."

"You and I will take a walk in the sunshine. We cannot have you wasting away in the gloom."

I was suspicious, but had no choice but to go with Lady Fairfield, followed by Miss Knowles at a discreet distance.

"There," she said as we walked through the formal gardens. "Is this not perfectly civilised?"

"Superficially," I said. "I would say I'm like one of your spaniels, only I know my life is far less valuable to you."

"On the contrary, Thomas. You are most valuable. I will explain why."

"Please do."

"But first I must tell you a little about myself. I may risk boring you, but then again, I have a captive audience, don't I?" She laughed, and then said, "Oh, how wicked of me – I shouldn't mock you. What I have to say is actually quite serious. I may have previously you given the impression that my marriage was a source of happiness. Well, I started with the aspirations and dreams of any bride, being in love with my husband, James. I admired his skill as a surgeon, and he was handsome and attentive. For whatever reason, I had not been the recipient of many serious offers from suitors, but James had seen qualities others had missed.

"James also seemed different from the various men I encountered, not least the family friend whose unwanted, intimate attentions had been the cause of much dread and misery. I had formed an extremely jaundiced view of men before I met James.

"To begin with, we were happy. I took an interest in his work, and he was flattered and instructed me in some of the techniques he helped to develop. So I was able to assist him in small matters. I became particularly adept at extracting and preserving brains. It became a source of fascination to me, to see the seat of all of a person's thoughts laid bare. The essence of men and women reduced to a mere lump of jelly – whatever status in life, whichever the sex, however rich or poor. That equality impressed me greatly."

"William told me he had seen your collection," I said.

"He looked as though he was going to be ill, poor thing!" Lady Fairfield said. We had reached the rose garden, and she bent down to take in the scent of a white rose.

"As my husband's professional reputation grew," she continued, "he became impatient with me. I was unable to bear him an heir, which was unforgivable in his eyes, and he began to belittle me, including in front of his guests. He no longer permitted me to help him in his work, and I became wretched. Not only did I not have the opportunity to create a family for James, I was in effect losing my husband too. We rarely spoke. It was especially bitter, since I had trusted James to cure me of my horror and contempt of men. And now he had betrayed me, and again confirmed my previous view of his sex."

"And this is why you started the Society?"

"To some extent, yes," she replied. "I had much time on my hands, and read and read, including works by Mary Wollstonecraft, Margaret Fuller, and other women with clear sight. I saw that this could be my life's work – to free women from the restrictions upon their liberty and choices, and to recast them as agents of their own destiny just as much as men are. In fact more so, as I believe women are superior in many ways that are more important than mere physical attributes. Men are fundamentally selfish and feral creatures, while women necessarily possess a caring, nurturing instinct."

"Really? My recent experiences don't bear that out," I said.

"These are exceptional circumstances," she said. "Anyway, I began to hate my husband. I found that hate and love are simply different flavours of the same thing, namely obsession. I was glad I hated him, since it gave me an energy and the motivation to create my own future. I am grateful to James – just not in the way people think."

"And now," I said, "you use his wealth against his sex. I expect that gives you a certain satisfaction."

"Precisely, Thomas. Perhaps I was a little impatient – you never know how soon it will be before God takes back what he has given. I had much to achieve, so I hurried things along."

I winced. "You mean you murdered your husband?"

"Not murdered, precisely. But he over-indulged in many

ways, and he had an unhealthy blood pressure and weakened heart. I knew just how to make him angry, so I refined it over time. In the rare times we spoke, I would goad him about how well his contemporaries' children were doing, or how his distinguished competitors had burnished their reputations. And one day, about two years ago, it worked – he became so angry, his heart burst. I recall the final blow was Mr Dunstone's son becoming a member of Parliament at the tender age of twenty-two. Mr Dunstone also being a distinguished surgeon, it was the perfect weapon, especially when the news was delivered jubilantly, inducing a spirited row, and thence a final failure of his diseased, loveless heart."

"My God," I said. "And you feel no guilt about this?"

"Not really," Lady Fairfield said, breezily. "It was necessary. I will show you his brain, if you wish. I bribed the undertaker to ignore the signs of surgery."

"You extracted his...?"

"Oh, yes – it was highly satisfying," she said, smiling. "My insufferable husband reduced to a floating blob of tissue in a jar. I almost wish it were still sentient, so I could tell him about all the ways in which I spend his money."

I stopped on the north lawn where we were currently walking, and Lady Fairfield and Miss Knowles were forced to halt also.

"You do realise you're a soulless, godless monster?" I said.

She shrugged. "I expect to be called names. I do what I need to do. Besides, to most people, I'm not in the least a monster – I am a benefactor, a guide – an inspiration. So it entirely depends on your perspective. And your perspective, I'm afraid, is a little prejudiced by your unfortunate situation."

"And what unfortunate situation did William find himself in?" I demanded. "What did you do to him?"

"I did not give you the privilege of this walk to talk about William," she said. "You're becoming tiresome. Are you going to let me finish, or must you be sent immediately to your room?"

"As you wish."

"Thank you. As I said, I could not produce a family. But lo and behold!" She gestured towards the house. "I have made myself a different kind of family, one that is superior to the usual sort because we are united by the same goals and ideas. And yet – this cannot be sustained. If women are to dominate – as I believe they will in due course – men are a necessary evil, for the purpose of breeding. And so I wish to conduct an experiment that I hope will show the world how it can be managed."

"You wish to breed from the Sisters?"

"Those who are vigorous, intelligent and of child-bearing age, yes. Their progeny will be brought up in an atmosphere where they will take for granted all the ideals we have to work so hard to inculcate into the common mind. They will then go forth and act as a kind of beneficial infection in society, spreading the word."

"Well, unless they develop minds of their own or simply revert to convention."

"Nonsense!" Lady Fairfield snapped. "The truth of our philosophy will overwhelm all else. I have already started to plant seeds in the minds of our young at their schools. The clergy are eager to be seen to be advanced in their thinking, so they are a willing instrument of conversion: they already possess the skills of oratory, and have the confidence of their congregations. My teachings – and of course those of like-minded women – are being received well amongst certain distinguished thinkers and writers. Hawksbridge is merely a model for what might be achieved in the rest of the country."

"And do your teachings include the savage ruthlessness you have demonstrated here?" I asked.

"There is no room for weakness in this campaign," she said. "So naturally my teachings will gently emphasise the strength of women and the degeneracy of the male mind. I hope that the aggressive, misogynist character that we are used to in the prominent leaders of government and industry will become unfashionable. As religion shows, humans can easily be shamed into submission. There is a point when an idea has sufficiently penetrated into society that it becomes too costly for an individual to resist."

"So you will achieve your results by a kind of terror."

"Persuasion, Thomas. Sustained persuasion, helped by the deep desire people have to display their conformity and goodness."

"I hardly dare ask," I said, "but what exactly is your vision of society, once your goals have been accomplished? I suspect equality is not your goal."

"How perceptive of you," Lady Fairfield said, smiling. "No – I wish to see women take the lead, of course. After all, men have had the advantage for far too long. They will finally resign themselves to lesser roles, recognising their inferiority."

"And all for revenge on the men who have harmed you?"

"That is to demean the loftiness of my aims. Particular men have taught me harsh and valuable lessons, to be sure; however, my experience is not so different from that of the majority of my sisters. I merely have more will than they to enact the inevitable restoration of balance."

Lady Fairfield stopped and folded her arms, gazing at me as if choosing a horse at market. "But you have missed my point – how all this relates to you."

My sense of dread had been growing for the last few minutes. I had not missed her earlier point.

"You, Thomas, will help me with my breeding plan. I might almost believe that you were sent here by Providence. It is perfect: there will be no conventional fathers, no messy emotional ingredient. I know you to be an intelligent man of decent looks and no obvious physical deficiencies. You will be dedicated to this task, with no distractions. Unlike a husband, you will do your duty as many times as it takes without drunkenness or the trauma of infidelity. And it makes it so much easier for me that I have a use for you. I would hate to... well, you know."

Yes, I know, I thought grimly – turn me into a specimen for you to gloat over.

"Isn't there a major flaw in your plan?" I said with as much bravado as I could muster.

"Oh? Enlighten me."

"A man must be... motivated to perform. He is not like a bull, or a tup. Or to put it another way, you can take a horse to water, but you can't make him drink."

"I have thought of that, naturally, and Miss Knowles has advised me of some excellent herbs that can help. I believe ginseng is one of them. And besides, much of the means to achieve a... result is in a person's head. You will be encouraged to make whatever pictures in your head are necessary. And if you lack imagination, actual pictures can be provided. Ultimately, I will provide motivation for you to make an effort and do as I ask."

"But the Sisters – do they have any say in this? What if they don't want to? A stranger impregnating them – it's cold and heartless, not to mention highly immoral."

"They will be glad to help further the aims of the Society. Its discipline has helped them – saved their lives in some cases – and now they must do their duty. Yes, it may be a sacrifice for some. But the results in transforming human society will be well worth it. And don't talk to me about morality – I see precious little of it in the way men treat women, and their fellow men for that matter."

I wanted to scream, "You're stark staring mad!" and run as fast as I could, away from this lunatic asylum, through the outsized gates, along the country roads, all the way back to safety in Ramsburgh and the loving arms of Phyllis. But I could not let them harm Mrs Milburn, and they would no doubt have hunted me down anyway. A shiver went down my spine then, as I realised there was a good chance Mrs Milburn would herself be a candidate for childbearing. I had admired her pansies, sipped tea with her, eaten the shortbread she had kindly given me. To now force myself upon her... it was unthinkable.

CHAPTER TWENTY-EIGHT

MY SECOND night was worse than the first. I had lost my freedom and the comfortable life I had known, and now Lady Fairfield wanted my very soul. How could I take part in this unholy experiment? Perhaps there were men who were suited for such a task, who would relish the affirmation of their prowess and simply fix upon their own pleasure. But while I had been tempted by strangers in the past, this was an entirely different matter. This was a transaction that had nothing to do with the natural affinity between men and women. These women would be coerced, with myself as the instrument of a gross abuse on their person. The result: spiritual torment, a troupe of fatherless children, and no doubt deaths during childbirth, especially if medical supervision were lacking, as I suspected.

I had no real doubt that Lady Fairfield's empire would fall, badly, sooner or later. But much damage might have been done by then, and the longer it took, the lower my chances of my survival.

I wondered at what point Phyllis, Flora and others would start to worry about me. They were probably unconcerned at present, due to my misdirection. I had followed Lady Fairfield's orders to the letter even when a free man. It had been beyond foolish and threw into question any iota of mental acuity I imagined I possessed. But there was no sense in chastising myself, when I needed all my mental energy to find a path through this, the most miserable and dangerous period of my life thus far.

I heard some voices and noises in another part of my vaulted jail for some time, but could not make any sense of it.

As the sun's rays moved around the cell, I shifted my position to soak up as many as possible. It was a small but significant comfort. Just as my spot of sunshine was becoming inaccessible, Lady Fairfield let herself into the cell.

"Good morning, Thomas. I hope you have reflected on what I said, and will cooperate with my plans with good grace."

I nodded, since there was no point in antagonizing her. "But it occurred to me," I said, "that I can hardly conduct myself as you wish from this cell. Horses are stabled better – this room is filthy. I need to keep myself healthy and clean."

"Of course. I have thought of that myself," Lady Fairfield said, "and I have been working on a new home for you. Come and see."

She and Miss Knowles escorted me to another area of the basement, where a suite of three rooms was secured behind a heavy door. The rooms were similar to the one to which I had been confined, but they were cleaner, and one was designated as a lavatory and wash room, another as my bedroom – with the luxury of an old chest of drawers – and third as a parlour, containing a table and two chairs. A plate of bread and ham had been placed on the table.

"What do you think?" said Lady Fairfield, smiling. "I will have your bed brought through shortly."

What a ridiculous situation this was, I thought. My jailer was actually proud of the new accommodation she had organised for me, and expected me to be grateful for it. Which, to my chagrin, I was.

"This is a considerable improvement," I said. "Thank you."

"My pleasure," she said. "Mrs Milburn even brought you a vase of flowers for you. I let her help with the furnishing, to bring her back from her state of melancholia."

"That is good of her," I said, feeling the tears pricking my eyes at the thought of this act of human kindness, which I had not known for what seemed like a very long time.

"There is a jug of hot water in your wash room," Lady Fairfield said, "and a change of clothes. Yours will be cleaned, except where the blood renders them irretrievable. I will come back later, when you are refreshed. I confess I don't like to see you looking like a tramp!"

~

Once washed and dressed, I felt a little of my dignity return. I could not shave, but naturally they would not supply me with a razor that could be used against them, so I would have to get used to growing a beard. I feared that my new clothes had once belonged to William, but it could not be helped, and there was a scrap of comfort to be had from this association with my lost friend. I was sure that he would, in the not so distant future, be avenged.

True to her word, Lady Fairfield returned, and we sat in my stony parlour on hard chairs in an absurd impersonation of a polite social encounter.

"Yes, you're looking much more presentable," she said. "How will you suit a beard, I wonder?" She reached out and touched my stubble. "Interesting. I quite like that."

In normal life, I would have interpreted this as outrageous flirting, but since all rules were suspended here, I did not know what to make of it. I supposed she was playing with her new toy. Dolly... It brought to my mind the innocence of little Matilda Belford, engaging in earnest conversations with her dolls. Lady Fairfield too must have once been in that blissful state of naivety, only to be corrupted, little by little, by the haphazard, contaminated stream of life flowing around her.

"I see no reason to delay my plan," she said. "I would like to make a start this afternoon."

I shuddered, hoping fervently that Mrs Milburn's name would not be on her lips.

"Thanes has agreed to receive you," she said. "Indeed, she was honoured to be the first."

"I see," I said. "Are you sure she wants to become a mother – an unmarried one at that?"

"Perfectly sure. She relishes the opportunity."

"And if I may ask... how does this... work, exactly?" I closed my eyes in shame and horror.

Lady Fairfield laughed. "Oh – I assumed you knew the facts of life, Thomas! I can't believe you have led such a sheltered life."

"I mean," I said, as patiently as possible, "I'm not familiar with the protocol of loveless intimacy. Is it to happen here...?"

"No, definitely not here," she said, grimacing. "Thanes will be ready for you in the Listening Room. You will be brought in and lie with Thanes – you may take as much time as you need. I – or Miss Knowles – will be on hand, but not in the room, to verify that you're performing your duty."

"My God," I said. "You will be listening?"

"I assure you we will take no pleasure from it. We must simply ensure it all happens as it should, whilst reassuring Thanes of her complete safety."

"And what if I fail to perform – especially with someone spying on us, and with a woman I have no passion for?"

"Then we shall employ herbs, and you must use whatever methods you can to excite yourself. Remember that ultimately, you *must* perform, or regrettably, Mrs Milburn will pay the price."

"How are you able to do this?" I asked. "One moment, you're taking pastoral care of Mrs Milburn. The next, you're threatening her with violence."

"It is curious, isn't it?" she said, as if talking about a change in the weather. "But determination and compassion are not mutually exclusive. I'm still a human being – an exceptionally single-minded one, I grant you."

~

Miss Knowles brought me to the door of the Listening Room, and said, "Please be on your best behaviour, Mr Rufford. If you try to run, it will be futile. And the window is too high to climb from. Good luck."

I nodded, knocked, and went in, closing the door behind me. The shutters were closed, and as my eyes became accustomed to the gloom, I saw Miss Thanes under the covers in her nightdress. She wore an expression of pained resignation that I fancied I had seen on paintings of martyrs.

"Good afternoon, Miss Thanes," I said, sitting on the edge of the bed.

"Good afternoon," she whispered.

"I need to say first that I have not agreed to come here of my own free will. I regret the need to be intimate with you in these circumstances."

"It's for the best," Miss Thanes said. "It will be glorious to be able to serve Lady Fairfield, and the Society, in this way."

Was she saying this for the benefit of the Listener, to avoid trouble, or did she really believe it?

"I see," I said. "If you're really sure?"

She nodded, and said, "You had better get undressed."

Reluctantly, I stood up, removed my clothes, and got under the bedclothes. I had no clue how to begin, and I was certainly not yet primed to accomplish my mission.

"What would you like me to do?" Miss Thanes whispered.

"Perhaps you could turn over, and I'll hold you, if you don't mind."

"No, that's all right."

She turned to face the wall, and I tentatively pressed myself against her, putting my arms around her. Miss Thanes' tense body relaxed after a few moments as she got used to my presence.

"The rose garden is looking fine at present," I said. "Mrs Milburn is quite an expert."

"Yes," she whispered. "She told me you took an interest in her garden at home. She said you were a good man."

She turned her head towards me. "That's why I wasn't frightened about this. Well... I was nervous, but I knew it would be all right."

"I try to be a good man," I said, "but they make it exceedingly difficult in this house." I hoped that our lowered voices would not be audible. I supposed they only really wanted evidence of louder exertions.

Miss Thanes took my hand and squeezed it. It was a touching gesture of reassurance; she must have had some sympathy with my position and I wondered how deep her loyalty ran. But it would be too dangerous for both of us to test it now.

I squeezed back, and then stroked her shoulder a little. It felt odd, as I was only accustomed to this intimacy with women with whom I was well acquainted, but I was beginning to like Miss Thanes, and the intimacy was not entirely objectionable, especially to one recently denied all affection and respect.

"It's a good thing you're not remotely unattractive," I whispered to her, and she laughed.

"I might say the same thing, Mr Rufford," she said. "It does make this easier."

I unfurled myself and gently rolled her onto her back. "If you don't mind..." I said, and pulled her nightdress up before kissing her breasts. Her quickened breathing signalled that she did not mind at all.

Contrary to my expectations, my caresses put us both in

the proper disposition for further activity, and when I enacted the required union, it was surprisingly effortless. I sensed no discomfort on Miss Thanes' part, and it seemed that the animal element of me overwhelmed the sense of guilt I should have felt. No doubt, I thought to myself, that will come later. I lost myself in hedonism and the smell and feel of a woman who, happily, was not threatening to kill me. For the first time in several days, I felt no fear or pain.

My vigour was all the more pronounced due to a long absence of congress, and the Listener would have heard the confirmation of our transaction.

We both caught our breath, and I was not sure what to say or do next.

"Thank you," I said, getting out of bed and starting to get dressed.

Her eyes still closed, she smiled. "I have known much worse," she said.

~

I had been lucky with Miss Thanes – I was sure that not all the women in the Society would be as amenable or put me in the required frame of mind. As I had anticipated, I immediately began to reproach myself for acquiescing to this crime against morality. It had been too easy, too pleasurable, even – how had I not been more inhibited? But the touch of human skin had been like a feast presented to a starving man. With the threat of extinction hanging over me, I had clung desperately to life and to this pretty, warm, soft woman, blotting out for a brief moment all the evils of my situation. Was it really any wonder?

And yet I had suppressed thoughts of Phyllis, whether by necessity or guilt. Could she reproach me for what I had done?

Perhaps only for my enthusiasm in carrying out Lady Fairfield's instructions, not the need for it.

I hoped Miss Thanes was not consumed with mortification at what she had done. I supposed that if she did not immediately conceive, I would be brought to her bed again. The three of us – Lady Fairfield, Miss Thanes, and myself – would drive another nail into the coffin that contained my engagement to Phyllis. For there was hardly a shadow of doubt that should I survive, I must release Phyllis from our contract. It would not be fair to expect her to understand or tolerate my deeds.

A sudden and unexpected feeling of relief came over me. Now that I was no longer obligated to Phyllis, nor she to me, my crimes were of lesser importance. It was some solace to know that besides the pain of our parting, I could no longer hurt her with every lapse, every sin, every degradation that it was my lot to perpetrate.

~

The next morning, I was in the middle of washing myself when Lady Fairfield came in. She seemed unconcerned by my partial nakedness, as I slapped water over my torso.

Leaning by the wash room door, she said, "You did well last night. You are to be congratulated. To think you doubted yourself so!"

I grimaced. "It seems you're correct about us being the weaker sex. I hate myself for it."

"But you did as I asked, and you got a little pleasure from it too, didn't you? Everyone here is happy."

"Everyone here will burn in Hell," I said.

"I'm sure you don't believe that," Lady Fairfield said. "I brought you some apples to show my appreciation. I have put them in your dining room."

"Thank you," I said, furious that she could make me grateful to her.

"Would you like to know about your next assignment?" she said, archly.

"Not particularly," I said. "Was it you listening, yesterday?"

"I'm afraid so," she said, smiling. "It was most interesting."

"I thought you said you wouldn't get any amusement from it."

"It seems I was wrong," she said. "After all your gloominess, your enthusiasm and vitality yesterday was refreshing."

I glared at her. "Privacy has little meaning to you, has it?"

"Modesty has its place," she said. "But in this instance, supervision was entirely necessary."

I dried myself, and put my shirt on. Or quite possibly, William's shirt.

"What happened to William?" I asked. "Are you going to tell me? You may as well, if I'm to be forbidden from returning to the outside world."

"Are you sure you want to know?" she said.

"Of course."

"Then come with me."

Lady Fairfield took me out into the main corridor, and we returned to where she had pointed out the specimen room. She reached into her bosom and took out a key on a chain, and removing it, she unlocked the door.

"This is a very special room to me," she said. "The key against my skin reminds me of it."

My wildest imaginings could not prepare me for the horrific sight that greeted me. On shelves around the room, and also lined up in the centre, were specimens of many kinds, including foetuses, lizards, eyeballs, monkey heads and shapeless masses I could not identify: but the greatest part of the collection was made up of brains, mostly human. The jars were neatly labelled.

Lady Fairfield looked at me to gauge the extent of my disgust. "Here is my esteemed husband," she said, pointing at a jar and then tapping it. "Hello, James! Nothing to say for yourself, as usual. How blissful, when compared with before."

I thought I was going to be sick, but worse was to come.

"And dear William," she said, indicating another jar. "He was altogether a more interesting man than James – but perhaps a little too interesting." She turned back to me.

"I confess I lost my head over him. Oh – no pun intended! He came to interview me, and he was extremely charming, and flirted tremendously. And so we got to know one another quite well. Very well," she added, looking back at William's remains. "We became lovers, didn't we? What a passionate fellow you seemed to be, at the beginning."

I started to retch. "Oh dear," she said. "You poor thing. We will return to your rooms, and I will explain."

When I had recovered a little – although still afflicted by nausea – she resumed her tale in my parlour.

"I knew about his wife, of course, but it was only after a few weeks that I learned about his whore in the country. This put a different complexion on William's character. It was one thing to be sole mistress of a witty and handsome man, but quite another to be second to an ignorant little shopkeeper's daughter. I sent my driver to pick him up, which it seems no one saw, and when he got here, I offered him the chance to explain.

"He apologised, but said it was simply in his nature to be drawn to interesting females. I pointed out he hadn't been especially discriminating when it came to Miss Belford. He said that they were genuinely in love, and that he was unable to stop himself falling in love with more than one woman. I asked whether he was in love with me, and he looked very uncomfortable, and said nothing.

"You may imagine how that made me feel – that he could fall in love with a piece of trash, but when it came to me, it was simply a matter of his lusts. That his response was just an automatic reaction of his loins to almost any woman that crossed his path. Or worse – it was mere habit."

"Perhaps," I said, "your personality dazzled him, and he confused the excitement of it with love."

"That may very well be the case," she said, "but it doesn't excuse his behaviour."

"So what did you do?" I wanted to get the revelations over with as quickly as possible.

"In my anger," she continued, "I marched out of the room and tried to evade him. He followed me to the gallery that overlooks the Great Hall. He grabbed my arm and told me I had been as persuasive with him as when talking to my followers, so it was at least half my fault. He didn't want to hurt my feelings by refusing me, he said. I said that it was absurd to say that what we did happened out of simple courtesy. Foolishly, I asked him: if he was just being polite, exactly what was it that he thought about when making love to me?

"He shrugged and said 'My wife'. It was the cruellest possible thing to say. I felt as though he had stabbed me: that the memory of his dull, mousy wife was more arousing to him than his mistress, when she was present, naked, and offering herself up to him. In a fit of rage I pushed him over the rail of the gallery, which is rather low. And that was that. Of course, I regretted it instantly."

"Why? Because of the mess?" I said, bitterly.

She laughed and said, "That, and because he really was a fine man in many ways, and I felt a little sorry for the inexplicably alluring Clementine Lowick. Not for Miss Belford, of course – I doubt she's capable of grief, or any other noble emotion."

My nausea returned, and I rushed to the wash room.

"I warned you that you might not want to know," Lady Fairfield said as I was kneeling over the bucket. "I'm sorry, but that's what happened, and what's done is done."

I looked up. "But the man's brain, for God's sake, woman!"

She shrugged. "It amuses me to have a part of him still with me. It's odd to think that his thoughts about me, and you, and everyone else, are locked up forever in that small blob of jelly."

I was immediately sick, and when I caught my breath and turned around, she was gone.

CHAPTER TWENTY-NINE

IN THE afternoon, languishing in my parlour – if a bleak stone cell can be so described – I heard the sound of horses and carriage wheels. I pushed the table to the wall and climbed on it, and my heart leapt when I saw the arrival of a familiar carriage. It belonged to the police, so it was likely that Inspector Simmons had come looking for me, unless he had suspicions about Lady Fairfield's link with William.

If the Inspector and his constables conducted a full search of the house, I would be saved, and there would be justice for William. But with every minute that I heard no footsteps in the cellars, I lost a little more hope. After a half hour or so, I once again heard the sound of the carriage, and climbing on the table, I saw it retreat. It was a crushing blow, and I went to a corner of the room and sobbed.

A few minutes later, Lady Fairfield appeared.

"It seems your absence has caught the attention of the police," she said. "Perhaps you were not sufficiently convincing with your story. We shall have to do something about it. I would like you to write to your fiancée."

"What do you want me to say?" I said. "How about, 'I decided to take a break from the civilised world in order to conduct research into lunacy and moral degradation'?"

She smiled. "Simply say you are in London and more information is coming to light about the trade in arsenical wallpaper. And that it will take a few weeks. I leave it to you to add the appropriate sentimental remarks."

"And when a few weeks are up?"

"We shall see," she said ominously, and placed paper, ink and a pen on the table. "Please make it believable. And I shall notice if you make any hints as to your location."

~

My letter to Phyllis was especially hard to write given that I no longer had any rights over her feelings, and no right to tell her mine. But I knew there would be consequences for refusal – Lady Fairfield did not have to spell them out. My letter read as follows:

> *My darling Phyllis,*
>
> *Knowing you would worry about my sudden absence, I wanted to assure you all is well. I am conducting some research into arsenic wallpaper following a tip from my kind and long-suffering acquaintance, Mr Nesbit. His condition has improved slightly, although his wife's terrible symptoms are no better, alas. But I cannot believe no more can be done. I pray for a medical advancement.*
>
> *Currently I am hopping from one location to another so eventually I will send my address if I stay in dirty old London for more than a few weeks. My darling girl, I long desperately for your embrace. I wonder how Effie is. All that rest, and the succour of her friends, will surely restore her to health before long.*
>
> *I think about you every day and look forward to hearing how your adventure story is progressing when I return. I was most intrigued by the little you mentioned of it at Francesca's.*

All my love,

Thomas

When Lady Fairfield came to collect my letter, she stood with furrowed brows reading it through a couple of times, and then grunted her approval and marched away with it.

In the morning, she returned with Miss Knowles, and said, "Have you washed?"

I nodded.

"Good. Then I would like to introduce you to Miss Knight."

It was obvious what kind of an introduction that would be, and to what end. I was led again to the Listening Room, where Miss Knight was huddled in bed. To my horror, I saw she was barely more than a child – I estimated somewhere between seventeen and nineteen. As I approached, I could see that her cheeks were streaked with tears. I froze a few feet away from the bed.

"Good morning, Miss Knight," I said. "I am Thomas Rufford. I..."

I could not continue. I turned and ran towards the door, which I found had been locked. I banged on it. "I won't do it," I shouted. "I won't do it! Let us both out!"

I heard Lady Fairfield's calm voice from behind the picture that hid a grille. "You must, Thomas. Remember what we discussed."

Poor Miss Knight had disappeared entirely under the bedclothes. I strode to the picture, removed it, and looked around for a weapon. I took a chair and with all my might, hurled it at the grille. It smashed through the ancient, crumbling wall it was mounted on, and I heard a scream behind the wall.

I kept attacking the wall, demolishing as much as I could with the remains of the chair. I was blind with fury and had no thought of the consequences. I only knew I had to destroy this evil chamber, this cursed tool of corruption. The door opened, and Lady Fairfield and Miss Knowles rushed in.

"How dare you!" screamed Lady Fairfield. The two of them tried to grab me as I continued to smash the wall, and then I lashed out, knocking Miss Knowles over. Lady Fairfield ran out and came back with several Sisters, who managed to pin me to the floor.

As I writhed on the floor, Lady Fairfield picked up the leg of the broken chair, and brought it down hard on my still aching skull.

~

When I awoke on my bed, I was in a monstrous amount of pain. I felt my head – it was bandaged. This time Lady Fairfield must surely have fractured my skull. I would have been content to be left to die, to blot out the pain, the humiliation, and the bleakness of my future. But it seemed Lady Fairfield still had plans for me.

"That was exceedingly foolish, Thomas."

Through blurred vision, I saw the shape of Lady Fairfield sitting on a chair near my bed.

I groaned. "What do you want with me?" I said. "My brain is nearly out of its pan already. Do what you will with it."

"I want to give you another chance," she said. "I accept a little of the blame for what happened this morning. I had not prepared you sufficiently for Miss Knight. I know she is very young, and she was nervous. You are a sensitive man. It's hard for you."

"How could I possibly be prepared to ruin such a young woman? How did you become so unspeakably cruel?"

The effort of speaking had worsened the pain, and my

eyeballs felt as though they would explode.

"You have it quite wrong, Thomas," she said. "Far from being ruinous, it is a kind of enlightenment, in which you are an important participant. You will turn her from a girl into a woman, and then into a mother – and most crucially, the progenitor of a wise family who will in turn spread the word of the Society."

"Wise – do you intend to teach your brand of foul 'wisdom'?" I said, wincing with pain. "The sort of wisdom where any action, no matter how heinous, can be justified in the name of your precious principles? Do you not see any irony in that?"

"Changing society is not a matter for the faint-hearted, Thomas," Lady Fairfield said. "Conventional morals must be overturned. Lives must be sacrificed. Otherwise, nothing will happen! The same smug men will rule over the world, making the same mistakes, inflicting the same subjugation on women. To take on the ruthless, we must be equally ruthless!"

"I can hardly wait for your new society," I said. "But if you think I'm going to lie with the likes of Miss Knight, you are mistaken. The poor creature was terrified."

"And yet you managed perfectly well with Thanes, did you not?"

"Miss Thanes is older and more experienced. She seemed to know what she was doing." I realised that I was being hypocritical. It had hardly been more acceptable with Miss Thanes.

"Well," she said, "I will let you recover, and then we'll talk about it again." She sighed. "Perhaps I was wrong about you. You are becoming more trouble than you are worth. But I shall give you one more chance."

~

It took a couple of days before I felt well enough to wash myself and remove my blood-soaked bandage. The bleeding had stopped, and my headache was receding slightly. It seemed that my skull was still intact – perhaps Lady Fairfield had struck only a glancing blow in the confusion.

I had one chance left, I thought, as I slowly dressed myself. How would I deal with being presented with another Miss Knight? Would my wrongdoing be mitigated by the prospect of making amends to everyone against whom I had sinned, and avenging those she had destroyed, either in body or in spirit?

I was weighing up my limited choices when Lady Fairfield appeared in my parlour with a bag.

"Ah! You must be feeling better," she said. "Good. Please go into your bedroom."

"What on earth for?"

"Go!" she commanded, following me.

"Lie down," she said, and after I had obeyed, she took an empty jar out of her bag.

I looked at it with alarm, and sat up. Exactly what was the purpose of the jar? Was she going to add me to her collection already?

She pushed me down again. "We are going to make things easier for you," she said. "You may remain down here in your quarters, and still prove useful. Miss Knowles and I have been reading about a method for producing a pregnancy without the need for the woman's husband – just a little present from him."

"Oh, my God," I said. "Surely that has only been done with animals?"

"Mostly, yes, but the principle applies equally to humans. A Scotsman – Mr John Hunter – demonstrated that it could be done successfully. It is another advance the Society can pioneer – removing an act that for many is distasteful, humiliating and prone to spreading disease. What a great gift to womankind this will be!"

"So you want me to... God in Heaven."

"Don't be so dramatic about it, Thomas. I will help. It will all be over shortly, and Miss Knight will be the happy recipient – all without the fuss you insist on making."

She proceeded to unbutton my flies, and exposed me so quickly that I was too surprised to react.

That one chance, I thought, as I bit my lip in mortification – take this one chance. I can stand this if it means I live, and I do not have to degrade any more women.

Her massaging had an effect, and despite myself, I began to feel an unwanted pleasure. I stared at the ceiling and tried to think of anything that might blot out reality. It was imperative that I bring this humiliating scene to a close as soon as possible, so I allowed myself to recall my past dalliances with Bess, and her delight in undressing before me. Surely there was no harm in these thoughts, I reasoned, if they could truncate this torture.

"You really are a fine specimen, Thomas," Lady Fairfield said, with a slight husk in her voice. "I'm beginning to regret hurting you." From her breathing, I got the distinct and disturbing impression that she was enjoying her task.

Just as I found myself on the cusp, she cried, "Oh, Miss Knight can wait, damn it," hitched up her skirts, and leapt onto the bed, straddling me.

"What in God's name!" I began, but she was already successful in her intention and was taking her own pleasure.

When I struggled, she raised a finger in front of me and screamed "Last chance!" and so I was forced to let her continue. My body was being seduced, and therefore wanted to respond, and yet my spirit was repulsed beyond measure. This was a woman who would no doubt become notorious as a female criminal fiend, and she had made me give up my pride, my hope and now my body. All she had left to take was my brain, and who knew how soon that would be?

To my dismay, she began to make a guttural noise, a primitive cry that swelled as she bore down on my person ever faster, compelling nature to take its full course with me. That consummation seemed to turn her cry into a roar, and just as her body began to quiver in her final convulsion, the door was flung open, and several men rushed in. Lady Fairfield was unable to stop herself, and so her scream of pleasure took on the added desperation of a cornered animal.

"Good afternoon, Mr Rufford," said Inspector Simmons as the dying sound echoed around the cell. "Are you absolutely sure you need rescuing, sir?"

~

Fortunately, my friends had not been permitted to follow the police into the basement. The Sisters had been herded into the Great Hall under guard, Lady Fairfield and Miss Knowles included, and having been escorted to the drawing room by Constable Taylor, I flung myself into Phyllis' arms and wept uncontrollably. "You're safe now," she whispered, tears running down her own cheeks. "Your head! Is it hurt?"

I nodded. "It'll mend," I said. "At least physically."

When I had recovered myself a little and disentangled myself, I saw that Francesca and Flora were also highly affected, and I went to embrace them.

"Thank you," I said, finally allowing myself to sit. "Thank you, all of you. I truly thought I would never see any of you ever again. I assume it was my letter that...?"

"Yes," said Phyllis. "I thought it sounded a little odd. I wondered if your memory was playing up when you said I told you about my story at Francesca's. But of course it was on the way to see Mr Belford. And you have never referred to my novels as 'adventure stories'. It all seemed quite unlike you."

“I thought so too,” said Francesca, “when Phyllis was visiting Effie and showed me the letter. I said it was almost as if someone was dictating to you!”

“And yet they were all my own words,” I said.

“I realised that,” said Phyllis, “but not until Francesca got me thinking – especially after William’s disappearance. What if the same thing had happened to you? And then I realised why you were talking specifically about that story. The code! When I found your message, I think I screamed.”

“You did,” said Francesca, “and I dropped a rather nice jug I bought in Dorchester.”

“I’m sorry about that,” said Phyllis.

“I still haven’t seen this letter,” said Flora. “Do you have it?”

“I took a copy before I gave it to Inspector Simmons. Here it is. The first letter of each line.” She handed it to Flora, who spelled out the two words I had hidden.

“Clever,” said Flora. “Thank goodness Lady Fairfield didn’t notice.”

“I think she must have been too concerned about Thomas hiding a clue in the meaning of the words to imagine anything as childishly simple as my code,” said Phyllis. “She’s going to be furious when she finds she made it so easy for us.”

“Why on earth did she kidnap you, Thomas?” Francesca asked. “What happened to William Lowick?”

My headache was returning with a vengeance and I put my head in my hands. “I will tell you all I know, later,” I said. “I just need to get home.”

There was a yell from the Great Hall and I heard the clatter of feet. “Get her back!” I heard Mr Simmons cry. “Get her, you idiot!”

We looked at each other.

“She must have escaped,” I said. Despite my headache, I instinctively leapt up and followed Taylor into the Great Hall. As I passed the staircase, I saw Simmons and Constable

Gawley pounding up the stairs. The stairs dwindled into a much smaller, narrower staircase, and we ran up those until we reached an open door to the roof.

Lady Fairfield had reached the stone parapet that topped the west tower, and was climbing over it. Standing on the other side, with one hand on the parapet, she raised the other to warn us from approaching.

"I will jump!" she shouted. "Stay away!"

"Do as she says," Simmons said, and we retreated a little.

"I will jump," she said, "unless everyone but Thomas goes back inside."

"I'm afraid I can't allow that, ma'am," Simmons said.

In response, Lady Fairfield raised her other hand as if about to fall.

"All right, all right," said Simmons. "We'll go. Mr Rufford, please do what you can. But don't put yourself at risk, sir. We'll be just inside here, by the door."

Simmons and his men hid themselves, and I was left standing a few yards from Lady Fairfield.

"Well done, Thomas," said Lady Fairfield. "I don't know how you did it, but you managed to save yourself. It appears I have lost. But womankind will be the real losers. It's a tragedy."

"The tragedy that will be written," I said, "will have you as the protagonist. Your place in criminal history is assured."

She shrugged. "It makes no difference. Come a little closer, please, Thomas. I want to have a proper conversation."

I stepped forward.

"That's better. I can see your handsome blue eyes."

She sighed. "I'm sorry about William. I allowed myself to be goaded by him. That's the point where everything went wrong."

"I think the rot started before that. You hurt people who trusted you. They will need to learn to trust again."

"I hope I will be forgiven," she said. "It was for a fine

cause. But it doesn't really matter. We all get so agitated – and nothing really matters." She once more let go of the parapet. "Goodbye, Thomas."

"Lady Fairfield, no," I said, "please don't –"

"I don't have the patience for a trial," she said, "or the courage to face the noose. But I can still make one last decision for myself."

"You might be found not guilty by reason of insanity," I said. "Surely that's worth hoping for?"

She shook her head. "This is where my story ends," she said, looking into my eyes. "Where will yours, I wonder?"

Still holding my horrified gaze, and with a calm smile on her lips, she gently toppled back, and in a second she had disappeared from view. In another moment, I heard a sickening, crunching thud and the sound of people rushing outside.

CHAPTER THIRTY

OF ALL that I had experienced over the last five days, the worst horror was Lady Fairfield's act of self destruction. If she had intended to haunt me with her final gaze, she had succeeded. On the roof, I had been unable to move, and had to be guided back down by the Inspector, where I shivered under a blanket in the drawing room. I could not escape Lady Fairfield's eyes. And while she deserved punishment, the grim manner of her demise was difficult to dismiss from my mind.

After sending for a doctor to examine Lady Fairfield's body, and making arrangements for constables to guard the house and its occupants, the Inspector came back into the drawing room.

"You've had a terrible shock, sir," he said. "I'll come to your home tomorrow, sir, and get an account of your experiences, if you are amenable. I won't trouble you today. Taylor will escort you and your friends back to your homes shortly."

I nodded, and cast an alarmed look at Phyllis at the thought of being parted from all of my friends so soon. She understood, and said, "I'll stay with you at Ramsburgh tonight, Thomas. You shouldn't be on your own."

I took her hand and squeezed it in gratitude.

"Just one thing, sir – is there anyone staying here who was especially responsible for the... goings-on, apart from Lady Fairfield?"

"Yes, Inspector," I said. "Miss Knowles was effectively her deputy. She was responsible for covering up William's disappearance, and helped to imprison me."

"Thank you, sir. Could I trouble you to identify her?"

"I'll do it," said Francesca. "I have had the displeasure of entertaining Miss Knowles. I never liked her." She strode into the hall, followed by the Inspector.

"That was satisfying," she said on her return. "The supercilious harridan!"

I thought of Rachel's hardness and eagerness to serve her mistress, and shuddered. "She poisoned Effie, I'm sure of it," I said. "She gave Sylvie herbs to give to Effie. Arsenic tea."

"God almighty," Francesca said. "I think I know where she got the arsenic. There was a piece missing from the left-over roll of 'Hedgerow'. She must have taken it at the dinner party."

"And scraped off the pigment," said Flora. "I hope she hangs."

I had begun to have suspicions about the missing wallpaper during my many hours of incarceration. "There were plenty of other places she could have got arsenic from," I said, "but this way, there were no purchases to trace the poison to her."

"What did she have against Effie?" Phyllis said.

"I think she was jealous," I said. "She and Sylvie had become close, and after Effie's explosion at the party, she must have been smarting. She will have known that Sylvie and Effie were too close to be prised apart naturally, so this was an attempt to get Effie out of the way."

"Perhaps Lady Fairfield gave her too much confidence," Flora said. "She felt invincible. Especially if, as you said, she organised the cover-up over William's disappearance. Is he definitely... dead?"

I struggled to speak. "Yes. Lady Fairfield..." Phyllis handed me a handkerchief and I blew my nose. "Lady Fairfield killed him when she found out that William had been toying with her affections, as she saw it. She pushed him off the gallery into the Great Hall." I could not bring myself to add the final, disgusting detail of William's fate.

"Oh, God," said Phyllis quietly.

"Poor, poor Mrs Lowick," Francesca said.

"And Miss Belford," I said.

"Of course," Francesca said. "They'll have to release Mr Belford now. I'm so relieved for him – he's a good man."

Constable Taylor came in and led us to one of the police carriages, past the blanket that covered my dead persecutor. I saw Miss Knowles in the other carriage, sullenly staring at us. Francesca drew a finger across her throat as she passed.

"Oh, Francesca! How ghoulish!" said Flora.

"Well," Francesca said, "she nearly killed Effie. It'll be good riddance."

~

"Mr Rufford! Thank goodness!" cried Mrs Felton as I came in with Phyllis and Flora, Francesca having been taken back to Halfpenny House. "They found you!" She hugged me warmly, nearly crushing my bruised ribs, which were still tender from my struggle in the Listening Room, exacerbated by Lady Fairfield's enthusiastic attentions.

"It's exceedingly good to see you, sir," Shipley said. "We were sick with worry, truth be told. I thought meeting the carriage at the gates was peculiar. I should have spoken up."

"Flora said you might be at Lady Fairfield's," Mrs Felton continued, "and in some kind of trouble. Is that right?"

I nodded.

"Merciful Lord! What in God's name has she done to you?" she said. "You look half-starved!"

"No doubt he will explain in good time," Phyllis said. "We must get Thomas to bed. He's had an awful time."

"Of course, of course – let me get some supper for you. How does chicken broth sound?"

"That's very kind, Mrs Felton," I said. "But just a couple of pieces of toast and a cup of tea are all I can manage." The horrors of the day had dulled my appetite, despite the fact I had not eaten for many hours.

"I shall bring them up shortly. Oh, my dear!" She squeezed my arm and hurried off to prepare my supper.

My own bed felt blissful. I looked at Phyllis, who had pulled up a chair near to me, and sighed.

"I didn't expect to come back to this bed," I said. "Or even to see you again."

"Don't," Phyllis said, wiping her cheek. "I can't bear it."

There was a knock at the door, and Mrs Felton came in with an invalid tray and placed it on my bed.

"There you are, my dear. And you just ring if you need anything else."

She pressed Phyllis' shoulder. "Lovely that he has you to take care of him. I'm so glad you're going to be Mrs Rufford! I can't wait for you to be the lady of the house. Oh – if I'm not being too forward, my dear!"

Phyllis looked up at her and smiled. "Of course not. Thank you!"

I felt deeply uncomfortable at this, and when Mrs Felton had left, and after I had consumed a slice of toast, I said, "Phyllis, I have something difficult I need to say."

"Oh? You don't have to talk about it now," Phyllis said. "You must rest."

"I do need to, or I won't be able to rest," I said. "I love you so much..."

"I know – and I love you too, Thomas!"

"But that's not what I had to say." I closed my eyes and tried to summon courage. "You have to release me from our engagement."

Her smile turned to incomprehension. "What? What on earth can you mean by that? What has happened?"

I struggled to find the words, and remained silent.

"Have you found someone else?" she said. "Someone at Kirkheaton Hall? Surely not."

"No," I said. "You are my only love. There is no one else I would remotely like to marry."

"Then why did you say that beastly thing?"

"Because of what happened at Kirkheaton," I said. "I'm not the same person."

She stared at me. "Well, you must have had a terrible time, even though I don't know exactly what happened. But I don't see how –"

I screwed up my face in self-disgust. "I was forced to do things," I said.

"What kind of things?"

"Things that make our engagement impossible. Things that you should not have to forgive or even hear about."

She was silent for a moment. "I believe I have a great capacity for forgiveness. You must tell me what I need to forgive. You don't know me well enough to say how I will – or must – respond."

"Forgive me," I said. "I didn't mean to be presumptuous. But it's not only how *you* will feel, but how my own capacity has been damaged."

"Your capacity for...?"

"For passion. For physical love."

Phyllis flinched at this. "Help me understand, Thomas. You're talking in riddles."

I tried to think how I might better express myself. "I haven't been in this situation before," I said, "nor do I know any man who has, so it's hard for me to entirely understand and convey. But I need time to forget these events – or at least diminish the power of them. I feel damaged, dirty – not myself."

Phyllis nodded. "Perhaps I'm expecting too much, but I must know what happened to you."

"Very well," I said. "Let me try to explain. Lady Fairfield

couldn't bear her own children – so her 'Sisters', as she called them, fulfilled some of the role of family. But then she wanted children, who could be brought up at Kirkheaton and indoctrinated, before going forth and spreading the word of the Society. And you may guess who she found to help with the paternal side of this plan."

The colour drained from Phyllis' face. "Yes. Yes, of course," she said. "I see. How many women...?"

"Two," I said, "and nearly a third, but I threw a tantrum and destroyed half a wall." The memory was satisfying. "But one of them..." I took a sip of tea. "One of them was Lady Fairfield."

"Lady Fairfield? But I thought you said she couldn't bear children."

"Yes. But nevertheless, she forced herself upon me. Just before Inspector Simmons found me."

"Oh, Heavens," Phyllis said, her bottom lip trembling. She put her head in her hands for a minute, and then sat up and said, "But none of this is your fault."

I shrugged. "And yet it happened. It's unthinkable that you should take me on in these circumstances. I couldn't live with myself if I debased you by marrying me."

She thought for a moment, staring at the floor. "You're not using this as an excuse, because there's some other reason you don't want to marry me? Perhaps the idea of marriage doesn't appeal any more."

"Phyllis, no! That's not it at all. Please don't think that of me. I'm just not suitable for marriage at present."

"Will you ever be?"

"I certainly hope so," I said. "But who knows?"

She was silent again, and then, taking the ring off her finger, said, "Well, if that's what you wish. I will absolve you of your obligations. I don't know what to think. I do find the idea of you with other women disgusting – I'm sorry. But I can't help also thinking that if we both love each other, it's stupid to throw it all away."

"I know," I said. "It's utterly mad. But we have no choice."

~

Lady Fairfield plagued my dreams. When sleep came, Lady Fairfield's penetrating, chilling eyes would sooner or later appear, and again I would watch her fall away to her death. She may not have had the opportunity to put my brain in a jar, but she had still contrived to capture my mind. Scenes from my captivity, some real and some imagined, played out remorselessly in my nightmares. One minute I was naked and being beaten by a pack of murderous nuns, and the next I was in Lady Fairfield's chamber of pickled horrors, being denounced for my immorality by William's angry, wild-eyed head, from which I was powerless to run.

Knowing that Phyllis was in the bedroom next door was a comfort. I wanted to go to her, and take her hand and talk, even seek shelter in her bed, but I knew that I had renounced the right to physical consolation. However, we had agreed that our friendship was not in doubt – that was a fact I clung to with all my being.

As promised, Inspector Simmons arrived the following morning and I chose to receive him in my study downstairs. This room represented a suitable mood, somewhere between the cool formality of the dining room – the Inspector's preferred place of inquisition – and the cheerful frivolity of the drawing room.

I sat behind the bulwark of my desk, and Simmons made himself comfortable in a small armchair. Mrs Fenton brought coffee, and Simmons took out his trusty notebook.

He smiled as he tapped his aide-mémoire. "I'll rather miss

this, sir. I've almost filled it up, and you appear in it a surprising amount. I sincerely hope that when I get a fresh one, you will be blissfully absent from it – and I say that with kindness, sir, as I know the last few days have been trying for you."

"Thank you, Mr Simmons," I said. "I hope to stay out of your pages too." I took some coffee, and then said, "Are you horribly cross with me, Inspector?"

"About this business with Lady Fairfield and Mr Lowick? I have no right to be, sir, when you have been so helpful in this case. Of course, I have a few opinions, when it comes to information that might perhaps have been better shared. But that would be quibbling."

I was surprised at his indulgence, but then, he knew a little of what I had endured at Kirkheaton Hall. Such things gave a man perspective.

"Again, thank you," I said, feeling unwelcome tears welling up at the Inspector's unaccustomed kindness. "Let me tell you everything, and if you then wish to judge me, I'll accept it. I've been foolish, I realise, and it has nearly cost me my life."

So I told my tale as completely as I could, without sparing my own embarrassment. Most of this the Inspector already knew, in general, but there were details that raised his eyebrows.

"— You say Miss Knowles was jealous of Miss Harris? Regarding her friendship with Miss Dubois? Ah – I see, sir. Yes, I gather that can happen."

"— Lady Fairfield came to visit you, and asked you for information about William? Interesting. Did it not arouse your suspicions, sir?"

"— So Mrs Milburn knew both Miss Knowles and Miss Dubois. Yes, I will have to interview Mrs Milburn, sir, but I agree that considering her mental fragility, she is more victim than conspirator."

"— Arsenical wallpaper? No, I had no idea it was so widespread, sir. This is alarming news. And Miss Knowles used a scrap of it for...? Well, I'll be damned."

"— It was unfortunate you followed Lady Fairfield's advice to visit her secretly, wasn't it, sir? But plenty would have trusted her, just like you."

"— I'm sure you had no choice about it, sir. We will make sure Miss Thanes is cared for, whether with child or not."

"— Good God! She pickled his what, sir? I have already instructed my men to search the estate for Mr Lowick's body, but if what you say is true, they are in for an unpleasant surprise. I will write, as delicately as I can, to Mrs Lowick."

"— It's rare indeed, sir, for a female to be the perpetrator of such a... personal crime. You cannot be blamed for Lady Fairfield's perverted behaviour. I assure you this part will not go in the police report – you will observe that I have laid down my pencil. And I have sworn my men to silence on the matter."

~

I was at Mrs Milburn's door. It had been three days since I had talked to the Inspector, and Phyllis had returned home. Although I still frequently shook with the dismal memories that churned in my mind, I had decided that engagement with the world beyond my fortress, formidable though that seemed, might be a cure – or at least a distraction. I could not yet face a visit to Halfpenny House and the prospect of seeing Miss Dubois, being so closely associated with the dreaded Miss Knowles. I was not sure enough of my composure. But I thought I could manage Mrs Milburn, and I was anxious to see how she was recovering from the trauma of her leader's death.

"Oh!" said Mrs Milburn, when Mrs Spillings showed me into the drawing room. "Mr Rufford! I... I don't know what to say."

"Good morning, Mrs Milburn," I said, shaking her hand. "I hope you're beginning to reconcile yourself to recent events. It has truly been a terrible time."

"Thank you," she said. "I'm calmer now, but I've been so confused. How can such a good person turn out to be so wicked? And how could I have helped her? I have been complicit in your torment – how you can even bear to look at me? If you have come to berate me, then I deserve it, and more."

"I have come to do no such thing," I said. "We are both her victims. You more so, perhaps, because of the absolute trust you placed in her."

Mrs Milburn's chin quivered, and she dabbed her eyes with a handkerchief. "You are too kind. I hardly dare to imagine what you went through, in the cellars. All I could do was to gather some flowers..."

"And it lifted my heart immensely, I assure you. You could do nothing more."

Mrs Milburn sniffed. "If you want to ask me anything, please do. I don't know what I've told you, and what I haven't. Oh – but I'm so glad you came to see me, because I have something I must say!"

"Yes?"

"I know what happened to Harold, up on the ramparts! It's as though the fog has cleared. It was when I came home, after Lady Fairfield... after she died. I was forced to see what I previously could not. And suddenly I remembered that moment, that was just a dark smudge in my mind before. We were happily walking, when Harold took a leaflet from his pocket and asked if I believed in what it said. I told him I did, and he frowned and said I had a tendency to get embroiled in crackpot notions. Well, I confess I have indulged in tarot readings, and I do believe the stars have an influence over us – not everyone believes in these things – but I protested that the Society was nothing like that, that it was simply trying to make the world treat women better.

"He said, 'Don't I treat you well enough already?' as a joke, and he teased me that he would burn the leaflet. I tried to grab it. He moved towards the edge of the rampart, holding the leaflet out of reach, and then he lost his balance. I could see him beginning to fall, and tried to grab him, but it was no use."

"How utterly horrific," I said. "I am so sorry. No wonder it made you ill."

She nodded. "I see it as clear as day now," she said. "It was an accident. So I'm not quite such a bad person as I thought – or at least, not until I fell in with Lady Fairfield. I was lost, and I thought the Society was the answer."

"I understand perfectly. It's a good sign that your mind is clearing. Did you tell the Inspector about this?"

"Yes. He was gentler on me than I deserved. He said I would not be charged for my stupidity in Mr Belford's shop. That I'd suffered enough, and I had been coerced by Miss Knowles and Lady Fairfield.."

"The Inspector seems to be mellowing," I said. "He was similarly kind to me. Do you have any plans?"

"I think I will get away," said Mrs Milburn. "Harold and I never made many friends – we had so little time together here. I know you have been my friend, but I must go where I'm not reminded of... well, everything. I've always rather fancied living in Whitby, where I have a cousin. It's very pretty, and I would like the fresh sea air. I have a little family money, so I will be all right."

"I'm sure a fresh start is sensible," I said. "I've heard Whitby is delightful. You deserve to be happy. Perhaps you might send me a letter when you're settled, and tell me how you're getting on?"

Mrs Milburn smiled. "With pleasure. Thank you, Mr Rufford. I won't forget your kindness."

~

As I rode back to Ramsburgh, Mrs Milburn's optimism, and the abundance of nature that was burgeoning as the summer advanced, lifted my spirits. There seemed hope that the darkness inhabiting Hawksbridge in recent weeks was beginning to lift. After I had stabled Celeste, I found a stranger in my drawing room, who leapt to his feet as I came in.

"Ah, Mr Rufford! Mr Timothy Knowles. I'm very pleased to meet you. Your man said I could make myself comfortable, I hope you don't mind –"

"Not at all, Mr Knowles. How might I help?"

Mr Knowles was a slim, earnest young man. My heart sank at his name, as I did not want my good mood to be punctured, but I was also intrigued.

"Well, I hope I might be able to help you a little," he said, sitting down again, "after all you have been through. First, I want to apologise with all my heart for my sister. I know she could be headstrong, and unconventional, but if I had had an inkling that she might..."

He shook his head. "She has been wicked, and you have suffered greatly, Mr Rufford. Our family owe you a great debt."

"You are not responsible for the sins of your sister," I said. "But I appreciate you coming to see me. It can't be easy for you to endure, either."

"I will manage," Mr Knowles said, "though my parents have taken it very hard. But what I wanted to talk about was your interest in wallpaper."

I laughed. "Sorry, that sounds so frivolous, but I know it's not. You refer, of course, to wallpaper with arsenical pigment?"

"Indeed," he said. "I'm a clerk at Forrester's. I have been concerned for some time about the direction of our manufacturing processes. I've been following poisoning cases in the press, and I discussed it many times with my sister. I'm afraid, sir, that I'm to blame for putting the idea of poison into my sister's head." He clenched his hands around the arms of his chair. "It's too awful."

"Don't think of it that way, Mr Knowles. Only Rachel is responsible for her actions. I'm glad to say that Miss Harris is on the mend. But certainly, if you have any information about Forrester that I could use, I would be more than interested. I intend to write an article – the piece that Mr Lowick planned to write."

"Then you will want to read this," Mr Knowles said, retrieving a letter from his jacket pocket and handing it to me. "It's from Mr Forrester to my manager, Mr Cook, who has expressed similar worries to mine." He stared at me intently as I read it.

MEMORANDUM FOR THE ATTENTION OF MR COOK (ACCOUNTS DEPT.)

Mr Cook,

I appreciate your concerns about certain of our products, but you put too much weight by press reports. Journalists are apt to exaggerate.

As you know, we have received high praise for our recent designs, especially 'Hedgerow'. That praise is partly due to the vivid colours we are now able to achieve. Were we to start selling paper with the experimental formulation, our customers would rightly feel cheated, after they have made their decision based on the original colours.

Furthermore, we have built up a large stock of these papers, which represents a considerable investment.

When the time is ripe, and we have further developed our arsenic-free pigments, I may consider a change of direction. But for now let us remember that the number of affected customers is small, and any harm that comes to them is their responsibility for having undue contact with their wallpaper or having applied it in unsuitable conditions. I would go as far as to say that the suffering of a few is acceptable, even necessary, for the many to benefit. After all, many products on sale today are hazardous if misused, so there is a strong whiff of hypocrisy from those protesting about wallpaper.

When we are ready, we will launch a prepared campaign in which we will profess our newly-discovered knowledge of the problems with arsenic, and encourage our competitors to follow our lead so we are not disadvantaged. Indeed, we may be able to make a virtue out of it. But meanwhile, letters from *our legal department are quite sufficient to keep trouble-makers at bay.*

Again, thank you for your concern: you may leave it entirely in my hands.

Gabriel Forrester

Having read the note, I looked up in amazement at Mr Knowles.

"The man has no ethics," I said. "In a way, this doesn't surprise me – it's entirely in keeping with the conversation I had with him. On the other hand, his brazenness is breathtaking, and he has created a powerful weapon against himself. May I hold on to it for a while?"

"By all means," said Mr Knowles. "Do whatever you need to do with it. From your reputation, I know you to be a man of principle. But please don't mention my name, as I would certainly be booted out of the company without a reference, and I'm not ready to leave yet."

"You have my word, Mr Knowles. And thank you – I believe this letter will do a great deal of good."

CHAPTER THIRTY-ONE

ALTHOUGH the trauma of Kirkheaton Hall had occupied most of my mental and emotional capacities, the arsenic problem had been nagging at me. I did not know how to proceed, except to write down what I knew in an article; but Mr Knowles had brought me a key with which I might unlock the might of public opinion. I would need to carefully consider how best to use it, but in the meantime, I felt strong enough for a trip to Halfpenny House, which I undertook the next day.

"Thank goodness you're looking less wan and thin," Francesca said as she embraced me in the hall. "I can feel it, too. Mrs Felton has been feeding you up!"

"She's doing her best to coax an appetite out of me," I said, "and largely succeeding."

"Wonderful! And the nightmares? Phyllis told me you were suffering from them."

I winced. "Still bad," I said, extricating myself from her embrace. "But I'm distracting myself. I hope that by cramming as many different thoughts into my head as possible, I will push out the monsters."

"A fine plan," Francesca said, leading me to the small sitting room. "I'll help you as much as I can. Will you be up to a dinner party here? We must celebrate your triumphant return from those dreadful cellars. And Phyllis must come, of course."

"Most certainly I'll come. But what about Effie?"

"You shall see for yourself! She is improved enough to attend at least for a little while. And you won't believe who else will be there!"

Francesca smiled and waited for me to guess.

"I have no idea. I hope not Miss Knowles," I said.

"No, for heaven's sake! She's in jail, where she belongs."

"I can't guess."

"Flora and Victor!" she said triumphantly.

"Good Lord," I said. "However did you manage that? She said nothing to me. Does that mean...?"

"Yes!" she said, and clasped my hand with both of hers in her excitement. "Isn't it glorious? They are reconciled – in no small part thanks to you."

"I'm... amazed," I said. "And so very happy for them. Flora has forgiven you?"

"I'm not sure I would have in her shoes, and I'm unworthy of it," Francesca said, "but by some miracle, she has. She came over yesterday to say that if she could forgive Victor, then she could forgive me. And she had the grace to say that I had good taste in men!"

"Well, you do," I said. "After all, you're friends with me."

"True," she said. "And she told me that Mr and Mrs Harris were asking kindly after me – that they hoped I would come to dinner soon. After what I did! They are such kind, generous people."

"They truly are," I said. I was particularly relieved, as circumstances had meant that I had not been able to carry out my promise to put in a good word for Francesca with the Harrises. I imagined that Flora had done this instead, and that the Harrises – who had always had a soft spot for Francesca – had been keen to forgive and forget.

"So it seems that we might soon have two weddings in Hawksbridge," said Francesca.

I sighed and said, "I'm afraid one of them won't be mine. I have made Phyllis break our engagement."

Francesca looked at me in shock. "Oh, no! Thomas, what happened?"

I struggled to think how to explain. "I had some

experiences at Kirkheaton Hall that... well, they have made me indisposed to marriage at present."

"Oh, Thomas, that's too bad. I won't pry, but do you think this condition is permanent?"

"I hope not," I said. "I'll give it some months and see how both of us feel. We are still on good terms."

She squeezed my hand. "That's something," she said. "And don't forget that there may be others who see Phyllis' qualities – and she may not wait forever."

"I fear that may be true," I said. "And now I must see how Effie is doing, if she's up to it."

"I'm sure she'll be delighted to see you," Francesca said. "Let's go up."

Francesca knocked on Effie's door. "Hello! Can I come in? I've brought someone to see you."

"How lovely," Effie said. "Please come!"

Effie was sitting up in bed, propped up by a multitude of pillows and making use of an invalid tray covered in sheets of paper.

"Thomas! You poor thing, how are you? I've heard such dreadful stories. Come and sit by me."

Francesca left, and I sat in the chair next to the bed.

"You look a hundred times better than when I last saw you," I said. "And you're working again! That's such a relief."

"And to me," she said. "I still have a lot of pain, especially in my head, but it's nothing like before. Francesca said Miss Knowles tried to assassinate me – and used my friend against me! That's the last time I drink herb tea."

"She managed to use two friends against you," I said. "She stole a piece of Francesca's wallpaper, and then got poor Sylvie to feed you the scrapings."

"Thereby implicating the famous Mr Forrester," she said. "I gather you are on the war-path where he's concerned. But after the last few days, you're entitled to a holiday from your investigations."

"Perhaps, but they help keep my demons at bay," I said. "I have a plan for how to deal with Mr Forrester. I will let you know how it goes."

"How exciting," she said. "I also have interesting news."

"Yes?"

"I'm working on a piece for you, Thomas! As I said, you have inspired me, even without – well, you know. It has been coming to me in bursts, while I lie on my bed of pain. I've been dreaming it."

"Thank you – I'm honoured," I said, greatly touched by this. "Are you getting help from Sylvie? I haven't seen her today."

"After the Inspector had finished with her, I insisted she have a break from me," she said, "so she's gone to Paris for a while. She's been so worried for me, and I've been tiring myself worrying about her. I've been managing on my own for now. I may find someone to help me with a neat manuscript."

"Ah. Do you have a name for this piece?"

"Certainly," said Effie. "It will be called 'The Ramsburgh Variations'."

~

The police found William's remains in the grounds of Kirkheaton Hall, amongst the beloved dogs populating the Fairfield family pet cemetery. Although his funeral brought back many bad memories, I tried to concentrate on the companionable times we had spent – alas, far too few. We should have become firm friends, I mused, although there might have been a little too much liquor involved. As I listened to Mr Benton conducting the rite of committal in his usual sing-song staccato, behind me a familiar voice seemed to say drily, "I just hope all of me is in there, Thomas, or resurrection is going to be a very rum affair." At least that is what my disturbed imagination conjured up.

As I was leaving the churchyard, a stout middle-aged man – who I noticed looking at me during the service – hurried up to me.

"Mr Rufford – my name is Frederick Stanton," he said, extending his hand. "I'm the proprietor of The Hawksbridge Herald."

"Pleased to meet you," I said, shaking his hand. "In fact I wanted to speak with you about an article."

"And that, Mr Rufford, is just what I wanted to talk to you about. But first I must thank you for finding William's murderer."

"Finding, and then losing, I'm afraid," I said. "I would have preferred justice to be done."

"Well, it's a kind of justice and better than none. About William's article – Mrs Lowick told me you wanted to finish the work he started."

"I do," I said. "Would you print an article about Forrester's lethal wallpaper?"

"I welcome it," Mr Stanton said. "By the bye, we found a box of his research in a cupboard at the office. You may find it useful. And if Mr Forrester wants to sue me, let him. He may not want the publicity."

"I think you're right. He's quick with a lawyer, but it's time to call his bluff. First, though, I'll have another word with him. It may change what I have to write."

"You think he'll listen? He's a tough bugger, that one."

"Yes," I said. "I have reason to believe he'll listen to me, this time."

~

Arriving with Phyllis at Mr Forrester's imposing house and stepping down from the hired carriage, I had a little more confidence than previously.

"Oh, it's you, sir," said Greene. "I assume you don't have an appointment?"

"Correct," I said. "I would be grateful if you could show us in, Greene. Your master will definitely want to speak to us. Besides, I come bearing an apology."

"Very good, sir, ma'am," he said. "Please wait in the hall." The footman went to fetch Mr Forrester.

"Impressive," Phyllis said, looking around her. "I wonder if he has any arsenic wallpaper in his own house."

Heavy footsteps presaged the appearance of Mr Forrester. "You are bold to return, Mr Rufford. Good evening, Miss Drummond. It's an honour to welcome such a distinguished writer into my home."

Phyllis bent her head in acknowledgement.

"An apology, I gather?" he continued. "Well, that is splendid news. A rapprochement, by God! Let's go to my study, and we'll drink on it."

He poured three sherries, and I said, "I must apologise, sir, for implying you might have been responsible for Mr Lowick's disappearance. As we now know, Lady Fairfield was entirely to blame."

"Ah, Esme, Esme," he murmured. "What were you about? So promising and advanced in her views, and with the energy of a hundred women! She must have become unhinged. Relations between men and women can do that, you know."

"Indeed they can," I said, "and lead to callous acts of revenge, whether murdering a lover or merely the English language."

Mr Forrester laughed heartily. "Oh, Mr Rufford, I have underestimated you! You are a wag, after all." He swallowed his sherry. "Yes, mea culpa. It was not the best verse I have ever written. My talent lies in other directions. Well, we have cleared the air – capital."

"Not entirely," I said. "I have some requests."

"Do you? Fascinating," he said, refilling his glass. "Carry on."

"I would like you to stop using arsenic in your wallpaper, pay the medical bills for all those affected by your products, and issue an apology."

Mr Forrester spilled his drink, his astonished look turning into a huge grin as once more he bellowed with laughter.

"Very good, very good," he said. "I can't breathe!" After a moment he continued: "Miss Drummond, marry the fellow immediately, since he's the funniest man you'll ever meet."

"Mr Rufford is entirely serious," Phyllis said, unflustered. "I think you are going to do exactly as he says."

"Why on earth would I?" he said. "We have already had a similar conversation the last time you were here, Mr Rufford. My patterns excepted, I do so hate repetition."

"Because of this," I said, and handed him the note.

He frowned and took it to a lamp. "Oh, this. Where did you get hold of it? So there are spies in my company. I shall have to root them out."

He ripped it into shreds and put it in the bin. "There. The matter is resolved. Did you have any other business? Because I'm a little tired, and wish to retire for the evening."

"Obviously that is just a copy," I said. "And your bluster is futile. Unless you meet our demands, I'll have to publish that note. You may imagine what that will do to your reputation and your business. You will be completely ruined, as you have condemned yourself out of your own mouth."

The confident smile faded from Mr Forrester's lips. "You are trying to blackmail me, Mr Rufford. The police will be most interested."

"It seems I have recently earned some leniency with the police," I said. "Inspector Simmons was most concerned about the wallpaper when I mentioned it. So you are correct.

The police will be interested – in investigating you and your company. Whether your marriage will survive a public interrogation of your character is also a question you must ask yourself. You stand to lose everything."

He sighed. "And you kindly offer me a way out of this bleak future?" he said bitterly.

"Precisely," I said. "How futile it is to merely ruin a man's reputation, when instead, the lives of some of his victims – those still living – might be eased, and the possibility of future victims eliminated."

"What you demand will ruin me financially," he said, running his hands through his hair. "Once I admit liability, any rogue could come after me with a spurious claim."

"It's a risk you will have to take," I said. "There will need to be oversight, of course. For those claiming to have become ill as a result of your wallpaper, an expert such as Dr Peter Henrick may be invaluable in validating the claim."

"That old fraud has got it in for me," he said. "He'll be delighted to drum up business and get rich on it."

"I don't claim this will be easy," I said. "But perhaps you should have thought of this before being so careless with a deadly poison."

"You sanctimonious little pipsqueak!" he exploded. "Have you any idea what it takes to build and run a successful business? Of course you don't – you sit idly in your castle looking down your nose at everyone else, everyone who puts in a hard day's work for the benefit of the world! How can you possibly understand what pressure I'm under? How the devil do you expect me to find the money for this? I shall have to burn thousands of pounds' worth of stock."

I shrugged. "Perhaps write another book about your vision of Utopia? That could raise some funds. You can write about a wonderful world where the inhabitants don't poison their fellow men for money."

CHAPTER THIRTY-TWO

I COULD see the excitement in Flora's eyes. She was wearing the same daring crimson dress that had so impressed Victor at Ramsburgh; Francesca had placed them next to each other, and the understanding and affection between them was palpable.

I was happy to see it, but I was also aware of the comparison with Phyllis and myself. Although Phyllis did her best not to show it, seeing their closeness must have hurt. I cursed myself, and then cursed Lady Fairfield, the true origin of this fracture. How long would she have a grip over us? I still felt too sullied to entertain the thought of forming a sacred alliance. And I was sickened, too, by the knowledge that the world must be gossiping about what had been forced on me. It was, after all, the stuff of salacious news articles. How could I possibly allow Phyllis to also be the target of such speculation? It was simply dishonourable to bring her into it. And of course, she had her own considerable reputation to protect.

"Thomas? Tho-mas!"

I became aware that my name was being called. "Now, Thomas, I don't know where you are, but we need you back," said Francesca brightly. "I'll do far too much talking otherwise."

I started. "Sorry," I said. "I was just thinking how delightful my sister is looking."

"Isn't she?" said the Captain. "I'm a damnedly lucky fellow. Of all the victories I have known, this is by far the sweetest."

"Well said!" said Francesca. "I've been dying to know what your plans are, if you are at liberty to say."

The Captain nodded. "I think we can say – can we, my dear? Good. Well, given we are the subject of prurient interest, we will have a very quiet, very quick wedding, and then we are going away for a few months. Perhaps longer."

"Going?" I said. "Where?"

"We haven't yet decided," the Captain said. "In a way, it doesn't really matter. India, North America – most probably Brazil. The jungle holds a fascination for me. Our country, beautiful though it is, is only a tiny corner of Creation. I want to further my study of natural variety, but we also both need a fresh start, away from tittle-tattle."

"Quite," I said, avoiding looking at Francesca. "This is extremely exciting."

"And terrifying," said Flora. "But I've been rotting away here for too long. I shall miss you all dreadfully – but I shall write. That is, where there is a postal service."

"So the explorer got his companion in the end," said Effie. "I had a feeling you would. But you had better bring Flora back in one piece."

"I shall indeed," said Victor. "I cannot guarantee that we will be quite the same people, of course."

"I should think not," said Francesca. "You will have tales galore, and be so much wiser, and will think us all exceptionally parochial in Hawksbridge."

"I expect it will be a great relief to return," said Flora. "But I'm ready for an adventure. If it's not too morbid to say, you never know what's around the corner, and how much time is left."

I nodded, and said, "I have been made all too aware of that lately."

"And I," said Effie. "But on a more cheerful note, has anyone else seen The Hawksbridge Herald this morning?"

No one else had. "Aha! Let me fetch it," she said, and she left the room.

"She's looking so much better," said Victor. "You have

done a splendid job nursing her, Francesca."

"Thank you," said Francesca. "Yes, she is nearly her old self. Of course, I can't forget that if she hadn't been staying here, she wouldn't have become ill in the first place."

"I don't see why not," I said. "Sylvie and Miss Knowles might still have got together, and Miss Knowles might have chosen another method – perhaps an even more deadly one."

"True," said Francesca. "That is some comfort."

Effie returned with the newspaper and handed it to me. "I expect you'll find the same in the national press. Look at page four."

I opened up the newspaper and read the half-page advertisement aloud.

AN IMPORTANT STATEMENT FROM FORRESTER & CO.

We would like to announce that we shall no longer be selling papers containing arsenic pigments. This affects all colours of 'Hedgerow', 'Rose Garden', and 'Wildflower Meadow'. We will be switching to a proprietary pigment formulation forthwith, so there will be only a small interruption in supply. The differences between old and new papers will be noticeable but slight, and unquestionably worth the welfare of our customers. We hope other manufacturers will join us in this important advance in public safety.

We advise customers to talk to their decorators about replacing paper in the ranges mentioned above, at no cost to them, as soon as is practicable.

We would also like to take this opportunity to apologise to all customers who have been adversely affected by the chemicals in our paper. Naturally the public's health and happiness are paramount, and we regret any unforeseen harm. If customers wish to discuss compensation for severe disease that they have good cause to believe has resulted from our papers, they should write to: Forrester & Co., Amble Road, Hawksbridge.

"Thank goodness," I said, swigging half a glass of claret

by way of celebration. "The blighter's seen sense."

"You did it!" Effie said, getting up again and embracing me. "You clever chap. Is there anything you can't do?"

"Good God!" said Victor. "How bloody extraordinary. Excuse my language – but are you telling me this change of heart is entirely due to Thomas?"

"Not at all," I said. "I had crucial help from an employee of Forrester's, who was horrified at reports of death and illness caused by the papers. He gave me the means to persuade Forrester that this would be the best course of action for him. And Phyllis backed me up with her usual poise when we went to speak to him."

"Beautifully devious. But the cost, man!" said Victor, cutting up his lamb chop. "I wonder if he can even stay in business."

"We shall see," I said. "But his reputation is more important to him than the money. He still sees himself as a distinguished political philosopher, and chief guardian of public taste."

"He doesn't deserve any sort of reputation," said Phyllis, "but this is the most practical outcome. People like the Nesbits will be able to make themselves a little more comfortable. And others won't have to suffer just for wanting a beautiful pattern on their walls."

"You still have your work cut out, though, Thomas," Victor said. "Are you also going to have arsenic removed from other common objects? Lotions, paint, book covers, that sort of thing."

I made a sudden realisation. "Of course! How stupid of me. He wasn't mad!"

"I'm sorry?" Victor said, startled. "Who wasn't?"

"William – he burned some of his wife's books, and so she thought he may have been suffering from some kind of disorder of the mind. It seemed odd and arbitrary behaviour. But he must simply have been protecting his family against the possibility of arsenic poisoning."

"How wise," Francesca said. "Well – I'm going to check my library tomorrow, and I advise everyone else to do the same. But what are we looking for, exactly?"

"Very vivid blues and greens, I believe," I said. "Of a similar intensity to your wallpaper."

"So it's not just Mr Forrester who's murdering us with arsenic," said Francesca. "What I still can't comprehend is how such an awful man can create such wonderful designs. We associate beauty with goodness – but we must be quite wrong about that!"

"It's no different in Nature," said Victor. "A beautiful animal can also be a violent predator. We assume beauty is laid out by God for our delectation. But in fact, pattern and form in nature are simply tools in the raw struggle of life. Sorry – that's a little unromantic, I realise."

"Hu and Pru are good examples," said Effie. "That whole shimmering, hypnotic display, just to catch a mate. Does that mean we share a bird's idea of aesthetics?"

"An interesting point," said Victor. "That says something about the selection of characteristics across species. One would expect dissimilar creatures to have totally different responses to the same stimuli, surely. I must give that some thought."

"I refuse to be put off enjoying natural beauty," said Flora, "just because it's not there purely for our benefit."

"Quite right," said Francesca. "And I hope the good Captain will not become jaded with all his scientific knowledge."

"Not me," said Victor, leaning to kiss Flora on the cheek. "I enjoy beauty in all its many forms."

~

Effie went upstairs to rest, and when the remainder of us retired to the drawing room, I was surprised to find that it had been painted a plain, if attractive, turquoise blue.

"I was fed up with decorative decisions," Francesca said, noticing me looking at the walls. "And besides, I don't want anything that remotely reminds me of that awful man."

"I like it," I said. "Your pictures look good against it."

"You know," said Victor, "I heard a shocking thing that Miss Knowles apparently confessed to. Or is it too grim? Perhaps it's better left unsaid."

"Oh, come now, Victor," said Francesca. "You can't leave us hanging."

"Very well," he said. "Lady Fairfield was planning to endow a trust to help with the victims of arsenic poisoning."

"Is that shocking?" Phyllis said. "Hypocritical and cynical, yes, but it sounds like the sort of ostentatious gesture she was fond of."

"Not of itself, I agree, but when you hear the name of it..." He grimaced and took a draught of port.

"Well?" said Flora. "Out with it."

"Supposedly, she wanted to call it the William Lowick and Thomas Rufford Memorial Trust, or some such."

A shiver went up my spine.

"Good grief," said Francesca.

"Oh, Victor, you should really have kept that to yourself after all," said Flora. "That is just horrible."

"My apologies," Victor said. "That's why I hesitated."

"So she did intend to do away with me after she had finished with me," I said. "And then appear all sympathetic and magnanimous. She was even more of a monster than I realised."

"What will happen to her Society, do you think?" said Francesca.

"Disbanded, I imagine," said Victor. "I can't imagine anyone would want to lead it now. I expect she's put back the women's emancipation movement by years."

I wondered how much the others knew about Lady Fairfield's breeding plans. I hoped nothing at all. Miss Thanes had been good enough to write to me and assure me that she had not conceived, which was an almighty relief. All in all, things might have been much worse. I might have created an army of Rufford bastards, all to be inculcated with her ideology. Even though it had not happened, the mere thought was still the perfect fodder for nightmares.

~

Ramsburgh felt strangely quiet after Flora's departure, which had swiftly followed her necessarily discreet marriage to Victor, so unfussy and brief that it bordered on elopement. I had become accustomed to her guarding the old tower and it was odd to see no light at the window in the evening. I was beginning to miss our lunches together. Even old Mrs Northcutt, Flora's housekeeper, had gone off to live with relatives, and I was left with Titian, Flora's cat, who now had the run of the whole house, and was dashing about exploiting it to the full. Fortunately Fox was more curious about him than peeved at the intrusion, so they blithely coexisted, and Titian was too intimidated by Hu and Pru to harm them.

Diverting myself from the melancholy of Flora's absence, I started my article for The Hawksbridge Herald. Now that Mr Forrester had fulfilled his side of the bargain, I could not communicate my rage at his negligence. With gritted teeth, I praised Forrester's new approach, but I did not desist from condemning the use of arsenic in products manufactured by other companies. (It is a matter of profound regret than even as I pen this memoir, few such companies have been similarly enlightened, but I hold out hope that sustained pressure will eventually wipe this scourge from our shops and homes.)

With extraordinary speed, as if to reverse the time lost to illness, Effie had finished her composition and had written it out with the help of none other than Bess Shannon, whom I had suggested, having heard her arrangements for the harp. Bess had eagerly accepted this considerable challenge – a welcome respite from her duties at Myrtle's – and in order to accommodate Effie's desire for haste, her methods and her residual infirmity, had installed herself in Sylvie's bedroom at Halfpenny House. I allowed Catherine more time at Myrtle's to take over some of Bess' duties. That the collaboration was a fruitful one, there was no doubt, since within a matter of six weeks, Effie had arranged to conduct the première of 'The Ramsburgh Variations' at the Town Hall using the same assemblage of musicians that had done such justice to her first symphony.

Phyllis agreed to accompany me; however, Francesca was not yet ready to face public life. I was intrigued to see the movements listed in the programme: 'Curiosity', 'Hubris', 'Prudence', 'Courage', and finally 'Fantasy'. I understood the references to the peafowl, but surely 'Courage' could not refer to me. 'Curiosity' could be a musical rendition of Effie's own interest in Ramsburgh, and 'Fantasy' might simply describe the looseness of the musical form – but knowing a little of Effie's passions, I suspected that this was not all that it conveyed.

When Effie stepped up to conduct, it was hard to believe that she had recently teetered on the brink of death. She had regained her energy and her confidence, and when she bowed to the audience before the concert began, she seemed to emit a glow of pleasure. She caught my eye and smiled before turning and raising her baton.

Unlike the beginning of the previous concert, there was no great blast of noise to herald 'Curiosity', but instead a gradual swelling of strings, mounting in intensity and then overlaid with a melody on the cello – her Ramsburgh theme.

As the melody was taken up and varied on other instruments, an oboe seemed to pose an unresolved question with an upward flurry of notes, and this was repeated, with varied harmonisation, producing surprising changes in effect.

The piece gradually reached its peak, the questioning theme becoming a resolved statement, and then like a receding tide, the constant flow of sound faded until it disappeared altogether.

There was no sound at all from the audience, as they strained to hear the end, and then when Effie relaxed, everyone remembered to breathe and move and cough.

'Hubris' elegantly caught my peacock's strutting, the Ramsburgh theme being coaxed into something resembling a march, brassy chords depicting his pride and exuberance. 'Prudence', on the other hand, drew a hesitant and delicate picture of a reluctant lover.

In 'Courage', the theme was reworked to depict – as I interpreted it – the quality of determination, amongst moments of musical violence. But 'Fantasy' was the most interesting variation.

A soprano stood up, and waited for her cue. A single violin toyed with the Ramsburgh theme, giving way to a romantic waltz. As the waltz faded – making me think of a ghostly dancing couple, disappearing into the mist – a low, velvety hum of strings provided the cue for the soprano to start a song without words. It had an improvised quality that reminded me of the moment I discovered Effie singing in front of Halfpenny House, and it managed to convey her passion for life. It built slowly in intensity, and yet the melody became simpler, and eventually, several highly sustained, fortissimo notes rang out – the same note – that proved quite uncomfortable for the audience. There was fidgeting and even a little nervous laughter. When they were echoed in a quieter form, dying out gradually to a serene string accompaniment, I blushed at the association that came into my mind.

Surely Effie would not dare to depict such a thing knowingly, I thought. I looked around as the applause filled the hall, but no one was prepared to betray themselves with anything but an appreciative smile. Then it was surely my own mind at fault, twisted by recent events.

Effie bowed, delighted at the reception to her piece, before encouraging the orchestra and the singer to take their own bows.

"Interesting," said Phyllis. "Effie doesn't take a conventional path, does she?"

"I suspect she would hate being cast into any mould," I said.

Then Effie held up her hands to stay the applause, and after wiping tears from her eyes, said, "I don't normally say anything at a concert – it spoils my mystique!"

There was laughter, and she continued, "But I have something on my mind. As you may know, I have recently recovered from arsenic poisoning. Writing this piece was an immense help to me during my convalescence. Many people have been kind to me over this period, but I want to thank one in particular who has cheered me, and also successfully fought against the use of arsenic in wallpaper. As if that were not enough, he solved the case of poor Mr Lowick, imperilling himself dreadfully in doing so."

I covered my face with my hands and wondered if I could slink out before anyone realised who I was. Phyllis looked most amused.

"Finally, he and his beautiful home inspired tonight's piece. I know he doesn't like to take credit for the things he does – and he has been a quiet friend to many in Hawksbridge – but just this once, I want him to be publicly acknowledged. Thomas, could you possibly come up so I – and we – can thank you properly?"

I would sooner have wrestled a bear, but it was too late to run. If it was important to Effie, then I would do it. I stood up and walked to the front of the room, feeling as though I was going to fall over my own feet in my self-consciousness.

I stood next to Effie, who shook my hand and turned back to the audience. "Please help me thank my dear friend and inspiration, Mr Thomas Rufford!" and to my intense embarrassment, I received a warm round of applause. I bowed, and then Effie turned to me, and with a mischievous smile, whispered in my ear: "Did you enjoy my fantasy, Thomas?"

EPILOGUE

THE clouds had cleared, and the midday sun was making us grateful for our hats as the carriage laboured up the dirt track. Mrs Lowick glanced nervously at Phyllis, who smiled back reassuringly.

"Oh, she won't want to see me!" Mrs Lowick said, her gloved hand at her mouth. "This is a mistake. Should we go back?"

"I don't think it's a mistake," I said. "You have much in common. And you don't ever have to return after today, if you don't want to. You will at least have tried to be a friend to her."

"Yes, yes, of course," she murmured.

We reached the familiar cottage, and for a moment I worried that Miss Belford and her daughter had moved on. But then, hearing the sound of the carriage, Miss Belford appeared at the door. She was now heavily pregnant, and walked slowly.

She frowned as the carriage stopped and she saw us.

"Good morning, Miss Belford," I said. "I hope you don't mind us visiting. Mrs Lowick, I don't believe you've met Miss Belford."

"Bugger me," said Miss Belford, before correcting herself: "I mean, pleased to meet you, Mrs Lowick."

"The pleasure is mine, Miss Belford," said Mrs Lowick, shaking her hand. "I do hope we haven't caught you at a bad time."

"No worse than any other," Miss Belford said. "My father's visiting for a few days, so he'll be glad to have someone to chat to, I'm sure."

"Good," I said. "I wanted to speak with him. Mrs Lowick has brought a few more things for you and Matilda. And for the baby."

Mrs Lowick offered up two bags of clothes and toys. "I hope these are all right," she said.

"Thank you, ma'am. That's very decent of you. I did like the other stuff you sent. Made me cry, didn't it, Mr Rufford?"

"Oh – I'm sorry!" said Mrs Lowick, alarmed.

Miss Belford smiled and laid her hand on Mrs Lowick's arm. "No need to be sorry. I get all emotional so easily these days, that's all. Probably this one's fault." She gestured at her distended belly.

Mrs Lowick nodded. "I wanted to express my... I just wanted to say..." She could not continue, and extracted a handkerchief from her sleeve.

"About William?" Miss Belford said, and Mrs Lowick nodded again. "I know. I'm sorry too. He was a right one, wasn't he?"

Mrs Lowick laughed and dabbed her eyes. "Exactly, Miss Belford. He was a right one. But he was our right one. We loved the silly fool."

"Yes," Miss Belford said. "Yes, we did. I will joke about the man, and I will curse him, but you had better believe... I loved him! I loved him more than I can say."

She broke down, and Mrs Lowick, her lip trembling, instinctively opened her arms and held her gingerly, mindful of her delicate state. They stayed locked in embrace for a minute, weeping, until Matilda came out and stared up at them with wide eyes and open mouth.

"Who's she?" she said to me.

"This is Mrs Lowick," I said. "She's a good friend of your father's. And she's brought you some more things."

"Will I see Daddy soon?" Matilda said.

Lillian separated herself from Mrs Lowick and stroked Matilda's head. "Not for a long, long time, my angel."

"Tomorrow?"

"Longer than that."

"Oh," Matilda said, pouting.

"Hello, Matilda," Mrs Lowick said, bending down. "Mr Rufford said you had some lovely dolls. Can you show them to me?"

"Yes," Matilda said. "Come with me. And you," she added, pulling at Phyllis' dress. And she marched into the house, with Mrs Lowick and Phyllis in tow.

"How are you keeping, Mr Rufford?" Lillian said. "I've heard some very rum things about you. I'm glad it was you who found William. Someone kind, who knew him."

The fact that I personally only found part of him was better left unsaid. "Yes, I'm glad too. I'm all right – and I'm alive, which I'm thankful for every day. It was finely balanced, though."

"I'm truly sorry, Mr Rufford. It all sounds foul. Good thing her Ladyship didn't get her hooks into me – but I had enough on my plate. And I'm not nearly hoity-toity enough."

"I think you would have been a match for her," I said.

She smiled. "Too right I would," she said, raising both her fists.

Mr Belford emerged from the house.

"Ah – Mr Rufford," he said. "You find me in better circumstances than before." Then he looked back at Lillian's cottage with an expression of distaste. "Though not much better, to be frank."

"I wish I had been able to do more," I said. "In fact, I think our talk at the police office did you more harm than good. I'm sorry about that."

"Ah well, never you mind about it now," said Mr Belford. "If you hadn't found out about William, I dare say I'd be at the assizes. Or six foot under." He shuffled at the dust on the garden path. "I know I said some harsh things about the man, but I was wrong. If a man can inspire both of his women –

rivals, mind – to put things right, well, he must have had something about him, mustn't he?"

"He did," I said. "He may have let his passions get the better of him, but he was nevertheless a fine man. He heartily loved both of his families. And he was damn good company."

Lillian came rushing out of the cottage. "Papa! I'm moving! No more of this stinking cottage!"

"How's that, my dear?" Mr Belford said. "Found yourself another fancy man?" He chuckled.

"No," she said, playfully whacking her father on the arm. "It's Mrs Lowick. She's got a house for us in Hawksbridge, and we don't even have to pay any rent!"

"I bought a pair of terraced houses with family money," Mrs Lowick said, coming out of the cottage holding Matilda's hand. "I haven't had a tenant in one of them for a while, so you will be doing me a favour looking after it, for as long as you like, Miss Belford. I already have plenty to live on."

"Hear that, Papa? No more trudging up the lane to see me. And no more rats. You don't have rats, do you?"

Mrs Lowick laughed. "No, we don't have rats, I'm happy to say. And your children and mine can play together, if you like. We won't be far away."

Miss Belford did not reply immediately, but went to embrace Mrs Lowick again as firmly as her size permitted. "I should like that, Mrs Lowick. I should like it very much."

"That's right," said Mr Belford. "Take whatever blessings you can, when you can."

I suddenly realised that last night, for the first time in many weeks, I had not woken up in a sweat with Lady Fairfield's eyes searing into my brain. Today, I had not been haunted by feelings of being either a victim or a perpetrator. Perhaps the old Thomas Rufford had finally returned. And Mr Belford's words rang true – I had the right, indeed, an obligation, to take the opportunity laid so obviously in front of me.

I dug into my pocket. The object I kept on me, always, was still there. I took Phyllis by the hand and led her a little way down the track, by a field where a flock of dirty-looking sheep looked up briefly from their grazing.

"Thomas? Where are we going?"

"Nowhere. Oh – everywhere! Phyllis..." I tremblingly fished out the little box, opened it, and offered it to her. "I love you so, so much. Will you be my wife?"

"Are you sure? Are you well enough now?"

"I am, I know I am – if you will have me? But I've been disgraced – can you overlook these terrible things?"

"Of course I can!" she said. "It was never truly an obstacle for me – shocking, yes, but something to be put from our minds. What happened was not your fault."

"Thank God," I said. "Then will you forgive me for letting you go? It was a more witless thing than anything else I have done – more foolish even than trusting Lady Fairfield."

Phyllis took the ring and put it on her finger.

"Yes, my dear Thomas. I can forgive even that. Of course I'll marry you."

I wrapped Phyllis in my arms and kissed her. We stood locked in embrace, oblivious of the knot of people staring at us.

"Why are they sad?" I heard Matilda say.

"They're not sad," her mother said. "Sometimes you cry when you're really happy."

"That's silly," Matilda said.

"Yes, it is," said Mrs Lowick said. "And yet rather wonderful."

"I want to give you everything you need," I said, still holding Phyllis. "We'll make a writing room in Ramsburgh for you. I know you fret about what will happen with your work."

"The library will do just fine. I'd rather like to do some redecoration, though, if you don't mind."

"The house needs it," I said, "but please, nothing by that

wretch Gabriel Forrester!"

"I promise."

"I didn't tell you," I said. "Hu and Pru have chicks! I saw them on the roof. I hope they won't be too noisy. There must be four of them, at least."

"I'm sure they'll be a delight," Phyllis said. "I can imagine Mrs Felton saying it's a good omen. We can always find someone to take one or two if they threaten to overrun the place. But I don't want to sweep in and change everything. Certainly not you – I wouldn't rewrite your character, even if I could."

She touched my cheek and kissed me again. "As for the house, it just needs a few... well, Ramsburgh variations."

~ THE END ~

DRAMATIS PERSONAE

Ramsburgh

Mr Thomas Rufford: owner of Ramsburgh

Miss Flora Davison: niece of the previous owners, the Kingtons

Mrs Margaret Northcutt: Flora's housekeeper

Mr Matthew Shipley: Thomas' butler

Mrs Norah Felton: Thomas' housekeeper

Mrs Catherine Wakeley: Thomas' cook

Old Howard: the groom and dogsbody

Jenny: a pony

Celeste: Thomas' horse

Fox: Thomas' dog

Hawksbridge

Miss Phyllis Drummond: a novelist

Dr Anthony Drummond: a doctor and Phyllis' father

Mrs Francesca Campbell: friend of Thomas

Mr David Harris: a former banker

Mrs Olivia Harris: Mr Harris' wife

Miss Euphemia Harris: the Harris' daughter, and a composer

Captain Victor Harris: the Harris' son and amateur zoologist

Miss Sylvie Dubois: Euphemia Harris' assistant

Inspector Ralph Simmons: a detective

Constable Taylor: a policeman

Constable Gawley: a policeman

Mrs Bess Shannon: the proprietor of Myrtle's coffee shop

Mr Frederick McPhee: a director at the Pottery

Dr Philip Weldon: a doctor

Mr William Lowick: a journalist

Mrs Clementine Lowick: Mr Lowick's wife

George Lowick: the Lowicks' 9-year-old son

Amelia Lowick: the Lowicks' 6-year-old daughter

Mrs Angela Beatty: the Lowick's housekeeper

Mrs Ninette Milburn: a widow

Mrs Julia Spillings: Mrs Milburn's housekeeper

Mr John Belford: a jeweller

Miss Lillian Belford: Mr Belford's daughter

Matilda Belford: Lillian Belford's 3-year-old daughter

Lady Esme Fairfield: a philanthropist and women's rights campaigner

Miss Rachel Knowles: a friend of Miss Dubois

Mr Timothy Knowles: Miss Knowles' brother

Mr Gabriel Forrester: renowned designer, painter and socialist

Mrs Penelope Forrester: Mr Forrester's wife

Mr Winston Eagle: proprietor of the Conundrum Print Works

Mr Frederic Stanton: proprietor of The Hawksbridge Herald

Elsewhere

Mr Jonathan Nesbit: a patient

Mrs Emily Nesbit: Mr Nesbit's wife

Dr Peter Henrick: a doctor

ABOUT THE AUTHOR

Julian Smart was born in Nottingham, England, and studied Computer Science at the University of St Andrews. He has a doctorate from the University of Dundee. Julian has worked for the University of Edinburgh, the Artificial Intelligence Applications Institute, the Scottish Crop Research Institute, and Red Hat UK.

Julian started the wxWidgets open-source GUI toolkit project which is used by many organisations and individuals worldwide, and by Julian for his own projects, including the e-book editing software Jutoh. Jutoh was used for creating all books by Julian and Harriet Smart.

Julian collaborated with Harriet Smart to write *Emma Vernon's Northminster Ghost Stories*, a spin-off from Harriet's Northminster Mysteries which he has edited since 2010.

Julian is currently working on *The Thomas Rufford Mysteries*, a series set in nineteenth-century Hawksbridge, a fictional town in the north east of England.

Printed in Great Britain
by Amazon

13708692R00214